The Whiskey Creek Water Company

A Depression Era Novel

November, 1932, Burke Bay on Puget Sound—
Local Indians called the natural spring burbling up
in the forest *spirit water*. Scandinavian settlers took
that to mean whiskey and named the stream flowing
from the spring *Whiskey Creek*. Rumor has it the
creek's name attracted the dark stranger who
disrupted life in the community.

The Great Depression was a worldwide economic
depression that began in the United States in late
1929 and lasted to the middle 1940s.

Also by Jan Walker

Romar Jones Takes a Hike (teen/adult fiction)

A Farm in the South Pacific Sea (adult fiction)

An Inmate's Daughter (YA fiction)

Dancing to the Concertina's Tune: A Prison Teacher's Memoir

Parenting From A Distance (for incarcerated parents)

My Relationships, My Self

The Whiskey Creek Water Company

Jan Walker

Plicata Press
Gig Harbor, Washington

Plicata Press LLC
P.O. Box 32
Gig Harbor, WA   98335
www.plicatapress.com

ISBN: 978-0-9848400-5-2
LCCN: 2013916343

Walker, Jan
The Whiskey Creek Water Company / Jan Walker
1. The Great Depression – Fiction 2. Moonshine – Fiction
3. Scandinavian Families – Fiction 4. Burke Bay – Fiction
5. Kitsap County – Fiction 6. Bremerton, WA – Fiction

For Eva Marie Nelson Olsen and John Olsen
In Loving Memory

1

~ The Teacher ~

*T*he harsh north wind whipping down Puget Sound kicked up whitecaps and tore limbs from cedars and firs overhanging South Bay Beach. A branch dipped low, snatched the knit cloche from Maeva Swanson's head and dangled it out of her reach. She left it hanging and jumped across the small creek separating the Swanson and Jenson properties where the *Aggie J* waited. The passenger launch rocked alongside Jenson's pier, her engine churning, her bow rope straining.

Axel Jenson, boat captain and Maeva's fiancé, blew the whistle loud and long, his way of yelling at her to hurry. They were already late and bucking the wind would slow them more. Burn more fuel, too, Axel would remind her.

"Go on without me," she shouted, but he couldn't hear and it wouldn't make any difference to their current tiff, this one about Roosevelt's election. Axel and his family were staunch Republicans, quick to point out FDR's shortcomings each time Maeva mentioned the man's plans to bring the country out of the Depression. She and Axel had been involved in one tiff or another since she moved home in July to teach grades one through four at Burke Bay Grade School.

She picked her way along Jenson's icy pier, let Axel pull her onto the bow deck and usher her through the wheelhouse to the passenger section. The engine groaned as the *Aggie J* plied her way to the cove where South Bay schoolchildren boarded. Maeva settled them by age and size, youngest closest to her, oldest in eighth grader Wesley Wiley's charge.

The launch eased into the wind, heading almost due north for Burke Bay Dock. Maeva wrapped her arms around the four smallest children, two on each side of her. Wesley helped the others plant their feet on the wet floorboards and grasp the bench front with both hands.

Children screamed when a wave washed over the bow, sending sea water through the wheel house into the passenger section. They screamed again when the launch leaned to port, the side on which they sat—the side closest to land and deemed safest by Maeva's sensibilities.

She reassured them with praise for the *Aggie J's* sea-worthiness and Axel's expertise as her captain. If her words were tinged with ire toward Axel, the children didn't notice. They trusted her to keep them safe.

She felt more than heard a thud, likely a wave tossed log, and calmed the children once again while the boat slogged on, reaching its destination late, perhaps somewhat bruised externally. It was a sturdy boat, one of many that shuttled passengers to and from piers and landings on Puget Sound.

Axel gave the *Aggie J's* whistle a long blast to let all Burke Bay know they'd arrived. Maeva kept the children seated while Wesley helped Axel secure the bow and stern lines. Once tied, Axel handed children down to Maeva and Wesley who carried them from the wave tossed float to the gangplank without letting their feet get wet.

Helmer Persson and his dairy truck that served as a makeshift school bus in the morning, waited for the children on the dock at the top of the ramp. He helped children scramble into the back of the panel truck, with Wesley last, closest to the door. Maeva stood to the side until Helmer tested the latch and waited again while he walked around to open the passenger door for her. It had a tricky handle.

"Mornin', Maeva," Helmer said, once they'd both settled on the truck's bench seat. "Nasty weather."

She nodded, still trying to catch her breath and slow her pulse. Carrying some of the sturdier children across a float awash in icy sea water had been worrisome and taxing work. Two of the boys wanted to splash in the waves to test their skill at maintaining their balance as the float dipped and rose with the sea.

Helmer kept the truck in low gear the length of the dock and onto Dock Road, beeping his horn as they passed the Burke Bay Tavern. He let the truck roll to a stop where Whiskey Creek ran under the road and emptied into the bay. There he tromped on the brake, shifted into neutral, and turned to face her.

"You'll be having a new student today, Maeva. Daughter of our hired hand. Farley Price. Moved here from Kansas. Me and the Missus know you'll take a liking to the child, see to her learning her letters and numbers."

They sat in silence for several long seconds, burning precious gasoline to go nowhere, the truck's sputtering heater delivering more moisture than warmth.

"A new student?" Maeva said, thinking about how that would complicate her day. She had sugar cookies in a tin in her canvas tote, two for each student to be handed out when both classrooms gathered with her for special events, two for the principal to take with her tea. She could have brought extra, but times were such that extra anything came at a price. Her mother shared all their baked goods with Axel's family and with widowed neighbors, two or three of whom stopped in at the Swanson's for afternoon coffee— *eftermiddagskaffe* they called it—almost daily.

Helmer's face was framed by the driver side window and backed with a view of churning water on the normally serene Burke Bay. He stuck a matchstick between his teeth.

"The child's name is Farley?" Maeva thought it an odd name for a girl. The child would be given two cookies, leaving none for the principal, Miss Truax, who looked forward to such treats.

Helmer frowned. "Nah, the hired hand's named Farley. I'll leave the explaining to the Missus, she's more up on the child's name and needs, and what have you."

"Farley Price," Maeva mused.

A chill that had nothing to do with Helmer's temperamental truck heater swept over her the moment she spoke the man's name. A cloud formed and dissolved above Burke Bay, an apparition

3

fabricated in her mind. She experienced premonitions at times and gave them proper heed, but a misty figure hovering over the small bay made no sense.

Helmer put the truck in gear, beeped his horn for the garage and mercantile, and turned onto School Road. The road ran west from the bay past Burke Bay Grade School to Hidden Valley.

The truck bounced over the roots of twin bigleaf maples positioned as though planted to guard the drive and drifted to a stop near the school stairs.

"There's the Missus now," Helmer said, pointing the matchstick he'd been chewing.

Ebbe Persson, a large boned woman with cheeks rosy from outdoor work and Scandinavian genes, stood under the porch roof at the top of the broad stairs. She wore a faded house dress and man's heavy wool sweater. Her hands rested on the shoulders of a waif-like child surely too small to belong in school.

The child had soft dark curls and a small round face. The sleeves of her coat stopped two inches above her wrists. The woman and child resembled photos used by newspapers to remind readers how others fared during these hard times.

"Good morning, Miss Swanson," Ebbe said in her thick Swedish accent. "Meet Hannah Price, a new student for you. Go on now, Hannah, on into the foyer. Hang up your coat alongside the others. Line up on the right hand side and wait for the bell."

Miss Truax, principal and teacher of grades five through eight, scowled from her post in the left side classroom door. She clutched the heavy brass school bell in both hands. Wisps of thin gray hair escaped the coil at her nape. Her small mouth in her dried apple face puckered with disapproval. Protocol dictated that Ebbe Persson should have brought Hannah to her for enrollment.

Maeva greeted Miss Truax before addressing the children. "Have you all heard the good news about our new president elect?"

The children, rigid in Miss Truax's presence, relaxed and grinned. They'd cast a unanimous vote for FDR in the mock election Maeva conducted the day before, the younger ones to please her, the older ones believers in the hope for change. Their eyes moved to her canvas bag, certain she'd brought cookies for special events.

Ebbe said, "Leave the president business for class time, Maeva, and come change out of them boots while I tend to explaining. We've some worries over to our place. Over Farley Price, the hired man who'd also be Hannah's father. Appears he likes his drink a mite too much. Odd though it sounds, I'm thinking he came out here to Whiskey Creek looking for liquor. Came all the way from Kansas in a car that don't look like none other I've ever seen."

Maeva tugged off boots and poked her feet into black pumps new two years back, recently resoled.

"How could a man in Kansas possibly learn an unofficial name for one of Kitsap County's unnamed creeks?"

Maeva pictured Kansas as she knew it from geography books, the yellow-brown shades used for plains and prairie, with a little blue at its northeast corner where the Missouri flowed by. "Somehow ships and Kansas don't fit together, Ebbe."

"No, and neither do Farley Price and his wife and child. That's the reason you need to be putting little Hannah in that empty seat in the window row. Move the others back one desk, place her in front, she's bound to be the youngest. Might be the brightest, too."

That odd chill swept over Maeva a second time. "How young?"

"Six soon enough not to argue," Ebbe said. "Putting her in school will clear the way for Mrs. Price to help with harvesting our turkeys. Bremerton markets are about ready for them what with Thanksgiving two weeks off."

Maeva whispered, "You want the child off the property while turkeys are being killed? That's why you brought her here?" She glanced at Hannah, waiting in the foyer, eyes on her scuffed shoes.

Ebbe gave Maeva a nod and Hannah a wave. "Go along in now, Hannah. Miss Swanson will see to things from here on. I'll be back when school lets out, you just mind what Miss Swanson tells you."

"Yes, Mrs. Persson," Hannah said, her head tipped back, her eyes squeezed almost shut.

"There's the other reason for putting her up front," Ebbe said. "Them eyes of hers."

Maeva tried for a stern look, one that showed concern for the rules, though she felt a grin form. She turned to the board, chalk in hand, and saw the flag. Dear God, she'd almost forgotten The Pledge of Allegiance, an omission that would earn another demerit in the dossier Miss Truax kept.

The storm had abated and the seas calmed by the time the *Aggie J* made its return trip to South Bay Beach that afternoon. Axel helped the children board and debark without speaking a word to Maeva. When they reached Jenson pier, he resumed his rant against Roosevelt where he'd abandoned it the night of the election.

"I hope you're prepared for what FDR will do to this country, Maeva."

She considered saying *Yes, FDR will bring the country out of the Depression*, but that would only deepen his anger. Instead she said, "I'm tired, Axel. It's been a challenging day. Let's agree to disagree."

He grabbed her forearm. "Hoover had an economic recovery plan in place, but that's lost. Thanks to voters' idiocy, the economy will only get worse."

She pulled her arm free. "Whose economy? Jenson's, with your two passenger ships and your family's other business interests? Your father's political position? Or struggling families like mine? We're lucky I got called back home to teach in Burke Bay where I can help Mom and Nels with our farm now that both Jonas and Berta are married and gone."

She stomped down the pier and across Jenson beach, enjoying the satisfying crunch of clam shells, and waded through the stream that defined the southern edge of Swanson's' ten acres.

Axel dogged her steps, calling her a socialist and Jonas a stingy lout. She ducked under a fir tree the storm wrenched from the bank, already planning how she and Nels could cut it into lengths for firewood. Axel circled the tree and followed her up the trail to the Swanson yard. She spun around to face him.

"What do you need tonight? A quart of our milk? Fresh eggs? A loaf of Mom's bread?"

He threw up his arms and left empty handed, a rarity. At the least he grabbed a handful of cookies or a jar of jam on his way out the door. He ignored her the next day, an act she found peaceful. Though she enjoyed intelligent discussions on most any topic, the FDR argument no longer qualified as a discussion.

Thus she was surprised when Axle showed up for dinner, his pleasant smile in place. Nels, Maeva's younger brother, had invited him for clam chowder. Nels had graduated high school that year and did all he could to help the family. He was the family peacemaker. He'd dug the clams for the chowder by lantern light in the wee hours, he reminded Maeva, and rowed most of them to sell at Poulsbo's fish dock, a distance of over six miles.

Axel sat beside Nels at the round oak table where candles burned low, their sleeves filling with wax drips. While her mother sliced warm bread, Maeva ladled clam chowder into bowls and told the story of Hannah Price's first two days in school. She considered it a safer topic than anything political.

"My new student, Hannah, is young but very bright. She read the entire first primer, cover to cover, before she told me Ebbe had given her a copy. I sent them home with a stack of books this afternoon. Hannah's only five and so nearsighted she has to hold the book this close to her eyes."

She held a hand two inches from Axel's face, daring him to back away.

"Her birthday isn't until late March. I warned Ebbe that the school superintendent will likely order me to send her back home when he sees the date. Ebbe said 'Just write 1926 on the form to make her six.'"

"My," Alma Swanson said, a word used to cover Swedish thoughts when finding English would take more than a moment.

Nels asked, "What did you think when you met the mother?" He was cutting a slab of butter their mother had churned.

"What mother?" Maeva had been thinking that their mother's face looked too red from her long day with a hot fire in the cast iron stove. She opened the door to the cool room off the kitchen.

The long narrow room, built over a stream, had cement walls, a low ceiling and slotted floor boards that could be lifted out of the way to set food directly in running water.

"The Price girl's mother," Nels said.

Axel rose from the table. "Another story, that. The chowder is excellent as always, Mrs. Swanson. May I help myself to seconds?"

Chowder dripped from the ladle sides as he asked.

"Another story?" Maeva watched Axel, who liked to drop hints of local gossip into conversations to catch her interest.

Nels stood to replenish his own bowl. "Rumor has it Mrs. Price was seen with blackened eyes and bruised cheeks. There're all sorts of Farley Price stories floating around Burke Bay. One's that his car, a tan coupe, is a good color for hiding out in Kansas wheat fields when running from the law."

Their mother placed a hand over her heart. *"Gud i himmel."*

"Sorry, Mom." Nels gave her an innocent grin. His hazel eyes, a Swanson trait, twinkled.

Maeva squinted at Nels. "Stories or facts, Nels? I can't imagine Ebbe Persson permitting such a man on her property. Helmer either, for that matter."

Axel shook his head. "For a school teacher you can be so naive, Maeva. The Perssons hired a hand to kill turkeys and milk cows. What control do you think they have over him?"

She stared at Axel. "Perhaps Helmer could give the hand a blackened eye."

No wonder Ebbe, not Hannah's mother, brought the child to school and came in the afternoon to take her home.

"Then what happens to little Hannah?" Nels asked. "Not yet six and oh so smart she can read all five words in the first primer? Or is it ten words?"

"I didn't write the book, Nels. By second grade, she'll be reading the newspaper."

Hannah's penchant to get lost in a book reminded Maeva of herself as a child. Hannah *needed* to read.

"Turkeys soon won't need feeding," Axel said. "Persson can let Price go, take his family back where they came from."

"Why couldn't Mrs. Price and Hannah stay on with the Perssons while Mr. Price seeks work elsewhere?"

Axel set down his spoon and groaned. "Women are not hired on as milkers."

"And why not? Look at Mom and me. We milk and plow and chop wood."

"Mrs. Price belongs with her husband and child, Maeva, That's the meaning of marriage. Two become one, women care for home and family, men earn the living and make decisions about important matters. Voting matters, for instance. It's time you got that into your head."

He finished his chowder and bread, grabbed his top coat from the hook by the door and went through the living room to the front porch for a smoke.

He looked so confident, so Swedish with his blue eyes, blonde hair, broad shoulders. She wanted to follow him, make him take back the pronouncement that Mrs. Price belonged with her husband. No woman belonged with a man who hit her.

She wanted to remind him that she was an educated and intelligent woman who would not be content only caring for home and family. She decided to keep her peace. There were times when she suspected Axel enjoyed battling with her more than he enjoyed snuggling out on the huge front porch, listening to the wireless.

Her thoughts moved to financial matters, the factor that prevented her from marrying. She'd spent most of her first two years teaching salary repaying Jonas for her college education. Given the Depression, she feared it could take Nels several years to find work that would support their mother and the farm. She liked living back on the farm, helping her mother, teaching young children. Teaching nourished her soul.

She turned her attention to the kitchen, to her mother, widowed before Maeva turned four. Alma Swanson had gotten a plethora of obligations and a dearth of pleasures from marriage. Her entire widow's pension went toward flour, sugar and coffee, the basics that helped create the warmth and comfort all found in her home.

"You go put your feet up, Mom. Read your Swedish newspaper. I'll clean the kitchen."

Water heating in coils at the back of the stove trickled into the sink. She washed, rinsed and waited for Axel to come in from the front porch for cookies and a quick kiss.

When she heard him laughing with Nels, she grabbed the soapy dishcloth to attack chowder drips and bread crumbs spattered and scattered on the table.

"Men," she muttered, and found Farley Price, a man she'd never seen, in her mind's eye.

She went upstairs to retrieve her notebook. Sketching and writing cleared her thoughts, helped her see truths she otherwise missed.

She sketched a faceless man, fists clenched, hovering over a beaten woman with hands hiding her face and, in the background, a child with dark curls and frightened eyes. She'd captured Hannah's likeness well enough that any who'd met the child would recognize her in the drawing.

Angry heat swept Maeva's chest and neck. After a long moment she ripped the page from her notebook, crumpled it and tossed it into the stove. Flames caught, burned, faded back to holding coals she would stir up in the morning to make coffee and toast.

Later that night she wrote a story for her column in *The Kitsap Weekly*. They paid her with free newspapers and an occasional quarter or fifty cents.

That done, she drew the same faceless man floating above a choppy sea, the apparition she'd seen. Beneath the drawing, she wrote *Farley Price Roils the Waters of Whiskey Creek and Burke Bay, November,1932.*

2

~ Whiskey Creek ~

Whiskey Creek originates in Hidden Valley, meanders through farms and behind the grade school, fills two ponds and spills into Burke Bay. Some folks say it's not a creek at all, but just a rill that broke through the earth's crust after loggers removed the trees. Others say it flows from an artesian well that produces the purest water in the county.

Maeva Swanson for The Kitsap Weekly

Orval Blevins read those words and darn near fell off the sofa where he'd stretched out to ponder how good luck put a man with a need for drink in his path. He found Maeva Swanson's mention of his artesian well perturbing. Like walking into a nettle patch while hunting down wild blackberries, it left a sting.

Not two whole days had gone by since Orval stood eyeball to eyeball with that thirsty man, the new hired hand at Persson's Farm.

Yessiree, he read the hired hand's need clear as print on the newspaper. They came eyeball to eyeball at the Burke Bay Mercantile, each man seeing something in the other that made the chance meeting worth more than a nod.

Could have been the sugar Orval set down on the counter about the time the stranger walked in. Could have been the stranger's coat that didn't come from the Sears & Roebuck catalog. Orval might dress in flannel and denim, but he could recognize fine wool and the money it took to make it fit just so when it walked past him.

"Ma'am," the stranger said to the store owner. His eyes moved from sugar to Orval with but a glance to Mrs. Bakke back behind the cash register.

Not that Orval meant to brag on himself as a reading man, though he'd taken his schooling proper like. Learned from an old maid school teacher who kept a paddle on her desk, not a young one like Miss Maeva Swanson who'd taken to writing stories for the weekly paper.

Local lore, the paper called her stories, and made a big to-do about her growing up on the beach over to South Bay where she'd made friends with an old Indian chief who camped on Swanson's beach during fall salmon runs.

> *"Lum chuck, our people say. Spirits' Water. Swedes took hold of that translation and turned the name into Whiskey Creek."*

Maeva Swanson wrote that as a quote from the chief who'd been known to spend a good bit of time with loggers, being as they were the ones who used the water to make brew of all sorts.

Orval had half a mind to demand his nickel back, cost of the paper, for mentioning an artesian well in Hidden Valley. That came darn close to naming him and his business. A family man like himself deserved some privacy.

He could take the paper into the Burke Bay Mercantile where he bought it along with the sugar, slap it down on the counter and state his protest. Might do just that if the outhouse wiping supply hadn't run low and his pretty little wife taken to hiding her private roll from him.

He could write a story or two about Indians his own self. Stories told by his old grandpap who started the Blevins' distillery business back before Prohibition came along to give it a boost.

Orval heard talk from the time he was knee high about Indians who believed their ancestors' spirits made the water bubble out of the ground the way it did. Darned tribe thought they could wander up the creek onto Blevins' land anytime they liked, seeing as that's where the bubbling-up occurred.

Grandpap put up barbed wire fences, but that didn't much matter to Indians who came and went as they pleased.

One gal, a half-breed who had a hankering for his grandpap, hung around for a year or so after the old man died. Stayed until she got tired of all the work Orval expected from her. She'd taken to liking his whiskey some too good. Lazed around drunk most of the day while cows and chickens went untended and started seeing to their own needs, grazing or pecking their way into his garden.

He'd found a new gal, a pretty one younger than him by half when they first met, him thirty-two at the time and her sixteen. She understood his business, coming from a family that supplied product to a couple two three old logging camps out to the canal.

She married him soon as she finished her schooling. It was her idea to round up some help for him when it came to moving product.

This new man down to Persson's farm hailed from Detroit, by way of Kansas, and drove a darn spiffy car. When Orval stopped by to check things out, the man met him in the driveway. He patted the hood of his car, a sure sign he had some extra horses harnessed.

"Name's Farley Price," the man said. "Heard about your doings, Blevins. Heard you mention you could use some help."

"Could be. Carried a little of my product to hold you over while I ponder the matter."

Orval lifted a jar of beer, brewed with his mash tailings, out from under farm tools and what have you in the back of his truck. He had half a dozen jars wrapped nice as you please in brown paper his smart little wife pressed out with her hands and saved in a cupboard.

"Got yourself a gunny sack? Gunny sack's good for cooling brew such as this. Stick it in the creek out back. I'll hang on to the paper sacks for my wife."

Farley Price opened a jar. "Bring anything else? Any of the good stuff I heard about?"

"Enough for a taste." Orval produced a jelly glass sealed over with waxed paper held on with a rubber band. He planned on carrying glass, paper and band back on home. "Plenty more where it comes from, if things work out. Cash and carry, that's how I do business."

"Carrying's the dangerous part. Keep that in mind if you're looking for a legger."

Orval was looking for a legger, one good man to carry his product to Bremerton and points beyond. Of late he'd found it downright perturbing to rise up out of a warm bed for delivering purposes.

"Could be, like I said. Depends on whether you last out the month milking cows."

Farley Price narrowed his black eyes. "You're not the only man providing product."

"Only one with spirits already in the water," Orval said, "and customers lined up for the taking."

3

~ Persson's Farm ~

Out of the corner of one swollen eye, Eleanor Keane Price saw the clutched knife dripping blood, the turkey flopping about in the rain, unaware it was dead. Blood-stained rain water puddled under the eaves of the poultry shed.

Inside, where dead turkeys waited to be scalded and plucked, the odor of innards and alcohol burners and singed flesh lingered despite Ebbe's scrubbing and Helmer's sloshing buckets of water.

Farley had dragged Eleanor out to watch the turkey slaughter so she could see what their reduced circumstances made him do. He blamed her for their trip west, though he'd bragged when they drove away from the Keane ranch that he'd pull down good wages in the Bremerton Navy Yard. He still insisted he'd get hired on, it was just a matter of time.

Time. Eleanor would bide hers, tuck away any money she could until she had enough to take Hannah and disappear in a city. Seattle first, across Puget Sound, accessible by ferryboat.

When she'd saved a little more money she'd travel south to Portland, then east until she found a rancher who believed her when she said she could ride, rope, drive tractor or a plow team, cook, sew and whatever it took to earn her keep. Hers and Hannah's.

By the time she worked her way home to the Keane Ranch, Papa and Mama would help her get a legal divorce. Surely they would let her come home and suffer with her the shame of divorce when they knew the whole truth hidden behind Farley Price's handsome exterior.

The ranch raised wheat and cattle, and now supported three families—her two brothers and their wives and children, her father and mother.

"Barely supports," her mother said, "since the Depression set in."

That was their stated reason for sending Farley, Hannah and her on their way. Their unstated reason had to do with Farley's need for drink, and more on cattle going missing at the camp Farley managed.

Heavy boots sloshing through puddles reminded Eleanor she was in western Washington on a dairy and poultry farm, not western Kansas. She turned from Farley's rant to see Helmer Persson, face ruddier than usual and a scowl that lifted his hat scalp-high.

"What the Bejaises! What's goin' on out here? Mrs. Price, your help's not needed out here, you go on now, go on inside the shed, the Missus is on her way back from delivering Hannah to the school teacher, scalding water's coming on hot enough."

Eleanor sidled away, entered the shed where she listened while Helmer informed Farley that women did not kill turkeys on Persson's farm nor did men leave marks on women, it was only because of Mrs. Price and little Hannah that Farley hadn't been given his walking papers.

Turkey blood spattered the tattered sweater she'd pulled on over a new apron made from feed sacks. Ebbe Persson gave her a stack of washed feed sacks and had Helmer carry a sewing machine down from the big house to the hired-hand's cottage.

She shivered though the small wood-burner, an oil barrel turned on its side and reshaped, glowed red. Steam from a copper canning kettle atop the stove fogged the air.

If Helmer fired Farley before she saved enough money to run, they would be back in his car, likely stuck at the edge of a shanty town searching a dump for something to sell, something to eat. No stove, no boiling kettle of any sort.

They'd spent two nights in Bremerton in Farley's fancy car while he went looking for work and came back with drink and plans.

"Whiskey Creek," he said. "Someone needs a farm hand out in the country. Persson's Farm on Whiskey Creek."

She'd grown to like the farm with the creek tumbling by its northern edge and the narrow fork running away from it to cross the pasture. The fork trickled along behind the cottage. She liked falling asleep and wakening to its sound.

She sensed Ebbe's presence in the shed, felt the older woman's eyes take in her blood-spattered clothes and shaking hands.

"Merciful heavens, what have you gotten into? You needn't be handling these birds till I've dipped them. Now where are the rubber gloves? Plucking takes a toll on the hands, you wear gloves. The mister's having a word with your husband. There will be no more nonsense on this farm."

No more nonsense. Did she mean drinking? Or hitting? One led to the other. Eleanor doubted the Perssons could stop the drinking but they might threaten Farley into controlling his fists.

She hadn't known that side of him until after they married. Never in her experience or imagination had a man hit a woman. Men worked fields, handled cattle and horses; women ran ranch households, taught children lessons when snow drifts closed schools.

Farley came west to Kansas from Michigan, showed up at the ranch looking for work, escorted her to a town dance and did the foxtrot better than any local lad. She found him dashing with his dark hair, watching eyes and sharp chin.

She'd let him dash her through courtship to marriage, not told her parents of that first beating when her pregnancy began to show, and suffered the decision. By the time she hinted that Farley's temper led to the use of his fists, her mother said she'd made her bed.

Her mother, who'd been reared on a southern plantation and missed her life there, tried to warn her away from Farley. "You never know where a stranger might haul you off to settle, so take care with your choice."

To her regret, Eleanor hadn't listened.

She plucked turkeys and drew shallow breaths to combat the sour stench of innards collecting in an old watering trough. Now and then she moved to the door for a swallow of rain drenched air. She'd never known so much rain, so much vertical greenness, such a colorless sky.

"This weather's some different to Kansas," Ebbe Persson said as she pulled a scalded turkey from a boiling pot and dropped it on the scrubbed board that served as plucking table.

"Yes." Eleanor returned to her task. She knew Ebbe waited for an answer that encouraged her to say more, but conversing required deeper breathing.

After a space of time with the only sound that of feathers leaving flesh, Ebbe spoke again.

"Maeva Swanson, she's the teacher, Maeva remarked on two things this morning. Hannah's reading which is beyond her age, and her eyesight which is none too good. I suspect you're knowing both. Helmer's seeing to a desk apart from the others so Hannah can get near enough the black board to see what the teacher writes."

Eleanor felt her chin drop and lift in a weak nod. "Hannah needs glasses, I know that. But she needs new shoes and a winter coat first."

"There's a couple wool coats tucked away in mothballs in a trunk in the attic. Might be you could cut one down for Hannah, handy as you are with sewing. Cut the other down for yourself, if you like."

Eleanor let her eyes touch Ebbe's. "I'd need to pay for the fabric in them. You could take it from our wages. From the part I earn, not from Farley's."

A frown touched Ebbe's forehead and disappeared. "Not if I choose to give them to you. Belonged to my two girls in their teen years. Both outgrew them. Built like me, those girls, buttonholes don't reach far enough to catch the buttons. I saved those coats figuring they'd serve somebody someday, and that day's at hand."

Eleanor suffered a combination of shame and urgency at having such a need. She swallowed the taste of feathers resting at the back of her throat.

"I'll accept for Hannah, with the understanding I sew something for you." In her opinion, Ebbe could use a new dress, even one made from flour sacks. A new apron, at the least.

"That would do better than pay from your small earnings. There's plenty fabric pieces stored up, some from dresses seen better days but already took apart at the seams."

Their eyes met again. Eleanor read something in the older woman's that she'd never seen in her mother's or any of her mother's friends, something she'd define as collusion.

For all those Kansas ranch women managed, they felt indebted to men who worked the land. They catered to men, fed them well, housed them. Hired hands didn't bring wives and children to the ranch.

Eleanor had expected to stay on the Keane Ranch when she married. Neighboring ranchers' daughters lived in small houses built close enough to the main residence to assist their mothers with women's responsibilities. In time, with deaths or failing health of parents, daughters even took over the main house. But she had older brothers, and they had wives.

Until she started west with Farley, Eleanor had never been more than fifty miles from Keane land, never met anyone whose life didn't revolve around cattle and grazing or wheat planting and harvest.

As she plucked pinfeathers from a turkey's wing she felt an inner warmth that had nothing to do with the overheated moist air. Ebbe Persson lived in a different world, and now so did Eleanor. Ebbe's words said there would be no more nonsense on this farm; her eyes said she'd help Eleanor take charge of her own life.

For the first time since Farley's fists last connected with her flesh, Eleanor felt hope. She'd make Hannah a decent coat, buy her shoes that fit and pay for an eye exam. She finished plucking one bird, started another.

But what was she thinking? Thanksgiving was two weeks away, the birds would all be dinner for those who could pay the price, the turkey processing on Persson's farm finished.

And Farley had already found a place to buy drink.

4

~ Burke Bay Grade School ~

By afternoon recess the day before Thanksgiving, Maeva longed to breathe fresh air, rain or no. She could not face another fifteen minutes with children trapped in the basement, their voices echoing back from cement walls, the benches scraping cement floors.

They needed playground activity, and Maeva needed time to observe Hannah Price at outdoor play. She wanted to strengthen her argument against Axel's declaration that the Price family should move on now that Persson's turkey slaughter was over.

The night before, Axel had said, "Everyone in Burke Bay agrees they don't fit in this community."

They'd been cuddled by the fire in the Swanson living room, soft music from the wireless in the background. She was beginning to see a pattern in his behavior. A few kisses, some promising caresses, and then a statement of how things should be or what she should do.

Fresh air and watching Hannah might help her think that through, too.

When the recess bell rang, children crowded into the foyer, waiting to be led downstairs.

Maeva said, "Put on your coats, we're going outside to the playground shelter."

Miss Truax, nostrils flared, said "It's raining rather hard, Miss Swanson. I do not approve of outdoor activity in such weather."

"They need the fresh air and an opportunity to release some pent-up energy."

"Do see to it they all stay undercover. Mind you, I won't be responsible for a case of sniffles due to wet clothes."

"Germs cause sniffles. A little rain won't hurt us."

Some children shouted, some jumped into mud puddles. Virginia Holmes, a first grader who didn't fit in with the other children, grabbed three fingers of Maeva's gloved hand and held so tight all circulation ceased.

Her father, the Reverend Seely Holmes of the Burke Bay Church, had sent a formal letter to the school stating that Virginia, a delicate child, needed to avoid strenuous activity. Though Miss Truax reminded Maeva of the child's condition, she didn't offer to watch Virginia during recess.

While other children ran to the open shelter, Virginia crept on tiptoes and got wetter than most.

The shelter, supported by peeled poles and roofed with cedar shakes, had been donated the year before by two bachelor brothers who'd built a house across Whiskey Creek from the school.

Boys shinned the smoothed poles, swung on rings hanging from cross beams and tossed a worn, leaking basketball at a steel hoop at the far end of the shelter.

Girls who gathered for hopscotch found their squares erased by rain and dappled with fir cones that blew in under the roof. Maeva pried Virginia's fingers from her own and gave the girl a gentle pat on her shoulder.

"We'll use a fir bough to sweep away needles and cones and the broken branch end to etch new squares." Maeva brushed the damp earth and redrew the lines. Virginia shuddered.

Seventh and eighth grade girls, their hopscotch days behind them, hovered near the swings, deep in conversation punctuated by giggles that all but drowned Virginia's small voice calling, "Miss Swanson, Miss Swanson."

"Yes, Virginia, what is it?" Maeva, coat and skirt hems gathered around her legs, crouched to the girl's level.

Tears filled Virginia's eyes. She held her mittened hands in prayer. "Father said I'm not to get my mittens dirty. That rock is dirty."

"Virginia passes," Maeva said. "Hannah, I believe it's your turn."

21

Virginia gasped, her hands reaching for the heavens. "Miss Swanson, she might damage her new coat."

"Her coat will survive. Go on, Hannah."

Maeva was less concerned about Hannah's new coat, velvet-trimmed, satin-lined tweed, than her ability to see the lines defining the hopscotch squares. Hannah squinted and managed just fine.

A fifth-grader jerked on the feet of a fourth-grader who'd parked halfway up a pole and wasn't taking turns. Maeva glanced at her pocket watch, handed down from her older brother Jonas when his wife gave him a new one. She considered it a luxury and kept it on a crocheted chain so she could wear it around her neck.

Five more minutes. She scanned the grounds for Wesley Wiley who helped with boys' spats and kept her updated on happenings in Miss Truax's classroom. "Wesley?" she called. How could she lose Wesley, almost sixteen and six feet tall?

The older girls giggled into their hands. The boy who'd parked up the pole slid down so fast he landed on his bottom. The basketball, dropped by another boy, thwomped on the packed earth. All stood still, watching, until Louanne Strom, a plump and clumsy fourth-grader, broke the silence.

"Him and my brother's off in the woods. Ralph knows where to find whiskey stuck in the crick."

"He and Ralph are in the woods," Maeva corrected, "and we say creek."

Dear God, rumors older than prohibition about moonshiners floating whiskey down the creek in wooden casks for runners to collect from the ponds. Rumors based on truth about a long-established operation at the top of Whiskey Creek.

Children waited, still and silent, while Maeva decided what to do about Wesley and Ralph. A window scraped open. Miss Truax rang the old brass bell. From the corner of her eye, Maeva saw the two boys dash from their evergreen hideout. She put the seventh and eighth grade girls in charge of leading the others back to their classrooms.

When the boys had come too far to retreat, Maeva walked toward them. "Wesley, Ralph, did you forget the playground boundaries?"

"Yes Ma'am," Ralph said at the same moment Wesley said, "No, Miss Swanson, we heard something in the trees. Thought it might be a bear. Wanted to scare it off."

Wesley stood with shoulders rounded and coat clutched.

"I presume that's a bear club you're holding to your chest, Wesley."

Ralph backed away. Wesley reached his left hand inside his coat and brought out a blue-green Mason jar with a zinc cap. "It ain't whiskey, if that's what you're thinking. It ain't even good beer. You gonna kick me outta school?"

"Would you like me to do that, Wesley?"

He shrugged, looked at the jar. "Nah, Miss Swanson. You got me persuaded toward learning since catching me up over the summer."

"Good," she said, waiting a moment while Ralph pushed a rock around with one foot. "I believe Miss Truax takes away recess time for tardiness, one recess for each minute. You and Ralph will have more time for learning since you're going to show me where you found the jar."

She took it from Wesley's extended hand, unscrewed the cap and sniffed its contents. It looked murky, with a layer of foam at the top from shaking when Wesley ran. It smelled sour, not at all pleasant like beer she'd helped Jonas brew. She dipped in a finger and touched it to her tongue.

"You're right, Wesley, it is beer. It likely belongs to the men across the creek, the brothers who built this nice shelter where we can get fresh air without getting wet." She stared just long enough at Ralph and Wesley's wet trousers and shoes. "We'll return it to where you found it."

Wesley, with Ralph at his heels, headed for the woods, stopping where the clearing ended. "Gets thick in here, Miss Swanson, you want to watch your silk stockings. Might be I should take the jar back where we found it. With you keeping an eye out."

"The creek's about ten steps in, Wesley."

Her stockings were sensible cotton rather than silk. Still, they would get snagged. She could see moving water, hear its soothing song, the nuances of its tumble over rocks and roots, its rush along smoother ground. Damp earth and cedar scented the air.

"Jars are hid some farther upstream, Miss Swanson. Up to Persson's fence post, almost, this side of the creek," Wesley said. "Ain't the Nordlund brothers' brew."

"Hidden, not hid some, and we don't use ain't, Wesley." She could imagine two bachelors putting homebrew in canning jars and cooling it in the creek, but that didn't fit Helmer Persson.

"It ain't . . . is not Persson's brew neither, if that's what you're thinking. It's the property of Farley Price, father to that new girl you got in your class. He'll drink anything, so says my dad who's took a sip with him."

"I see," Maeva said. She made scooting motions with her hands to get the boys moving, but Wesley wasn't through.

"He gets it from Orval Blevins up in Hidden Valley, him being known for using his wife's jars and bottling up beer he squeezes out of used mash. Whiskey making's more his line, but he's not above selling beer to a paying customer. Word is Farley Price pays him cash."

"*Gud i himmel,* Wesley, we are not out here in the rain along Whiskey Creek for a discussion on brewers and consumers. Return the jar to the spot where you found it. Ralph and I will wait right here."

"Righto, Miss Swanson." Wesley grinned, all cocky innocence. "Sure you don't want a real sip to settle your nerves? A little something to get you through the rest of the day?"

Maeva tried for her best stern teacher look. "Right now I want you to put the jar back in the creek."

Miss Truax stood just inside the foyer, clock in hand, while Maeva and the boys climbed the school steps. "Boys, wait on the porch. Miss Swanson, a word, if I may."

The foyer reeked of coats damp with rain and children's sweat, some items passed from older child to next and next without being washed or cleaned.

"No, no whiskey," Maeva whispered. "A fruit jar full of something liquid, but not whiskey."

"Well, then," Miss Truax said, and called the boys to join them. "Twelve minutes late. That will cost you boys twelve recesses. You will face separate back corners of the classroom during that time and remain absolutely silent. The reason for your tardiness may earn further punishment. It may increase if you're given to braggadocio."

"What's that?" Ralph asked.

"You are not to discuss the commodity you found in the creek."

"Can't be bragging," Wesley said. "Or naming names, such as that of Farley Price."

Maeva coughed to cover a laugh and turned her face toward the row of wet coats.

"And you may pray Miss Swanson hasn't taken a cold."

Maeva coughed harder. She lacked the stern quality expected of teachers, though students responded to her directions. Miss Truax questioned some of her teaching methods that came from nature and wonder, and current events, but she agreed to permit them in the name of experimenting.

"Return to your seats, boys. Miss Swanson, we will talk further after school is dismissed."

When the day ended, Ebbe Persson was there with an umbrella to collect Hannah Price. Before Maeva had finished pushing the dust mop between desks, Ebbe returned.

"Hannah's been telling me some tale about the big boys finding whiskey in the creek this afternoon."

Miss Truax joined them, tucked a straying hair into her netted bun, directed them into Maeva's classroom and settled at Maeva's desk. "I've had to take a digestive powder, I'm that unnerved."

"Wesley said it's beer," Maeva said. "He thinks it belongs to Hannah's father. I didn't ask how many jars."

Ebbe's plump rosy face darkened. "Farley Price needs to be gone from our farm. Only trouble, that leaves Eleanor and Hannah at his mercy and me to take up the slack on the milking. Like I told Helmer, leastaways we offer Eleanor some protection if we keep Farley on. Could be the good Lord sent them to us for that very reason."

Miss Truax clutched a wad of eyelet at her throat. Holding down her bile, Maeva guessed. Her own stomach churned with worry for Hannah. She said, "The child is very bright," to encourage Ebbe's commitment.

"Looks like Romstads, down to the tavern, might give Eleanor some work. Cooking, sewing new curtains for their summer cabins out back, mending sheets, cleaning, whatever. Astrid's got the rheumatiz in her hands, they're all swole-up."

"I think that would be good for Hannah," Maeva said. "Staying on with you and continuing in school."

To Maeva's surprise, Miss Truax said, "I concur. Heaven only knows what will become of that poor blind child if we don't keep her occupied."

"Nearsight I think it's called." Ebbe pushed her body up from the child's desk. "We'll see, then. Maeva, you better get a move on, you don't want to be missing your boat. Helmer can finish putting things to order when he comes over to shut down the furnace."

Maeva saw the *Aggie J* still at the float when she rounded the bend on School Road. She would thank Axel for waiting, linger with him in the wheel house after they tied up at Jenson's Pier, laugh at the story of beer in the creek. In their childhood they often rowed over to Burke Bay to sip creek water. She'd convinced Axel that it gave them uncommon powers.

She drank in the cold salt air wafting off the bay and listened to the gangplank's squeak as it scraped the float. Axel stood on the *Aggie J's* bow deck ready to cast off.

A man looking her way waited on the dock. A man who watched her, seemingly without blinking. As she drew near, she saw his eyes were blue. Seafarer blue, if such a color existed.

"Watch your step, Miss Swanson. Ramp's slick." The man took her hand in his with no protest from her. The conversation she'd been conducting in her head dissolved.

"I don't believe we've met," she said.

He nodded. "True enough. Hauk Nordlund."

They proceeded down the gangplank, her hand still in his, he a step ahead.

26

"One of the Norwegian brothers who built the school shelter? Off fishing in Alaska or logging somewhere when I first moved home?" She'd imagined them older, near their sister Ilsa Bakke's age.

"The same."

"Step lively," Axel called, "we're running late." He reached out a hand to help her onto the boat's deck.

In the same moment, Hauk Nordlund placed his hands on her waist and lifted her. "Oh," she said. She wasn't a small woman and couldn't remember ever being lifted off her feet.

"Hauk'll be piloting the *Aggie J* for a few days next week while Dad and I look into some business matters." Axel planted a kiss on her cheek and slid open the wheelhouse door.

"Hauk Nordlund." Maeva said. "He couldn't look less hawk-like." Except, perhaps, in the way his eyes watched her walk toward him, follow him down the ramp, startle when he lifted her.

She stifled a groan at her interest in his intense eyes. She'd spent too many late nights reading romantic novels after Axel broke off a promising kiss and went whistling into the dark.

5

~ Burke Bay Tavern ~

*H*ope, when it visited after a long absence, felt like the first warm spring breeze at home, with disappearing snow and green grass and just-soaped saddle leather. So thought Eleanor as she peeled and sliced apples for pies. A peeling curl trailed from the apple in her hand to mound with others already turning brown in a chipped white enamel dishpan sitting in the large porcelain sink.

She smelled promise in the apple slices (almost smelled cinnamon even before it was added), and the heady perfume of safety in the warm tavern kitchen where turkey soup burbled on the huge black stove.

Beside her, Astrid Romstad massaged fingers with knobs big as drawer pulls.

"Pies bring folks in nearly much like liquor did back before this Prohibition nonsense. Them who want liquor find it easy enough. You're knowing that, according to Ebbe."

The refrigerator hummed. Rain dripped from the roof overhang. Burning wood rearranged itself in the stove.

Eleanor looked through condensation on the window over the sink to a grassy slope cut through with a narrow lane and two rows of cedar-shake cabins, roofs green with moss Astrid said needed removing. Did she expect Eleanor to tackle that once the pies were in the oven? Or would that be nonsense, a favorite word of both Ebbe Persson and Astrid Romstad.

"Summer cabins, but for the one with two bedrooms at the top of the lane. The Baptist Church rents it for Pastor Holmes and his family. Church itself sits on a rock ledge just beyond." She broke into song, sweet-voiced, words altered: "The Baptists built their house upon a rock."

"Oh," said Eleanor, a now and then Episcopalian.

"No one will pay much mind if you don't attend. Most drive to the Lutheran Church over to Silverdale. Never met a good Swede nor Norwegian neither who took to Baptists. The ones who built it done so to save loggers from sin, but most don't see sin quite the same as them Baptists."

Eleanor didn't answer, having already worn out *Oh*. She wondered if Astrid Romstad and Ebbe Persson were sisters with their sturdy bodies and rosy faces, and accents that required an attentive ear.

She covered the huge bowl of apples with a damp flour-sack towel, dumped the peels into a dented bucket on the porch out back for Erling Romstad to collect, and opened the gate-leg table to roll out piecrust.

Astrid laid out a pastry cloth thickened with collected flour and lard from former rolled crusts, smoothing it flat as best her bent fingers allowed. "This here table should serve for your daughter as a place to read or make paper-dolls while you're going about your work."

"Thank you, Mrs. Romstad. Thank you for Hannah, especially."

"Call me Astrid. No need to stand on formality around here." She hobbled the length of the kitchen and opened a door at the far end. The door's nice brass knob was dull with use and steam and sea air.

"There's an iron frame bed in the room back here where Hannah can sleep if you're working late. We'll not ask Ebbe to watch her much beyond today. Big enough bed for you and Hannah side-by-side, if need be."

If need be. Assurance from a woman she'd met the day before, in a community close to two-thousand miles by car from her Kansas home.

Eleanor didn't know what to make of these Burke Bay women, Ebbe Persson and Astrid Romstad, both born in Sweden and transplanted in America by choice, both equal to their men.

Partners to them, a bit impatient with them if they forgot to wipe their feet on the doormat or wash their hands all the way to their elbows, she'd observed that with Ebbe more than once and yesterday with Astrid when her husband came to the tavern kitchen with fish dangling from his hands.

"Nice fish, wipe your feet."

Ebbe Persson said Hannah's teacher was Swedish, too, from a good family along the beach at South Bay, and swept an arm to show where she meant.

The beach across the bay from the tavern ran south along a plank road toward Bremerton; the beach this side ran north toward Keyport, the creek west toward a valley somewhere beyond Persson's farm, beyond hills and trees all dripping green. She would learn.

The letter from home, delivered to the Burke Bay Mercantile that also served as a post office, and from there into her shaking hands by Ebbe's work-reddened ones, dashed her belief Papa would welcome her and Hannah back on the ranch. He wrote of banks foreclosing on farms, cattle prices so low they didn't cover the cost of feeding, and her good fortune to have a husband who had any work at all.

Had he misunderstood her intention to leave Farley? Or ignored it? Either way, she had his answer.

Her good fortune included Thanksgiving ruined by Farley, drunk the night before, asleep through the day until evening milking, then gone through the night. Gone again this day, looking for work at Carlson's Mill. Looking for work more fitting, in his thinking, than milking cows.

Astrid's turkey soup with homemade noodles, Ebbe's bread with slabs of butter, Eleanor's apple pies and pot after pot of coffee moved from the tavern kitchen through a double-hinged door to the high ceiling public room where mingled aromas made stomachs rumble.

Five men sat at the mahogany bar on fine mahogany stools, their feet on the bar's long brass rail. Two of the men looked like twins at first glance, though on closer study Eleanor noted slight differences. Astrid had named them and every other patron, but names went past her ears without entering, names pegged onto a wash-line and reeled off to catch the wind.

One of the look-alike men smiled more than the other; she smiled back without meaning to. She glanced at them on every trip from the kitchen, drawn to their blue eyes that looked as polished as the bar and stools and brass rail she'd labored over while pies baked. Eyes bluer than she'd ever seen, as though lighted from behind with knowledge beyond that available to other men.

Four booths along the end wall that looked east to the dock and sea beyond held men and women, two couples each plus an extra man at one, a bachelor. Astrid made much mention of bachelors who especially liked her tavern fare and kept business going.

Six of the eight tables that filled the space between the bar and front windows were occupied. Conversations knew no boundaries. Table patrons shouted to those in booths who, in turn, called out to the men at the bar. Burke Bay folks out for Saturday night, dressed in their best, some of that less than fine but all clean and pressed.

If a patron or two lingered beyond closing to have a nip, as gossip suggested, she wouldn't know about it. Helmer and Ebbe Persson were there to see her and Hannah safely home. Hannah, asleep in the iron-frame bed, worn out with worries brought on by a drunken father and burdened mother.

Erling Romstad, in denim overalls and a blue chambray shirt with fraying cuffs, opened the piano set up a few feet from a potbellied stove. Eleanor could turn those cuffs, the collar too, and wondered if she should offer. Not to Mr. Romstad but to Astrid, with whom she already felt comfortable.

The crowd quieted. One of the blue-eyed men at the bar, not the one with the ready smile, plucked a harmonica from his shirt pocket and picked up Erling's tune. Men moved tables. A couple rose to dance, then another. Eleanor's eyes smarted. She'd liked dancing. Liked it so much she'd let Farley dance her away from everything familiar.

The front door opened, the bell above it tinkled. A voice called, "Hey there, Axel and the teacher."

The man, Axel, dance-stepped around the room shaking men's hands, kissing ladies' foreheads. He had flaxen hair, fine as silk,

31

splendid as a crown. Along with dancing she'd liked handsome cowboys, had liked them before she should her mother said, and this man was handsome.

From beside her Astrid said, "That's Axel Jenson, captain of the *Aggie J*, and Maeva Swanson, your Hannah's school teacher. I'll do the introductions."

Eleanor forced her eyes from the cowboy of the seas to the teacher and released the breath she'd held. Nerves settled with one look. Maeva Swanson need not circle the room. The room circled her.

Dark hair cut just below her ears, clean part on the right, smooth on top, waves on the sides, high forehead and thick brows framing intelligent eyes. A pretty oval face, but it was the eyes that drew Eleanor in and held her much as a mother lifts and holds her infant. Not their color so much as their depth, the comfort they offered, the confidence they projected.

Eleanor carried pie and coffee to the table where Maeva sat. Two tables pushed together, three old men vying for Maeva's attention, their voices loud, edged with dissension, a name batted about. Wesley. The creek. Wesley. Brew.

Piano music in the background. The harmonica. Requests for coffee refills. She brought the pot, filled mugs. When she'd finished, Maeva spoke to her, giving Eleanor time to note the eyes were green with gold flecks. She'd never seen eyes quite like them.

"Excellent pie, Mrs. Price."

"It's Mrs. Romstad's recipe." Eleanor looked at the coffee pot she held, warmed by the words. Embarrassed. Pleased.

"A recipe's success rests with the cook." Maeva touched Eleanor's hand, a light touch and release. "I've grown very fond of Hannah. She shares my love of books."

Eleanor nodded. Axel spoke before she found a response.

"Maeva could spend less time reading and more learning to bake pies like this." He winked at Eleanor. She felt her face heat and turned away.

"I'm capable enough when there's a need," Maeva said, and then to Eleanor, "My mother is an excellent cook but most of her recipes are stored in her memory. Those written out are in Swedish and call for dabs or handfuls, and her hands are much smaller than mine."

Without wanting to, Eleanor looked at Maeva's hands, not large so much as long-fingered, though both her little fingers curled to point at her ring fingers.

"You can see why I don't play the piano," Maeva said, "which is almost unheard of for grade school teachers. I don't sew either, though bent fingers are no excuse there. It never interested me until I saw the coat you made Hannah. My mother has trunks filled with lovely garments, if only I could remake them."

"I could help you." The words flew past Eleanor's lips before she could bite them back. Mr. Romstad moved from scales to a schottische. Axel stood and pulled Maeva to her feet.

"I'd like that," Maeva called over the music. "So would Mom."

Eleanor backed out of the way as table and chair legs scraped the polished wood floor, and more dancers circled the room. The harmonica player's eyes followed Maeva, of that Eleanor was certain. His almost twin stepped away from the bar and extended a hand toward Eleanor.

"May I have the honor, Mrs. Price?"

"Oh, no, I can't. I'm working." She felt heat in her face again, another blush tinged with fear. What if Farley should walk in?

"Give me that coffee pot," Astrid said. "You go on and have a dance, Lang's a gentleman, him and his brother Hauk both. We're all of one in this here place, and you're part of us now."

The man called Lang danced her into the space between piano and tables, between tables and door, around past the booths to the end of the bar. She relaxed, forgot the fear, and would have let him hold her closer if the door hadn't blown open.

"Fire," a man shouted, the teacher's brother Nels, she later learned. "Fire. At Carlson's Mill, not too bad spread so far, just the burner."

Men rolled out the door. Women watched them go. Astrid hugged the blue enamel coffee pot against her breasts. Maeva lifted the harmonica from the bar, from the neatly placed cloth napkin where the man named Hauk had left it. Ebbe went to the piano and lowered the cover over the keys.

Eleanor heard car engines cough and catch and drone, and the silence that followed, but her mind's eye saw cowboys grabbing horses' reins, poking one booted foot in a stirrup, swinging into saddles and riding off.

When the shock waves settled, Eleanor gathered stoneware cups and dishes, carried them to the kitchen, washed, dried and carried them back out. Women clustered in the center of the room, finding comfort in closeness, in passing cream and sugar. Spoons clicked as they stirred and stirred. Clicked again when they settled on saucers.

"Not like Irv Carlson to let the burner go unwatched," Astrid said. "Nor to miss being here of a Saturday night. Maybe he just let sawdust stack up, what with so little work of late. Little call for all the shakes and lumber he's got cut and stored."

"Where . . . where exactly is the mill?" Eleanor asked, her voice ragged with fear that Farley might be involved. Not in fighting the fire, but in starting it. Things had a way of going wrong with Farley around.

"Over to the lagoon on past Ilsa Bakke's store," Astrid said, with a wave of her hand. "Along the road on your way here from Bremerton."

Maeva arranged cream and sugar containers, cups and spoons, and drew imaginary lines on the table. "This is Bremerton. The main highway runs directly to Burke Bay. Here, about a mile beyond the Mercantile, there's a man-made pond hidden by a stand of maple trees.

"The first mill owner dug the pond between Whiskey Creek's south fork and the Bay's lagoon to provide water-power for his mill. The present owner, Irv Carlson, uses steam power but the pond's always full, just in case."

"I remember ponds on both sides of the road on our way here," Eleanor said, "but it seems more than a mile back."

Astrid chuckled. "That would be the marsh. Road floods there every November, and stays flooded clean to April."

Maeva spooned a little coffee onto the table to show the marsh in relation to Bremerton and Burke Bay, and placed one small drop at the spot she named Carlson's Pond. "We call the road through the marsh the new road to Bremerton, built to connect with the new Manette Bridge."

Astrid moistened a swollen finger and drew a line perpendicular to the highway. "And this here's the old road, the one you see along the beach across the bay from us. A mile of it's planks set on pilings along the beach, the whole length built by Swedes across the lagoon inlet and beach without the help of the state. South Bay Road, it's called. From there it's paved clear on to Manette."

Astrid handed Maeva a used paper bag and pencil. Maeva drew a map of Burke Bay, with squares for buildings, straight lines for roads, curved lines for Whiskey Creek and its south fork. She sketched the dock with the abandoned building at its end, the Baptist Church and the rock it sat atop, the tavern, mercantile, garage, and Carlson's Mill, with scattered X's for homes.

"You can see why she's called The Teacher," Astrid said. "She makes sense of things, and she's got some talent for drawing."

Maeva laughed. "Some talent, but not much."

That made Eleanor smile and relax a bit. She felt comfortable with these women.

For the next hour women drank coffee and chatted, now and then excusing themselves to use the wash-house, a building out back with shower, flush toilet, washing machine and laundry tubs that served cabins and tavern. Every few minutes eyes turned to the door. Twice Astrid went to the window, wiped off steam with a dish towel and peered out.

Eleanor was on her way to the kitchen with an empty coffee pot when the tavern door opened to frame Erling as though he'd waited off-stage for his cue. He shook his head, took cigarette papers and tobacco bag from his pocket.

"Burner's shot. Irv pulled the pond gate, saved most the rest except the shakes. They're burning like kindling. Likely some cured lumber will need drying all over again. It'll need watching for a few days. Them Nordlund brothers saved Irv when the chute come down. Few fellows got skin burns. I come for some lard, some old sheets, Astie, we can spare some."

Astie. An endearment Eleanor found touching. Under her breath, speaking only to the clutched coffee pot, she said, "What have you done now, Farley Price?"

6

~BURKE BAY MERCANTILE ~

*O*nce they had the fire under control, Hauk and Lang Nordlund and Irv Carlson gathered in Ilsa Bakke's living quarters behind the Burke Bay Mercantile. The rooms were cool and quiet, a pleasant respite after the mill fire.

Hauk selected a curved needle from his sister Ilsa's sewing box, threaded it with darning cotton and dropped it in water coming to boil on an electric hot plate. Her wood stove, last fed hours earlier, remained warm to the touch but not hot enough to boil water. Nor did its ashes produce the lingering odor and taste of wood smoke that filled Hauk's nostrils and rested at the back of his throat. That came from himself, his brother, and Irv Carlson, cut up and smoked almost to cure-stage.

Irv reclined in Ilsa's kitchen rocking chair, rockers blocked with firewood from the box by the stove. Ilsa held his head in her strong square hands. Lang placed an eye-cup filled with boric acid over Irv's left eye. Ilsa tipped Irv's head back. Irv emitted a deep primordial sound that ended with one recognizable word.

"*Konjakk.*"

Ilsa patted Irv's face. "One minute. Hauk's warming it."

Irv's moan raised the fine hairs on Hauk's arms. He held a jelly glass of warmed brandy in his palms, waiting for a nod from his sister, remembering another fire.

He'd been almost three, following Ilsa and Lang who were rounding up the family's dairy cows to change pastures. Hauk stopped to chase a garter snake and ran to catch up, taking a shortcut across blackened earth where their father had been slashing and burning. He remembered the warmth of the ground beneath his feet, the sensation of his legs unable to move, the smell of burning flesh.

Scars, two dotted rows from knee to ankle on both hairless legs, and the way they ached in cold weather and every morning on rising from bed, reminded him daily. Ilsa said their dad plunged him feet-first into a watering trough to cool the burning leather before he peeled it from Hauk's legs.

"Boot leather and your hide come off in Father's fingers, but the little metal lace eyelets stayed stuck to your shin bone," Ilsa said. "They're still there. New skin grew up over them."

He'd believed that until he was eight or nine.

At Ilsa's nod, he carried the warmed brandy to Irv, held the glass to his lips, and watched him suck it down. Ilsa lifted a cloth she'd soaked in boric acid from Irv's forehead. The gash ran from his receding hairline through his eyebrow, now shaved clean by Ilsa's steady hand.

Hauk rinsed his hands once more in the antiseptic, poured boiling water from needle and thread, and found a spot beside Ilsa, who secured Irv's head in her vice-grip hands, squeezing so the gash edges almost met.

With steady, practiced proficiency, Hauk poked the needle into flesh on one side of the wound, pulled it out on the other, and tied a knot. Lang reached in to snip the thread. Hauk repeated the process every one-eighth inch, just as he had on many a cow or calf who found her way into uncleared land or tangled up in barbed wire.

He worked without talking, leaving Ilsa to counter Irv's curses and moans with soothing words. Soft voice for a big woman. When Hauk finished sewing, Ilsa moved to the front of the chair, pillowed Irv's bloodied head on her chest and spoke to his left ear.

"He sews good, my baby brother does. Taught him myself, beginning when he was but a lad. Eleven children we were in our family on that Snohomish Dairy Farm, me the last girl, four boys behind me. Them darn cows were always tearing their hide on barbed wire and blackberry vines. I saw to Hauk after he had a mishap with fire. Dad figured he might never walk right so he'd need to come up with ways to use his hands. Teaching him sewing made sense to me. He got good at all sorts of tasks. I saw to Lang, too, since he never left Hauk's side. Cut one of them, they both bleed."

Lang poured brandy into the glass Irv clutched, then into three more jelly glasses lined up by the kitchen sink. His hands and arms were blackened, the hair singed or gone completely, his eyes red and weepy. He'd placed himself in front of Hauk at the fire, stepped out in front of him every time Hauk moved, so there'd been little for Hauk to do until Irv slipped and fell against the burner's ragged edge just before it crumbled and dropped the chute.

The brothers lifted their glasses, drank, nodded appreciation. Their sister's blackberry brandy went unequaled. Not sticky-sweet like some they'd tasted. She added gooseberry juice to the blackberries to temper them. Hauk gave Lang a nod that said 'You do the talking.'

"Irv," Lang said, "now you're stitched up good as new, tell us how that fire got started."

Ilsa backed away. Irv said, "Aw, hell," maybe missing her bosom-pillow, maybe regretting the truth. "Hell, all I done was take a nip or two with a man come looking for work."

Lang studied his brandy and Irv at the same time. "Man anyone we might know?"

Irv's fingers tested his shaved-off eyebrow. "Helmer's hired hand. Peculiar name. You heard about him?"

"We've heard," Lang said. "He have anything to do with the fire?"

"Not direct. He didn't do nothing but ask how the dang burner works. Thought I could hire him to keep watch over that, help him out a bit. He give me some of his snake-bite, you boys might want to look out for where he's doing his cooking. Could poison the whole dang crick with that witch's piss."

Irv's jowls reddened to the color of his bloodshot eyes. "Sorry, Ilsa, only meant to say it's powerful stuff, not sipping whiskey, that's for dang sure."

Hauk chuckled and let Lang keep the conversation going. No need for both of them to talk when their thoughts and notions matched.

They'd asked around, nosed around some would say, after Price crossed the creek to their property and knocked on their kitchen door hoping to be invited in for a drink. They'd offered him venison stew with potatoes from their own garden, and warm biscuits. He'd eaten, licked his lips, looked around for the cook like they had someone hidden in the rafters.

"Man's name is Farley Price," Lang said. "Near as we can figure, he gets his hooch somewhere up the creek. Spends about all the cash he earns without much thought for his wife and child."

"*Ja,*" Irv said, "it starts up the crick. It's Orval Blevins' whiskey, I'd sure enough bet, or his all but used up mash. Either way, Price is adding extender. Cow liniment, it tasted like." He held out his empty glass for a refill of Ilsa's brandy. "I hear-tell Price's wife's helping out the Romstads. Hear-tell she's a pretty woman. Not Norwegian, though. English, Helmer says."

"She's pretty," Lang said.

Ilsa looked at Hauk. She heard the weight of Lang's words much as he did. Farley Price had an adversary such as no one would want.

Neither brother had a quarrel with those who brewed drink for profit or drank for pleasure, nor were they inclined to poke their noses into others' personal lives. But a page turned in Lang's book yesterday, the first time he saw Eleanor Price step out of the Burke Bay Tavern kitchen into the public room's light, and another turned this night when he asked her to dance.

"Hear tell the child's next to blind," Irv said. "Man blames his wife for that."

Ilsa patted Irv's face. "Eye glasses can likely take care of the child's sight, Irv. Keep that in mind when you collect on your fire insurance. While you're at it, buy yourself a pair and watch who comes around looking for work."

"Hell, there's no sense milling timber that don't sell. I'm thinking about closing down, taking up fishing full time, least it's food for the table."

"That requires a decent boat," Ilsa said.

Irv narrowed his eyes and winced at the tug on his stitched wound. "You're right about that. Think your brothers can build me one?"

Ilsa gave Irv an impatient look. "And why not? If I ever learn of anything these two boys can't do, I'll publish it in the *Bremerton Searchlight* and *The Kitsap Weekly* both."

Hauk got caught up in a grin at that statement and almost missed his sister's next words, a sign that life moved on.

"Might make better sense, though, for them to fix up Skipper Bakke's boat hiding out in the shed down below here. Seems a shame to let it rot. Could be one of you'll want to take this Farley Price fellow on a fishing trip one of these days."

7

~ Hidden Valley ~

Orval Blevins reckoned he needed to make a trip down to Burke Bay, a good two miles from his own place as the crow flies, after his busy little wife passed along rumors about a fire at Carlson's Mill.

"Mrs. Strom tells me it's been said the hired hand at Persson's Dairy started the fire," Thelma said. "More than likely drunk, though she's not sure where he's getting his liquor. I took that as a hint that she has her suspects."

Orval pondered that a bit before answering. "Now, Thelma, don't you be paying no never mind to Trilby Strom." He let it go at that, busy as he was chewing on what Grandpap would say if he knew Orval had dealings with that hired hand.

According to Grandpap, there'd been trouble in Burke Bay ever since some fellow built the tavern with a bunch of cabins out back. First off folks came across from Seattle to rent them cabins, bathe in the bay's shallow waters and hold clam-bakes on the sandy beach. Next thing they filled jugs with water from the ponds at the end of the creek and hauled it back to Seattle.

All too soon folks took to buying up land along the creek, trying their darndest to drain it dry with wells dug here, there and everywhere.

Them folks peeved Grandpap on account of his distilling business relied on that water for its success. The peeving passed down to Orval right along with the business. When Prohibition came along, Grandpap figured it was time for Orval to get acquainted with the folks that owned the tavern.

"You hie on down to the Bay and sidle up nice like to them Romstads at the tavern. Let them know you've got good product. Hell, give them a bottle free to whet their interest. Not a jug—a quart'll do."

Grandpap figured the Romstads, who'd bought the tavern and cabins back along about 1912, would need his product to keep afloat, so to speak. Turned out they were Swedes of the worst order, more stubborn than the Swede woman who'd been Orval's grandma. They refused all offers of local product. Must be they did their buying business with runners out of Canada, though no one ever caught them in the act, what with steamships and fishing boats navigating every which way on Puget Sound.

Romstads kept a dinghy, sails and oars both attached, tied up to a drift log right across Dock Road from the tavern. Erling Romstad like as not rowed or sailed out onto the Sound in the dark of night for Canadian product. Either that or he relied on home brewed beer, not real liquor.

~

Orval's wife broke right into his thoughts about Grandpap to say, "There's all sorts of rumors flying up School Road with the Strom's youngsters. You might take time to listen."

He nodded and squinted, signs he was doing just that. She kept up her end of their marriage bargain, tending the garden, canning up stores for winter and producing a child. A girl-child, not his first choice, but she was carrying another, one he trusted would be a boy, he'd put that much work into holding himself in check until his brain nearly burst. The seed for the girl got wrung out too fast, his wife being so young and pretty.

"You'd be wise, Orval Blevins, to pay close attention to what I'm saying. The mill fire problem's one thing, what's going on at the school is another altogether."

He paid attention enough to stop off at Strom's place on his way down to the Bay. Walt Strom, a Swede smart enough to keep to his side of the fence that separated their places but not smart enough to put a stopper to a new baby every year or two, had a chatty wife and a big batch of offspring. There were Stroms in their twenties and Stroms in diapers.

Lucky for Orval, the Strom's youngest daughter, Louanne, by name, chattered up a storm about the school teacher. Louanne's voice was annoying as a stellar's jay but good for carrying facts back up the creek from the school. Not ABC facts, rather news-facts about art projects, the latest being colored maps of the entire Kitsap Peninsula, along with one of Burke Bay and Whiskey Creek blown up big as all outdoors. That one had a blue circle set right smack dab in his woods. He saw the thing with his own two eyes, over to the Strom kitchen.

"This here's where the crick starts," Louanne said, her stubby finger on the blue spot in his woods, "and this here's where it ends." She pointed at Burke Bay, also blue but bigger, with upside-down vees. "These here are waves on the water. And these here circles are the upper and lower ponds at the end of the crick. Miss Swanson says the lower one gets salty from the tide coming in."

Orval took a close look at the blue line Louanne called the crick, blue circles she called ponds, the blue spot smack-dab in his woods. "You call this here an art study?" he asked.

"A project," Louanne said. "Miss Swanson gives us art projects two times a week. She drawed outlines for us and we colored in the parts. I picked blue for the water parts and green for the tree parts and white for the houses. White's the hardest to color. My dumb brother Ralph made the crick black."

Orval chewed on that for a full minute before saying, "Ralph's not in your school room, now is he? He's about to be graduated out of eighth grade and you'd only be just starting to school. Don't seem to me Ralph would be coloring pictures."

Louanne sniffed in twin nose drips, wiped her pointing finger crosswise above her mouth and stood her tallest, though that didn't get her head much above the table. "I'm in fourth. Miss Swanson teaches art projects to the whole school, first through eighth. It's her job. She's the best teacher ever. I hope she teaches fifth to eighth next year."

"Project, you say." Orval drew a kitchen match up the seam of his pants and held the flame over his pipe-bowl, but the tobacco there had burned its last, leaving him with nothing to draw in but dead ash.

"You run along now, Louanne, give your mama a hand with the wash," Walt Strom said, giving his daughter a little push.

"What you make of that?" Orval asked.

Walt shrugged. "That teacher, she's a smart one. Kids come home last week with pictures made by settin' toadstools' undersides on paper. Spore-printing, the teacher called it. Ralph got into that project. Went off back of the pasture pickin' them stinkin' things, packin' them up onto the porch."

"Be damned," Orval said, and added a snicker. "Never heard of no such thing." Spore printing sure as shooting didn't give cause for concern same as drawing a map with his creek on it. Damned accurate map at that. Could be he'd need to have a word with the teacher, let her know her own daddy did business with Old Grandpap back before she was born. And, in more recent times, Oval'd met up with her brother Jonas and his high school buddies in Bremerton in the wee hours. Like father, like son.

"That's not the worst of it," Walt said. "Ralph said the Wiley boy found some brew in the creek and brought it onto the school grounds. Ralph went along on the adventure so he took his punishment same as young Wiley. Brew stored in canning jars."

Orval rubbed his chin. "I hadn't heard that story." He'd need to have a word with Farley Price about those Mason jars. Them things belonged to Thelma, his fussy little wife, who'd be fussing aplenty if those jars went missing.

"What I come by about is your take on the fire down to the Bay. I'm about to head down that way, pick up a thing or two at the mercantile."

Yessiree, he'd buy an item or two before he tried to get any news out of Mrs. Bakke. Now, there was a woman that scared him half out of his wits. First time he called in at the store after she bought it, she looked him down and up, did some odd thing with her mouth and gave her head a shake before he'd said more than his name. "I don't give out merchandise on credit, Mr. Blevins."

"I wasn't askin', now was I?" he said, though he'd been about to do just that. A business man needs sugar and more than one place to get it, and them that run the mercantiles had the wherewithal to get a good supply. He'd kept his foot in Mrs. Bakke's door, giving her a little business here and there, careful to count out his change like he didn't have wads more stuck down inside his work boots.

Took Thelma down to Mrs. Bakke's every so often just to let Burke Bay folks know he had him a woman up there at the top end of Whiskey Creek. Introduced her by first name and last.

"Meet my wife, Thelma Blevins."He'd expected Mrs. Bakke to answer with a proper 'pleased to meet you,' but no, not her.

"Thelma," she said, extending her hand, not to shake like a man would, but to grab hold like a mother. "I'm Ilsa Bakke. If you ever need anything, anything at all, you let me know."

Thelma had looked at him with an odd little smile forming, then looked back at Mrs. Bakke, and said. "Thank you, Ilsa Bakke."

Damned if her smile didn't stretch up and put a light in her eyes. While he was trying to catch hold of the conversation's meaning, Mrs. Bakke made a point of telling Thelma there was a telephone in the back room that folks sometimes used when they needed a doctor's appointment or such.

"We'll be going now, Thelma," he said. "Just wanted you two women to meet, being as you're at opposite ends of the creek. You draw your drinking water from the creek, do you, Mrs. Bakke?"

"Drinking water," Mrs. Bakke said, her thick eyebrows lifting above her specs, "cooking water, floor scrubbing water, toilet flushing water, they all come from a private source."

Orval had that visit on his mind when he parked alongside three cars in front of the mercantile. He still hadn't figured out that private water source message. He ambled into the store and made his way toward the meat market counter in the back where Irv Carlson was wrapping a package. Smelled like fresh smoked bacon.

"*Ja*," Irv said to the waiting customer, "you heard it true. Hauk Nordlund sewed me up. Fire's still smoldering, if you want to take a look at the damage. All but put me out of business. Looks like I'll be clerking here for Ilsa."

Orval took a good look at Irv's stitches. His pesky little wife hadn't heard the sewing up part of the story or she'd have let him in on it. He'd linger a bit, see what more Irv had to say on the matter. See what else them Nordlunds might be up to now that they'd planted themselves in a house alongside his creek.

Darn nice house, he'd heard, for two men getting along without wives. Darn good well they'd dug. Could be they wanted to cut in on his business.

8

~ Carlson's Mill ~

*T*he Sunday after the fire Maeva went with Nels and Axel to view damage to the mill and stored lumber. Charred remains of the burner and chute-feeder were stuck hither and yon in mud left by low tide. Haze lingered over the site like fog sometimes clings to the bay long after sun shines overhead.

The acrid smell created by smoldering debris permeated the soft tissue of her mouth and throat, and carried with it a sense of sorrow at Irv's loss. The main working part of the mill remained intact though the front of the building facing the burner sported charred spots.

"Looks like it could flare up again," Nels called from somewhere out of her sight. Axel answered, "There's some hot spots over here, too. Cedar shakes."

She didn't understand their excitement, their frequent calls to come look at this, go look at that, as though every separate charred item and mist from a steaming pile of shakes deserved museum space.

She jotted a few notes on her tablet, filled the page with a sketch she hoped conveyed the ugliness of nature scarred not by a fire in a mill but by the mill itself. The backdrop of second-growth evergreens forty or so years old, some majestic, others struggling for sunlight, and the bare maple tree branches lifting toward the sky were easy for her untrained hand. She drew in the main building, the scattered blackened remains, and ghost mists dancing above smoldering shakes.

That evening she began composing an article for *The Kitsap Weekly*. As she studied her sketches she thought about the time before loggers and lumber mills, the time when local Indians camped along creeks and around lagoons, cutting only trees they could use for sustenance. She wove a bit of their history into the article, sidebar material the paper welcomed.

That done, she wrote a poem atop her sketch. Her brother Jonas insisted poetry writing wasted good paper even more than sketching. She combined them to save paper. To save money. Her own money.

She was reading through a draft of her article aboard the *Aggie J* Monday morning when Wesley launched into his account of the fire. He'd wedged himself in beside her, his left thigh beside her right. She half-listened until he mentioned the boat captain sewed up Irv Carlson's head with a darning needle.

"What did you say, Wesley?"

"Hauk Nordlund's at the helm this morning. You know that much, right?"

She scowled at Wesley. "I am able to distinguish between Mr. Nordlund and Mr. Jenson."

"Righto," Wesley said, and winked, a wink she read to mean he knew what went on between her and Axel.

"I said, Miss Swanson, that Hauk Nordlund, who's our captain this morning, sewed up a gash on Irv Carlson's head with a darning needle and thread."

"Now where did you get that story, Wesley?"

"See, Miss Swanson, that's your problem. You know all sorts of book things, but you don't know half the people things going on around you. Everybody along the beach and all the way up Whiskey Creek heard about the sewing and the screaming and the brandy drinking it took to keep old Irv still long enough for Hauk to do the stitching and tie the knots."

"By whose account?" Maeva wanted Wesley to see rumor for what it was.

"If you mean who said, it was Irv his own self. Him and my dad and some other men got together in the mill office last night to talk about damage and salvage. I went along to see my dad got back home. My dad figures he can make use of some charred timbers or shakes, keep from tossing them on the trash heap."

"Wesley, your grammar is slipping again," Maeva said, then couldn't recount his errors; she was too busy processing the fact that Wesley, for all intents and purposes, was one of the local men. Whiskers sprouted on his handsome face. He drove his dad, at his mother's insistence, to get Wes Sr. and the car safely home.

When Hauk Norldlund handed her down from boat deck to float, she asked if the story were true. He gave one abrupt nod without so much as a grin. Something in his eyes sent the next question out of her mind. He seemed to study her lips, as though he might touch them with his.

Wesley rescued Maeva during morning recess when Virginia Holmes announced she was not allowed to play with Hannah Price because Hannah's father set the fire. Virginia said more, something about drink, or perhaps drunkard. Maeva and most of the children missed it because Wesley swooped in, lifted Virginia off her feet and whirled her around.

"Buzz, buzz, busy bee," Wesley sang. Virginia screamed in fear, and clung sobbing to Maeva's coat after Wesley put her down. Girls clustered around Wesley, begging for a turn.

"Look at that, Virginia, you got to be first in the bee game." Maeva cast a weary glance at Miss Truax's classroom windows, still in their closed position. Of course Miss Truax would hear about the game and Virginia's screams from someone. "Wesley, a word, please."

"It was meant to turn her attention, Miss Swanson. To help you protect Hannah. Some folks, Pastor Holmes included, want Farley Price run off Persson's Farm. Others, you included, want him left alone on account of Hannah and her mother."

"Wesley," she said, preparing to lecture and discarding the notion in the utterance of his name. "Never mind. I'll have a visit with Pastor Holmes after school. Please tell Mr. Nordlund not to hold the *Aggie J.*"

How on God's green earth had Wesley figured out she wanted to protect Hannah? Axel must have said something to Wesley's dad.

~

An oil stove with its thin walls glowing red struggled to heat the Baptist Church sanctuary and the pastor's small office behind the altar. The air smelled of heating oil and dust. Maeva studied Pastor Holmes while he stared at whitewashed walls in need of paint. He had watery gray eyes set too close to a nipped-in nose on a narrow face.

"I've come about Virginia," Maeva said, without preamble. "About her announcement on the playground this morning that she's not allowed to play with Hannah Price."

The pastor fidgeted. Maeva thought about Wesley's warning that she'd be walking home. *"Pastor won't be taking his car out after dark on account of his bad eyes, but more on account of his need to hand out misery to all who don't fall at his feet."*

"Miss Swanson," Pastor Holmes said, his laced fingers atop his desk, "you of all people should understand my position. We, you and I, are without doubt the only adults in Burke Bay with education beyond that offered by public schools. I, a man of God, must protect my children—indeed all God's children—from evil. Farley Price, in all regards, is an evil man."

Maeva leaned forward. "By what regards? He works for the Perssons, he has a lovely daughter, he . . ." The pastor interrupted her while she tried to formulate further argument.

"Those in this community who are considered reliable. I have it on such reliable authority that Farley Price went berserk when Mr. Carlson refused to hire him, attacked and seriously injured Mr. Carlson, robbed him and set the fire to cover his tracks."

She blinked, taking that in. "The reports I've heard from several men who attended the fire, including my brother Nels and my friend Axel Jenson, differ drastically."

Attended the fire. She could have said fought or managed or controlled, but *attended* fit her mood at the moment. "I'm here to discuss Virginia's shunning of Hannah Price, and her proclamations that you have declared Hannah the daughter of evil. I have informed Virginia she must not again voice such an opinion on school grounds."

Anger stained the pastor's cheeks and drew his lower lip into hiding behind a stingy upper one. "Miss Swanson, I will not permit my daughter to associate with the Price child. Is that clear?"

Maeva began the silent count she practiced to delay her tongue's quick response. Though she wanted to question his Christianity, his position as a man of God, she focused on the issue at hand.

"Pastor Holmes, I am sad to report that until Hannah joined us, Virginia had no close friends in school, though I worked to see others included her in activities. I fear her actions and statements will again isolate her, for Hannah Price possesses an elfin charm that drew other children to her defense when Virginia made her announcement. Your decision harms your own daughter, not the daughter of Farley Price, a man you've chosen to defile without due cause."

She'd succeeded at sounding sad and worried for Virginia, and considered adding amateur theater to her interests. She could write and direct plays with several Burke Bay characters portraying themselves.

The pastor rose to his feet. "The man is a drunkard, clearly drawn to this place on the map by the creek's unfortunate name. Others have said as much. For my part, I have initiated a campaign to strike *Whiskey Creek* from the records and legally christen it *Burke Creek*.

"I have prepared a letter to your friend Axel Jenson's father, Mr. Emil Jenson, whom, as you know, is involved in county government. I plan to carry this crusade to our capitol in Olympia at the next session of our state's legislative body."

Maeva stood, too. "*Whiskey Creek* is not the name of record. It's simply a local appellation, almost a metaphor. It grew from Indian history. It must be honored."

"It invites evil. Sin and evil, personified by Farley Price, who arrived here with an unquenchable thirst for whiskey and all that comes of imbibing. Fire has rained down on our fair community, a warning from God, sparked by the evil hands of a man sent to test our faith."

Pastor Holmes jabbed the air with a clenched fist. His jacket sleeve slid down his raised arm to expose a fine-boned wrist. He, not she, won the actor's prize. For a moment she felt sad for him, a man too delicate to work the earth, log trees, mill lumber or cast heavy ropes from a ship's bow. How out of place he seemed; how east coast seminarian.

"Has Irv Carlson accused Farley Price of assault?"

"Irv Carlson." Saliva spewed from Pastor Holmes mouth. "Another swiller of whiskey. Scandinavians know no bounds when it comes to drink. Consider the reputation of your own brother, not Nels, the older one whose name I can't recall. I was called to this place to cleanse the creek of the likes of such men, to bring the word of God to those accustomed to using might rather than mind. I'd hoped you'd join me in my crusade, but it seems you fall short of your reputation as learned and intelligent."

Maeva felt fire in her own face and forgot her momentary concern for his puniness. Jonas did drink too much, but he'd worked his way to leading-man electrician in the shipyard. She wouldn't listen to an outsider, a Baptist outsider, malign her brother. Or her friends.

"Not only will I not join you in your crusade, Pastor, I will fight any efforts to change our creek's name. I am Scandinavian, and I know no bounds when it comes to speaking my mind."

On that note Maeva buttoned her coat, picked up her canvas bag and left the church she'd never attended.

Dusk had settled over Burke Bay. Romstads' cabins were on her right, their hilltop home on her left. Silvered planks of the dock stretched out over pewter water and blended together somewhere in the distance. A lone golden light let her see inside the tavern's kitchen. She wondered if Eleanor Price worked on an evening meal for local bachelors who scraped up enough money here and there to eat out rather than cook for themselves.

What would happen to Eleanor and Hannah if Pastor Holmes succeeded in driving Farley Price from their community?

She turned onto Dock Road, covered the distance from tavern to garage to mercantile with ease thanks to her long legs and the energy fueled by fury at pomposity cloaked in invoking the name of God. She turned left onto South Bay Road and stopped for a moment to survey its geometry. Planks and rails, slightly angled to fit beach, bay, and tree-covered hillside, stretched ahead for a mile. Swedes, and possibly Norwegians, had driven the pilings with strength of their bodies, hammered home spikes with hand-hewn mauls.

She grasped the rail, gave it a hearty tug. It didn't budge.

"Scandinavian might," she said, eyes lifted to the heavens where she assumed her Swedish father's spirit rested, "and Scandinavian ingenuity. They know no bounds, these Burke Bay Scandinavians."

The night chill drew heat from her face. Headlights approached as she reached the end of the plank road and started the climb up Indian Hill. She moved to the road's edge without breaking stride. The car stopped, the window on the passenger's side lowered.

"Miss Swanson? Hauk Nordlund, here. Young Mr. Wiley said you'd made other travel arrangements; he didn't say you'd be walking."

"I didn't clarify my arrangements to young Mr. Wiley."

The car door opened. "Climb in. I'll drive you home."

"Thank you, but I'm quite capable of walking." She sounded churlish, and added, "You're headed the opposite way," and continued up the hill.

She heard the door close, the car move on, the sound of it being turned in the middle of the road, the man's voice again.

"There, now I'm headed the same way. I know how far you have to walk."

She crossed in front of the car, climbed in and offered an apology that slid into defensiveness. "I didn't mean to sound rude or unappreciative. I've walked the distance enough times to manage, dark or not."

"You're certainly a Swede," he said. "So *sta*. Such a heritage."

"*Sta?* Is that Norwegian for stubborn?"

"Something like that."

When the silence became uncomfortable, she said, "I had a rather unpleasant meeting with Pastor Holmes, whose oldest daughter is one of my students. He maligned all Scandinavians, Norwegians and Swedes alike."

"Called us all drunkards, did he?"

"Yes," Maeva said, her mind already on another thought. "May I ask you a rather personal question, Mr. Nordlund? About your land deed?"

"Name's Hauk. You may ask."

"Not all that personal; not the price, at any rate. Did any of your property's legal papers name the creek?" She waited through what seemed interminable gear shifting.

"I'm trying to recall. Stream, I believe. Yes, just that."

"Stream." She wondered what an official naming would require.

Hauk shifted into a lower gear, turned left onto Swanson-Jenson Road, a dirt lane that led from South Bay Road down to the water. "Pastor Holmes is a bit like a wood splinter buried in a finger. Annoying, but not threatening. If half of what I've heard is true, he's no match for you."

"Because I'm so *sta?*"

"Because folks respect you."

That left her silent until they reached the Y. "Left here. Our road is narrower than Jenson's."

She directed him to pull into the turn-around at the upper pasture, though the lane continued in a sharp descent. "Thank you for the ride. I do appreciate it. Would you care to stay for dinner or a cup of coffee? My mother is an excellent cook."

"My brother is expecting me, but I will walk you to your house." He opened the glove box and retrieved a flashlight.

She noted the emphasis on will, liked it but protested all the same. "That's not necessary."

"No, Miss Swanson, it is a courtesy."

"Please call me Maeva, if I'm to call you Hauk. Leave the 'Miss Swanson' for my students." She opened the gate. He ushered her through and closed it behind them.

"Maeva," he said. He played the beam from his flash along the fence on their right, forest on their left, the old barn when they cut across the lower pasture, the wood shed along the crushed shell path to the house, the Royal Ann cherry tree with a simple bench under it, her mother's flower beds settled into winter rest.

Light of a kerosene lamp shone through the kitchen windows.

"We haven't yet brought electricity down from the road," she said, as the door opened to frame her mother. "My older brother wired the house. It's up to me to provide poles and lines."

"My," her mother said. She'd been worried.

"Mom, meet Hauk Nordlund. He came upon me walking and turned around to drive me home. He's piloting the *Aggie J* for Axel. Mr. Nordlund, my mother, Alma Swanson."

Hauk nodded. "Mrs. Swanson."

"Please, come in, Mr. Nordlund. We will add another potato to the pot."

"*Tack*, Mrs. Swanson, but I must go. My brother and I see to ourselves, and it's my turn to cook our dinner. I'll latch the gates behind me." He gave an abrupt nod and turned.

Maeva watched him go, his flash turned to illuminate his surroundings, not just the path he trod. He'd said 'thanks' in Swedish. Or likely in Norwegian; some words were too similar to distinguish.

Behind her, her mother said, "Hauk," and something more in Swedish. Born with eyes wide open, or born with an eye to the truth. Maeva didn't know for certain, though she knew it mattered to her mother and would likely matter to her.

9

~ The Tavern and the Reverend ~

Though she'd heard nothing of his physical description, Eleanor recognized the man on the customer side of Burke Bay Tavern's bar as Pastor Holmes. She identified him from the picture she'd formed of a person more out of place in Burke Bay than she herself felt; a man who hid behind the church's veil.

Hannah had told her what Virginia Holmes said on the school playground and asked, "Is it true Farley set the fire?"

"Of course it isn't true," Eleanor said, "and you must remember to say father or dad."

She ignored Hannah's protests much as she'd tried to ignore the hurt that lodged under her breast bone when the pastor's wife knocked on the tavern kitchen door earlier. Mrs. Holmes poked her head in to look around but kept her feet firmly on the porch.

"You should know, Mrs. Romstad, that the teacher interrupted the pastor in his study for the sole purpose of defending Mrs. Price's husband in that mill fire matter. I overheard the exchange from another room and watched Miss Swanson leave red-of-face with shame and without a ride home, her just desserts."

Eleanor eased past Astrid to the back room, where she sat on the edge of the bed and wept into cupped hands.

"Dry them tears," Astrid said. "That's nonsense talk, pure and simple. The Reverend's wife trying to cover for his failings. Maeva left hell-bent with fury. And she could walk that distance in freezing rain or blinding snow and still milk the cows when she got home, need be."

"How far?" asked Eleanor, who added distance-walked to her worry pile. In her mind, the nice teacher suffered to protect Hannah.

"Oh, I'd say three-odd miles to the Swanson-Jenson Road, maybe a mile or so down from there."

"Four miles." Eleanor pictured four miles in Kansas where one climbed on a horse and rode off in the straightest line possible.

"Now don't you take to worrying about Maeva. First off, she can see to herself and any number of others. Second, that nice Hauk Nordlund passed her on his way back to Burke Bay from running the *Aggie J* for Axel Jenson, and he up and turned his car around and drove her on home. I got that direct from Ilsa Bakke, up to the store, she's a Nordlund by birth, she's the reason those two nice Nordlund men moved here."

Those two nice Nordlund men, one of whom danced Eleanor around the tavern the night of the Carlson Mill fire, a fire quite possibly caused by Farley, though it wouldn't do for Hannah to believe that.

And now Pastor Holmes stood about where the Nordlunds sat that night. He pulled a folded paper from inside his black gabardine suit jacket and snapped it open. His suit needed a good brushing and damp-cloth pressing.

"You would be Mrs. Price?"

"Yes." Eleanor tried to muster up the pose she'd seen her mother assume with ranch hands over the years, one that declared without undue words who held the authority. Eleanor represented the pastor's landlords. Astrid had told her to put a little starch in her spine and quit worrying about matters she couldn't control.

"I have a concern I'd like to address to Mrs. Romstad," the pastor said.

"She is unavailable. May I help you with your concern?" Eleanor hoped Astrid's faded bib apron, starched stiffer than her spine felt at the moment and spotted with holes here and there from wood-fire sparks, didn't diminish her position. She'd tied the apron over her chambray blouse and split denim riding-skirt with the hope of wearing them two days before washing. Serviceable wear, clean and pressed by her own labors with an agitating washer and electric iron, the first she'd ever used.

"You . . ." the pastor looked over his left shoulder and then his right, "are part of the problem, Mrs. Price. Or perhaps more accurately, you are wed to the problem. To a drunkard, if I may be so bold."

Eleanor's heart pattered like a bird's she'd once rescued from a barn-cat's jaws. The bird had looked at her with one frightened eye while its other eye sought escape from her hands. Burke Bay represented safety from Farley's shortcomings. She remained rigid, her eyes on the pastor while her brain sought a response, a way to defend herself and her daughter. Behind her, the door from the kitchen whooshed open.

"Bold?" Astrid said. "You call yourself bold?" She rubbed knobby purple knuckles on what Eleanor had come to see as loving hands.

"Ah, Mrs. Romstad, I have a petition here to officially name our little creek Burke Creek, thus ridding our fair community the shame and blasphemy of its current name. I'd like to post it on your dining counter, so to speak, so your patrons can add their signatures."

"Only blasphemy, far as I can tell, has to do with troubles visited upon us by this Prohibition nonsense. Wouldn't near so many folks drink bad liquor if they could buy good in a decent place such as this one the mister and I maintain."

"Are you suggesting God condones drinking liquor?"

"I am suggesting, Pastor Holmes, that you save your sermons for church. This building is a tavern, a place of rest for visitors seeking a good meal and drink to wash it down. This counter's a bar, and a fine one. Solid mahogany. Now if you'd like a cup of coffee, we can serve you. That's about all we have to offer these days, though it's my understanding that could change when Roosevelt takes over the country and the congress. So says the teacher who got it from reading umpteen dozen newspapers and magazines."

"I see. I'll just leave my petition with you."

Astrid shoved graying hair off her forehead with one swollen hand.

"Won't do us much good. Not big enough to wrap all the potato peels and carrot scrapings it takes to make a pot of stew. Not much meat these days, but we still make the best stew around. Mrs. Price opened a jar of canned venison for tonight's meal. You might bring the family in for dinner, Pastor."

"I think not, Mrs. Romstad. I think not. Nor shall I waste further time with you." He re-folded the paper, tamped it into his breast pocket and turned to leave without a formal goodbye.

"Fact is," Astrid said to the pastor's parting back, "you can give most anything, including people, a formal name, but folks'll use a nickname if it suits them. Whiskey Creek suits Burke Bay folks. Indians named it. I got that from the teacher, too."

The bell jingled as the pastor opened the door and jangled as he closed it.

Eleanor, who'd been reared to act reverent in the presence of a man of the cloth, experienced an odd thought: to heck with posture and poise, go directly to words.

"Let's give the stew a stir," Astrid said, "and poke some more wood in the stove."

"I'll see to it. You warm your hands with a cup of coffee." Eleanor wondered if she'd ever be able to speak directly to defend herself or a principle. She'd cast her lot with Farley Price, succumbed to his kisses and caresses, borne Hannah and brought her to what seemed the earth's edge when they arrived in Burke Bay.

Eleanor lifted the lid on the wood stove, shoved in a length of split alder and dropped the lid in place. Her face warmed from shame more than flame that leapt forth. She relied on strangers to protect Hannah from Farley. She stirred the stew, so far just venison pieces simmering in juices with onion for early flavoring.

Pastor Holmes was right about one thing: Farley Price was a drunkard. She peeled and quartered potatoes, cutting away black spots Astrid called *svarta*, and dropped the quarters in an enamel pan of cold water. Like the meat on the stove, Eleanor stewed in her own juices.

The tavern door's bell tinkled again, followed by Hannah's voice, excited and pleased.

"Mama? Mama, come here."

Hannah's simple greeting lifted Eleanor from her pot of worry as sure as the slotted spoon lifted meat from the kettle. "I'm here, Hannah, in the kitchen." She turned to smile at her small, squint-eyed daughter and wondered how soon her earnings could cover an eye doctor's fee and a pair of glasses.

"Come meet my teacher, Mama. She borrowed me some books to read."

"Loaned you some books, you mean." Eleanor wiped her hands on a towel she wore draped over her left shoulder, squatted for a hug and followed Astrid into the tavern's public room. Maeva Swanson and Ebbe Persson stood side by side, their arms loaded with Ebbe's bread.

"No, borrowed," Hannah insisted. "She borrowed them from the big library."

"In Bremerton," Maeva said. "Hello, Mrs. Price, hello, Astrid. Ebbe planned her bread baking so she could deliver me to the dock with a few minutes to spare."

"Time enough for a nice cup of coffee." Astrid departed and returned in a blink, one hand on the enamelware pot's handle, the other supporting its spout. She set it on the work counter behind the mahogany bar and lined up cups.

Eleanor retrieved loaves of warm bread, breathing in their fragrance and studying Maeva at the same time. The teacher's eyes held Eleanor's attention. They sent a message, one to do with Hannah.

"Maeva takes cream," Ebbe Persson said, "and I've some fresh in the truck. Hauk Nordlund's running the *Aggie J*. We know he'll wait for our Maeva without a grumble, now don't we, Astrid."

"Mama, I have a new friend. Her name is Beatrice and she is seven and she helps me with hopscotch."

Maeva put a gloved hand on Hannah's shoulder and squeezed. "Hannah is able to keep her balance while hopping on one foot, though she has to squint to see the squares. Beatrice coaches a little, which lets her feel like a big sister. She's the youngest at home."

"Oh," Eleanor said, her eyes on Maeva's gloves as the teacher removed them and put them in her coat pocket. Carefully darned gloves, hand-knit scarf inside her collar to save the coat from wear and a tone that said squinting was a condition, not a fault. It wasn't until later, after Maeva left running for the boat and Ebbe drove off in Helmer's dairy truck, that Eleanor sifted out the other message, the one that passed between the two older women. The one that had to do with Hauk Nordlund waiting for Maeva Swanson without a grumble. She didn't know any of them well enough to be certain, but her somewhat frayed romantic instincts told her Ebbe and Astrid discerned something about Hauk that Maeva might not recognize.

Eleanor Keane Price's heart beat lighter through the rest of the afternoon. Maeva Swanson had selected library books for Hannah. Maeva didn't judge her and her daughter by Farley's failings.

Had Eleanor arrived in Burke Bay by some design beyond Farley's search for work in the Navy Yard? Had she brought Hannah to the threshold of something promising rather than the edge of the earth?

Oh, she'd keep one eye—the distant one—on escape, but she'd train the other on Burke Bay to see if she could find peace within herself and a place for Hannah to grow.

10

~ Bachelor Brothers ~

$\mathcal{H}$auk and Lang sat across from each other at their dining nook table in the house they built on the north side of Whiskey Creek, a sturdy house set on the high point of their five acres. They'd logged the land, cleared stumps for the building site and a large vegetable garden, dug a well ten feet deep and piped water to their house and their sister's mercantile.

"Darn good well," one said to the other at least once a week. "Enough water for yet another family, when the time comes."

They'd finished the serious business of cooking and eating their evening meal. Lang rolled cigarettes while Hauk washed dishes. The dim rays of an electric lamp Ilsa gave them reflected back from French windows on three sides of the whimsical nook Hauk added to their kitchen.

"Salvaged some windows from a tumble-down place," he'd said to Lang when they were framing the house. He drew the nook plans on a cedar slab ready for the shake froe.

Though Lang shook his head at the notion of so much glass, he went along with the change and grew to like how light, electric or oil lamp depending on circumstances, danced on the panes.

They used electric power to pump water from their well to storage tanks for gravity feed and more sparingly for light. If times got tougher, they would carry water from the well and use oil lamps. Electricity was a luxury. They'd lived their entire lives, twenty-seven years for Lang and twenty-five for Hauk, without luxuries.

Lang rubbed his cheeks, measuring his need for a shave. "You spend any time talking with the teacher when you docked the *Aggie J* this afternoon?"

Hauk gave one shake of his head. "Axel waited on the pier to walk her up the trail. You spend any time talking with Mrs. Price at the tavern?"

"Never got away from Ilsa's store. Customers in and out all afternoon, some more than once, looking for gossip about Pastor Holmes. Word is he's called the sheriff to help smoke out brewers of every ilk to save us from hell and damnation."

"Ah," Hauk said, permitting a smile, "that's what had you rooting around in our cellar. Seemed to take you a long while to come up with one quart of beer."

"Moved a few bottles here and there. Took a count while I was at it. Good thing we're not planning to sell, we'd run out before week's end."

Hauk struck a match on the lamp's wrought iron base and let it burn clean before holding it to Lang's cigarette and then his own. Each smoked three cigarettes a day, one after each meal. "I see in the paper that Hoover's program has the Navy Yard ripping out wood walls and timbers in the dry docks and replacing them with concrete."

"Guess they won't be buying the peeled logs we've got stockpiled, then," Lang said. "Could be we'll have to go back into the brewing business. Good timing, the way I see it, with the pastor stirring up interest in the creek's name. Once we get Skipp Bakke's boat fixed up, we could sell surplus beer offshore. I hear tell that's been done."

Hauk studied his older brother's face for seriousness and found a hint of smile in the corners of his eyes. "If you're meaning to supply Farley Price, see him drink himself into an early grave so you can court his widow, I doubt it's worth the risk."

"Nah, I'll mind my manners where Price is concerned. I'm just thinking economics, pure and simple. Couldn't take up courting without income for supporting. No mills are buying our logs, nobody's calling on you to put up a building of any sort, brewing could pay the bills."

"We agreed and swore to Ilsa we're through with brewing for other than our own needs."

Ilsa had been more mother than older sister to them since the year she opened a shop in one end of her Snohomish home not far from the Nordlund Dairy. There she sold dry goods alongside her own jams, jellies, canned goods and pies. The boys helped her craft shelves and a sales counter, and managed the store when she had other commitments. Lang had been eight and Hauk six.

Four years later they moved in with her to stay. Both their parents had died and an older enterprising sister took over the dairy and sent them packing.

Once they'd settled in, Ilsa began teaching them her beer and brandy making secrets. Her bottled products, considered superior by those she trusted enough to accept as customers, never made it onto the shop's shelves. None but Hauk and Lang saw it in the brewing stage, done in a vented cellar accessible by ladder from her bedroom floor.

They learned to can venison for their own use. In later years they carried canner and jars to hunting camps with them, and brought canned product back to her.

With Ilsa's blessing, Lang stayed out of school for two years, working in the woods while Hauk caught up. They went through high school together, graduated and took over Ilsa's brewing business when she married Skipp Bakke and left town.

After graduation both logged for a living and sharpened saws in mills in their spare time. They sold brew for extras—vehicles, dress clothes for Saturday night dances, a wireless radio—until the day a stranger in town asked too many questions.

That night they emptied a twelve-gallon crock of green beer into the Pilchuck River, refilled the crock with apples they'd stored on the back porch, and nailed down the loose boards on the bedroom floor.

The next day they listed the property for sale.

Two weeks later, cash in their pockets, they loaded their possessions including their crock of wrinkled apples into a pickup truck, delivered the money to Ilsa and headed to Oregon, where they worked in logging camps and mills until news of Skip Bakke's death reached them.

"I want my boys back with me," Ilsa wrote.

They packed up again, drove to Burke Bay, purchased the five acres of land and upper pond along Whiskey Creek, and settled down.

By the time Farley Price came on the Burke Bay scene, the Nordlund brothers were known as men who could do just about anything a person needed: carpentry, plumbing, wiring, roofing, cement work.

They milked Persson's cows for a week when Helmer fell ill, clerked for Ilsa when she went to Seattle on a buying spree for her store, captained the *Aggie J* for Axel Jenson now and then, and helped Irv Carlson at the mill when he needed a hand.

Folks who assumed the brothers moved to Burke Bay so Ilsa could cook their meals soon learned they cooked for her often as not, and kept the tavern in venison, both fresh and canned, through the winter. Erling Romstad hired them to make some repairs on his cabins and soon Astrid had their help at the stove on a day when her swollen hands couldn't heft a cast iron skillet.

No one in Burke Bay knew the two men had a good cache of heavy brown beer bottles filled with brew from Ilsa's old recipe. They made just enough for themselves, Ilsa, and Irv Carlson.

Lang thumbed through the *Bremerton Searchlight* to the crossword, folded the paper in quarters and sharpened a pencil with his pocket knife. "Yep, we're through with brew selling." He printed a word in down squares and pushed the puzzle back to Hauk's side of the table.

Hauk studied the puzzle a moment. "Got everything we need to get us through the winter with or without fishing in Alaska. Good solid house, enough to eat, plenty dry wood, decent pair of calk-boots each and next to new dress-shoes. And no wives to fret over."

"No girlfriends either," Lang said. "I've been thinking a girlfriend would be nice."

"Girlfriends expect a man to have something to offer. Steady work of some sort. And it seems the one you've taken an interest in is already married."

"Seems so. Might be I'll have to take an interest in Maeva Swanson, give Axel a run for his money."

Hauk watched Lang try to hide a smile and waited for him to say more. The smile grew into a chuckle.

"Not that I'm interested in pursuing her since it's clear you find her to your liking," Lang said.

"That right?" Hauk watched his brother for another full minute, the time it took for Lang to nod.

"That's right."

"Seems to me she's spoken for, too," Hauk said.

"Spoken for, but not yet wed, which makes your task an easier one than mine."

Hauk grinned at that. "Speaking of tasks, Astrid tells me she could use a little fresh venison. A couple roasts. Some chops."

Lang narrowed his eyes. "S'pose we could make a run out to Lena Creek. Camp a night or two, see what wanders down out of the hills. Poaching's not near so dangerous as selling brew."

"True enough. Nor so dangerous as separating women from men who don't deserve them."

"The women in question will have to do the separating. Our task is waiting, or to cast our sights elsewhere."

11

~ The Christmas Pageant ~

In her years away from home, Maeva had missed the solitary comfort of December nights in her bedroom under the rafters, wrapped in the down quilt her mother made for her tenth birthday, a stack of books nearby, rain tapping her window.

On such a night, she wrote the history of Carlson Mill, the story of the fire, owner Irv Carlson's injury and stitches, and sent it along with a sketch of the aftermath to *The Kitsap Weekly*.

> *The mill's location, known as Burke Bay Lagoon, is the mouth of a narrow and shallow tributary that branches off Whiskey Creek along the west edge of Persson's Dairy Farm. It flows under School Road through a timber culvert built by Helmer Persson's father, Oskar, circa 1901. Helmer says the tributary is a natural water trough for his dairy herd.*

She would counter Pastor Holmes' campaign with stories of Indians and loggers conversing about the creek's name. She'd fight the pastor with written words and call on her long-time relationship with Axel's father to stop any legislative action.

The article finished, she created a program for Burke Bay Grade School's annual Christmas Pageant and printed *On Whiskey Creek* in small letters below the school's name.

The next day students duplicated the program on half-sheets of tablet paper to carry home to their parents.

Miss Truax's hand flew to her throat when she saw the program title.

"Truly, Miss Swanson, do you deem that appropriate?"

Maeva did but before she could support her reasoning, Miss Truax spoke again.

"You've assigned a rather large part to Hannah Price. An eight-line recitation by such a child is inviting disaster, don't you agree?"

"Such a child?" Maeva narrowed her eyes, and studied the older woman, worn down by years of pouring or pounding knowledge into young minds. "Her age, you mean?"

"Legally too young, one might say, to be enrolled in school. And a source of community friction, given the circumstances."

"Young, yes, but bright."

Along with fighting for the creek's name, Maeva would do battle for Hannah by defending her father against those who wished him gone from Burke Bay.

"Hannah recites her lines without faltering. I will be nearby to prompt her should she require help. I'm more concerned for Virginia Holmes, who suffers stage-fright. Her father pressures her, I fear."

Maeva watched for Miss Truax's reaction to that and saw the almost indiscernible tic in the older woman's left eye.

"Rightly so. Children need a little pressure, a sense of high parental standards, or they slip into laziness, don't you agree?"

"No, I don't agree. I believe children need support and encouragement and opportunity to explore their world, not rigidity." Her mind thought pomposity; her tongue found rigidity in the nick of time.

"I hope your trust in Hannah doesn't spoil the event for other children and guests. Our school pageant is a community event, please keep that in mind. We see a rather impressive turn-out here."

"Yes, I know. I grew up here."

"I am aware of that, Miss Swanson, having taught you in your youth. You were a demanding student, far ahead of your peers, but I believe I was equal to the task." Miss Truax sniffed and searched for her hankie. "I do hope you made adequate arrangements for refreshments. We always provide a lovely spread."

A lovely spread indeed. Rich Scandinavian cookies and pastries, some made by Maeva and her mother the night before, ready to be frosted this evening. Together they rolled and cut cookies in shapes of Christmas trees, Santas and stockings. The cutters, hand shaped tinware darkened with age, had been crafted by Maeva's father. She handled them as if they might reveal secrets about him.

"All is in order," Maeva said. "Ebbe Persson put herself in charge of the kitchen. She and Mrs. Bakke are seeing to special treats for the children. An orange each, nuts and hard candies."

Maeva had stopped by the mercantile to give Ilsa Bakke money for the treats and ran into Norwegian stubbornness more than equal to any she'd encountered with Swedes.

"Put that money right back in your pocket, Maeva Swanson," Mrs. Bakke said. "I know you're supporting your mother and caring for her to boot, with her bad hip and all that farm she has to tend."

"I insist," Maeva said.

"Insist all you like, but if you leave even a penny on my counter I'll use it to send two pennies worth of goods to your mother's place. Long as you're here, take her this nice candied fruit for her *Jule Kaka*. If she's of a mind to send me back a wee bit to share with my brothers, I won't complain, nor will they. Good cooks themselves, those two boys, but not so much for baking."

The night of the pageant, the school basement lunchroom filled with children, parents and grandparents while the kitchen filled with cookies, spiced nuts, divinity candy and assorted plates, glasses and cups. Ebbe Persson heated milk for hot cocoa. Astrid Romstad brewed coffee in large pots she brought from the tavern. Treats wrapped in tissue and tied with ribbons waited in a corner.

"I'll be right here in the front row," Maeva said to the students. "You may look at me first before you look at the audience. When you finish your part and look back, I'll still be right here."

Christmas trees decorated with paper chains, strung popcorn and bits of tinsel, stood at either end of a low platform Helmer Persson brought out each year. Children sat in the front rows, lined up by grade, their shoes polished or at least brushed to remove dried mud and manure. Girls wore their best dresses and bows in their hair; boys dressed in pants with creases pressed in and dress shirts they'd outgrown or hadn't quite grown in to.

Wesley Wiley and Ralph Strom, in charge of arranging the room, had slicked-back hair. Wesley had shaved his whiskers. The Strom family, Orval Blevins with them, filled one entire bench.

Maeva wore a dress of wool challis the green of cedar branches, with fitted bodice and waist, and skirt yoke with one pleat on the left front. She pinned her mother's wedding brooch of clustered garnets high on her right side.

Axel, who'd run his fingers over it and a little lower to tease her breast while helping her into her coat in the Swanson living room, had whispered, "I like how the dress shows off your figure."

She felt a rush of heat, a hint of impatience with him. He liked to tease and arouse to wring promises from her. She'd pulled away, headed for the door and responsibility to her students.

Miss Truax rang her bell, fiddled with the lace at her throat and squeaked out words of welcome and wishes for a glorious Christmas season. She called on Pastor Holmes to offer a blessing. He veered from blessing the event to invoking the help of God to save them all by renaming their creek and removing illegal drink from their midst.

Maeva lifted her head, opened her eyes and glared, to no avail; the pastor's eyes were on heaven, or on the school basement's ugly ceiling.

Two or three children experienced what Maeva called a tripping over the tongue in their recitations, but recovered so well they gained extra admiration in the eyes of their audience. Hannah recited her eight lines with proper inflection and without squinting until the end when she looked hard for her mother.

Miss Truax rose to offer thanks and an invitation to visit the classrooms upstairs while the older boys made the basement more comfortable for refreshments.

In that moment, Maeva caught a glimpse of a man leaving Eleanor Price's side. A man in a black overcoat, with hair dark as the lump of coal promised in Christmas stockings of naughty children.

Her fingers itched to take up pencil and paper, to sketch the image. She saw something indefinable in the man. Not evil or even a propensity for drink. Despair, she thought; a man clinging to the moment out of fear for the future.

Though she wanted to watch him, her eyes moved against her will to meet those of Hauk Nordlund, seated at the rear between his sister and look-alike brother. Hauk gave her a nod and spoke to his brother without moving his eyes from hers. Lang nodded in turn, one sharp lowering and lifting of his head. Neither smiled.

Children swirled around her. She bent for hugs. Axel appeared at her side, placed his hand on her back, whispered he'd be outside for some air. His lips touched her neck.

"Later," she whispered, wanting to follow him, experience the masculine privilege of escape, talk about the pastor's words, unravel the secrets hidden under Farley Price's dark demeanor.

She turned to the children who needed one more word of praise.

Miss Truax called a not quite gentle reminder that Miss Swanson should repair to her classroom to greet guests. Maeva glanced at her mother working alongside Ebbe Persson, Astrid Romstad and Ilsa Bakke arranging plates of cookies, removing skin from a pot of hot cocoa, filling coffee cups. Those three women knew about Alma Swanson's hip pain. They would keep an eye on her.

Maeva circulated in her classroom, listened to children tell their mothers about assignments, watched for fathers finding their way back from the parking lot. Some came to their children's sides. Others lingered on the porch, perhaps remembering their own school days with discomfort. She looked for Farley Price, hoping for a word, a chance to form an opinion not based on hearsay. He didn't appear, nor did she see the Nordlund brothers or several other men in the lunchroom when Miss Truax led all children and parents back down for refreshments.

When the crowd dwindled, Maeva moved into the kitchen to help clean up and found Eleanor Price with the older women, Hannah under the counter with a third-grade reader.

"Hannah, wouldn't a chair be more comfortable?" Maeva said.

"I like it here."

Maeva smiled at her, and more at memories. The child felt safe tucked into the corner of a kitchen filled with women.

"Like you," Maeva's mother said. Astrid and Ebbe agreed. "Like Maeva as a child." Hannah looked up, squinting.

Yes, Maeva saw herself in Hannah, had seen herself in the child since the day when life filled Hannah's squinted eyes the moment a book opened in her hands. Did it follow that she saw her own father, a man she couldn't remember, in Farley Price? She tried to retrieve comments she'd heard Jonas make about their father's dark side.

She turned at a soft "Oh," not much more than a breath, and saw tears streaming down Eleanor's cheeks.

Maeva turned away, an act of courtesy and restraint. She wanted to comfort Eleanor, to say, "I understand," though it would have been a lie.

Orval Blevins's itching feet had told him it was time to check out some things down to the bay. School things for one, Farley Price for another. He found it easy enough to let Walt Strom and his missus talk him into attending the Christmas Pageant. His pretty young wife got wind of his plans and wanted to go along, but he nixed that.

"You're too far gone with the new babe you're growing to be out amongst school children, now aren't you Thelma?"

She'd shed a tear or two, not near enough to salt the stew, ironed up his best shirt and pants and heated water for his wash-up while he loaded some odds and ends into the back of his truck. Farm things, it looked like, if anyone lifted the canvas.

He had a knack for tucking bottles inside a sack of feed or tossing around enough ripened down pea-vine silage kept moist under oiled canvas tarps to deter most snoops. Any silage would do but, to his nose, pea-vines carried a particular wallop.

He backed his truck into a spot near the road where he could drive out in leisure or haste, whichever might be called for, and waited in the shadows until he saw the Strom family making their way up the school steps. He fell in beside them so as not to be conspicuous, perched at the end of their bench, and took to watching the adults while they eyeballed their offspring.

Best thing he saw all night was Farley Price looking back at his glance without a spark of recognition. The man knew his stuff. Worse thing he saw was Mrs. Bakke at the back of the room, her two brothers alongside. Something uncanny about those two, not near so big as their sister but delivering a clear-eyed double whammy when both looked the same place at the same time. Auger eyed, his Grandpap would have called them.

Orval paid more mind to the teacher than the children. The young teacher, Miss Swanson, not the dried-up prune. Strom had let it be known that his boy, Ralph, and Wes Wiley's son had a major hand in the production, setting up the lunchroom and all.

Easy enough to see Miss Swanson had those boys doing her bidding and no small wonder, no small wonder a'tall. She cut a fine figure, did Miss Swanson, but when he got himself an up-close look, he saw something that rocked him right back on his haunches. Same thing he'd seen in Mrs. Bakke, another woman who didn't know her place, who looked too directly at a man and took the wind out of his mainsail.

Mrs. Price, now there was another looker. Almost fell off her chair when the daughter said her piece. Small boned, Farley Price's wife, with hair the color of a chestnut rubbed up till it shines. Not near so scared looking as he'd expected, given stories coming from Strom's. A good sign, that. He wanted no truck with a man who used his fists on a woman.

When the pageant ended, men high-tailed it outside for smokes and nature's call. Orval took his time, getting that good look at Mrs. Price and Miss Swanson, then ambled out, pausing on the steps to light his smoke. When he figured Farley had him in his sights, he headed off to the trees at the upper edge of the clearing and took up his wait.

"Blevins?" a voice said out of the dark.

"Price?" he answered, some pleased the man had come up on him without a sound.

"It is. You given any more thought to a deal?"

"Some thought. Got some ideas. You interested in hearing me out?"

"I'm listening," Price said.

"Last time we talked you said you'd done some running down from Canada."

"To Detroit. With my old man. I know big cities, how they're laid out, how to work them. Seattle's easy, waterfront towns always are. Bremerton, too, though small towns can be a risk."

"You know how to pack a car so revenue men don't find nothing when they pop a trunk? Not to say a trunk's not a handy item for safe runs, but now and then a man's got to be cautionary."

"My old man taught me tricks haven't yet made it west of the Rockies."

"Shoulda taught you to keep your fists off your wife. Least off her face." Blevins heard the man's breathing deepen. He'd found his mark.

"Told you once, that happened when I'd been dry for a long spell. Hasn't happened since."

Not where folks could see bruises at any rate. Orval gave him that. "Then, here's an idea to fit that fancy car you drive. Go get yourself a salesman job. Fire and casualty insurance, some kind of elixir, brooms, whatever. Part-time job. Don't be giving up your milking, that works for my business. Add a line that makes your car known for legal trade. You with me?"

"You bring me down some insurance tonight, like you mentioned?"

"Could be."

"Could be with you then."

"You going back inside, visit your kid's teacher, drink yourself some hot cocoa?"

"I'm through inside."

"Best let our whereabouts be known to others, roll a smoke with the neighbors. Save our business till folks clear out."

"Car's unlocked, like I said it would be."

Orval felt Price leave, though he neither saw nor heard him. Good man, dark of hair, long black coat, light on his feet. Could work, moving some product in that fancy car.

Farley Price, out of Michigan woods, said he's at home in forests and along waterways more than he ever was in Kansas, that's just where he ran out of gas one morning when he'd found a need to leave Detroit. Never ran homemade liquor before, only legit stuff coming down from Canada. Said the feds, or maybe some other runners, got his old man. That helped; Farley Price had his score to settle.

Only problem, he'd given in to drink to take the edge off bad memories. He'd need close watching.

Eleanor cried in front of all those women in the school kitchen; cried tears of pride when Mrs. Swanson compared Hannah to Maeva. The look on Mrs. Swanson's sweet round face said so much more. Said she loved and admired her daughter, and that mothering such a daughter made her own life worthwhile. Or maybe Eleanor read on Mrs. Swanson's face what she felt in her own heart. She would endure for her daughter.

Farley came to their bed that night with an odor of drink on his breath. A stronger odor than beer, and less sour. He pinned her to the mattress as he'd taken to doing on such occasions, clamped a hand over her mouth so she couldn't protest, forced her legs apart with one knee and pumped his anger into her body.

And his sorrows; she felt sorrows in him, though he never spoke of feelings and she'd stopped asking long before they left Kansas. Afterward, when he slept, she crept from the bed to douche and clean herself. She'd gotten a pessary not long after Hannah was born and slipped it into place before bed every evening, just in case. Her love for Hannah didn't mean she wanted to bear another child to Farley Price.

She checked on her daughter, asleep on the davenport that served as settee during the day, then returned to bed swaddled in an extra blanket Ebbe Persson had given them. Cocooned, protected until the alarm sounded.

She would rise before Farley, stir up the fire, start water for coffee, cook him oatmeal. He would grumble at the need to rise so early for a bunch of stupid cows, and at the lack of bacon and eggs. She would slice and toast bread on the stove top and open a jar of blackberry jam Ebbe gave her.

"Blackberries for the taking, come summer," Ebbe had said.

76

Summer. Would they still be on Persson's Farm? She'd been so anxious to leave, to take Hannah and run. Now she hoped to stay, to persevere with Farley so she could have the pleasure of friendships she'd found. Ebbe Persson, Astrid Romstad, Ilsa Bakke to a lesser degree. And, hopefully, Maeva Swanson. They were of an age and Maeva showed a fondness for Hannah.

But it wasn't a friendship as Hannah's mother and her teacher for which Eleanor longed. Rather, for a woman her age—one who held her own with men. Indeed, was admired by them. A woman who'd known childhood in this wet, green place.

Almost Christmas and no snow.

*H*auk and Lang's kitchen held heat and the fragrance of soup bones they'd left simmering while they attended the pageant. Hauk stirred the coals in the stove's firebox and added a piece of fir. "Lot of cigarettes being smoked outside the school tonight."

He'd found himself craving a smoke for the taste and even more for the distraction. He'd never before attended a school Christmas pageant, not even when he attended school, and wondered why. There must have been such things in his youth. Could have been at milking time.

He'd milked morning and night more years than he cared to remember. Milked up to and beyond that day his oldest sister moved in and said there would be some changes.

Changes that moved Lang and him off the dairy farm to live with Ilsa, but kept them going back to handle milking. Two young boys without parents, two older sisters who had them in a tug-of-war of sorts. One who loved them enough to give them a home; one who exploited them. He'd forgotten some of those bad times. Best leave it that way. Memory could be unreliable.

"Liquor being passed too," Lang said, staring out into darkness from his post at the kitchen sink. "Being bought and sold. Something not quite right about that, to my thinking."

Hauk grinned at his brother's back, knew Lang would catch the image reflected in the dark window and grin back in time. "Drank some on school grounds once. At a dance senior year, if memory serves. Want me to roll you a smoke, pour you a drop of Ilsa's brandy?"

"We had girlfriends then. At that dance. Still think a girlfriend would be nice."

"You see any prospects tonight?" Hauk watched his brother's reflected face for the truth. Lang's eyes had wandered off to Mrs. Price enough times during the program to worry their sister. His own eyes stayed on Maeva Swanson, with occasional glances at Axel Jenson. He thought the man might be over-confident where Maeva was concerned.

Since meeting her, Hauk spent time plumbing the depths of Axel's character, searching for substance beneath the charm. Axel Jenson grew up privileged, had a business partnership with his father earned by virtue of being male and, if rumor could be counted as truth, a doting mother and three pretty sisters at his beck and call.

"Prospects?" Lang said. "Might have. Ilsa mentioned a pair of twins from up toward Keyport. Could be you saw them. Seated a couple two three rows in front of us."

"I saw them from the back same as you. Ilsa only mentioned them to take your eyes off Eleanor Price."

"No more so than to take yours off the teacher."

"Maeva was in charge of things. Most eyes were on her, watching to see their children got a fair share of the program and proper coaching."

Lang chuckled. "Logical reasoning, poor excuse. We're a sorry pair. Missed out on Christmas pageants in our youth, missed out on introductions to those twins due to that other sorry business."

"Your long-winded conversation with Farley Price when we followed him to his place?"

Lang gave his head one shake. "Seemed a good idea at the time. Polite thing to do, since the man invited us to stop by. Gave us a chance to take his measure, see how he lives. Who would have known he'd yammer on about needing more work, did we have any prospects, could we hire him, help him get a toe-hold in the Navy Yard? What gives him the notion we've got answers?"

Hauk grinned. "Ilsa. Our sister touts our talent to any and all. She and the Romstads. Perssons, too, come to think of it. As for Price, he seemed sincere in his interest. And in his concern for his daughter."

"Seemed antsy, if you ask me. Wanting us to offer him a drink or wanting us gone so he could have one alone. I'd wager he had more than enough for the three of us tucked inside the seat springs and hidden trunk of that fancy car. Not that I hold that against a man. Having a drink."

No, Hauk thought, but that wasn't what had Lang staring out a window into darkness. They hadn't ridden the short distance to the Persson's farm in Price's little coupe to spend time with the man. Lang wanted to see the place Mrs. Price made her home. Hauk cataloged it all, more or less from inside Lang's head, looking through his eyes. Flour sack curtains at the windows, crocheted doilies on tables, floor scrubbed clean, kitchen put in order.

Lang went on talking without turning around. "Man has a right to a drink, true enough. Long as he sees to his family first. Man doesn't do that, it creates a set of memories his family best forget."

"Ilsa erased most of our bad memories," Hauk said, knowing it was only half-true. "Or covered them over with good ones."

Lang turned from the sink, looked at Hauk. "Like her brandy just sitting there on the counter waiting for us to put Farley Price out of mind. You got them smokes rolled yet? Shame to sip without a smoke."

Sometime after midnight, Hauk came awake to the acrid smell of smoke drifting through the open bedroom window. Lang was already on his feet.

"Must have overloaded the stove with bark before I dampered it down," Lang said.

"Doesn't smell like smoldering bark." Hauk took their flashlight outside for a look at the chimney.

Lang followed. "Not the stove, not our place."

"Across the pond," Hauk said. "The tavern, maybe one of the cabins."

"Maybe the church," Lang said. "We'd better pull on some clothes."

12

~ Church Fire Aftermath ~

Eleanor moved from tavern sink to stove to main room and back, making coffee and toast, peeling potatoes, tossing coffee grounds and peels and starting again. Each time she looked out the tavern's steamy kitchen windows, she saw more debris piled and corralled on Church Road.

Men roped chunks of the church's burned walls and roof, and dragged them down the road for a bonfire at the water's edge north of the dock, away from the bathing beach. The workers looked like cowboys roping stray calves, dragging them to a holding pen. Wood, glowing in spots, hopped and skipped, leaving jagged char lines on the oil mat road.

She'd let Hannah view the church's smoldering remains, then settled her in the back room with books, pencil and paper, and a stern warning to stay out of the kitchen until things quieted down. Until gossip settled, but Eleanor didn't say that to Hannah.

To a couple old bachelors, fire meant Farley Price, though Irv Carlson had cleared his name in the blaze that brought down the mill burner. Eleanor's face flamed when she told Astrid that Farley had been there when she got home from the pageant, had shared their bed and slept through the night.

"Pay them no mind," Astrid said. "They cackle more than chickens who just laid their eggs."

Rumor countered rumor, some fueled by drink from a flask passed amongst those that talked too much and worked too little. Eleanor listened to those she considered reasonable. Irv Carlson, for instance, who said the church floor had "burnt clean through" where the oil heater stood, but remained thick enough for a man to stand on in the room's corners. He and the Nordlunds took that as proof the fire started with the heater and blazed hot enough to melt most of its parts in the process.

A wrinkled and whiskery faced man Eleanor didn't know said, "Started with the stove, but how? Could be someone found his way inside and helped the stove overheat. Could be a clever man, maybe someone who likes fire. Two fires inside a month."

Another old man with toilet paper patches where'd he'd bled from shaving sat across from the speaker, nodding and calling for coffee by tapping his empty cup with his spoon.

Astrid set the coffee pot down, none too gently, on their table. "Nobody got hurt. That's all that matters. The children are safe, the parents too. Might be time some of you ask Pastor Holmes about the amount of oil he burned all week long to heat a building used only on Sunday. Might be the men cleaning up the mess out there could use a couple more hands."

The tavern door opened before the men could respond, and there stood Maeva Swanson, dressed in wool pants tucked into boots, hair under a cap and heavy sweater doing little to hide the fact that it covered a woman's body. One of the men snorted like an old horse stuck in a small corral.

"I came to help with the cleanup," Maeva said, "I recently visited the pastor and noticed the oil heater's walls were thin and glowing red. We should have discussed the matter at the time."

Eleanor, who stood in the doorway between kitchen and public room, smiled for the first time that day. Only Maeva Swanson, with her reputation for taking charge of community events, would dare show up dressed in men's pants prepared to join in men's work.

The tavern closed the next two days, Saturday and Sunday, for Christmas, though Romstads offered to keep it open and heated for Pastor Holmes use. He declined, meeting instead in his home.

"Thank God for that," Astrid said to Eleanor. "We get a quiet Christmas."

Monday morning, when Eleanor returned to work, the tavern windows had frosted over inside and out. Astrid fussed at Erling over the kitchen stove going cold.

"Fire in the stove wouldn't keep the blamed pipes from freezing, woman." Erling shoved another piece of wood in the firebox. "Cedar, this piece, get things popping, get water going for thawing out them pipes."

"Get water going for coffee, you mean," Astrid said, her jaw set, her eyes narrowed. "I didn't carry water down from the house for you to thaw pipes. For coffee, that's what, and peeling some spuds for frying up for lunch. Spuds and eggs, that's about all we'll have to offer."

"There's plenty bread, Astie, and butter and jam."

"Do you think I don't know there's bread, Erling? There's always bread, we never turn folks away for lack of bread, now do we? But there's no stew or chowder, and no time for getting any ready."

"Not likely many to eat it neither, times being what they are."

"Times haven't changed that much since Friday, when we had a good fire going."

"Sure enough have, Astie." Erling sidled up to her and nuzzled her neck. "Rain stopped and freeze moved in that very night."

"Off with you," Astrid said, with a gentle push on Erling's shoulder.

Eleanor yearned for love of such depth, love that allowed spats to clear the air of frustrations. Love she'd never found beneath the lust that led her into marriage. Any chance of love further poisoned by a sad Christmas.

The little money Farley brought home, plus her earnings from the tavern, went for shoes, not toys, for Hannah. Eleanor had fretted aloud over the gift of shoes and soon had an old doll and fabric scraps to dress it, a stack of children's books and a spinning top to wrap, thanks to Ebbe Persson, Astrid Romstad, and Ilsa Bakke. The top, hand-carved cedar, scented the air when Hannah spun it.

"Where ever did you find such a top?" Eleanor asked Ebbe.

"Ilsa Bakke came up with that," Ebbe said. "From her brothers."

Eleanor went to the front of the tavern, put up the shades, propped the OPEN sign in the window and stared across Dock Road to the bathing beach. Blue water, deeper blue than the sky, winked at her, a thousand winks on every ripple.

Would Burke Bay folks call the surface *rippled*, or was that word reserved for river surfaces? Until that moment the water had always been gray, almost black and frightening. She could not imagine plunging so much as one foot into the sea regardless of color.

"What are you looking at, Mamma?" Hannah asked.

"The water. It's turned blue with the cold weather."

"Mrs. Romstad said I can swim there in the summer. And make castles with the beach sand and hunt for shells."

Eleanor shivered with fear. "Oh, Hannah, you must never go into the water here. Sea creatures live in the water."

"But Mrs. Romstad said." Hannah whined, uncommon for her.

"Sand castles and shells are another matter. I'll help you with those, but not bathing. That's not for us, sweetheart. You must promise you'll never go over there without me. Promise, now."

"I promise," Hannah said, head lowered.

Did Eleanor detect an impatient sigh? She put a hand under Hannah's chin to raise her face. "What is it, Hannah?"

"I like the sea. It smells good. The air is better than at Big Papa's ranch."

Eleanor stared at the sea. From Hannah's birth she'd pictured her on a horse, the two of them racing against the wind. "Let's start the pies. I'll give you some scraps for tarts."

The tavern still held a chill when Lang and Hauk Nordlund delivered a truck-load of firewood and a gunny sack Eleanor supposed held potatoes. She felt shy in their presence, a result of her short dance with Lang. She noticed a piece of carved wood in Hauk's shirt pocket where men carried tobacco and papers for smokes.

Later, when all had been fed and Hannah crawled under a quilt on the iron-frame bed, Eleanor discovered the tavern refrigerator held several packages of fresh meat, the gunny sack was gone and the potato supply had not increased. As soon as she saw it unwrapped, Eleanor knew the meat was venison.

"From Mrs. Bakke, roasts and what have you," Astrid said. "There's mincemeat too, made and preserved by Lang and Hauk, there in the box under the table. For New Year's pies. Today we just make apple. Tomorrow, Nels Swanson brings more apples from over to their place so we have plenty.

Eleanor didn't say a word then, nor did she wonder aloud when more roasts appeared for the New Year's Eve celebration. She'd grown up on a ranch that raised cattle and grain; she knew a cut of beef from a cut of venison. So would the tavern's customers who came for dinner, though all would order roast beef, mashed potatoes and gravy.

So, those nice Nordlund brothers killed deer out of season and gave meat to the Romstads. They'd fixed up Irv Carlson's boat and done more than all the other men put together to clean up the fire debris. Did they do it for money? Neither had steady jobs.

She pictured them as she'd seen them several times, sitting in the tavern booth or at the counter, two silent men watching others, maybe drawing conclusions about their lives. In her mind's eye she saw the piece of wood in Hauk's pocket. Cedar?

And then she knew how Ilsa Bakke came up with the cedar spinning top.

13

~ SWANSON CHRISTMAS ~

Maeva wakened the morning after Christmas to a house gone cold, outdoor temperatures in the low twenties, a hint of pink in the eastern sky. The living room fireplace had burned down to ash, the kitchen stove nearly so.

While Nels coaxed milk from Edwina and Elbertina, Maeva got both fires going and put the coffee pot on to boil. She left the pot to its work, went out into the crisp morning for a barrow of wood, worked to the rhythm of morning sounds: birds lifting from trees, mice skittering in the wood pile, Edwina mooing her thanks for filled trough and emptied milk bag. A quiet morning to reflect on the past few days.

"You made the event a grand success," Axel whispered the night of the Christmas pageant, his mouth near her ear, his breath warming her neck. They were cuddled on the daybed on the shuttered end of the front porch, wrapped in an old quilt, listening to night sounds. He'd kissed her well enough to earn forgiveness for all the times he hadn't kissed her when they argued over wedding plans. While she insisted they postpone their wedding for a few more years so she could continue teaching, he argued they could marry in secret.

She leaned into him, seeking more warmth, words of love, kisses that would weaken his resolve.

His lips stopped moving. "Listen . . ."

Her mother? She stood.

"The emergency horn at Andersons' garage," he said, grabbing his coat and running for the door.

"Wait, I'll go with you," she said, though he gave no sign of hearing her She thought about bundling up and walking the beach, or taking the row boat. Instead she moved into the living room to sit by the fire where she wrote a poem about love gone wrong. She meant her words to show sadness, read them back and found only anger. But anger at whom? Axel, for being less than the man she created in her thoughts? Or herself for wanting something that didn't exist? She tossed the page on the burning logs and opened a novel, her favorite way to escape disappointment.

"You made a spectacle of yourself in Jonas's old pants and that sweater plastered to your body," Axel said the next night. "Why can't you be more ladylike? My mother was shocked when word reached her."

Those words whipped up her anger and made her pulse pound so hard she heard it. She'd gone into a rant about his mother, his three proper sisters, his unrealistic expectations of her, all a ruse to avoid the truth. She'd helped with the cleanup to overhear and dispel rumors about Farley Price. She'd done it to protect Hannah and Eleanor from gossip. She'd done it because Hauk Nordlund was right. She was respected in Burke Bay.

"Actually you cut quite a figure in those pants and sweater" Axel said the morning of Christmas Eve. "All the Burke Bay men are talking about you." He laughed when she ordered him out of the kitchen, picked up the box of cookies her mother wrapped for his family and left whistling.

He had charm, which must be what she loved in him, though she wondered at times if she mistook arousal for love. Hadn't the kisses of men she dated in college made her feel much the same? Even Hauk Nordlund's lingering looks at her brought a rush of heat. A rush, followed by shame.

Christmas Eve, eight gathered around the Swanson dining room table: her older brother Jonas, his delicate wife Cynthia and her mother, Mrs. Hiram Smith; her older sister Berta, and her husband Garth; her younger brother Nels, their mother, and Maeva herself.

Cynthia's mother kept her beady-eyed foxtails wrapped and draped about her shoulders to ward off the chill while they ate. To Maeva, the dining area felt overly warm. She assumed it felt the same to Jonas, whose face wore a ruddy flush.

Jonas produced a bottle of good brandy to serve with cookies and coffee, poured drinks for all and remained standing to make an announcement. He raised his glass and said, "Cynthia will make me a father before summer."

In the midst of congratulatory toasts with glasses reflecting candle light, Jonas said, "And that brings us to the topic of power poles and lines. We need to get electricity down here before the baby arrives so Cynthia will be more comfortable when we visit. Maeva, I trust you've saved enough money by now."

To Maeva it seemed that Jonas, a tall, broad-shouldered man, towered over her even when seated. His eyes looked hard in the candle light. "You and I can discuss that later, Jonas. Mom and Mrs. Hiram Smith are going to be grandmothers. Let them savor the moment."

Maeva's mother smiled and said, "My." Cynthia's mother, who kept Hiram in her name to honor her husband who'd owned the first auto dealership in Bremerton, downed her brandy and extended her glass for a refill. She seemed unfazed by Jonas's announcement. Perhaps Cynthia had told her. It would be natural for a daughter to tell her mother before other family members.

"Can we propose a toast to Cynthia and the baby?" Maeva asked, but Jonas wouldn't let the electricity issue go. Before they'd finished their brandy, he handed their mother a card with gilt edges and glitter on its face, and a parchment note inside.

To the three of you from all of us ~ an electric stove and an electric wringer washing machine ~ Merry Christmas ~ Love, Jonas & Cynthia, Berta & Garth.

"There, you'll be set, once poles are in place and wire strung," Berta said. "We want to make life easier for all of you."

Jonas added, "No more excuses, Maeva," his tone and look meant to intimidate.

Later, when the others had gone home and their mother was in bed, Maeva and Nels recapped the night. "Used appliances," Maeva said, "given to Mom so Cynthia can acquire new now that's she's expecting a baby. I wonder how much money Jonas wrangled out of Berta. One of them could have shopped for a personal item for Mom. A vase, an embroidered hankie, even a dishtowel she didn't have to make for herself."

"We're talking about Jonas here," Nels said. "You can bet he talked Berta out of more than she and Garth can afford." He grabbed a handful of cookies, poured a glass of milk, stretched out on an oak kitchen chair and continued.

"They'll be back tomorrow, Jonas with more brandy and Berta assigned to explain about how hard they worked and how easy you got off. Jonas flips the switch and Berta recites her part. They'll be on me about work, too, but they know I'm not ever going to spend money on college."

He washed the cookies down with a gulp of milk while she pondered and nodded. Jonas had a history of manipulating all of them to suit his needs.

"Brace yourself," he said. "You'll always be the one Jonas attacks. Jonas and Garth will drink too much and get into an argument. Berta will try to intervene. Mom will say *'Tyst,'* but no one will hush, not for a moment."

The annual Swanson Christmas Day Smörgåsbord, attended by their South Bay neighbors, swirled with family and friends eating traditional Swedish fare, sipping hard cider, their mother's fruit brandy, endless cups of coffee with fresh cream, and conversing in mixed Swedish and English. Maeva stayed busy replenishing serving plates and washing dishes so her mother could remain with their guests.

Axel caught her around her waist when she brought clean dessert plates to the dining room, kissed her forehead and murmured, "Mmm, you smell sweet. Stay put for a minute. Dad has an announcement."

Emil Jenson stood by the fire, a bottle of Jonas's brandy in his right hand. Emil's golden hair had silver threads that enhanced his good looks and gave Maeva a pleasant glimpse of how Axel would age.

"I have news to share, my dearest neighbors. Axel and I are expanding our transportation business to include bus service between Poulsbo and Bremerton, with stops along the way. We've formed a partnership with a Seattle family who, like us, have two passenger boats operating on the Sound."

He drew his wife Aggie, for whom the launch *Aggie J* was named, to his side. "And, with my wife's blessing, we're thinking of broadening our political horizons. A legislative position for me, let Axel take over my spot as county commissioner. We need to lay the ground work for his political career. There's a good chance Axel will be governor one day. Maeva's golden tongue and pen will help put him in the capitol building and the governor's mansion."

Maeva felt her mouth drop open. Literally. Axel as governor one day? He'd never shown any interest in politics, at least none beyond berating her for supporting FDR.

She heard her mother say, "My," and then a round of applause. Before Maeva could speak, Berta, who'd sipped a good bit of their mother's brandy, stood and tapped the table with a spoon.

"Hold on a minute, Emil Jenson. Surely you know Maeva's tongue and pen could do you more harm than good unless you're ready to declare yourselves Democrats."

Axel snickered at that, and Emil grinned. Berta ignored both.

"And, if you're talking marriage, keep in mind Maeva has a farm to run. She owes Jonas, and me to a lesser degree, for all the years we've put in here, all the times she hid out in the madrona grove or the woodshed with her books. All the times Mom said 'Let her be,' when she and Axel went off to walk the beach. She promised us she'll continue teaching and seeing to the farm for another five years before she marries."

Maeva wanted to pull Berta into a hug, but Emil raised his glass and broadened his smile.

"Maeva can teach and write speeches at the same time. She and I recently struck a bargain. I'll pull some strings to make Whiskey

Creek the official name of a currently unnamed stream, and she will put pen to paper for my humble cause."

He paused for all to drink. Axel planted a kiss on Maeva's cheek. Berta scowled.

"As for marriage," Emil continued, "let's just say there are ways around that silly rule requiring teachers to remain single. We're looking forward to making her a part of the Jenson family and our political endeavors. Now, if a baby comes along . . ." Emil left that dangling.

Garth quieted Berta, who had more to say. Jonas called for a toast to the new Jenson transportation company. Mrs. Hiram Smith petted her fox tails. Glasses clinked.

Maeva said, "Excuse me," and retreated to the cool room off the kitchen. She'd agreed to write political speeches for Emil in exchange for making the creek's name official. That was the extent of their agreement. Axel had been there.

True, when they were alone later he'd said, "We can marry in secret, live with our families, yours for dinner, mine for the night. The school district will never know."

She'd pulled away from him, told him to stop. Stop talking nonsense, and stop distracting her with lovemaking.

How dare Emil make such a declaration? How dare Axel let him?

They dared because they were Jensons.

Though the weather remained crisp and clear through the week between Christmas and New Year's Eve, an ugly cloud hovered over Maeva's conversations with Axel. When she challenged him on the idea of going into politics, he said, "Why not?" and left it at that. When she broached what she considered the outlandish idea of his becoming governor one day, he gave the Jenson family view on how to attain political office.

"Jenson money and influence, and your way with words, Maeva. You've been given the gift of the golden tongue. Why waste it on school children?"

When she refused to cuddle by the fire, he shrugged and left whistling, only to return the next morning ready to forgive her for her stubbornness. She had fleeting moments of questioning whether he loved her or only her ability to help him reach some political goal she hadn't known existed.

He wore through her resistance to his charms by New Year's Eve. They began their celebration at the Burke Bay Tavern where Erling Romstad beat out tunes on his old piano and the Nordlund brothers accompanied with their harmonicas. Axel gave tailor-made cigarettes to the men and kissed every woman in the room.

They were due at the Jenson gala by ten, about to leave so she could change from her black gored skirt and white scoop neck blouse to a more formal dress, when Hauk put down his harmonica. "I would like the honor of a dance with the teacher before the boat captain dashes her off to a finer party."

His blue eyes, his serious look, disarmed her. Though she didn't answer, he took her in his arms and waltzed her away from Axel. They were almost the same height—he somewhat short for a man, she tall for a woman—perfect for dancing cheek to cheek, though of course they didn't quite touch.

"You dance very well," she said, to keep from resting her face against his. He smiled, a rarity. She felt his eyes settle on her mouth as though he might taste her lips, the second time she'd allowed her imagination to run in that vein.

And there was Axel, frowning at her, speaking to Hauk. "Sorry, but I've got to cut in. There's an engagement to be announced. We mustn't be late."

Did surprise sweep over Hauk's face before it settled into the look no one could read? "His sister's engagement," she said. "Marjorie."

Axel planted a wet kiss in the general vicinity of her mouth before she had a chance to turn away.

"That could change by midnight if I play my cards right," and steered her out the tavern door.

"Were you jealous? Or just rude?" Maeva asked once Axel started the car.

"Jealous? Of Hauk Nordlund? An unemployed laborer?" He chuckled. "Don't be ridiculous, Maeva, we're running late, we both need time to spruce up a bit and change clothes."

At home she made a quick change into her best party dress, a pre-Depression silvery blue taffeta with dolman sleeves, draped neckline, and flared skirt she'd purchased from a college acquaintance who never wore a party dress more than once. Axel showed proper appreciation for her appearance, though he frowned at her shoes, still her only decent pair.

Sometime before midnight, Emil Jenson turned off the Victrola, rang a crystal bell and formally announced the engagement of Marjorie Jenson to William Anslow, the son of Jenson's new partner in land transportation. Toasts with Emil Jenson's good whiskey and brandy, and a plentiful supply of fruit punch laced with something that gave it an odd taste, lasted twenty minutes or more.

Maeva found herself being kissed by several men, a pleasant experience. She looked around for Axel, certain he'd be a bit jealous since some of the men were strangers to her. Surely he'd been jealous earlier when she'd danced with Hauk. She found Axel asleep in an overstuffed chair shoved into a corner so the Oriental rug could be rolled aside for dancing.

Only later, home in her bed heaped with quilts against the frosty air creeping in under the eaves, did she wonder why she'd hoped Axel would be roused to jealousy though his flirting never caused jealousy in her.

And why she'd so wanted to feel her cheek against Hauk's.

14

~ *Inauguration Day* ~

Eleanor brewed and served three pots of coffee, peeled and fried dozens of potatoes and lugged in a box of apples for pies before Roosevelt's inauguration began. Erling fiddled with the tavern's radio, turning the volume so high Astrid threatened to drag the contraption across Dock Road and pitch it in the bay.

At ten o'clock Astrid told Eleanor to put down the peeling knife and come out front. "If we had any sense about us, we'd sneak out and find a quiet place to put up our feet. Must be plenty places, what with all them folks hovering around that radio. Church in the Mill, for one."

Irv Carlson, at Ilsa Bakke's urging, had offered his mill office space to Pastor Holmes for church services, with the stipulation it be called *Church in the Mill*, without Baptist in the name. The Nordlund brothers crafted pews with Irv's milled wood. The Holmes family stayed on in the largest Romstad cabin same as before.

"Is Farley out there?" Eleanor asked. He'd paced the floor the last few nights, snarled when she urged him to sit, closed his hands into fists more than once.

"Him and Orval Price, both in top coats and fedoras down to their brows, looking like they could be in cahoots with Al Capone," Astrid said. "Axel Jenson and his dad decked out in suits, like as not campaigning for the next election. They'll not have a kind word for Mr. Roosevelt or any that voted for him, but they'll keep that fact tucked away in their inside pockets on this day. Emil Jenson's a master of keeping facts tucked away."

Rumors Eleanor heard about Emil's mistress in Bremerton reminded her of those circulated about ranchers and their town girls, something her mother called a sad fact of life.

"Is Maeva with Axel?" she asked. She and Maeva had become friends over the last two months, a friendship built around Hannah getting fitted with glasses, and added to as each woman opened her closet of secret feelings long enough for the other to catch a glimpse.

"No, no Maeva yet," Astrid said, "but Irv Carlson's there dressed out in the flannel shirt you sewed up for him, about to bust his buttons, he's that proud. Hauk and Lang Nordlund come in a minute back, if you're wondering but not about to ask. Ilsa's there, too."

Eleanor took another swipe at the sink. She wouldn't show pride in the shirt she made Irv, though the plaids matched, and the flat felled seams were perfect. The shirt was part of a spoken contract to repay Irv for Hannah's glasses.

Nor would she have asked or said a word about the Nordlunds. She hadn't taken a dislike to the brothers for hunting out of season, as Astrid supposed. Rather, she felt uncomfortable around them. Their watchful blue eyes sensed truths Eleanor let Maeva see but didn't share with others. Things about Farley that she didn't know for certain; things that men figured out.

She wrung the cloth, set it on the counter and followed Astrid to join the group watching the radio like they could see Franklin Delano Roosevelt as he spoke, his voice deep, strong, fatherly.

I am certain that my fellow Americans expect that on my induction into the Presidency I will address them with a candor and a decision which the present situation of our nation impels.

This is preeminently the time to speak the truth, the whole truth, frankly and boldly. Nor need we shrink from honestly facing the conditions in our country today. This great nation will endure as it has endured, will revive and will prosper.

So, first of all, let me assert my firm belief that the only thing we have to fear is fear itself - nameless, unreasoning, unjustified terror which paralyzes needed efforts to convert retreat into advance. . .

Eleanor heard other parts of the speech as independent phrases.

Values have shrunken . . . farmers find no markets for their produce . . . plenty is at our doorstep . . . the money changers have fled from the temple of our civilization . . . action now . . . put people to work . . . raise the value of agricultural products . . . strict supervision of banking . . . broad Executive power to wage war against the emergency . . .

She looked at Farley, the man she chose to marry not by careful consideration of his worth as husband material but by her body's response to his. She wished she'd been like Maeva, who admitted to kissing several men while she'd been away in college. But hadn't Maeva also admitted kissing didn't tell you much about the man himself? And that she hadn't chosen Axel as her intended as much as accepted it as fait accompli?

So it had been with her and Farley, in a sense. He'd ridden into her life at the very moment her womanhood emerged. She felt as though she'd gone to bed one night a girl, wakened the next morning a woman and found him waiting on the doorstep.

Farley glanced her way, turned his back. The right shoulder of his long coat lifted. She read the movement. His right hand reached into his left inside pocket, removed a flask, raised it to his lips. Farley would always put drink first. She accepted that fact while Roosevelt addressed the nation as President of the United States.

Maeva and her mother leaned toward the wireless, each weighing Roosevelt's words on scales of their individual experiences. Alma Swanson's Swedish language newspapers told her life was better on the west coast, on Puget Sound, where the sea aided and abetted the land in food production. She said there would be enough to see her through her days; her worries centered on Maeva and Nels struggling to care for her when they should be saving for their own futures.

"Not to worry about the electric poles," she said when Roosevelt closed his speech with an invocation to God to guide him. "We have a good life."

Alma Swanson nee Eriksson was born in 1878 in a Swedish sea town near Malmö, to a family with too many children and too little land. At age eighteen she left Sweden to wed Anders Swanson, thirty-nine, a man she'd met as a child and didn't recognize when she stepped off the train in Iowa, where a cousin arranged a proper wedding.

Alma's family, wanting to give her a better life, paid her passage to America. Anders, an old family friend, had a home ready on the shores of Puget Sound west of Seattle. The Sound was an inland sea much like the Baltic, Seattle a prosperous city much like Malmö.

Alma saw little of Seattle, for she was soon pregnant. Her first pregnancy ended in a still-birth, a son named for his father who tried to breathe life into him; her second pregnancy ended one cold morning in the outhouse before Anders, who worked in Seattle and remained there week-nights, realized Alma was expecting. She never told him.

Her third pregnancy produced Jonas. She'd had eight pregnancies to bear four living children; she became a widow in her thirty-seventh year.

A widow with a small pension, four children, a decent house with a bathroom added after her second child's birth, ten acres of land, tilled ground to raise vegetables, forty mature apple trees, two cows in the barn, a chicken coop full of laying-hens and enough timber around to fill the woodshed with firewood.

Maeva, who understood Swedish, learned details of her mother's history by listening when neighbor women came by for a pound of butter, a dozen eggs, apples or fresh beans. She heard her mother's unspoken thoughts along with the spoken, never noticing her heavy accent—v's for w's, rolled r's, Swedish words mixed with English.

That morning she followed her mother into the cool room at the back of the kitchen. Her mother closed the door to preserve the chill, lifted the floor-board over the rock lined creamery to expose the depths where cooling waters of an underground stream trickled over smooth stones. She lifted aside the paraffin-coated wood butter box that defined the left corner of the creamery. Her arm disappeared up to her elbow, reappeared with a silver cream pitcher blackened with tarnish. She handed it to Maeva, who flinched at the weight and chill.

They returned to the kitchen, to the round oak table, where her mother poured flannel and sock-wrapped coins onto the scrubbed oilcloth. Gold coins, some saved from the first hours of Alma Swanson's widowhood.

"Not to worry, we be fine without electric. You earn for your own life, not this farm."

Maeva busied herself with the flannel, reluctant to touch the creamery-cooled ten and twenty-dollar gold pieces she imagined being plucked warm from her father's pocket moments after his death. She saw her mother's shaking hands lift a child's sock from atop the heap of laundry fresh from the clothes line, drop in the coins, tie a knot. Her father, an older version of Jonas, lay prone on the floor, his hands crossed on his chest, arranged by her mother's hands just moments before they reached into his pockets.

Familiar objects around her blurred. Had she witnessed her father's death? Or conjured it from the accounts she'd heard spoken in Swedish to other women?

Anders Swanson had come in from milking, deposited the milk in the cool room, sat at the table. Alma Swanson, arms filled with clothes, followed him in, spoke to him about sitting down too hard. The clean laundry, smelling of sea air and spring blossoms, dropped from her arms to the table in the same moment her husband fell from chair to floor.

In the quiet aftermath of Roosevelt's speech, Maeva heard a chair scrape, a thud, odd sounds she couldn't describe, and over them the sound of gold coins dropping into an old sock.

"Oh, Mom. This is my life. You, our little farm and teaching."

"You will marry one day, maybe soon like the Jensons hope. Save for that." *You vill marry vun day. Save for det.*

"I am saving. In my own way, I'm saving by teaching." She didn't know how to tell her mother her fears about marrying Axel; fears he and the Jensons would suffocate her with the power of their money and politics much as Jonas had suffocated her with the superiority of his years and earned wages. She admitted those fears only to herself and, of late, in hints to Eleanor Price. She watched her mother's eyes and saw one truth; her mother experienced similar fears before she left Sweden. Life with Anders Swanson had not eased them.

Together they returned the coin bundles to their cream pitcher, the treasure to its hiding place. They closed the door to the cool room and made a fresh pot of coffee.

During the next hour, three women from up the beach found their way to the Swanson kitchen, Swedish women who knew the president of their adopted land said something important, yet were uncertain what it meant for them. They sipped coffee, agreed a little chopped hard-cooked egg on Alma Swanson's good bread would be nice, took a cookie or two with the coffee while the eggs boiled. They drew the curtain of their native language around them so they barely noticed when Axel poked his head in the door.

"Romstads need another box of apples," Axel said. His color was high with March wind and celebration. He carried the smell of the Burke Bay Tavern on his clothes and in his hair. "The tavern's jam-packed. Looks like folks have settled in for the rest of the day. Playing pinochle, cribbage, whist. You ladies want to join us?"

"*Nej tack,*" the women said. No thanks. They were widows, long since adjusted to the comforts of widowhood, the ease of seeing to themselves without worrying about men. They would stay where they were, in the warmth of a kitchen so much like their own they might forget who had the right to offer sandwiches, more coffee, another plate of cookies. For a moment, Maeva envied them their age and privileges it earned.

Axel set aside his dislike of Roosevelt for the day. He loved parties, any reason to celebrate. With Axel, as with Jonas, celebrations required alcohol. Whatever he'd consumed lent to his high color and mood. He sang silly songs as they drove away in Romstads' Chevrolet, loaned to him to collect a box of apples and her help peeling in the bargain.

He'd left the *Aggie J* tied up at the Burke Bay Dock; no one expected him to keep a schedule on this day. His song changed to a whistle as he maneuvered the car into a spot between two others just like it, retrieved the apples from the trunk, and headed for the tavern's back door.

Maeva followed, her own mood pensive. Had she been under the kitchen table with a book when her father died? How many gold pieces had her mother saved?

Cinnamon and apple scented air seeped out of the tavern kitchen's whitewashed door much as sea air seeped in on cold days. It settled over cedar split for kindling, fir stacked and ready for burning, mud residue on the porch. Axel whistled, a gull squawked, an engine coughed and caught.

The door opened as Maeva grasped the knob. Eleanor said, "Maeva," and smiled like she'd seen the sun break through clouds after a long rainy spell. Maeva smiled back. Friendship.

Axel set the box of apples on the counter, swooped Hannah off her feet, dropped a kiss on Eleanor's forehead, another on Astrid's cheek, picked up the tune he'd been whistling, handed Hannah to Maeva and two-stepped through the swinging door to the tavern's public room. Maeva heard male voices and cards slapping tables, then the relative silence of a busy kitchen. Comfort-sounds; the pfft-pfft of a spitting pot, water running from a faucet and stopping, a rolling-pin at work.

"You can grab a knife and start peeling, if you've a mind to," Astrid said to Maeva. "We've been up to our elbows, and mine are aching with rheumatiz. Trouble with pies, you only get six good slices from each one and, from the looks of things, every male over ten from here to Timbuktu has taken up squatters rights out front."

"No women?" Maeva set Hannah down and picked up a paring knife.

"Only us left. Ebbe's gone on home to put her bread in the oven. Ilsa's back to the store. Few others here during the speech took themselves and their children home. Left the shouting to the men."

"They're drinking," Eleanor whispered. "They're in and out, opening car trunks, wandering up the cabin lane or down to the beach to refill their pocket flasks."

"There's drinking, sure as shooting, more than some of them women could tolerate," Astrid said, her hearing unhindered by rheumatism. The cup she used to measure sugar scraped bottom in the bin. "Erling was s'posed to get some sugar from Ilsa, but he's forgot. I'll send Hauk or Lang, one or the other, 'less they've taken to nipping along with the rest. It pains me places the rheumatiz misses to think what kind of money we could be making if we could sell good drink." She pushed her way, backside first, through the door to the public room.

Maeva held an apple in one hand, paring knife in the other. A peel-curl spiraled around her fingers. "Is Farley here? I've never met him, you know."

Eleanor nodded, glanced in the direction of the bedroom where Hannah had gone with her spinning top and a stack of books. She could speak openly to Maeva. "Take a peek out there. Black hat, long black coat. He's handsome, I'll give him that. If you see Orval Blevins, you'll see Farley. They've been together all morning. I guess you know what that means."

"I've heard stories about Orval for years." Maeva went into the noisy, smoke-filled public room, scanned the occupants, saw Astrid massaging her right hand and talking to Hauk and Lang.

Erling Romstad ran his fingers up the piano keyboard. Wes Wiley Senior called out, "Hey, there, Maeva, your mother ready for me to plow her garden? Won't be long 'fore it's time to plant peas. I just been telling Axel here it's about planting time, he could offer to help out, take up the slack with Jonas and Berta both gone."

She laughed at the look on Axel's face. He wouldn't offer help with gardening or any other tasks around the farm.

Erling's fingers moved the other way, lower notes, louder, ending with thump thump thump. "Speaking of gardening, you need to get some food out here, Astie, quit worrying about pies. Bread and soup, that's what we need."

"You'll get bread when Ebbe gets here with it. As for soup, there's not much makings left."

Hauk, on his way to the door, said, "I'll rustle up something from Ilsa."

Though Maeva knew he spoke to Erling and Astrid, his eyes seemed to rest on her. What did he see? Eleanor told her in confidence she thought both Nordlunds had some uncanny ability to look into souls. "They are quiet observers," Maeva replied, and wondered if she and Eleanor meant the same thing—that quiet observers saw what most folks missed while they were busy talking or readying their next set of words while they appeared to be listening.

A cloud of cigarette smoke hung in the air, fog over a patch of warmth. Maeva breathed in its acrid odor, smelled the tobacco that created it and, beneath that, the sourness of alcohol-breath.

Movement at the east-facing window caught her eye. There, in dark coats and fedoras like those she associated with undertakers or government officials, stood Orval Blevins and another man. She crossed the room, waved off Axel's calling her to join him and followed Hauk. Outside, she turned left, not right as he'd done, rounded the corner and called, "Hello," without a thought to what she'd say next.

"Why, hello there to you, little lady." Orval Blevins stumbled her way.

"Mr. Blevins," Maeva said, "and you must be Farley Price. I'm Maeva Swanson, Hannah's teacher." She extended her hand while she spoke, an unladylike act according to Emily Post, but a calculated one. She wanted to feel the hand she knew had been raised in anger at Eleanor and possibly at Hannah. She wanted Farley to know she and Eleanor were growing a friendship.

Both men shuffled their feet as they might on unsteady ground or a dance floor sprinkled with granules to help shoes glide. Farley's right hand left his coat pocket, reluctantly she thought, to meet hers.

"Miss Swanson," he said, his eyes on their hands for a long moment before they lifted to meet hers. Black eyes, difficult to read, in a chiseled face. Good cheek-bones, sharp brows and nose, strong chin. A tall man, handsome indeed. The sketch she'd made and burned hadn't done him justice.

Orval Blevins busied himself with tobacco pouch and cigarette paper. "You care for a smoke, Miss Swanson? Or a wee nip?" His breath reeked of both.

"Christ, Blevins," Farley said.

"No thank you, Mr. Blevins, I've heard tobacco dulls the taste buds, and Prohibition has yet to be repealed."

"You think that's in the wind? Repeal?"

"Most assuredly. I'd say the Romstads will soon be selling beer at the least. Once Congress acts, I expect closed breweries will reopen. Will you gentlemen find that to your liking? Legal beer sales?"

Farley shrugged and raised his brows. He had a tic at the corner of his left eye.

Orval coughed. "Won't make me no never-mind. I'm not much given to beer, nor taverns neither. How about yourself, Miss Swanson?"

"I'll be pleased for the Romstads. They've worked hard for years to make the tavern and cabins pay. All of Burke Bay benefits from the commerce they generate, don't you agree?"

"Me, I'm a farming man." Orval pulled a watch out of his pocket and squinted at its face.

"And a family man, I believe, Mr. Blevins. One of my students, Louanne Strom, told me a new baby will soon arrive at your home."

Blevins's look softened for a moment. "Hoping for a boy this time."

Farley muttered something and turned to look down the dock. Maeva took that as her cue to leave.

"Astrid and Eleanor will think I've run out on them if I don't get back to the kitchen. I'm glad we finally met, Mr. Price. I'm fond of Hannah, and of Eleanor. Give my regards to your wife, Mr. Blevins." She left them, wishing she could hear what they said once she'd gone.

She circled around to the back of the tavern to reenter the kitchen. Hauk stood at the sink, scrubbing and scraping potatoes; salt pork sizzled in a cast iron frypan. In minutes, its aroma mixed with cinnamon and warm-apple fragrance.

"We thought you'd up and left us, Maeva," Astrid said, "so Hauk took over your spot. Ilsa sent the salt pork so we could get some soup into those men out front. Hauk makes a good potato soup, you leave him to that for the time and give me a hand with pie crusts."

Maeva took the pastry cutter from Astrid. "Though my older sister has her doubts about my prowess in the kitchen, I'm fairly good with pies."

"You'll do fine when it's your own kitchen. Not that there's any need to rush into things. There's plenty pie-makers around, but not many good teachers."

"I plan to teach until the Depression is behind us. That could easily take Roosevelt's entire first term." Would she be secretly married and teaching? Would Jensons keep it a secret once they'd pulled off the marriage?

She cut lard into flour and salt. Astrid measured a little water, tossed it atop the mixture, and announced she'd look in on Hannah. Maeva watched her go, left hand coaxing left leg and hip.

Without looking up from slicing apples, Eleanor said, "I saw you outside talking to Farley and Mr. Blevins. I'm surprised either can still stand. Helmer won't like it if Farley shows up drunk at milking time."

Hauk moved the frypan to the coolest spot on the big stove. "Lang and I will milk, if need be."

Eleanor sighed the sigh of a weary woman coping with life, a sigh Maeva heard too often from her new friend. "Farley heard there were jobs out here, in the Navy Yard. That's what brought us this far. He thought he could get on in one of the shops. The newspapers back home were full of hope out west. I think they ran those stories so people would leave, times were so bad back there. They made it sound like a man just needed to be fit. '*Skilled laborers needed*,' the papers said."

Maeva rounded up pie dough, divided it into four balls, dusted Astrid's pastry cloth and rolling pin with flour while Eleanor poured out her heart, pled her case to Hauk, the man who carved a spinning-top for her daughter; one of the two men who provided fresh venison for a New Year's celebration at Burke Bay Tavern.

When Eleanor told her about the venison, Maeva said, "Good for them. Romstads are decent people. They deserve help from younger men." It took her another full minute to realize Eleanor didn't condone hunting out of season.

"How could this Depression go on for another four years?" Eleanor said.

Maeva turned to see both Eleanor and Hauk watching her. "I think the changes Roosevelt needs to make, and plans to make for that matter, are so extensive . . ." Maeva waved her hands to emphasize how extensive and sent flour and bits of pie dough flying. Hauk chuckled and Eleanor visibly relaxed. Maeva went on, expressing thoughts and reactions to the president's address.

"Roosevelt spoke almost poetically at times. '*Withered leaves of industrial enterprise . . .*' I wrote that one down in my notebook. Something about nature's bounty and human efforts. I believe, from all I've read and heard, that's where he intends to start the New Deal—putting people to work in nature, on the land. '*Happiness in the thrill of creative effort . . .*' I wrote that one down, too. It made me think of your sewing skills, the beautiful coat you crafted for Hannah from a garment no longer used. When Mom sews or knits, I see pleasure settle on her face. My brother Nels has a similar look when he tinkers with car engines and hears a smooth hum."

"You, when you're teaching, I'd be willing to bet," Hauk said.

"To a degree, perhaps, but it's not the same, not like crafting something with one's hands." Maeva collected dots of pie dough from the floor, dropped them atop apple peels, washed and dried her hands.

"Craftsmanship was lost to machines," Hauk said. "That's the Industrial Revolution run amok. That's what has to change, not just in our country but in Europe, too. Workers need to see honor in their work, value in men and women who manage the machines. Upton Sinclair said it best."

Maeva looked at him, the man known in the community as unemployed though able to do any task that needed doing. Until that moment, she'd seen him as a laborer, capable and competent but not necessarily educated. Goose bumps rose on her arms.

"Say that again. I want to add it to my notebook."

"Maeva writes poetry," Eleanor said. Her hand flew to her mouth as though she could stuff the words back inside. "I'm sorry; that's private, I had no right to speak."

"I don't mind, and I promise to never force it on you, or anyone. As my older brother and sister point out, I burn more lamp oil over words, reading and writing them, than the rest of the family burns over keeping the household running."

Hauk nodded. "Makes sense. Such pleasures are saved for hours of darkness, after the day's work is done."

Maeva turned her back on them and whispered, *"Gud i himmel."* Could it be Hauk Nordlund shared her love of books? Had a kindred spirit settled along Whiskey Creek in her absence?

But no, it couldn't be. He was a man.

15

~ Sobering Moments ~

*H*auk thickened the salt pork drippings with flour, stirred in cream until the mixture was smooth and poured it over the cooked diced potatoes. He thinned with milk, added pepper, a little more salt, and held a spoonful for Astrid to taste. She pronounced it excellent, ready to serve.

Lang opened the door and signaled that Hauk was needed out front. Ebbe Persson arrived with bread still warm. The tavern kitchen hummed with conversations. Hauk, who'd shocked himself when he spoke his thoughts about craftsmanship, slipped away while women ladled soup and sliced bread.

"Trouble brewing out back," Lang said, his mouth close to Hauk's ear so he could be heard over Erling pounding piano keys and men blessing or cursing their cards. "Preacher's been down a couple times, stuck his head in, nobody did much more than look up. Blevins drove off. Price's car is still out there."

"Feed Price? That what you're thinking?"

Lang nodded. "Soup. Bread with thick butter. Erling gave me the key to one of the cabins, said to feed him, get him up there if we can, let him sleep it off."

"You willing to help Persson with the milking?"

"Rather help Eleanor and Maeva with the cooking," Lang said, half-smile in place. Ilsa claimed they both did that, let a little light in their eyes, let their lips stretch a wee bit. Their sister liked the word *wee*, and found places to stitch it into conversations. It got them to smile a wee more yet, she said.

Hauk rubbed a hand over his chin. "Where's Price now?"

"In his car, far as I know. Key's for the fourth cabin up, out of sight of the kitchen."

"Give the women a hand serving. I'll head out with some food. Better me than you. Chances are you'd watch him choke."

Hauk found Price, breath rancid and overcoat stained, slumped over the steering wheel of his car. "Brought you some soup." He could have been speaking to a man sitting at a table inside the tavern or inside his own kitchen. "Mrs. Persson's fresh bread and butter. All good for neutralizing whatever rotgut you've been drinking."

Price lifted his head, opened one rheumy eye, then his mouth. So, the man hadn't passed into oblivion. Hauk spooned in soup, thick creamy liquid first, a small piece of potato when the first sip went down and stayed. Price slurped, dribbled a bit, rested his head between bites, took the buttered bread in his own hand when most of the soup was in him. "Got anything to drink?" he asked.

"Coffee," Hauk said. "And water. We'll get some of both in you, get you into bed." He helped Price from the car, walked as normally as a shorter man supporting a taller one could along the oiled dirt road that ran up toward the rock where the church had stood, across ragged grass to the fourth cabin. The skeleton key worked, the door opened to a musty chill. Hauk helped Price past a small table and two chairs to the bed, the main fixture in the room.

"Take off your coat, you've done it enough damage for one day," he said, and helped with the process.

Price settled on creaking springs, held the coffee mug in shaking hands, drank it down. Hauk took a tall glass from the open shelf beside the sink, rinsed it and filled it within an inch of the top. Price had slumped onto the bed. Hauk lifted Price's shoulders with his right arm, held the glass to Price's lips with his left hand and turned his own head away from the stench of the man's breath.

Price, half asleep, emptied the glass. Hauk stepped back, looked at the man for clues to his history, saw nothing telling. He untied and removed Price's highly polished mud-splattered shoes and placed them under the bed, helped him roll onto his side, better for sleeping off a drunk than flat on the back, and tucked the extra pillow behind him. He piled a heavy quilt, cold with winter air, over the man, packed another quilt atop the pillow-wedge and left the key on the table.

Lang waited by Price's car. "Leave him propped up a bit?"

"One pillow and one quilt worth."

Lang nodded, started walking toward the dock. Hauk fell into step. They were half-way down the dock, past the low-tide mark, before Lang spoke again.

"First time I've known Romstad to permit liquor inside the tavern. Least out front."

"Looked like he had a drink or two himself."

"A snootful," Lang said. "Pastor came down again. Came to the kitchen door while I was dishing up soup. Said he was going up to the mercantile to call the sheriff. Astrid's up in arms. Ebbe Persson took Eleanor and Hannah on home. Maeva gave the whole place hell. Gave them one minute to get all their alcohol off the premises."

"Sorry I missed that," Hauk said.

Lang nodded "Remember the time that she-bear came out of the woods over on the Dosewallips, we all sat still as stumps until she turned back, then we all took to scurrying around, hanging food twenty feet off the ground, burying garbage ten feet under? That's what happened inside back there. Everyone froze while Maeva spoke and snapped to when she headed back to the kitchen."

"Anyone eat?"

"Must have. Every drop of soup's gone, every slice of bread. Astrid hid back one pie. Maeva took charge of dish washing."

Hauk pictured Maeva talking to the crowd and felt the change in his eyes, his face muscles; the change his sister could see coming. Best news he'd had in months, better even than Roosevelt's election, was Maeva saying she planned to keep teaching. He liked the idea of her in the school building, hoped it meant she wouldn't marry soon.

"You think Axel's fit to run the *Aggie J*?" Hauk asked. He or Lang could take the helm, need be.

"Give him an hour or two. He pulled his coat up around his ears when Maeva started talking. Afterward, he filed out with the rest. Must be twenty thirty flasks in the pond."

They stopped at the end of the dock, studied the old building that had served as shelter for ferry-hands and passengers until ten years back. "Shame to let this place sit out here and rot," Hauk said.

Lang rapped on a wall. "Man could salvage some of the lumber."

Hauk poked here and there with a pocket knife. "Most, but not all. Window frames look soft."

"You're right," Lang said. "Want to make a run down to Belfair tomorrow? Maybe on to Tahuya? Check on the old camp, see if Trigg's around? See if he has any work."

Hauk let that idea roll around in his head. They rarely saw their older brother, a logger and boom man, and hesitated to look him up. It was akin to asking for help, which went against their grain. "Might be time to check in," he said. "Unless Persson still needs us tomorrow. Goldarn cows."

"Goldarn Farley Price," Lang said. "And goldarn Axel Jenson while we're goldarning. They're not worthy of their women."

*O*rval Blevins considered himself a brewer of spirits, a *bryggare*, the Swedish word used by his grandmother in his childhood. Walt Strom, close as any man came to being his friend, called him that. Orval never much cared for words he heard bandied about and saw in newspapers: moonshiner, bootlegger, rum runner. His grandpap called the alcohol they made 'shine' for short, and packed a pint in his boot top most everywhere he went. Shiner or legger—either word suited Grandpap just fine.

Been a rum runner or two somewhere back in the family, too, the Irish side, but Orval never had more than a taste of rum. He considered his liquor, brewed from the head-waters of Whiskey Creek, equal to any ever distilled legally, including that his grandpap bragged about from the old country. One day the old country was Scotland, another day Ireland, and what did it matter? It was the recipe that counted, that and the timing.

Now and then, when he came up short on the good stuff, Orval brewed up some quick beer from fermented mash he'd used to make whiskey, to tide him over. Not him, personally, he didn't often drink much. No sir, to tide over sales, that's what. Sold a quart or two here and there. Sold several quarts to Farley Price.

It was Price who brung him Seattle papers to read, one of them full of Congress wanting to repeal Prohibition, passing the Twenty-first Amendment to the Constitution of the United States.

Bank closings, twelve or thirteen million unemployed, gangland murders—those stories didn't get more than a blink from Orval Blevins, but the idea of Prohibition ending set his heart racing and his stomach burning. It kept him so stirred up he'd decided it was time for another trip down to the bay to see what folks were thinking about the new president.

Celebrate, that's what they'd been thinking, and Orval got caught up in the mood like every other man. He enjoyed his own product a bit too much and found himself in need of a nap. He left Price leaning against the steering wheel of his car and drove off home where he could listen to the waters of Whiskey Creek burble and tumble.

His truck wandered off the road a time or two on the drive up to Hidden Valley, but he coaxed it back before a ditch took hold of the wheels. His back porch had raised itself another foot off the ground in his absence and caught the toe of his boots. He landed hard, cursed loud and set his daughter to crying.

"See to it that girl-child stays quiet, Thelma," he said to his young wife on his way through the kitchen. She wasn't near so pretty with the new baby, the one he'd worked hard to make certain was a boy, stretching out her belly and dragging down her tits.

He stumbled on the rug Thelma kept by the bed, railed at all womankind, especially the teacher, walking up to him and Price like she had every right in the world to speak out. Too bold, that one. Knew too much about every dang thing.

He got himself sorted out and seated on the bed edge so he could worm his feet out of his boots. Cash money he'd collected from Farley Price spilled from his left boot onto the crumpled rug. Forgot he'd put it there. Hadn't meant to, not in front of Price. The room tipped on end when he reached down to retrieve the bills. He gave it a minute to right itself, stuffed the money inside his undershirt down close to his belt, and lowered his head onto a pillow.

Teacher and preacher, both showing up where hardworking men gathered to celebrate their country's new president. Teacher saying she expected Prohibition to end, folks would be drinking beer in the tavern again soon.

"Beer's one thing, whiskey's another altogether," he'd said to Price when the teacher went back inside the tavern. Back to the kitchen where women belonged, so said his grandpap.

> *In the kitchen, and in a man's bed, that's what the good Lord made women for, son. You marry up with one, you make certain to keep her one place or the other.*

Not that Grandpap managed that with Grandma, a strong Swede woman who took over Orval's raising when his mamma and daddy died. Orval opened one eye looking for his grandpap, the voice had been that clear. Sure enough, there the ghost of the old codger sat on a tree stump, one he'd sawed off himself. Grandpap never logged for real, but he felled himself some nice fir close to the crick so's the bramble bushes could start growing, make it less likely folks stumbling onto the property would go on up to the crick's headwaters.

Grandpap used some of them fir trees to build a slaughter shed and smokehouse. Told folks he'd set those buildings out at the edge of the property. In truth, the property went on a good bit farther, clean on into deep woods and another building protected with brambles and barbed wire both. The distillery where Orval made his whiskey.

Keeping one eye on his grandpap on that tree stump made the bedroom settle and allowed Orval to give the preacher some thought. Skinny man. Small soft hands with shaped fingernails. Girl hands. He'd had a good look at them when the preacher wagged a finger and spoke a warning. Said he'd call the sheriff if the drinking and shouting and piano pounding didn't cease.

"Ain't nobody drinking, Preacher, far as I can see," Orval said, "and ain't no law against shouting or pianos neither."

Once the Preacher headed back to his cabin, Orval got Price settled in the driver's seat of that fancy car, only car on the property not black, and got himself into his truck. No sense waiting around to see if the law showed up. Only trouble he could see in driving off like he done was leaving Price to his own devices. The man moved product and brung back money like a pro, but he drank too much. Orval could hear his old grandpap's warning: *Never trust a liquored-up legger.*

Grandpap and stump faded. The girl-child coughed; Thelma shushed. Orval laid a hand over the wad of bills tucked in his undershirt and let himself drift. Prohibition or no, folks'd buy good product.

16

~ Tears of Relief, Tears of Sorrow ~

Eleanor startled at the knock, three light taps, more polite than Ebbe's work-roughened knuckles made and not the pounding she expected from Farley when he found the door locked.

She accepted that Farley was involved with Orval Blevins and his bootleg whiskey operation. Ebbe and Astrid dropped hints, Astrid's more pointed than Ebbe's. They considered Blevins a local character, almost a necessity in the community, but they gave him a wide berth. Astrid said he wasn't the only source. She spoke of whiskey ships coming down from Canada, dodging through the San Juan Islands, hiding out in bays and inlets, sneaking into the Sound on the dark side of the moon.

Astrid's worries about Pastor Holmes' threat to call the sheriff made Eleanor suspect the Romstads had alcohol stashed somewhere, maybe at their home.

"Who is it, Mamma?" Hannah asked.

"Go into my bedroom and close the door," Eleanor said. "Stay there until I tell you to come out."

"Why, Mamma?" Hannah's eyes, already enlarged by her thick glasses, grew wide with fear.

"I think it's about the drinking. I told you men were drinking. Go on now."

The knock came again, tap-tap-tap. Eleanor edged aside the curtain. Two men stood on the small cement slab porch, to the side of the rug she kept there. Hauk and Lang Nordlund. Her thumping heart sought its normal rhythm. She turned the key in the lock, opened the door, looked beyond them for someone else. Farley, perhaps, still staggering. The sheriff, with news of Farley's arrest, politely waiting while friends offered comfort. Or with news he'd died.

Her face heated with shame when she thought about the relief his death would bring.

"Yes?" she said, her eyes focused on a flashlight Lang held at his side like cowboys held their guns. "What is it?"

"Wanted to let you know Farley's sleeping it off in one of Romstad's cabins," Hauk said.

"Come in." She opened the door wider. Night air took the heat from her face. She'd need to add more wood to the stove to make them coffee.

"Better not," Lang said. "Just wanted you to know he might be late. Milking's done. We'll check back with Helmer in the morning, make certain Farley's here."

"Thank you." Eleanor closed the door, held the curtain aside for a moment, let it go to wipe away tears. Tears of relief from one eye, tears of sorrow from the other.

How does a woman talk to a husband she fears? What does she say to another woman, a new friend, who senses her truths, tells her so with looks but swallows words before they form? Does she defend the man as decent when he's sober? She'd heard ranch women make such claims, heard her mother say drink unmasks the true personality, a neighbor say that it opens a door wide enough for demons to enter.

Eleanor wasn't a stranger to drunken behavior; she'd seen her father stagger and fall against a china cabinet and helped sweep up shards of her mother's precious china in the aftermath. She'd seen ranch hands empty their stomachs on Keane land and leave the mess for nature and women to clean away.

She'd scrubbed and aired Romstad's cabin, where Farley had vomited more than once. She spot-cleaned his overcoat with naptha, hung it in the wind, pressed it with wet cloths to keep shine from wear at bay. She washed his other clothes by hand to avoid fouling Ebbe or Astrid's washing machines, brushed mud from his shoes, poked wadded paper in their toes and rubbed on new polish once they'd dried.

She'd learned to clean up after men without knowing she'd been taught.

She was Farley's wife; she cleaned his mess and shared his bed. She kept her peace to calm his fists; she kept her douche bag ready for those nights when he reached for her before passing out.

Four months ago she'd plotted to leave Farley, to work her way home from this wet place crowded with trees and bordered by the sea. She'd believed she belonged to the Keane ranch, the only community she'd known. Now she yearned to stay in Burke Bay where she'd found friends, where crocus bloomed in February and daffodils in March.

Eleanor kept her peace until the late March night Farley asked for the wages she earned at the tavern, the money she'd squirreled away to buy Hannah something special for her sixth birthday.

"What?" she said, though she'd heard him. She stood at the sink, her hands in dishwater, her story ready.

"The money. Give me the money. Your wages from the tavern. From sewing for Irv Carlson and the others. I want you to hand over the money that rightfully belongs to me as head of this family."

"I don't get paid much cash, Farley, I work for trade. Food, some fabric and notions, firewood."

He grabbed her upper right arm, spun her to face him, squeezed until the pain in her arm bone ran down to her fingers and up through her shoulder to her head. She gasped, choked on too much oxygen and pain, shook her head at Hannah, who'd stopped the rocker where she cuddled with her books.

"Firewood. From them Nordlunds? What're you trading off for firewood in a place overrun with trees? A wiggle of your behind for their blue eyes? That why they spend all their time at the tavern? Or more than a wiggle? They following you into that back room? Taking turns at trade?"

Eleanor blinked, stunned by his words, and there was Hannah, tugging on Farley's shirt. "Go, Hannah, go into the bedroom," she said, but Hannah tugged again.

"You better not be mean to my mamma, Farley Price, or I'll tell Big Papa, and he'll come here and shoot you with his gun."

"You're not going to tell your Big Papa anything. He's a thousand miles away."

"I will so. I can write him a letter, Miss Swanson taught me how to write."

Farley's fingers dug deeper into Eleanor's arm and jerked. She waited for the bone to snap, for her arm to leave its socket. He swung his other hand, caught Hannah on the side of her head and knocked her into the wall.

"Give me the money. I need to put some gas in the car, I've got a job to do. Give me the money and tend to your daughter." He pushed her against the sink.

"You drink too much, Farley. It's going to be your ruin."

Freed, her arm pain increased. Eleanor lifted a can of coffee off the shelf with her left hand, poured the contents into a bowl, lifted the wrapped coins from the heap.

"Two dollars, Farley. That's all I've got. Two dollars and hate in my heart."

Farley shook the coins from the coffee-stained fabric scrap, stomped across the living area and slammed the door on his way out. Eleanor was on her knees beside Hannah, her left arm around her child.

"Shh, sweet one, it's going to be all right. I'll heat water for your bath and tell you stories about the ranch back home and riding Colby into town to see my friends. We'll put clean sheets on your bed. I'll sleep right beside you tonight."

Her lips swept Hannah's cheek and temple, testing the injury by the heat it gave off. There would be a bruise, a black eye. She straightened Hannah's glass frame, kissed the hurt, crooned while water heated, talked while undressing her daughter and helping her into the water.

"Will the Perssons send us away?" Hannah sat with her knees pulled up to her chest in the round galvanized tub. She cupped water in both hands, like balanced scales. She'd asked to look in the mirror, squinted at her reflection, patted the swelling over her cheekbone saying it didn't hurt.

117

"I don't know, sweetheart." Eleanor feared they would. Farley had been warned. If so, she hoped Astrid and Erling would let her and Hannah move into the tavern bedroom until she saved enough money to pay for a room in Seattle.

"I will say I fell, Mamma." Hannah tipped one hand so the water dripped onto her knee. "That way the Perssons will let us stay."

"No," Eleanor said, "you mustn't lie."

Hannah tipped her other hand. "It's not all a lie. I fell into the wall. I can say I got in Farley's way and he bumped me into the wall."

"Hannah, you must not lie, and you must not call him Farley. He's your father."

"I don't like him. I don't want him to be my father."

Eleanor closed her eyes, but lids made poor floodgates. Hate in her heart would serve no worthwhile purpose. It would paralyze her, subjugate her child to a life of sorrows and lies.

"Listen to me, Hannah. There are some things we cannot change. Farley Price is your father, I am your mother. Tomorrow morning I will tell the Perssons what happened. After that, I will walk you to school and tell Miss Swanson."

Hannah sucked air as though she'd been suffocating, and wailed, "No, Mamma. The Perssons will send us away like Big Papa and Grandma sent us away. No one will give us a house."

"Oh, my child. Oh, Dear God, what am I meant to do?"

17

~ Men Drive, Women Ride ~

Maeva and Eleanor were standing on the Burke Bay Grade School porch discussing Hannah's bruised face when wind ripped a branch from a Douglas fir and sent it caroming to the ground twenty feet from the tree. The break resounded like a gunshot while the branch rocked and settled.

"Widow-maker," Maeva said. "That's what loggers call out when a heavy limb breaks loose. They can be deadly."

Eleanor, eyes on the branch, said, "I'm not that lucky."

Maeva filed the comment in her mind as a truth shared by a friend, and accepted another truth: none of her efforts to quell gossip about Farley Price could protect Eleanor and Hannah.

"Do the Perssons know about Hannah's face?"

Eleanor locked eyes with her. "Hannah told Ebbe, just as she told you, that her father yelled at me and stomped out of the house. She got in his way and got bumped into the wall. Her father said he's sorry this morning."

"And Ebbe's response?"

"She said the Nordlunds are headed off somewhere to work a log boom with another brother, there's no one else to help with the milking. I think Farley would be fired by now if Lang and Hauk were here."

"Not necessarily. The Perssons are Swedes; they ponder a good while before deciding important matters. Both of them love Hannah like a granddaughter." Maeva looked at Jonas's old pocket watch hanging on its crocheted chain, aware of its weight on her neck, the weight of time ticking by. "I'll stop by the tavern after school, if you're going to be there. We'll talk about you and Hannah, and what's best."

Eleanor looked away. "You'd miss the boat. Axel won't wait for you. There's never time. Not for women."

"We'll make time. I'll find another way home."

Maeva lingered a few more seconds, studying the prints left by Eleanor's boots. Stairs and porch needed a good sweeping.

Laughter rippled from her classroom, and lifted the weight of worry she'd borrowed from Eleanor. Wesley had the girls giggling, Hannah among them. Only Virginia Holmes remained unmoved by Wesley's antics, her small lips pursed so she resembled her father when he stormed the tavern's kitchen with threats of the sheriff descending.

Hannah's friend Beatrice covered her mouth to stop the saliva that dripped past missing teeth when she giggled. Maeva hesitated outside the classroom, reluctant to interrupt. Wesley wasn't teaching grammar or math or penmanship, but something more valuable—a lesson these children might borrow in trying times without remembering the specifics of this day.

"See, her mamma won't let her wear rouge so she bonked her cheek against the wall for a little color." Wesley sensed her presence, turned, winked. "Ain't that so, Miss Swanson?"

"We all need to add a little color now and then," Maeva said. "Thank you, Wesley. I'll carry on. Try to avoid using 'ain't'. You've outgrown it."

She assigned tasks by grade level and ability, walked between desks, offered suggestions or encouragement, noted who needed hands scrubbed or fingernails cleaned before lunch. Wesley's aftershave lingered. She'd noticed it on the boat when he sat so close his thigh touched hers. He'd outgrow his crush soon enough. Next year he'd be among girls his own age.

Wesley, almost sixteen and trapped in eighth grade, lived in a world where fathers drank too much and used raised fists to maintain control. Wesley had started school late and missed entire terms. She'd tutored him over the summer, helped him catch up. This coming summer she would help him push ahead.

She hoped he'd develop a gentle side, such as she saw in Hauk Nordlund. Lang too, she supposed, but it had been Hauk in the tavern kitchen inauguration day, making potato soup for men who'd had too much to drink.

She'd replayed that pageant a dozen times, and wondered if she'd ever see Axel or Jonas stand at the stove longer than the time it took to snitch a taste of what a woman cooked.

Maeva kept a close watch on Hannah through the day, lest she withdraw during reading or spelling, or on the playground. She pictured Hannah as a woman; a bit stoic; easily lost in books and stories; uncertain of her role with men. She startled, aware she'd described herself.

At afternoon recess, while boys batted a baseball and ran to bases marked with tattered burlap feed sacks, Virginia Holmes planted her feet in front of Maeva.

"My father said you were inside the tavern when liquor was being consumed. He thinks you're unfit to teach young minds."

Maeva studied the child's face. Unlike Hannah, who would be attractive in womanhood, Virginia would remain plain. Maeva squatted, unmindful of her coat and skirt hems sweeping the packed earth.

"Virginia, repeating your father's words, especially if they are spoken in anger, is a habit I urge you to avoid. You've done so before. I will not tolerate such behavior from any student."

Tears formed in Virginia's eyes and a horrible wail rose from deep within her stodgy body. An intense dislike for the child surged through Maeva. She wanted to shake Virginia to stop the noise. Her legs went weak with awareness of anger consuming her. She blew her whistle and ordered the entire student body to form a line and return to the school building.

Wesley, with Ralph Strom's help, gathered up bat, ball and bases. Wesley yelled, "C'mon, you heard Miss Swanson, return to the building."

She gave Wesley her best stern look, the one she'd used in the tavern when she ordered the men to remove all alcohol from the premises. Anger at Pastor Holmes boiled in her now as it had that day and, like then, she spent the anger on others. What had those men done? Set aside worries for a few hours to celebrate the symbol of hope: a new president, born to wealth, but concerned for all mankind.

The returning students interrupted Miss Truax's afternoon rest. Maeva offered neither explanation nor apology. She waited for her class to settle, told them to put their heads down on their desks for five minutes, the remaining time of their recess, and utter not a sound. They did so, much as those men in the tavern had marched themselves and their illegal alcohol out the door.

While her students sneaked peaks at her and one another, she jotted thoughts in her notebook—thoughts of spiders she'd collected from the wood box and returned to the woodshed or garden where they could do their work, dead birds she'd buried in her mother's flower beds, barn cats she'd saved from being drowned. How could she possibly want, even for a moment, to shake a child?

Ebbe, her face redder than usual, stepped into Maeva's classroom before the last child left. "The mister and I, we're thinking Eleanor needs a trip to Seattle, a look around for safe places to hide for a time, if it comes to that. You'd be knowing Seattle better than most. Might be you could take her there of a Saturday. The one coming or the next."

Maeva nodded. Miss Truax waited for a word. Ebbe frowned and headed downstairs to put things there in order. Wesley rounded up Hannah for delivery to her mother at the tavern and the South Bay Beach children for their trip to the dock.

While Maeva explained the playground incident and interrupted recess to Miss Truax, her mind traveled to Seattle. Where could a woman and child hide? She could help a little with rent while Eleanor sought work. The Perssons and Romstads would likely contribute. Ilsa Bakke, too, if Ebbe and Astrid asked. Those three women had a way of handling matters without leaving ripples in their wake.

Maeva was still pondering when she turned onto Dock Road and saw Eleanor step off the tavern porch. They met at the dip where Maeva had first heard Farley Price's name. Her ear caught the music of water spilling from the upper pond on Nordlund brothers property to the lower pond owned by the Romstads.

"Astrid's entertaining Hannah for me," Eleanor said, "I'd be crazy to leave this place. Ebbe and Astrid both mother me. Ilsa Bakke, too. She delivered salt pork and ground sausage to the tavern, and told me to keep out a little for my own use." Tears ran down Eleanor's cheeks and dripped onto her wool coat. "Nothing Farley does to me makes me cry, but these women . . . they're so kind." She dug a hankie with a tatted edge from her pocket, daubed her cheeks, sniffed.

"We'll walk out to the old dock-house," Maeva said. "Tell me what Farley did. Tell me what you want to do."

"My arm, that's all. He squeezed and jerked it to make me give him the money I'd hidden. Then . . . then he hit Hannah."

Eleanor's tears grew to body wrenching sobs. Maeva put her arm around Eleanor's waist and steered her to the dock railing. A breeze wafting off the water ruffled their skirts. A gull swooped low, squawking protests. The *Aggie J* rounded Indian Hill Point and disappeared from sight.

"I hid my money for Hannah's birthday." Eleanor spoke in gasps. "How can Farley spend so much that he needs my dollar or two? Besides no rent for the Persson's cottage, we get milk and eggs from Ebbe. Bread and butter, too, and her blackberry jam. I take leftovers home from the tavern most nights. Astrid gave me some apples you and Axel brought. I made applesauce, so that meant buying sugar, but sugar's cheap. Coffee. I buy coffee from my earnings. And toilet paper."

Maeva knew how far a dollar went. She earned more than some men with families. Axel often remarked on her wages as though she were stealing from an innocent man trying to support his family. In her case, she did the supporting. For a moment the anger Maeva felt toward Farley stretched to include Axel.

"I don't know how men spend their money," Maeva said. "I doubt the Perssons pay Farley much cash, but it seems they would pay enough to cover regular expenses."

Eleanor's sobs settled into sniffs. "Let's keep walking. It makes my knees go rubbery if I look down through the cracks between the planks, but it's good for me. If I'm to live in this country, I need to grow accustomed to the sea and docks and boats."

"Bridges, too," Maeva said, though Eleanor didn't seem to hear.

"It's the drinking. That much drink costs money." A few steps later she added, "And the women. I wash his laundry, I know about the women."

"*Gud i himmel.*" The breeze caught Maeva's oath and carried it away. Eleanor and Hannah needed a permanent solution, not a place to hide.

They walked in silence to the old dock house, where they sat inside on a bench once used by passengers waiting to cross to Bainbridge Island or Seattle. The wood, polished by years of scooting bottoms, glowed in the half-light. Her own father may have contributed to the patina.

"I think you need to go home. To your family. We can get you train tickets so you can take Hannah home and see her settled. Once that's done, you can decide what to do about Farley. About your marriage."

Eleanor stared at a broken window in the end wall, the one facing east, while she spoke. "Papa said they may have to kill off some cattle to keep from buying feed. There's not enough grass. There's been dust storms. Papa said I'm lucky to be here where I can pluck fish from the sea, where rain waters the vegetable garden. Hannah and I would not be welcomed."

Maeva felt another anger wave sweep through her body. "Have you told them about Farley? What he's done?"

Eleanor released a long sigh. "They knew everything they needed to know about Farley before we ever left. He stole cattle from Papa; he's lucky Papa or one of my brothers didn't shoot him for that. He got alcohol back there, too, there's no place a man addicted to drink can't get it. He hit me before Hannah was born, when he'd had too much to drink; he'll hit me again. Last night was nothing, just a wrenched shoulder and a sore arm. Nothing, except he hit Hannah to push her away. How can I stay with a man who hits a child? How can I leave, with nowhere to go?"

Maeva closed her eyes, saw Farley standing beside his car, long black coat, brushed felt hat, dark good looks. In that moment she'd known she'd stand before him again one day, though when and what she'd say wasn't clear. She had no experience with violence and little with men beyond Jonas and Axel. She was looking into the future, seeing herself watching Farley's eyes while she lied to him about Eleanor and Hannah's whereabouts.

Another premonition? She shook it off.

"Ebbe suggested we go to Seattle Saturday, to acquaint you with the city," she said. "At least you'll know where the ferry docks and a bit about getting around from there."

Eleanor sniffed and nodded. "I need to do something, just in case. Right now, I'd better get back to the job I have."

Hannah met them on the tavern porch. "Mamma, you walked all the way to the end. Mrs. Romstad said you walked on water." She giggled, a child amused at the notion, and moved into her mother's open arms for a hug. "Mrs. Romstad said fresh coffee's on, come have a cup."

Coffee, the Scandinavian solution to all problems. Maeva had one cup and left for home, her heart heavy. Twenty yards or so along the plank road she felt the rumble of an approaching car and knew it would be Axel. Would he be concerned or vexed?

Vexed, to put it mildly. He stopped beside her, put on the hand brake, climbed out, leaving the car door hanging open. "Stay out of their business, Maeva. I don't care what that stupid bastard does, you stay out of it."

Axel had what Maeva's mother called fire in his eyes. "Hello, Axel," she said. "Did you come to offer me a ride, or just a warning?"

He opened the passenger door. "Get in the car."

Maeva looked at him, tall handsome blonde with a strong chin and a half-grin even when his patience was being tested. "All right," she said. "I'm a little weary."

Axel drove to the Burke Bay end of the plank road, turned around in front of the mercantile, hands and feet busy with clutch and gear shift. Maeva studied his moves so she'd be prepared when she got behind the wheel of a car herself. Clutch down, shift to second, clutch down, shift to third, back to second to climb Indian Hill. She mimicked his moves with her feet and right hand.

Neither Jonas nor Axel let her practice driving. Both were possessive with their cars, guns and assorted gear, but all too ready to share shovels, rakes, hoes or a wood splitting axe.

She said, "I've decided to buy a car. We need a working car at the farm."

"You'd never see it. Nels would have it all the time. Men drive, women ride, that's how it works."

"It would be my personal car to drive to school, the library, the ocean when I feel like it." She waved an arm to take in the entire country, thinking of where she could take Eleanor and Hannah.

"What's this about? Farley Price getting a little heavy-handed with his wife? I am warning you, stay out of their business. What a man does in his own home is nobody's business but his own, Maeva. The man is the head of the household. You're the school teacher, that's all. It's not your place to poke your nose into your students' scrapes and bruises."

He whapped the horn to emphasize his point, and sent dirt flying when he turned onto the Swanson-Jenson Road.

"What do you know about Farley and Eleanor?"

"I had a cup of coffee at the tavern, which Astrid had to pour. Eleanor could barely lift her right arm let alone a coffee pot. The Wiley kid showed up with the Price girl whose eye is going black. He told me the whole story on the way down the dock."

"What is the whole story, according to Wesley?"

"The parents were arguing, the kid tried to stop them and got in the way. It happens all the time with people of that class."

Axel stopped in the upper pasture, accustomed to staying at the wheel while she got out to unlock the gate, but driving through meant he'd accompany her to the house, perhaps stay for dinner.

"I'll walk from here," she said. "Thanks for coming for me."

"Don't I get a little kiss?"

"I'd rather not kiss a man who considers it appropriate for a husband to get a little heavy-handed with his wife."

She closed the car door, slipped through the gate, taking in deep breaths to calm her snit. She smelled manure and hay from the barn, cedar and decaying wood from the shed and, over it, clean sea

126

air from the Sound. She could live right here on Swanson property for the rest of her life and be quite content.

How, she wondered, did Axel's need to control her very thoughts differ from Farley's need to control even the small wages Eleanor earned? Control, that's what men wanted.

The night went dark, closing Maeva and her mother in their warm kitchen scented with fresh-baked bread. Her mother had spent the day sorting seeds, some collected from last year's crops, carefully dried and stored in jars in dark cool corners of cupboards; some purchased in growers' packets. She'd drawn a diagram of the garden plot, vegetable names written in Swedish on the back of an oft-used paper bag. Seeds and plan occupied half the round oak table, dinner settings for three the other half.

Maeva sketched the tableau in her notebook below the words she'd written that afternoon. Her notebooks filled in that manner, by chronology, sketches on lined paper. Though her drawings lacked depth, she found them helpful when she recalled scenes, added descriptions or sorted and arranged thoughts like her mother had arranged seeds.

If a poem one day grew from the words and sketch, it would be forever separated from the kernels of its inception. She couldn't leave blank lines, to come back to later.

Jonas, the first controlling man in her life, had seen to that.

18

~ Seattle Bound ~

*T*o Eleanor's surprise, once she realized each rumble of the big boat didn't forewarn an explosion, she enjoyed the ferry trip to Seattle. She fixed her eyes on Mount Rainier, rounded and pristine with snow, while Maeva named glaciers and rivers they fed. Further evidence why Ebbe and Astrid, and Burke Bay Tavern customers called Maeva *The Teacher*. Every conversation with her contained a fact worth remembering.

"We'll walk," Maeva said, when the ferry docked. "You won't mind the climb, will you? Seattle is built on hills."

Eleanor didn't mind, though Maeva set a fast pace. They left the waterfront with its ships and train tracks, and signs that said *No Help Needed*. They climbed Marion Street to 1st Avenue, turned left, naming cross streets. Marion and Madison, Spring and Seneca, University and Union, Pike and Pine. Maeva had her recite them in that order and then reversed, so she'd remember them when she wanted to find her way back to the ferry terminal.

"If it comes to that," Eleanor said, words so often spoken by Astrid and Ebbe.

They passed open arcades where sleepy-eyed barkers invited them in, painted-window cafes that advertised good food cheap, gated-front pawn shops with guns and silver tea sets side-by-side in their window displays.

They walked around panhandlers in tattered suitcoats and filthy trousers, sitting cross-legged so the cardboard stuffed inside their shoes showed through the holes in the soles. One man offered to sell a diamond ring, cheap.

"Not today." Maeva took Eleanor's arm and circled him. "We'll come back down on 4th Avenue, where the commerce is less seedy and possibly less lucrative, given the times. I thought you'd like to see this area first."

"Because of Farley? Is this where he'd sell bootleg whiskey?"

"Just because it's good to know areas you want to avoid when you're alone, especially after dark."

They slowed their pace when they reached the downtown shopping district. Maeva led them through Frederick & Nelson Department Store, where they behaved like shoppers with money to spend until they reached the business offices. It was the first place of many where Eleanor heard, "No, we're not hiring, not even seamstresses for alterations."

They ordered a sandwich and coffee at a drug store lunch counter and studied Maeva's Seattle map until Eleanor could point them out as Maeva named them: Puget Sound, Lake Washington, Lake Union, Capitol Hill and Queen Anne.

Seattle was all hills and water, with industry to match—a poor fit for a woman reared in Kansas.

After they ate, they walked south on 4th Avenue past Pioneer Square and Seattle's origins to the King Street Station, where they collected train schedules and fare information.

"Fares aren't so bad as I'd thought," Eleanor said, calculating how long it would take to earn enough for Hannah and herself to gain some distance from Farley.

"Can you hide enough money with Ebbe or at the tavern for two fares home, just in case? I can loan you enough so it's there."

Eleanor could neither swallow nor speak, so she nodded. She'd go far enough east to find a ranch, but not as far as Kansas. Maybe somewhere in Montana. "I'll hide my earnings at the tavern. If need be, I'll accept a loan from Astrid. She's offered. I can't accept money from you, Maeva. It could ruin our friendship."

By the time they boarded the ferry to return to Bremerton, Eleanor had a map of Seattle in her head and blisters on her feet.

Maeva opened the afternoon newspaper to the classified ads and together they searched Help Wanted. Two ads offered a room and one meal a day, no wages, in exchange for labor. Male labor. There were a few commission-only sales jobs, and a call for temporary hands on the docks—check the daily shipping news.

"No one needs a waitress, or cook, or seamstress," Eleanor said. "That's about all I'd qualify for in a city." She thought about taking Hannah away from Burke Bay. From Ebbe Persson and Astrid Romstad. From school and Maeva. Her stomach churned. "Restroom," she said, and made her way to the privacy of an enclosed stall.

When she returned to her seat, Maeva took her hand. "There must be other choices. Perhaps as a live-in maid with a doctor's or other professional's family. They'd be discreet. We'll look into that."

Maeva made it sound like the problem belonged to them equally. She had a look on her face Eleanor had never seen before. A frown that lowered one eyebrow.

Eleanor blinked back tears, found her hankie and blew her nose. Her mother would disapprove. Lace-edged handkerchiefs were for keeping moisture from one's face on hot summer afternoons at teas or church suppers. If a woman needed to blow her nose, she found a private place and used rags torn up for that purpose. She told Maeva that, hoping to lighten the mood.

"Better a hankie than a sleeve," Maeva said. "Mom supplies me with handkerchiefs for the classroom. She makes them from old petticoats or whatever scraps she can find, with white stitched hems for girls and dark stitched for boys."

"That makes me want to cry," Eleanor said. "That kindness."

Neither spoke for a time. Eleanor listened to the boat engine's hum. Seattle would be a temporary stop, if she did run. For now, she'd need a new place to hide the few coins she collected from tavern customers, the dollar or two she could safely hold back from the wages Astrid paid her. She'd take home enough to hand over to Farley.

He had hit her in early November, drunk on beer and angry over having to kill turkeys. After that he'd spent his anger other ways until March, after several late nights of heavy drinking what she supposed was Orval Blevins's whiskey. When she thought back over the six and a half years of their marriage, the pattern had been similar. Anger built, he exploded, hit or shoved or jerked her arm, and then stayed subdued for several weeks.

Papa had a similar pattern, stew for a time and then blow up, though he didn't drink daily and never hit her mother. Instead, he broke things: dishes, a spindle chair, a crystal vase her mother had washed and polished weekly and never used, deeming the prairie flowers of Kansas unworthy of such a container.

Her mother swept up those crystal pieces and stored them in a hat box. *One day I'll sprinkle them on your grave, Mr. Keane.*

Those long forgotten words, churned up by the boat's drone, brought along other memories of unpleasant moments between Papa and her mother. Why hadn't they come to mind before she fell for Farley's charm? Or when he waltzed her around the ballroom floor that had been nothing more than the school gymnasium dressed up for a dance?

"Maybe all couples have their bad times," Eleanor said, thinking out loud more than offering conversation. "Spats and all." She hesitated, for a moment, but wanting to know won out. "Do you and Axel ever have spats?"

Maeva laughed, a sound so pleasant people around them looked their way and smiled. Her eyes brightened, green with gold flecks like stars caught on a tree branch.

"Since I moved back home, our relationship has been one continuous spat. He's trying to shape me into a replica of his mother. Change my politics and basic notions about how the world goes around so I will be an asset as his wife. So far it's not working the way he hopes. I call them energetic discussions. Axel tries to end them by saying, 'I don't want to argue with you,' which of course means he wants me to give in."

"Energetic discussions," Eleanor said, trying to remember even one serious discussion with Farley. Would Axel and Maeva go on as they were accustomed, into marriage and parenthood, or would he take more drastic measures to make her into a woman like his mother? He wouldn't succeed, Eleanor knew that. Maeva was too smart and strong willed to be bullied.

The ferry's engines groaned into reverse.

"It won't work," Eleanor whispered, knowing Maeva couldn't hear. "Axel's the wrong man for you."

19

~ Business Matters ~

Orval Blevins got his son, Theodore Loyal Blevins, two weeks late, born in the Bremerton hospital like Orval's pretty little wife wanted. Thelma got herself a good long stay, twelve days, for complications of delivering his ten pound boy.

"No marital relations for at least a couple months," the doctor said.

Orval shook cash money out of both boots, and still had to dig up a buried coffee can to pay the bill. The complications, whatever they were, caused him to give in to Thelma on the boy's name, a deed he expected to rectify by skipping past Theodore and calling the boy Loyal, just like his grandpap called him.

You're a loyal one, son. Shame your mamma didn't name you Loyal.

Might take some time to get the boy accustomed to Loyal once he got big enough to be away from Thelma. She called him Teddy while he suckled at her breast.

"Teddy," he bellowed the first time he heard her cooing that name to his son. She upped and replied the name had been good enough for a president, one she admired, who happened to be a relative of the current president, whom she also admired. Now where in tarnation did all that admiring come from?

Orval held a different view of the current president, who seemed bent on making changes that interfered with a man's right to earn a living. Darned if the president hadn't made beer sales and drinking legal. He'd even hinted Congress would soon extend that to whiskey and wine, and every other decent beverage.

The Stroms tended to his daughter while Thelma and the baby rested up in the hospital, and that gave Orval time to tend to a vexing matter. There'd been a serious drop in product sales due to legal beer, but more so to some revenuers snooping around. Orval feared they might be on to Farley Price and his fancy car.

From what Orval could make of things, Price and another man got into a tiff over a street lady outside a Bremerton tavern, and both got hauled off to jail. Price made it out in time to help Helmer Persson with the morning milking, but not in time to prevent a police officer from connecting Price to the sand-colored car.

"Trade the car straight across for whatever you can get," Orval told Farley. They met up in Bremerton at a café popular with Navy Yard workers, and talked over a bowl of tomato soup and grilled cheese sandwiches. Yard workers tended to shout, like as not due to damaged ears from the work they did. Orval kept his voice low. Price did the same, the little he spoke.

Price shook his head and fixed his black eyes on Orval. "Nope, not giving up my car."

"Be the end of our doing business," Orval said. "Can't risk sending my product out in an automobile that's being watched." He figured that would get Price's attention, much as the man needed drink himself.

Price narrowed his eyes. "There's others cooking, other means of delivery. Car's part of me, it stays with me."

"You got yourself a boat, that what you're saying? You plan to sail across the Sound, drop anchor along Seattle's waterfront?" Orval's feet took to itching, a sure sign the conversation was headed off in the wrong direction.

"You're a small-minded man, Blevins. You make good whiskey, sell at a decent price, but you're short on savvy. I move your product, bring you back cash, that's the extent of our business. You don't need me anymore, just say so."

Orval shook his right foot, then his left. Damn boots made his feet too damn hot, and he hadn't had a clean pair of socks for days.

Thelma needed to get herself up out of that hospital bed and get on home to her wifely duties.

"You ever get yourself a salesman job?" he asked, hoping for more information from the dark and cold Farley Price, getting only a sly grin.

"Guess you could say so. I sell whiskey."

"Stay out of street altercations, Price, they'll bring you down."

Price's eyes narrowed to slits. "Drunk jumped me over a woman he claimed was his. Woman saw it differently. I defended myself. Only reason I'm telling you that much is the drunk got that way on your whiskey. Think about it, Blevins. I defended myself, the woman, and you. Your name never came into it."

"See to it you keep it that way. And keep them fists of yours to yourself. I told you that once before, concerning your wife. Street brawls are even worse. Get your name known to the cops. Name and car."

"Car's only a problem in your mind, Blevins. You mention it again, it's the end of our arrangement, and it'll come with a taste of my fists."

Orval Blevins was savvy enough to know when to shut up. He took a bite of his sandwich and thought about what to do next. Price had found other suppliers, he knew that for certain. He'd suspected that was the case, given rumors about how much the man was gone from home at night. That wasn't a bad thing. Transporters needed to keep transporting, and his operation could only produce so much.

"The whole of Prohibition ends like speculated, there won't be no business," he said, his eyes focused on the café window, but with Price's face there in the corner of his vision.

"Seems to me business will be better than ever, long as you keep the cost reasonable. Buyer sells government controlled stuff until the bottle's empty, refills with your product, sells for the same price. Your job gets tougher. You gotta keep the color right if you're calling it whiskey. Thanks for lunch." Price pushed away from the table, leaving the bill behind.

Orval had a son now, one he wanted to train as a distiller just as his old grandpap trained him. A man needing a drink wouldn't be looking at color. Or would he? Damn the new president for interfering with an enterprising man such as himself making an honest living. Course, Grandpap had been in business before Prohibition came along. There'd always be buyers for good product. Colored up whiskey. Damn, now he had to learn himself how to do that.

20

~ Three Nordlunds ~

𝓗auk and Lang leaned against the side of their truck to watch their brother Trigg work. They'd found him at his boom on the mouth of the Tahuya River, rounding up loose logs with a pike pole. A completed raft, secured with cables for transporting, lay tied to the boom pilings.

The Constance, Trigg's broad-beamed, bottom heavy boat used in the process, groaned when throttled down while he leaped from boat to logs, and back, uttering profanities neither wholly Norwegian nor English, understood only by those who knew him well.

Lang untied the canvas tarp covering the truck bed, pulled out two pair of boots and inspected the spikes on their soles. "Sounds like we'd better put on our calks and give him a hand."

Hauk nodded. "Long as he doesn't decide to do the two-step out there."

Trigg was thirty-five, had worked log booms for twenty years and been called Dance Man for at least eighteen. The last time Hauk worked on rolling logs he'd had a couple shots of whiskey first, to ease the pain in his shinbones left from deep burns in his childhood.

He dug around in a box of supplies for the salve Ilsa concocted for him to rub on his legs when he first got out of bed. Bear grease, she called it, though it smelled more like axle grease spiked with pepper. He shed his pants, rubbed on the grease, donned wool

Longjohns, suspendered tin pants and a heavy flannel shirt. He shoved work gloves in his hip pocket.

Lang dressed the same, greasing his own legs first. "Can't hurt," he said. "Cold as that water is, a man might be smart to coat himself stem to stern."

"Not enough grease," Hauk said, capping the jar.

They sat on a washed-up log to tighten and tie laces on their boots, their motions choreographed by genes and years together. Even the creases in their paraffin coated pants, legs cut off to fall above boot tops, matched.

They stood, raised their right arms in a wave to Trigg and stepped out onto the makeshift ramp their older brother used when he tied up to come ashore.

Trigg pulled them aboard, shook their hands and gave a Nordlund nod. "Thought about sending for you two. Had to let my crew go since nobody's buying the good stuff. Shelton mill wants hemlock for pulp. Figure I'll go back in, salvage what I can, haul it overland."

"Guess that's what gave me the notion to run out here," Lang said. "Something niggled my brain."

"This the last of what you've fallen up-river?" Hauk asked. Once Lang had mentioned making a run out to check on Trigg, he'd had the same sense of being summoned, a mind picture of logs stacked along the Tahuya waiting to be sent downstream.

"'nother two rafts worth or so up to the camp. Left Millie and the wee ones up there to keep an eye out. Nobody's buying, but plenty're thieving." Trigg motioned with his head toward the boat's cabin while he talked. Tobacco and papers and a bottle of Canadian whiskey sat on an upended wood crate. He uncorked the bottle, took a swig, handed it to Lang, who drank before passing it on to Hauk.

A Nordlund ritual among the brothers. Oldest to youngest with food or drink. Women first, if any were present, but only after children were fed and cared for. Hauk, youngest, entered the cabin last and left the door open for the breeze sweeping across Hood Canal. He could taste stale cigarette smoke, diesel fumes, sweat from Trigg's rumpled sleeping bag; he welcomed his turn at the bottle. Good Canadian whiskey Trigg picked up somewhere at sea when he towed a raft of logs up the canal to Port Gamble.

"Now we've burned the Ford we get to work," Trigg said. He called Hood Canal the fjord and referred to whiskey as *brenne*, the Norwegian verb for burn. Hauk and Lang had been working for him a few years back when a sheriff's deputy hiked into camp looking for information on illegal alcoholic spirits, Canadian or otherwise, being trafficked along the canal. A logger who'd been arrested for public drunkenness named the camp and Trigg as his source.

Trigg, in his best Norwegian accent, spoke mishmash, crafting new words on the spot, leaving the bewildered deputy to turn to Hauk and Lang for translation.

"We're younger, we didn't learn the mother tongue so well as Trigg," Lang said. "All I can make out is something about a Ford burning somewhere."

The deputy left them, muttered oaths about Norwegians trailing behind like smoke in the wind. Before bedding down for the night of that encounter, the three brothers drank to the burning Ford. They expected to do so on meeting and parting for the rest of their days.

Trigg hooked the pike pole into a log and jostled it into place inside the raft formation. "Rounding up logs is a dang site easier than rounding up cows. It's working the goldang chains that busts your knuckles. Goldang salt water gets in them cuts, you'll be cursing your maker."

"Brought gloves," Lang said.

"Brought smarts too," Hauk said. "Smarts enough to handle what we know and leave what we don't know to the one who owns the logs."

They set up a tent for sleeping and makeshift shelter for cooking, dug a pit toilet, and spent the rest of March and early April building splash dams upriver, floating logs down, rafting and securing them to ride out the wait until one mill or another put out a call. Hauk and Lang took turns in Trigg's upriver camp where Millie fed them meat and potatoes every day, followed with cake or pie for dessert.

She knit them new stocking caps and gloves, and retrieved her children from their laps before they grew tired of playing Uncle. She wrangled information from them, neither one knew quite how, so she had a good sense of their interest in unavailable women.

The brother who stayed behind at the boom kept a loaded shotgun ready, and trained his ears to listen for any change in the sea. All three of them could tell the level of the tide within an inch or two at any given moment. Twice, on rainy moonless nights, Hauk set a match to the kerosene lantern about midnight, an odd time for a fishing boat to pass. Once, when the boat took longer than he considered necessary, he fired the gun into the air and reloaded ready to fire again, but the boat's engine found new life and chugged on past.

When all the fir was rafted and secured, all the hemlock loaded and hauled, Hauk and Lang dismantled a bunk house at the camp upriver and reassembled it, somewhat reconfigured, near the mouth of the Tahuya. They set the cabin back from the flood plain in an area protected by cedar trees, and enclosed the pit toilet to create a decent outhouse for family use.

They stayed on an extra night to do a little Ford burning, discussing the ins and outs of Trigg keeping an eye on so many rafted logs without another man.

"Might be one of us needs to stay out here, spell Trigg nights," Lang said. "That or move the rafts to Burke Bay, float them into Irv's lagoon on high tide."

"We'll leave 'em be for now," Trigg said. "I got one man who'll spend a night now and then. Buyer'll come along one of these days."

"Lang and Hauk need to get home," Millie said to Trigg, a glint in her eye. "They left a couple women behind."

Lang gave a shake of his head. "One's married, the other's spoken for."

"Married is a problem," Millie said, "but spoken for doesn't count for that much."

"Married one works in the tavern?" Trigg asked. "And the other's the school teacher?"

Hauk felt his face heat up. "All this good food gets us talking too much, that's for certain."

Lang nodded. "Time we get on home and put our energies into planting spuds. That's something we can manage."

They increased their garden to grow enough potatoes to keep themselves, Ilsa's store and the tavern going for a year. They hauled sand from Indian Hill to loosen their soil and went to work digging. After turning soil for five hours, Lang said, "Sure could use some of Trigg's good whiskey long about now."

Hauk grunted. "There's a quart of beer cooling in the creek just where the next row you dig comes up against water."

"A quart, you say? What you planning for yourself?"

"Quart cooling the end of the row I'm digging."

Lang stuck his shovel into the earth and headed to the creek. Hauk followed, retrieved glasses he'd left on a mossy stump. Lang opened a quart and poured. They leaned against the cedar tree trunk, sipped, said "Ah."

"I've been thinking about Millie," Lang said. "She's made Trigg a happy man." He dug in his pocket for tobacco and papers, rolled a cigarette, handed it to Hauk. "Something about her working at that big old stove brought Eleanor Price and the tavern kitchen to mind."

"Hmm," Hauk said, leaning to his left to catch the flame of Lang's match. "I had an odd notion, watching her roll out pie crust, that she resembled Maeva Swanson some ways."

Lang shook his head once. "Guess that tells us both everything we need to know about darn near everything."

"Tells us there's been no shift in the wind."

21

~ Power Poles ~

Maeva wheeled a load of rotted cow manure mixed with straw up the incline from the barn to the vegetable garden where Nels waited for her, scowl on his face. He grabbed the pitch fork, none too gently, and handed her the hoe.

They were taking turns loading and wheeling up a barrow full, then hoeing it into the plowed earth. At each brief exchange they continued their argument, now in its third day, over acquiring peeled logs from the Nordlund brothers to use as electric poles.

Nels said, "You want those poles set so the power company can get electricity down here for Mom. Am I right?"

Maeva leaned on the hoe, a pleasure of gardening. She liked working the earth, didn't mind the pungent, oddly sweet smell of cow dung and damp straw, the muck on her boots and Jonas's old dungarees. She liked wearing pants and considered having Eleanor craft a pattern that fit her properly and sew a pair or two.

She searched for an answer that would get Nels on her side without telling him she was squirreling money away for train tickets for Eleanor and Hannah, just in case.

"Yes, absolutely. I just want them to name a fair price in advance. I need to budget."

"Budget away, Maeva. Take your time. They'll soon leave for Alaska, you'll still be budgeting, Mom will have another summer of baking and canning over a hot wood stove."

Nels pulled a bandana from his back pocket and wiped sweat from his forehead.

"Why can't they give us a bid, like any other workers? Why are they so stubborn?" So *sta*, she thought, and smiled.

"Hauk and Lang would be happy enough if all they ever got in pay was one of Mom's meals. They're good men, Maeva. Everything isn't about money, or what they can get in return. They're not like some people, always looking for an advantage."

Maeva studied Nels's face, bristled with light brown whiskers he hadn't bothered to shave for a couple days of gardening. He was referring to Emil and Axel Jenson.

"I've heard the Nordlunds cook well enough for themselves," she said.

"Seems so, but they don't bake bread or make butter, or have a cellar full of canned fruits and vegetables. They're planting potatoes for their sister to sell at the mercantile, and for the tavern to use, but that's about all. I'll see to watering and hoeing for them while they're gone. As a kindness, not for pay. Like they helped Irv Carlson refit that old fishing boat and fix up the mill for church services and replace some timbers on the dock. Not for pay, Maeva, for need."

"Which is exactly why we need to pay them wages, Nels. I earn wages for my labors, so I'm expected to pay when someone else labors for me." She stamped her foot—a manure coated, booted foot—and felt it sink in muck.

"Yeah, you earn wages, you budget for Mom to see a doctor about her hip, you put aside money for property taxes, you tell me to put what I earn into building myself a car. For all I know, you're slipping money to Eleanor. I know you, Maeva. You're all the time thinking things through, using your brain, working out what's right and fair and worrying about what might happen. You let Jonas's miserly ways and words eat away at you. You've paid back what you owe him, but it will never be enough. He wants to own us. Keep us doing his bidding until he departs this earth."

She looked at him, the brother she considered a sweet boy, now a nice man. His assessment of their older brother surprised her.

"And while you're at it, forget Axel, too. He wants to run your life. He wants you to be like his mother so he can be like his dad."

She started to protest, but Nels wasn't finished.

143

"Listen to the rumors about Emil Jenson, Maeva, and you'll know where that path leads."

"What rumors?" she asked, though she knew what he meant. She'd heard about Emil Jenson's women, his proclivity for gambling, his connections to the shady side of the street, but that didn't mean Axel indulged in the same activities.

Nels groaned, gave her a look she'd felt on her own face when she was provoked beyond words, and stabbed the pitchfork deep into the redolent earth.

"Go ahead," he said, "refuse help from the Nordlunds unless they accept money. But if they don't set the poles because of you and your stubbornness, it's on you that Mom goes without electricity for another year." He turned the empty barrow and wheeled away.

Maeva stared at his back, her anger dissolving. "Nels, you forgot something." She tugged the pitchfork free, caught up with him and said, "You work it out with the Nordlunds, I'll help Mom with the cooking."

"*How* much you figure a man could charge to dig a hole and drop in a pole, if a man were to charge?" Lang asked Hauk over breakfast of fried oatmeal mush, toast, and coffee. The mush was leftover from the day before. Planned over, the brothers liked to say.

They'd been discussing the Swanson job. Lang had a tablet beside his plate, a pencil behind his ear, and a frown on his face. Nels told them Maeva wanted a fair bill prepared for their services so her family could repay with goods. Accustomed as they were to trading services, goods too, for that matter, they'd never before been asked to write it down so it looked like a bill.

"Two-bits tops per hole," Hauk said, "if the man places the pole and tamps in the earth around it. Ten cents, maybe fifteen, for digging alone."

"Mile worth of poles ought to earn us a nice supply of fresh vegetables. Canned ones, too, and fruits and preserves, according to Nels. Meals while we're working. Dinner this Sunday coming, to meet the older brother and take a look at easements."

"How long you figure the job will take?" Hauk knew the digging and setting wouldn't amount to much.

"A couple two three days," Lang said, "unless we stretch it out. Word is Mrs. Swanson puts on quite a spread."

"We won't stretch it out. Might have to take out a tree or two before the power company strings the lines. That's additional work."

"Plus your surveying, keeping us in a straight line." While he spoke, Lang surveyed the loaf of bread resting on a cutting board Hauk had crafted, and cut a slice with the same motion and intensity he applied to sawing wood to length. "You want another toast?"

Hauk nodded. He'd gotten out the transit he'd owned since high school days and knew how to use, thanks to one of the men who'd tried to court Ilsa. Owned a nice collection of woodworking tools too, most of them stored under his bed.

Lang made a second precise cut through the dwindling loaf, gave the stove-top a fresh sprinkling of salt, placed the slices just so—all indications his mind was at work on the task. "We helping Nels and the older brother with the job, or they helping us?"

"You're in charge of the whole shebang," Hauk said. "You're the one knows the most about timber appropriate for power poles. You're the one who peeled the dang things. You might add that to your bill."

"Might at that. Could be worth a jar of raspberry jelly."

Hauk grinned along with Lang. They'd called the trees toothpicks when they brought them down and stacked them. Nice straight fir, too small for Irv Carlson to bother milling. Lang offered them to Nels for a dollar a pole, peeled and coated against weather and bug invasion. A bargain considering bark didn't come off fir easily. Not like cedar, which the brothers liked to say came off faster than clothes off a stripper, not that either of them had much experience with strippers.

Bark made a good holding fire overnight; that was why Lang peeled the dang logs in the first place. Let them get up to a warm kitchen.

145

Lang carried hot toast to the table. Bread and butter came from Perssons in trade for any number of tasks. Blackberry jam, too, which they made last. Lang took a bite of toast, set it down, pulled the pencil from behind his ear. "How many poles you figure it will take?"

"How many we have?"

Lang nodded. "That's kind of what I figured. Space them a little closer or a little farther apart than standard depending on what we've got ready."

"We'll walk it Sunday," Hauk said. "We'll know what we're talking about once we step it off."

"Better make the stepping off before dinner. Might not feel much like walking after."

Hauk and Lang stood on the crushed shell path that ran from the Swanson barn to the house, discussing pole placement with Jonas and Nels. One of them had trampled a bed of mint sending a layer of pungent fragrance over the barn odor.

Hauk let Lang do the talking, and would have believed his brother set power poles at least five days a week if he hadn't known better. Lang told them placing poles along the road down from the highway would be easy enough, though some trees would need to be topped and a dozen or so removed.

"Upper half of the road belongs to the county," Jonas said. "They should handle the topping and removing up there. They laid claim to it after Dad and Axel Jenson's grandfather turned what had been an oxen trail for loggers into a decent road for horse and buggy passage.

"Later, when Dad and Jenson purchased cars, they hauled in heavy rock to raise the surface, mixed crushed shells with fish oil and guts, and dragged chained logs over the surface to smooth it out. Winter rains develop a pothole now and then, but nothing near a washout. It's darn solid."

Hauk gave a nod and said, "A regular Swede road."

Neither Swanson brother so much as smiled. If he'd said that in Maeva's presence, he would have gotten a lively response.

He studied Jonas and decided the man was worried about his wife beyond the usual concern for a woman about due to give birth. When they arrived, she'd been hunkered under a blanket in a rocking chair in the kitchen, though the room felt overheated.

"I'm anxious to get the electric stove hooked up for Mom," Jonas said. "I wired the place almost two years ago thinking the county would get lines down to us, but they say we're on our own from the property line."

A light rain started to fall. The wind shifted, bringing cooking aromas their way. The men moved to the woodshed, a building Hauk eyeballed at twenty feet long and fifteen wide. It housed stacked wood and chopping blocks at one end, assorted lumber, tool boxes and work benches at the other, with a tarp-covered cider press in the middle. Jonas moved a few pieces of wood not yet split for burning and came up with two quart bottles.

"Cider. We'll have a sip soon as I show you the cellar." He retrieved a miner's flashlight from a hook by the kitchen door and led the way to the front yard. They ducked under a verandah which stretched across the front of the house, and descended four steps into a room with timber walls and packed dirt floor.

Jonas turned on his head lamp, located a kerosene lantern hanging from a floor joist, struck a match and gave light to what Hauk would later call buried treasure: filled jars, stored crocks, baskets and boxes with apples and potatoes.

"Mom preserves everything she can get her hands on."

Hauk heard pride in Jonas's voice as he named off items.

"Every fruit and vegetable you can imagine. Plus clams, chicken, beef and pork, venison when we're lucky enough to get one of the rascals before they get all the apples. Pickles of all sorts; sauerkraut; jams and jellies. Maeva wants you to know there's more than enough here so you'll be comfortable taking your pick in exchange for your work."

Lang said, "Digging holes and putting in poles doesn't amount to much. Dinner on workdays will serve."

"No," Jonas said, "it won't serve Maeva. If you're smart, you won't argue. There's more here than our family can use. Mom sees to three or four older widows along the beach, but none of them eat much these days."

They left the chill of the cellar for the warmth of the kitchen. Jonas opened the cider and poured it into heavy tumblers, forming a good head on each. "Mom?" He held forth a glass of the heavy golden brew.

Mrs. Swanson shook her head. "Dinner's near ready. Take your drink in by the fire."

Jonas turned to his sister. "Maeva? This is from your batch."

"Please," she said. "Check on Cynthia. She's in Mom's room."

A worry-shadow crossed Jonas's face and disappeared as though he'd pocketed it. "Gentlemen." He urged them ahead of him, asked them to sit and disappeared into a hallway.

They sat on overstuffed chairs arranged alongside doily covered tables. Kerosene lamps lit the room. One table held a stack of books, another a black glass vase filled with daffodils. Fire burned in the center of the large fireplace. Casement windows on either side of the fireplace looked out across the verandah to the Sound and Bainbridge Island.

A third window, in the side wall, faced the path they'd taken to and from the cellar. A flower bed beyond the path was filled with daffodils, primroses, pansies, and tufts of green plants Hauk couldn't identify. He wondered if Mrs. Swanson ever had time to sit and enjoy the view of the sea or her garden.

He heard Maeva and her mother putting the finishing touches on dinner, a discussion about seating around the large kitchen table so guests would be comfortable, not overly warm from the stove. A ghost's breath of sadness blew across his face and settled on his heart. He saw it touched Lang, too. They had once known such a kitchen, resplendent with baking bread, coffee, dinner about to be served. Lang gave one shake of his head in the exact moment Hauk felt his own move.

Jonas returned, more relaxed. "She's sleeping, she's just very tired these days." He retrieved his cider, poked at the fire, took a sip of his drink. "You can see how I did the wiring—up walls, across ceilings. They'd look better encased, but they'll serve."

148

"House seems well-built," Hauk said.

"My father was a carpenter," Jonas said. "I never picked up the finer points of the trade."

"Hauk's a carpenter. Self-taught, for the most part," Lang said. "Built our place. We milled most of the lumber at Carlson's, did our own wiring, chimney work, plumbed in a kitchen sink and a bath of sorts."

A slight smile relaxed Jonas's long narrow face. "So Nels tells me. Says he'll keep an eye on your place while you're off fishing in Alaska come summer."

Maeva stepped into the room, nearly empty cider glass in hand, color on her cheeks. She wore a dress Hauk would describe later as simple. Pale green. He would remember the belt, which showed off her waist and the flare above and below. Ilsa once remarked that Maeva Swanson was a handsome woman, too serious to be called pretty. Either word suited, in Hauk's eyes.

"Dinner's ready. Is Cynthia joining us?"

Jonas shook his head. "She wants to sleep."

"We'll keep some warm for her." She showed them where to sit, positioned with their backs to the sink, their eyes toward windows.

Hauk nodded, but remained standing. "May I seat your mother and you first?"

"My," Mrs. Swanson said. "*Tack så mycket.*"

"*Var så god,*" Hauk said. My pleasure, which indeed it was, to be invited to such a table. Crocheted cloth, lighted candles, steaming bowls of food.

Mrs. Swanson said, "Bless this food, our family and friends. Please, Lang and Hauk, to help yourselves."

Maeva handed Lang, who sat on her right, a large crockery bowl. "We'll start with the chicken and noodles. Mom makes her own noodles."

Lang helped himself, passed the bowl to Hauk. Maeva kept dishes coming. Creamed peas and carrots, green beans with salt pork, cranberry sauce, dill pickles, pickled crab apples, pickled beets, warm rolls, fresh butter. Maeva went to the stove to replenish serving bowls as they emptied.

"We'll soon get rid of that big old stove, Mom," Jonas said. "Get your electric one hooked up, and put in a trash burner you can use on cold mornings."

"*Nej*," Mrs. Swanson said. "I keep both."

Jonas scowled "You can't, Mom, there's not enough room."

Maeva brought a filled bowl of chicken and noodles to the table, set it on Jonas's right, gentled him with pats and rubs on his shoulders.

"We'll move the Hoosier to the outside wall, Jonas. Mom wants both stoves for now."

Hauk's eyes followed Jonas's to the large mix-center where it stood beside the stove, watched him mentally measure a space on the back wall. Jonas shook his head and shrugged.

When Hauk offered to help clear, Maeva touched his shoulder. "I know you're well acquainted with kitchen work, but let Mom and me take care of it this time. There's warm rhubarb cobbler. She'll whip some cream while I store leftovers."

Jonas pushed back his chair. "Leave the clearing to the women. Like I said before, you're better off not arguing with Maeva. I'll pour coffee."

Nels, who'd said little during the meal, and who'd out-eaten Hauk and Lang by half, handed his empty plate to Maeva. "Or be prepared to lose, if you do argue. Ask Axel. He hasn't won an argument yet, and I'd place bets on that never changing."

"That's not true," Maeva said.

"Name one time you thought he was right and you were wrong."

The golden lights in Maeva's green eyes sparked. She glanced at Hauk and Lang, and grinned at her younger brother. "That's another matter entirely. Sometimes he wins even though he's wrong."

Nels groaned. Lang chuckled. Hauk nodded. He found that news to his liking. Though he'd never been fond of arguing, he could give it a try, see where it went.

Behind them the beater whirred, stopped, whirred again.

22

~ A Buy, Sell or Trade Economy ~

Eleanor finished sewing her first ever pair of women's slacks cut from heavy cotton twill and a pattern made with Maeva's waist, hip and inseam measurements. Maeva declared them perfect. No more worn and patched men's pants with rope strung through the belt loops for her, except for gardening. The new pants Eleanor sewed would be too nice for that.

Beyond the chicken-coop cottage walls Eleanor heard wind soughing. Rain would soon tap the windows. Maeva said April on Puget Sound brought sunny days and daffodils followed by apple and cherry blossoms, all bearing up through cold rain squalls from the north or warmish ones from the south.

"Is that from a poem you wrote?" Eleanor asked.

They'd had too little time together of late, Maeva busy with spring garden chores, Eleanor at the tavern. Beer sales brought in more customers. The cabins needed to be cleaned and aired before Memorial Day opening. She took a sheet from the stack, cut a patch, pinned it in place and set the machine in motion.

Working the treadle calmed her, though it didn't take away her worries or stop her from listening for Farley's car. Nearly ten. Some nights he came in around eleven, others well past midnight, one night not at all, though he was in the barn for morning milking and never offered a word of explanation or apology. She didn't mind his lateness, but the tension of waiting, listening to night sounds, wore on her.

"Farley," she'd said to him after her trip to Seattle with Maeva, "we need to have a serious discussion. We need to talk about our future." She'd thought energetic discussion, Maeva's description of her talks with Axel.

Farley interrupted before she could say that she dreamed of a home of her own, a real house with at least two bedrooms, a fireplace in the living room, flower beds and a place to grow vegetables outside.

He said, "There's no future worth talking about right now, least not around here. I'm out working day and night, the less said the better. When the time comes to move on, I'll let you know."

He had that mean look about him when he spoke, eyes half-closed and fists clenched. She said no more. He was right; there was no future worth talking about. He whittled away at her hope with his sullenness, his hands either open to collect her meager pay or clenched into fists ready to hit.

He dropped in at the tavern from time to time, not on any schedule, to collect tips she received—nickels and dimes she dropped in her apron pocket. He didn't know she deposited half of her tip money in a fruit jar Astrid hid for her. That was her future, and Hannah's. Her secret, and Astrid's.

The jar was Astrid's idea, started the day after Eleanor's Seattle trip when Farley stopped at the tavern mid-afternoon. The Nordlund brothers and Irv Carlson sat at the bar drinking coffee and bragging about the fish they brought in earlier.

Red snapper, they called the ugly creature with bulging eyes and gaping mouth. Lang sharpened a knife, removed head, tail, and fins as easily as she herself sliced through a potato. Hauk pulled pliers from his hip pocket, grasped fish skin, gave a tug, and just like that all the ugliness disappeared.

They filleted the fish, talked about how many folks it would feed, then took their mugs of coffee to the bar where Irv had found the plate of ginger snaps baked that morning and displayed under a glass dome. He gave her a fifty-cent piece for the three coffees and cookies, and placed another beside his plate.

"For you," he said, just as Farley opened the door.

Eleanor felt her pulse start up in her neck like it awakened from a nap. "Hello, Farley," she said, and then to Irv, "That's too generous." She left the coin where Irv placed it, circled the counter and moved to her husband. He stepped around her, swept the half-dollar into his hand, dropped it in his pocket and nodded to the three men.

"I handle the money in our family. Eleanor, get me a coffee."

Lang Nordlund slid off his stool. Hauk placed a hand on Lang's arm. Irv stood, trapping both Nordlunds with his bulk and chairs of a nearby table.

"Well, boys, we got to finish cleaning the boat." Irv slapped Lang on the back and took him by the elbow.

Shame heated Eleanor's face and neck.

Remembering the scene while she stitched a rounded patch over a worn spot on a sheet brought the same intense heat. Shame, but not one iota of guilt for the fruit jar. Eleanor took home what she knew Farley expected and left the rest for safe-keeping. Not one iota of guilt for lying about what she earned turning collars and cuffs for those men and others, or for patching knees in their pants or elbows in their shirts.

She felt shame every time Farley entered the Burke Bay Tavern. Deep shame because Lang Nordlund wanted to protect her, and she feared Farley would hurt him. She'd set that problem in motion with one dance and kept it growing with smiles she couldn't hide every time Lang came into her sights.

She'd danced one dance in the Burke Bay Tavern; she'd been paying the piper ever since.

With a flick of her wrist Maeva sent Hauk's pocket knife into the blossom-covered earth under the Royal Ann cherry tree. The handle pointed heavenward. Hauk and Lang shook their heads. Both had scoffed when she said she was accomplished at mumblety-peg.

Scoffing involved a look that passed between them, meant to be unreadable by others. She'd studied the nuances of their glances, nods and conservative smiles during several evenings that included dinner, kitchen clean-up, Parcheesi, Chinese Checkers, followed by discussions of books, short stories and news journalists.

"By golly, you've got the wrist action down, no question," Lang said.

Hauk grinned.

Maeva savored the grin, uncertain why it mattered so much. Perhaps because she never won at the board games they played; she couldn't concentrate when there were serious matters to discuss and opinions to consider.

She pulled the knife from the soft earth. She sat between the two men on the weather worn bench under the tree, sipping raspberry *saft* and studying the enclosure they built on the kitchen porch. Just like that they'd created a utility room with an inviting door. They'd extended pipes and wires so the washing machine would be easy to use once the power company stretched lines and hooked them up. No more wheeling the washer into the kitchen to fill it, back out to drain it into the garden.

They'd rigged a drain, too, a French drain, they called it, where soapy water could leach into flower beds during dry seasons or be directed away when the rains came.

She'd paid little for the shiplap walls that enclosed the utility room and nothing for the door and window salvaged from a tumbledown shack. She looked the brothers in their blue eyes and asked if salvaged was a polite word for stolen. They chuckled and assured her the shack belonged to Irv Carlson who wanted it dismantled so they could build a house where it stood.

Maeva gave in on that point and took up her concern over the cost of their labor—five cents, ten cents, no charge. She played it their way, placed ridiculously low values on canned goods, fresh eggs, a sponge cake.

They inspected boxes she packed and asked what work she expected in return for all that food, and how she thought they could work with the added pounds they'd like as not put on from stuffing their faces.

Axel showed up for dinner every night the Nordlunds were there, showered her with attention like he'd shown summers when she spent two months at home, and slipped caustic remarks about the brothers' lack of steady employment into conversations.

"You should apply for work with the Civilian Conservation Corps Roosevelt created," Axel said. "It provides room and board, and pays a wage on top of that. You'd have a good size bank account after a year or two, thanks to our president playing Robin Hood with money generated by the business men and bankers he despises."

Lang studied Axel long enough for Maeva to see tension form along his jaw. "We're too old for the CCC. Least I am, and Hauk's too talented. Other than that, we don't qualify as an unemployed family."

"Conservation's admirable, though," Hauk said, a slight glimmer in his eyes. "Robin Hood, too, for that matter."

"The CCC is meant to save unemployed young men in cities, Axel," Maeva said, more than a bit impatient though she, too, worried about the brothers' lack of steady work. She paid too little attention to some of Hauk's remarks, remembered them later, pondered long into the night until she realized their sister Ilsa had played a major role in their upbringing.

Thanks to the brothers, she'd read and wept over *All Quiet on the Western Front*, a book she'd earlier shunned for its topic. Both said she should give it a try, though they understood she'd be saddened by reading about war, about men Nels's age dying horrible deaths for a cause they neither understood nor embraced.

"You read rather a lot, both of you. Is that Ilsa's doing?" she asked one evening in an attempt to get it all in perspective.

"Not much else to do after dark around here," Lang said. "Got no girlfriends to spark."

It was hard to know if he was teasing or serious. "How could you not have girlfriends? There must be more than enough young women available. The Federson twins, Iris and Rose. Axel's sisters, except Marjorie, who's engaged. Of course they're younger. Esther Olsson, Laura Larson . . ." she paused, editing her list of friends and acquaintances. Some wouldn't do for the Nordlunds. "There are others. They go to all the summer beach parties from Poulsbo to

Bremerton." She'd need to think about who might be worthy of these two men.

"We're particular about girlfriends," Hauk said. "That's Ilsa's doing for certain. And we're generally gone summers, worse the luck."

So, she'd been right on that count: Ilsa had shaped their views. Perhaps they held women in higher esteem than men with strong fathers and passive mothers.

"We're signed on with Alaska bound fishing boats," Hauk said.

Lang gave that a nod. "Can't manage without us."

She looked for a grin, a glint in his eyes that indicated he meant it as a joke, and saw none.

"Timing works out for us," Hauk said. "We'll get Romstad's row boats built and water-tested by the end of May. Nice little boats."

"I'd think boat building is a rather exact craft. Precise, that is, given the expectations placed on the end product." She'd heard about the row boats from Nels, who bragged about them and the rebuilt boat the brothers helped Irv Carlson outfit with parts they found here and there.

A look passed between the brothers, a slight move of their heads.

"We're building for summer folks, not the navy," Hauk said.

"Not that we couldn't build for the navy," Lang added. "Just need specifications. Decent set of plans."

"Do you have a decent set for these rowboats?"

Lang nodded. "Hauk drew them up himself. They're safe enough a man could row them across to Bainbridge without a concern."

"What about a woman?"

"You could, Maeva, without a doubt."

Hauk's eyes sent goose bumps up her arms, an odd experience for her, another thing to contemplate. She got out her notebook, but couldn't find words adequate to her feeling. Instead she wrote an article about the brothers buying brass oarlocks and sockets for the rowboats, saying some things couldn't be jerry-rigged. They accepted cash for the boat building but only goods from her in trade for their work.

She removed all personal names, titled the writing *A Buy, Sell and Trade Economy* and sent it to *The Kitsap Weekly*. It would earn her a quarter that would pay for coffee or flour, or another commodity they couldn't grow on their farm.

Or go into the property tax fund, her responsibility, one of the main reasons she couldn't risk marriage until the country came out of the Depression.

23

~ Rowboats ~

When Orval Blevins heard about Romstad's new rowboats and the christening party they planned to hold at their tavern, he decided it was time for a trip down to the Bay for a look-see. With legal beer flowing near free as water the last few weeks, his product sales were down. He'd expected a decline, but not near so much as Farley Price claimed. Last time the two met up, Orval's itching feet signaled something fishy, so fishy he could smell it even though they were deep in evergreens a good two miles from salt water.

"You in cahoots with that Silverdale outfit?" Orval had heard rumors about an operation selling product right out of the barn, and made a trip over the ridge to check it out. The barn sat smack dab in the middle of a hay field—five acres, give or take. Sign on the fence post at the road said *Hay For Sale*, with a backward *S*.

Sure enough, the big barn was filled with baled hay. Not a cooking pot or coiled tube in sight. That didn't surprise him; a careful man wouldn't brew in a barn out in the open, but he sure enough cooked somewhere. Orval could smell discarded mash, like as not hauled off to the hog farm back down the road.

A man dressed in overalls and a plaid shirt, with a sweat stained hat pulled low so the brim shadowed his eyes, came out from behind a partition-wall at the far end of the barn.

"Help you?" the man said.

"Thought I'd check your hay supply, case I run short," Orval said. "Seems you got plenty here, this late into spring. Name's

Blevins, I live up to Hidden Valley, got a couple cows eat more'n they're worth. Got my pasture grass chewed down to nubbins."

"Good bit of this here hay's spoke for. You want some, you put your name and money on it now."

Orval pulled a straw from a nearby bale, sniffed it, stuck it between his teeth and bit down. "I'll take my chances. No sense putting out good money for something I might not need."

"Suit yourself," the man said, and disappeared behind the partition.

Back home, Orval had been caught up in pondering the hay barn when his talkative wife told him about the christening party the Romstads planned, complete with rowboat races across the bay. She seemed all het-up with the news, which she'd gotten while drinking coffee with Strom's wife.

He listened and nodded, and rubbed his chin to show he had other things on his mind, a shave at the least, until she dropped a hint that she'd like to go. Not exactly a hint, truth be told.

"I'm going to that boat christening, and you're taking me like a decent husband. The babies, too. And I'm going to have a boat ride across the bay while you hold onto the babies."

"Now, Thelma . . ." That's as far as Orval got before she spoke up again.

"Don't you 'Now Thelma' me, Orval Blevins. I'm not going to settle for being stuck up here on this farm having one baby after another. I'm no Trilby Strom. I plan to travel down to the Bay once a week, and take the *Aggie J* to Bremerton now and then."

Next thing Orval knew, the boat christening day had come, so warm and sunny Erling Romstad dragged his old piano out to the tavern porch where he plunked away while one of them Nordlunds blew into a mouth organ. Folks did the two-step on their way inside and all over again on their way back out. Slapdab right in the middle of the day folks danced across a tavern porch. Orval tried a slip-slide step or two himself to give his itching feet some relief. Women folks seemed to like that, him dancing with his two babies in his arms.

Meanwhile, Thelma hied herself across Dock Road to the beach to have a look at them rowboats. Orval did a few more steps on the porch before following her. He set their squirming daughter, Norma, on her feet in the sand and grabbed hold of her wrist tight as he'd hold a dog's leash, no matter how hard she squirmed and tugged.

He took a good look at the boats. Just rowboats, painted white on their sides, their gunnels and oars left natural but shined up with some sort of varnish. All named Burke Bay, with Roman numerals for numbers one through four.

There'd been a time back when he was but a boy that his grandpap used a rowboat now and then to deliver product. Grandpap rowed and Orval bailed water that leaked or splashed in. Bailed with a rusty can, bent out of shape but always there where it belonged, underneath the stern seat where Orval sat.

Those had been good times for a boy, by golly. Might be worth having a rowboat himself, when his son got a little older. Might be he could get them Nordlunds to build him one.

Orval chewed on that thought and held tight to Norma, his daughter who'd like as not grow up to be pretty as her mother with just as many demands, if her tugging and wailing to be set free were any sign of times to come. He called Thelma's name, but she didn't seem to hear. Lucky for him, Louanne Strom came along and took over Norma's reins.

"Me and Hannah Price will see to Norma, Mr. Blevins."

"Hannah and I," the Price girl said. "Ask Miss Swanson."

Orval turned his head and found himself caught in the eyes of the school teacher, and odd eyes they were, with gold flecks that poked into him like needles. Made his teeth ache, or maybe they ached from being clenched so tight over his pretty wife talking to the Nordlund brother not blowing into a mouth organ. Irv Carlson and Mrs. Bakke from up to the store were in on the chitchat, but it was the Nordlund who had Thelma's attention. She didn't understand the concept of staying private.

A car bumped down Dock Street and pulled alongside the tavern porch so it blocked half the step. New Ford, shiny as all get-out, with a driver dressed up in a black suit, white shirt, striped tie and black hat, its brim turned down just so. A Revenuer if Orval'd ever seen one, dressed like that on a warm May day.

The newcomer nodded to Erling Romstad on his way inside. Orval's armpits and chest took to itching near bad as his feet, all of which told him he needed to follow the man, hear what was being said.

"Here, take my son for a bit, if you don't mind," Orval said to the school teacher, and handed off the bundle before she had a chance to say no. "His mother's just over there."

Off Orval went like Mother Nature had made the loudest call of all time; off across the road and porch where Romstad plunked away, into the tavern proper, never mind that the toilet was around back.

Sure enough, the Revenuer was behind the bar looking at beer labels, talking to Mrs. Romstad and Mrs. Price, neither of whom seemed bothered by the whole affair, but then they were decent ladies at work serving their customers.

Orval took a good look around the tavern to see who all was inside and ascertained for certain Farley Price wasn't there. A Revenuer worth his pay would take one look at Price's tan colored car and feel his eyes narrow and twitch to get a look at the engine. Orval knew Farley had that engine souped-up.

Orval scanned right and noted Strom and his wife talking to some folks from up to Keyport. He nodded, turned his head to scan left and got caught in the Revenuer's high beam. The man's eyes didn't have the color of the teachers, but they sure as shooting had the same needles.

Orval scratched his chest left side to right and back again. "Toilet," he said, as if he didn't know where it was situated, and waited polite like while Mrs. Romstad explained about going out the front door and on around the side to the first building out back.

He followed instructions, got inside, pushed the door's hook into the eye. Not much of a lock, no more'n a man might have on a screen door. He put his ear against the door to listen for footsteps. When none came, he decided to take care of business and get himself back out to the beach before Thelma, his ornery little wife, came looking for him.

First thing he noticed while crossing Dock Road to the wide sandy beach was the school teacher hunkered down beside a bonfire, talking to the Wiley and Strom boys, and without a baby in her arms. That got him a bit riled up. He thought a school teacher would know better than to lose a baby not yet two months old.

Next thing he noticed was the gunny sack resting on the sand alongside the fire. That gave him a start, thinking as he did for a moment that Price had dropped off some empties for filling. He forgot all about his son until Mrs. Bakke came up to him with a bundle in her arms, singing some nonsense or other.

"Here's your son, Mr. Blevins, and a fine boy he is. I took over so Thelma could have a boat ride and Maeva Swanson could help those boys get the fire right for roasting oysters and clams. Nels Swanson showed up with a bucket of clams, and Axel Jenson brought the gunny sack full of oysters over from South Bay."

That's when Orval noticed only three boats lined up on the sand. "Thelma's on a boat ride?" He had to squint and look off to the east to see the fourth boat.

"With my brother Lang," Mrs. Bakke said. "He's doing the rowing so she can sit back and enjoy herself."

She cooed at the baby and chattered about the liquor inspector. He forgot about his nervy little wife long enough to ask what did bring the liquor inspector out to Burke Bay.

"Why, Pastor Holmes, it must be, more undone than ever now beer sales are legal again. He's at Erling and Astrid all the time about the sin of selling drink. Neither pays him much mind, but Astrid's taken to worrying that he upsets Eleanor Price. It's as if the pastor thinks Whiskey Creek drew the likes of Farley Price to Burke Bay, and others given to heavy drink will surely follow."

"To my mind that don't make no sense." Orval took a good look at Mrs. Bakke so as to determine if it made sense to her. She was a hefty woman, one he liked to steer clear of, but now she stood so close holding his son he noted she had a pleasant face with nice blue eyes that didn't poke or prod.

"Pastor Holmes is a Baptist," Mrs. Bakke said. "It's in his nature to see the worst in folks, and not surprising he'd make an example of Farley Price, given the rumors. The pastor hopes to get some state legislators out here to acquaint them with our creek. He's petitioning for an official name change."

"Acquaint them with our creek?" Orval pictured stern faced men in tailored suits and vests. Like as not any inspection would be what they could see while standing on Dock Road, where Whiskey Creek's lower pond collected its end waters before spilling into the bay.

Legislators would never make it up to the valley where it all started. Never make it through his brambles and briars in their fancy shoes. Still, he didn't like the whole idea. No siree, he didn't like it one little bit.

"Where is this pastor fellow?" Orval asked.

"Astrid tells me he took his family off somewhere for the day to protect them from the goings on over the rowboats. Ah, here comes your wee one's mother, and a good thing. I think he's hungry and needing a change."

Orval took that as good reason to round up their girl child and get themselves into the pickup and back up to the valley, but his stubborn little wife seemed determined to try his patience. Stubborn but pretty, with her brown curls glistening and her best red sweater wrapped around her shoulders. Not wrapped near enough to hide herself from prying eyes such as those of Lang Nordlund who like as not took full advantage of looking while he rowed that boat.

"I'll take him into the tavern's back room," Thelma said. "Mrs. Romstad said I could make use of the bed in there. I'm not planning to miss out on the clam bake. You tend to Norma. Don't leave her to burden the Stroms, they've enough of their own to watch."

That's when he noticed Walt and Trilby Strom had moved from inside the tavern to take up a perch on the bleached drift log that rested up against the cement bulkhead. Trilby had Norma cuddled up in one arm and her own youngest snuggled in the other.

The folks from Keyport, Federson by name, had moved out to the beach, too, like as not to keep an eye on their twin girls, both trying to get a boat ride with Lang. Orval gave his full attention to the boats and those folks gathered around them, and discovered they were making up teams for boat races. Irv Carlson, tablet and pencil in his hands and coffee can at his feet, took bets, giving even odds on the four who would do the rowing, winners splitting the pot according to the amount they put in: nickels and dimes, a quarter or two.

Orval had never in all his life seen such folderol over rowboats.

Boats changed rowers and passengers for each race across the shallow part of the bay, no more'n 150 yards given the tide tended toward low. Full sun sparked the water churned up by all them oars dipping and pulling. The scene gave him pause till he thought on Thelma cavorting out there with that Nordlund.

Near on to every male from the Wylie boy and Ralph Strom took turns as rowers, with the Federson twins and other young ladies, some he'd never before laid eyes on, as their favored passengers.

The school teacher went out as passenger when Axel Jenson took up the oars against Nels Swanson and two of the Andersons from up to the garage. Swanson beat out the others by a second or two, and started on a return trip against Jenson and the school teacher, with the teacher doing the rowing. She kept pace so the two boats nosed onto the sandy beach neck-and-neck.

Swanson and the teacher took to laughing and hugging right out in the open. It took Orval a long moment to remember they were brother and sister.

Thelma, who'd left the baby sleeping on the bed in the tavern's back room, went along as passenger with one or another of the older Strom boys until she'd had her fill of rowboat rides. She settled down to helping Norma roast a wienie Mrs. Bakke provided for the children so as to save the oysters and clams for grownups.

Orval settled for a bowl of clam chowder, provided at no cost by the tavern and carried across from the tavern kitchen by Romstad. His missus followed with Orval's son resting against her chest and a smile on her face. Mrs. Price brought over bowls and spoons, and did the serving. Those who'd won a little money on the boat races handed over a few coins even though the Romstads announced that wasn't necessary. Those who'd lost the races promised a tip soon as they had a chance to win some money back.

After a second bowl of chowder, Orval offered to take his son from Mrs. Romstad, but she declined, hugging the baby close and kissing his head. Thelma had settled into helping Mrs. Price and the school teacher with food serving and dish carrying, so Orval sat on the bleached log and rolled himself a cigarette.

Later, after Thelma had nursed the baby again, she gathered up Norma and settled both children on a blanket near his feet. Hauk Nordlund rounded up Mrs. Romstad and Trilby Strom for a boat ride, and Lang invited Mrs. Price and her daughter.

Orval lowered himself down onto the blanket beside his pretty little wife, leaned his back against the log and allowed his eyes to fall shut. He dozed off, common thing for a man to do after filling his belly with good food and having a smoke, and startled awake to a ruckus.

Farley Price stood near the water's edge, so near his shoes were getting wet, shouting to the wind. Orval shot to his feet and got himself up onto Dock Road to see where Price had parked his car. It struck Orval as odd that he'd dozed right through an engine's sound, and odder still when all he saw were black cars and trucks lined up, some straight and some willy-nilly.

Price shouted again, most of it words not fit for women and children's ears, the least of it calling Lang Nordlund an unkind name, and goddamning his rowboat. Orval jumped back down onto the beach, intending to round up his family and get the hell and gone out of there.

Helmer Persson wandered down to stand beside Price. "Take it easy now, Price," Helmer said. "Your wife and little Hannah were about the only folks here still waiting a turn on the water. No harm done, now."

"Get out of here," Price said, and gave old Helmer a shove that knocked him onto his backside and brought Ebbe Persson, Irv Carlson, Walt and Trilby Strom, Erling and Astrid Romstad, and Ilsa Bakke on the run.

"Orval, you get on down there and help out," Thelma said, her look meaning business.

Before he could state an argument, she went on.

"Or you stay with the babies and I'll go myself."

"Looks to me like there's more help than Helmer can use, all those folks already down there."

"Every bit of that help will be needed when Lang Nordlund brings that rowboat into shore."

He supposed she was right, and got to his feet. He spent a full minute dusting off his backside, which was dry and sand-free from sitting on the blanket. He needed the minute to choose up sides— Price's or Helmer's. Soon to be Price's or Lang Nordlund's, with that little rowboat flying across the bay.

Orval picked his way past those who hadn't raced to Helmer's rescue and soon had his eyes fixed on Eleanor and Hannah Price looking toward shore while Lang rowed.

What happened next would be disputed for some time, though Orval knew his recollection would be better'n most. Lang nosed that little boat into the sand, lifted Hannah out and handed her to Astrid Romstad, all the while ignoring Farley Price's shouts and cursing which included some unkind remarks about Mrs. Price.

When Farley set one foot, shoe and all, into the water and reached for his wife, Lang lowered himself something like an angry mule might and drove his head into Price's gut. It took some time for Price to fall. Five or six steps backward, but fall he did.

"Get up, Price," Lang Nordlund said, "and apologize to your wife and the rest of these folks for your filthy mouth."

Price came up swinging. He had a few inches in height and reach on Lang Nordlund, but he never landed a punch. Nordlund spun 'round like a top, knees bent, and came up under Price's chin with his right fist. Made of steel, that fist seemed, against a chin made of glass.

Price went down. The good men of Burke Bay picked him up and carted him up the beach like he'd been laid out to rest, not just knocked unconscious. Romstad gathered up the gunny sack, wet it good in the bay, and lay it over Price's head.

Meanwhile, Mrs. Romstad, Mrs. Persson and Mrs. Bakke helped the school teacher get Mrs. Price and her daughter to the tavern. Thelma wanted to follow them and get into their women thing, but Orval put his foot down, so to speak, and near dragged her to the truck.

He had some serious thinking to do. A consult with old Grandpap at the least. Farley Price likely got himself fired from his cow milking job. That would mean him and his family moving on, leaving Orval without a legger.

The way he seen it, those rowboats and the ones who built them caused him no end of trouble.

24

~ Night Sounds and Safety Alarms ~

Eleanor perched on the edge of the iron frame bed in the tavern's backroom, remembering Astrid's words the first time they met. *Big enough bed for you and Hannah side-by-side, if need be.*

Hannah slept on the far side of the bed where it abutted the wall, the satin edge of a blanket across her cheek. Eleanor remained upright and rigid, listening to night sounds: water spilling from the upper pond to the lower; an owl calling from a nearby tree; the incoming tide lapping the rowboats' sterns; a dog barking.

Earlier that evening, when the women huddled around Eleanor and Hannah while the men dealt with Farley, Hannah had said, "Farley Price drinks too much. Mama said it's going to be his ruin. He's almost always drunk, plus he's mean."

Maeva had answered, "Drink does that to some people, when they consume too much. Do you know what 'consume' means?" Hannah nodded. Maeva said, "Let's curl up and read while the men help Farley sober up."

That had been during daylight hours when sounds and shapes could be identified. Even then, Eleanor saw fear on Ebbe's face, and later smelled it on Helmer's cooling sweat when he reported Farley's doings.

"He demanded the wages he had coming, tossed clothes into his car and drove off. Still and all, we're thinking it best you stay down here to the tavern for the night. Ebbe will pack up some of your things."

"Who knows what he'll do next," Ebbe whispered to Astrid, a whisper that carried on sea-scented air drifting in through the open windows and giving up secret thoughts they'd never spoken.

Farley Price meant danger to everyone along Whiskey Creek, from Orval Blevins on down to the bay, and to the families of every child attending Burke Bay Grade School.

Until the moment she saw Farley on the beach, almost in the water, Eleanor had basked in the warmth of self-pride for making the trip across the bay. When the rowboats arrived at the beach a few days before the celebration, carried there from Carlson's Mill and lined up on the sand by Lang, Hauk, Irv Carlson and Erling Romstad, Eleanor vowed she'd never set foot in one. Never, yet there she'd been, Hannah beside her, Lang rowing.

Before the boat ride, she'd removed her shoes and stockings and cooled her feet in the sea after swearing that would never happen.

She'd decided before the rowboat in which she rode ran up against the sand—even before she saw Farley there—that she would break a third vow, her marriage vow. She would divorce Farley Price without her parents' blessing or help. She'd take her chances in the world with the skills she'd honed.

Pressure had been building in Farley since his last outburst, the one when he'd hurt Hannah. Eleanor mentally charted the frequency and intensity of his flare-ups, much as she charted her monthlies, and saw rage rising ever nearer the surface.

Farley grumbled his way from bed to barn every morning, damning the world for placing such an onus on his shoulders. For the last several weeks, he returned to bed once the morning task was completed and stayed there until the cows came into the barn in the evening, later and later with the lengthening days of spring. After that milking, he ate whatever she'd prepared for his dinner, often something she'd brought home from the tavern, cleaned up and went out into the night for what he termed his other work.

Eleanor had been biding her time with Farley and his temper so she could save a little more money. Perhaps Farley had ridden off into the sunset like her father said ranch hands did, and she could stay on in this place she'd called home for six months.

She'd made friends in Burke Bay, the Nordlund brothers among them. She liked the warmth she felt in their presence, and the sense that Lang found her especially appealing. He showed his interest in all the little ways men use to charm women: lingering looks, a touch on a wrist or elbow, an offer to help with simple tasks that called for no help at all.

She didn't encourage his interest, didn't seek sympathy for her plight or openly flirt like some women she'd known back in Kansas when an especially handsome cowboy showed up asking for work. No, she didn't flirt, but she did smile. Lang had tugged loose something tightly bound and deeply buried; something she'd tucked away before Hannah was born.

Something she needed to tuck back away.

At the first hint of dawn, Eleanor unlatched the tavern's backroom door and went into the kitchen to stir up the fire and run fresh water into the small coffee pot. It was Sunday; the tavern wouldn't open until eleven, beer would remain behind the counter for the duration of the Sabbath.

She raised the blind on the kitchen window and watched the building at the end of the dock take shape, the sky and sea turn from gray to lavender to a golden wash that defined the trees on Bainbridge Island and turned lingering clouds pink. Then the sun burst forth above the trees. She could see its shape—a quarter dome, a half, and soon a full circle too bright for human eyes already drawn away to the path it cast on the sea.

The path dissolved, or perhaps it widened to cover Puget Sound in its entirety. Yes, she guessed that's exactly what happened. She'd watched daylight creep up over the trees on the Persson farm and felt the sun when it climbed high enough to shine down, but she'd never before witnessed day breaking over water.

In that moment, weary from a sleepless night filled with worries, Eleanor Keane Price felt her hands cross over her heart and tears stream down her cheeks. She'd been falling in love with a place. The sunrise cinched it; she didn't want to leave. Maybe Farley would stay away, free of her and Hannah and cows and milking.

"Like as not it won't be quite so easy as that," Astrid said a few hours later when Eleanor confided her hope, her decision to file for divorce. "Farley's gone from the farm, true enough, but chances are good he's still around these parts. Better we make a plan, that's why Ebbe's here early of a Sunday morning. We have an idea."

They sat at the table in the tavern kitchen, Eleanor at the end so she could look straight out at the dock and bay. She listened, awed by the two women, one on either side of the table. It would be better, Astrid said, for Eleanor to move off the Persson place, settle herself and Hannah in one of the cabins behind the tavern. The Romstads needed her help more than ever, what with the summer season coming on. The cabins required thorough scrubbing and airing after each use. Sheets needed a light bleaching and a run over with a hot iron. Towels took a little fluff-up with a brush Astrid kept for that purpose.

"The first cabin, just above the wash house," Astrid said. "It's smaller than the Persson's cottage, but it puts you close by all that needs doing. Erling will bring the linen cupboard down from the house. It can go in the back room here, along with the mangle and an ironing board and iron."

"You can keep the sewing machine you've been using," Ebbe said, "or Astrid will give you hers, it's up to you. Hers has a prettier cabinet."

Astrid nodded, her mind made up. "I'd as soon move mine down to the back room, right along with the rest of it. There's space enough with the bed up against the wall. Turn that room into a decent work room, leave the bed for nap taking. Saves me from tripping over help up to the main house when things get busy and the Federson twins come looking to help out."

Eleanor's eyes moved from Astrid to Ebbe and back again, with a pause between to study the dock and the bay. "What if Farley comes back and raises a ruckus?"

"He's not welcome anywhere in Burke Bay, far as I can make out," Astrid said. "Wasn't much welcome in the first place. Now he's drove off and left Helmer high and dry with them cows, he's seen the end of what need he met."

"But what if he changes his mind and comes back for Hannah and me?"

Astrid's eyes narrowed, and her jaw jutted forward. "You'll call for help if he gets past all of us. It's up to the men to set safety matters in order. They're starting today, rigging an electric bell system loud enough to rouse Ilsa Bakke and set her calling for help on her phone. Me and Erling would be on the run by then, and like as not the Nordlunds in the bargain. They'd hear the ringing on across the pond, there's no doubt of that. They're only a spit and a jump away."

"Chances are me and the mister would hear clean to our place," Ebbe said.

"Hauk and Lang will rig the alarm," Astrid said. "They've the knowhow from their days in the woods when such contraptions warned of smoke. They're seeing to some other things in the cabin, while they're at it. Extra lock on the door, something to keep the windows from opening more than four or five inches."

"But what if . . ." Eleanor stopped when Astrid and Ebbe each grabbed one of her hands.

"No more 'what if.' It's the best we can come up with for now," Astrid said. "I know how much money you've got hid away here, it's not near enough to keep you until you find a position with some rich family in Seattle. If need be, one or another of us will hide you out somewhere, we've all got relatives from here to Minnesota and back. Now, we'll start a fresh pot of coffee and fry up some spuds."

*H*auk and Lang lugged seaman's boxes filled with odds and ends from the back of Ilsa's basement, past stacked feed sacks to the light of day. The boxes, treated wood with heavy rope handles, belonged to Skipp Bakke, Ilsa's dead husband. They contained carved ivory and whittled wood along with ship hardware heavy to the heft. Ilsa said a ringer system of some sort should show up in one of the two dozen boxes.

Lang opened box after box, giving his head one shake each time. "All these brass fittings, Ilsa could run a ship chandlery on the side."

"Be a shame to sell it now," Hauk said. "One of these days you and I will think of a way to put it to use."

"That's true, some of it today."

Hauk opened another box and lifted out assorted rags. "Here we go; a good old fashioned set of alarms."

Lang took one of the saucer-shaped pieces from Hauk. "Minus a few parts."

"Keep digging. Chances are you'll find parts enough to rig something or other."

Lang gave Hauk a squinted look. "What do you suppose, other than too much drink, gets into a man and makes him mean to his own wife and child?"

Hauk ran his fingers through his hair and stared out at the bay. He'd given the matter considerable thought during the long night he and Lang spent in their pickup truck parked on Dock Road.

"Only thing I can come up with is a man figures he's owed something and expects his wife to provide it. Sees his wife and child as property, like slaves or indentured servants."

"Hmm," Lang said, "that makes better sense than anything I've come up with."

They'd decided on the pickup vigil with minimal discussion. Hauk nodded when Lang said, "You think we should keep an eye on the tavern?" They took one shotgun and a box of shells. Firing in the air would get attention; firing at legs would slow a man in his tracks.

They slept in turns. Both saw the sunrise and were considering whether it was time to go home when their sister came out of her apartment at the back of the mercantile and called to them. While she fixed bacon and eggs, and buttermilk pancakes, she told them about Skipp Bakke's treasures.

Ilsa's reminiscing veered off course, catching Hauk by surprise. "Personally, I think you boys should take Eleanor and Hannah on out to Tahuya, to Trigg and Millie, maybe add on to the cabin you described while you're there, but Astrid and Ebbe voted me down. Astrid needs help with the tavern, true enough, but still and all it may not be safe."

Ilsa flipped a pancake. Hauk shot a glance at Lang, whose lips had an odd set to them. So, all three had the same idea. No surprise there.

"Might have been better not to mention Tahuya," Hauk said.

"Or mention Trigg by name," Lang added.

Ilsa turned to them, a scowl on her face. "You both think I'm dumb? After all I've taught you? All those two women heard from me was a simple idea to load up mother and daughter and drive them off to a safe place."

Hauk felt his face heat up and saw redness on Lang's.

"Sorry, Ilsa, we weren't thinking straight," Lang said.

"Here, I'll take a turn with the pancakes so you can eat," Hauk said.

"Fair enough." Ilsa handed him the pancake turner. "I'm guessing that's where you'd want Irv to take her, if things come to a head while you're in Alaska. And I gather you're still set on going, come what may."

Hauk looked at Lang, who gave the nod. "Only way we can earn some real money," Hauk said. "Property taxes took a good share of our savings."

"Nothing more needs saying, then." Ilsa sat down beside Lang, and waited for a hot stack of pancakes to come to her plate.

Neither brother saw Eleanor while they worked on the cabin, though Astrid and Erling came and went a dozen times each. Astrid fretted that the alarm they were rigging, which they attached on an outer wall high under the roof-pitch, wouldn't ring loud enough to call for help.

"It'll be loud enough," Lang said.

"Rigged a similar one in an Oregon logging camp one summer when fire threatened," Hauk said.

"A buzzer system direct to our house and on up to Ilsa Bakke's mercantile might do better," Astrid said.

"We'll look into that, if that's what you're wanting," Lang said, "soon as we get this alarm operating. Once we run a test, you make the call."

Both knew it would be loud enough to bring Orval Blevins down from the valley, and scare chickens out of their roosts all the way to Keyport. They tested it with rags to muffle the sound, tinkered and fine-tuned, and finally told Astrid to give it a try.

She pushed in the toggle switch they'd wired to the wall by the bed where Eleanor and Hannah would sleep. The alarm went off; the cabin windows and door rattled. Astrid jumped. She slapped at the switch to silence the thing.

Eleanor and Hannah ran out of the tavern kitchen, fright showing on their faces. Pastor Holmes, his wife and their daughters came on the run. It took Erling ten minutes to calm them. Ten minutes and a rhubarb pie warm from the oven.

When all was quiet again, Hauk and Lang settled down with coffee and one cigarette each.

"What would it take to string wire for a buzzer from here to the Romstads' house without it sagging down onto Church Road?" Hauk asked.

"One of us climbing trees both sides of the road," Lang said.

"Guess that would be you, seeing as you're older and have more experience climbing."

"We'll give Astrid an hour or two to consider whether a buzzer system's necessary. Plant some thoughts, power outages and such, and ring that alarm one more time when she's not expecting it," Lang said.

Hauk grinned. "That should work."

"Wouldn't hurt to rig some alarm bells onto the tavern, with a switch somewhere inside the kitchen. Sounds as if Eleanor will be working there or the back room most of the time."

Hauk spoke to the worry he'd watched settle on his brother's face. "A man can cause a lot of harm in a few seconds, if his mind's set. Alarms aren't likely to stop a man angry as Farley Price."

Lang ran a hand over his face. "You suppose it would look improper to Burke Bay folks if I set up a cot on that cabin porch?"

"You and your shotgun?"

Lang gave a nod.

"You'd stay here through the summer? Skip Alaska?"

"I would, if Eleanor agreed, but she won't. She's embarrassed by the alarm. She's nearly stubborn as Maeva Swanson."

That made Hauk laugh. "No, no one's that stubborn."

"No, nor that given to thinking things through," Lang said. "Might be worth our while, and Eleanor's, to seek Maeva's advice on this matter."

Hauk nodded. "Advice that calls for something short of a loaded gun."

25

~ Sensibilities ~

Thursday, June 1, five days after the rowboat christening and one after the official opening of the Romstad cabins, Maeva saw the school children aboard the *Aggie J*, and told Axel she would stay behind for dinner and a visit with Eleanor. True to his spirit, he ordered her to board the boat, to stay away from the Burke Bay Tavern and out of the Price family affair. True to hers, she replied, "Eleanor is my friend, Hannah my student; both need me right now."

She didn't tell Axel that Hauk and Lang had come to the Swanson farm not long after she'd heard reverberations of the alarm ring down the bay. Come to seek her sensibilities, Hauk said, before they left on Alaska-bound fishing boats for the summer.

They told her the Romstads and Perssons feared Farley Price would return when least expected, snatch Eleanor and Hannah from their bed and drag them off. They measured his staying away and saw it as more suspect than making his whereabouts known.

"Hasn't been seen," Lang said. "Neither hide nor hair, according to Astrid, since disappearing into the night Saturday. Irv Carlson searched Bremerton for his car and asked in at various taverns and other night spots."

"I think she needs to go home until we find her a live-in position in Seattle," Maeva said. "I have money for train tickets. I know in my heart she and Hannah need to leave Burke Bay."

She closed her eyes against tears, already sad at losing her friend. How had matters gotten so frightening over a rowboat ride?

That Thursday afternoon she and Eleanor sat on the tavern porch in rocking chairs Astrid kept there for public use, Maeva with her notebook open in her lap. While they talked, she sketched the beach and bay with the rowboats resting on sand above high tide line. Sun hid behind low clouds, but no rain.

Maeva said, "What I don't understand is why Lang rammed his head into Farley and then rendered that blow that knocked him out, when he could have calmed him with words."

Eleanor bit at a piece of loose skin alongside a fingernail. "Because of what Farley said. Most of you didn't hear him."

"Inappropriate language?"

"That and worse." Eleanor's eyes filled with tears. She whispered, "He accused Lang and me of intimate acts. He called me a whore."

"Words can hurt even when they hold no truth," Maeva said, hoping but failing to calm Eleanor, who spoke again, still whispering.

"Astrid knows. It's been hard for her, but she's the one who insists I shouldn't take Hannah and run. She thinks Farley will stay away from the tavern, from Erling and her, because the liquor inspectors have been around. The Romstads know things about Farley. Astrid says he's connected to more than one moonshiner. How she knows is beyond me. She's betting at least one of them has given Farley fair warning to stay away from Burke Bay and trouble he stirs up here."

"Orval Blevins, you mean? Farley's running illegal whiskey for Orval who's sticking his nose into the store or garage every day looking for gossip. I got that report from Nels."

An eerie half laugh/half cry came from deep in Eleanor's throat. "Orval's not the biggest and far from the meanest, if snippets I got from Farley are true. There's one not too far from here that's rumored to be connected to the law somehow." The laugh/cry deepened. "I've imagined Farley dead. That's a sin, in any religion."

Maeva looked at the sketches she'd made. Such nice rowboats, sturdy and steady, with good lines and no scrapes from running over rocks and shells in the shallows. Scars would show up in time.

Sea water and rain would dull the paint. Looking at her drawing helped her composure. She took Eleanor's hand.

"I don't think you're safe here. Farley will come back to Burke Bay when he chooses. I've talked to Mom. We agreed I'd buy train tickets to send you home to Kansas. Nels and I will take you to the train. Once it pulls out, we'll wire your parents to tell them you're on your way; that you need safe harbor only until a position opens with a Seattle family. Emil Jenson is working on that."

Both of them were crying by the time Maeva finished her speech, fat tears running down their cheeks, noses plugged. Maeva stood, tugged Eleanor to her feet. "Come on, we better go down onto the beach, we don't want to upset early customers."

Eleanor sniffed and went along without protest. They trudged through silvery sand to a spot under the dock where no one would see them crying, or laughing for that matter, if Maeva could find something to evoke a laugh.

"Salt air," Maeva said after a deep breath. "When you grow up with the scent of the sea, you suffer its absence." She waited for Eleanor to say something about Kansas air, what she missed from home.

"Maeva, I think you're the best friend I could ever hope to have in life, and I know you're the smartest person I've ever met. Thank you for your offer of train tickets." After a silence broken by a gull's squawk, she said, "But I'm not going back to Kansas. My parents aren't strictly religious, but they don't condone divorce, and they've warned me to stay away. Not because they don't love me; because they're scared. They know Farley would show up in time. They know there would be bloodshed."

"*Gud I himmel.*" Maeva collected handfuls of sand and let if sift through her fingers.

"What if Farley killed Papa before Papa shot him? Or, God forbid, all of us? My brothers and their wives and their children? All because of me. I transgressed, not them. I married a man my parents warned me against."

Maeva swallowed the protest that marriage didn't require a woman to suffer forevermore. For all she knew, that's exactly what the oath of marriage required. *There would be bloodshed* replayed in her head.

"Come on, time to wash our faces." She went to the water's edge, squatted to rinse her hands, splash water on her face and rethink her strategy. She would promise to write speeches for Emil Jenson and all of his Republican cronies in trade for a safe and nurturing place for Eleanor and Hannah. She would marry Axel in secret. She would make a deal with the devil to save Eleanor and Hannah from the evil she feared lurked in Farley Price.

How odd that she had sensed that in him the first time she heard his name, spoken by Helmer Persson in his dairy truck idling a few yards from where she now swished her hands in Burke Bay waters. She'd denied her internal warning and argued on his behalf with those in the community who wanted him gone from the first.

Eleanor reached out one hand and then the other, like the water was an animal that needed taming. While Maeva lifted her face to the breeze, Eleanor daubed hers dry with a tatted edge hankie.

"I know you're probably right," Eleanor said. "I'm not really safe here, if Farley gets drunk, but I'm making my stand. I don't think he'd hurt Hannah, not any worse than he did that time she got in the way before."

"What about you? What do you think Farley would do to you, Eleanor? If he gets drunk and shows up at the cabin, even if you hear him coming and set off the alarm?" Maeva's voice had climbed. Sounds carried across the water. She lowered her voice to a whisper. "I want to know what you think he'd do."

"If he shows up, it will be for money. I think it will. He'll be on the run or just needing a drink. I'm keeping money for him in case he comes. I'm hoping that's all he wants from me."

Maeva doubted money would be enough but, in case it would, she'd work on an alternate plan—find the man, buy him off. Have Emil Jenson or Jonas locate him. Or Irv Carlson. She worked to soften her eyes, force a bit of a smile. "You're not going to change your mind, are you? You're determined to stay and take your chances."

"I am," Eleanor said. "And I need to get back to work. The dinner crowd will be coming along." She laughed a little. "If you can call Irv Carlson and the Anderson brothers a crowd. And you, if you're still willing to stay."

~

Hauk and Lang Nordlund rose from the rocking chairs she and Eleanor had vacated, Maeva's notebook in Hauk's hand. Maeva's stomach lurched; her notebook, where she'd written all sorts of things about people at the boat launching. What had she written about the Nordlunds? A bit about the Federson twins trying to get and keep the brothers' attention. She'd given almost a page to Orval Blevins's wife, a woman who intrigued her. A spirited young woman married to a man a good bit older.

Eleanor gasped. "Your notebook."

Hauk handed it to Maeva with one of his half-nods. "Good sketch of the boats."

"It is good," Eleanor said, "but she'll write across it, fill every line with words so the boats will hardly show up."

"I'm not good at perspective." Maeva closed the notebook and shoved it in the canvas bag that held her good shoes and children's school work. "I sketch just enough to remember events so I can write about them."

"A shame," Hauk said.

"True, that," Lang added.

"A shame you don't draw more, and a shame you write over what you've drawn," Hauk said, a slight grin on his face, teasing, she feared.

"Paper costs money, just like everything else. There's no need to waste an entire page with unimportant sketches." Her words circled around her head, in through her ears in Jonas's voice, and took up roost like chickens at dusk.

"Sorry to hear drawings of our boats are unimportant. We rather liked them," Lang said.

Hauk grinned, full-out, wonder of wonders, and Lang did too, so they matched like the four rowboats matched.

"Hauk hoped you might tear out the page, give it to him," Lang said.

Maeva looked from one brother to the other, to Eleanor, back to the brothers. "You're making fun of me."

181

"No, Maeva, we're not," Hauk said. "We're remarking on your talent."

Lang gave a nod, and Maeva saw it for what it was. Agreement. That's what the brothers did. One spoke, the other nodded.

"I need to go in," Eleanor said. "Astrid and Hannah have looked out the window a dozen times."

Lang opened the door and followed Eleanor, leaving Maeva alone on the big tavern porch with Hauk. He liked her sketch. She looked toward the dock, turned to look at the bay, darker than it had been in Saturday afternoon sunshine, rougher with the breeze kicking up.

"I didn't get the bay right in that sketch. I was working on the shading when Eleanor and I decided to go for a walk."

"You have time."

Her head turned. "Time for what?"

"To finish the drawing, get the shading right. Shading's easier on better paper. You draw well enough to deserve art paper."

Maeva looked away again, south toward the Swanson farm, and heard Jonas's voice washing up on the incoming tide, haunting her about the money she spent on herself, little though it was.

Jonas would become a father any day now. Would he be stingy with his child? Their mother had sewed a nice layette for the baby using fabric Maeva purchased. The day she bought the fabric she'd looked at a tablet of artist paper and a book on drawing. She'd wanted both but purchased neither. The baby's needs came first.

"Maeva? It didn't go well, did it? With Eleanor, I mean."

She shook her head. "No, not well. Kansas isn't an option. She's determined to stay here, to stand her ground, she says."

"Ah," Hauk said.

She waited for more, for a new idea, a magical solution. When he spoke, it had nothing to do with Eleanor.

"I would like your drawing. Something created by your hand. I'd like to carry it with me when I go north. Like to hear from you while I'm gone, if you'd take time to write."

"Write? A letter, you mean?"

"One letter would do. Two or three would do better."

"What could I write that you'd care to read?"

182

"Burke Bay news. The weather. Books you've read. What you think about when you fix your eyes on the horizon."

Maeva waited for a grin to show he was teasing. She looked south again, this time her mind on Axel. She'd rarely written him the four years she'd been away and worried not at all when she heard stories from Berta that Axel had taken some girl or other to a dance. When she did write, Axel didn't reply. He told her before she left each fall that he'd catch her up when she came home. How odd that she felt so pleased to be asked by Hauk to write him; that she, who suggested the Federson twins as potential girlfriends for Hauk and Lang, had found the girls' antics during the rowboat races so annoying.

"Will you write back?" she asked.

One nod. "I will."

"My," Maeva whispered, aware for the first time how much her mother covered with that one word.

26

~ Transactions and Transgressions

Orval's pickup bounced over roots and ruts in the stand of evergreens he'd used to transfer product to Farley Price back before Price got every man, woman and child in Burke Bay breathing fire down his neck. Fourth time he'd checked the spot and no sign Price had been by.

Orval drove in with his headlights off, like any cautious runner with a lifetime of experience. He shined his flashlight beam through the tail of his work shirt. No gunny sacks or canvas bags or wood crates of any description tucked away in the underbrush. Absolutely no nothing a`tall, and him with a good supply stored in the back of his truck under rotted down hay and various farm odds and ends.

He quit poking around, climbed back into the pickup and gave thought to all Thelma had said before he drove off and left her to nursing Loyal, their demanding son she insisted on calling Teddy. With the way the country was going, Loyal would need to learn old Grandpap's business right soon while there was still business to be done.

Could be some of what Thelma had said made sense. He set his mind to contemplating her words, now he was off by himself with time to think.

"You drive into Bremerton in the dark of night with sour smelling hay and rusting machine parts, you're sure to rouse suspicions. No decent farmer would truck about looking like that in the light of day, and only a derelict one after the sun's gone down."

He'd answered, "That's why I wait for the dark of night, now isn't it, Thelma. So's not to be seen."

"Bremerton's a city, with street lights and all. You're going to stick out, Orval Blevins. Sooner or later someone's going to order you to lift aside all that smelly mess. You'd be wise to take me up on my suggestion before we run out of money to feed these children."

"Never you mind about my business, Thelma, you don't understand a thing about the ways of men and how they work."

"I understand plenty. Don't I have two young ones to prove that?"

Enough of remembering. He'd grumbled something at her last remark, stomped out the door, slammed it good and hard and driven off. A distiller such as himself should not be expected to deliver product. Shouldn't never have trusted Price, who took to keeping customers' names tucked into his own pocket. Chances were Price was selling them some other shiner's product.

Customers needed loyal suppliers. Truth was Orval broke his own chain of connections when he handed legging over to Price. Thelma was right; he had his own self to blame.

He started up the truck and drove on into town. It hadn't changed much since his grandpap's day. Sailors kept to taverns near the waterfront. Long skinny taverns that kept the lights dim.

He parked his truck on First Street to look like he was there meeting someone coming in on the ferry from Seattle, and climbed out to stretch his legs. He lit his pipe and sauntered across the street to the corner tavern, noisy as all get-out. Sure enough beer drinking going on. Shouting, too.

"You planning to sell one bottle at a time to drunken sailors?" Thelma had said in a not so nice voice.

He'd answered her patient like. "Word gets around, Thelma, one bottle leads to two and then to four and then to eight." He remembered his times-two tables up to sixteen but didn't go that far; he'd made his point.

The tavern's barkeep gave Orval a look that said come in and order up, or move along. He moved along, being smart enough to know what happens once a man stops to drink one beer.

"Looking for whiskey," he said, more statement than question, to the first man he came upon walking toward the waterfront, and managed to negotiate a sale of one bottle. One measly bottle and his feet were on fire like he'd stepped barefoot into a hill of red ants.

After thirty minutes of wandering up this street and down that, poking his nose in doorways of wide-open taverns selling beer left and right, he went back to his truck to give the situation serious thought.

Back during the days when no alcohol sales were legal, back before Price came on the scene, Orval sold most of his product to private businessmen with connections to finer clientele—druggists, bankers, attorneys, one dentist, several small grocers.

Nowadays grocers could sell beer legal out the front door. Most like as not quit selling distilled product out the back, might as well cross them off his list. He'd best reacquaint himself with druggists since that's where folks went looking for something to handle pain.

Damned if he hadn't lost all touch with the customers he'd known close enough to sidle up alongside with an offer. Oh, he remembered their names clear enough and their places of commerce, but none of them were waiting on street corners for Orval Blevins to drive up with product hidden under a load of sour hay.

Could be Thelma was right; he needed to drive her and the babies into town, let her call in a few places, ask a few questions, get business going again.

He drove on to Charleston, parked on a side street and meandered along, pipe clamped in his teeth, to a tavern with its door open wide and noise pouring out. Noise made for a good cover.

Every bar stool was occupied, another good sign. Orval walked the length of the bar, ears open more'n eyes, ready to let it be known he had whiskey available. No one paid him much mind, them being men younger'n himself for the most part, and well on their way to having their bellies full of beer. He checked out their smokes. Them who rolled their own didn't interest him so much as them with tailor-mades.

When he came upon a couple likely candidates, men who looked like they enjoyed a good drink but hadn't gotten too far gone in the tavern's offerings, he said, "Sipping whiskey would be good about now."

"Ain't that the truth?" one man answered. He was a hefty man, balding, red of face and built close to the ground. Short legs, no neck to speak of, big chest and belly.

"There's such to be had," Orval said. "I'll give you five minutes." He went on around the joint, casting his eyes here and there, squinting like a man looking for a friend. After circling the place, he meandered on out and found a dark doorway to take up his wait.

No-neck came along just as Orval was about to give up, bought two quarts, and went on his way. His partner didn't follow him. No one followed. Orval got into his truck, peeled off his boots and then his socks into which he stuffed the cash. He gave both feet a good scratching and drove on home barefoot.

Damned if Thelma wasn't up awaiting an accounting. He argued good and hard over the idea of her calling in on those former customers, giving in to her in the nick of time. He put on his best downtrodden look so she'd never guess he was letting her win, and handed her his dirty socks, one with the cash he'd collected that night. He considered it good strategy to let go of some money so she wouldn't get to searching high and low for his real stash.

He went off to bed thinking women sure knew how to make a man pay for what he got from them. Then he thought about Loyal, his son, and reckoned the cost might be worth it.

27

~ Fourth of July ~

As June came to an end with no sign of Farley, Astrid and Erling began fretting that he might show up on the Fourth of July, their busiest day of the year with full cabins and fireworks on the beach.

"He could show up right in the midst of things, and then what would we do?" Astrid asked.

Maeva, too, seemed concerned that a holiday gathering might serve as cover for Farley's reappearance. She wanted Eleanor to see the Swanson farm and know her way there on foot in case she sensed a need to get away from the tavern.

"Nels will drive you over and I will walk you back. We'll make it Sunday when there are no beer sales. Nels has use of the Nordlund brothers' truck while they're in Alaska."

Eleanor agreed, with Astrid's blessing.

Nels drove Eleanor over the plank road along the waterfront and along dips and bends when they reached paved road, naming driveways and pointing out landmarks: the old cemetery where pioneers and Indians were buried, huge cedar trees the road circumvented, a steep lane that wended its way to Wiley's Landing.

Once they reached the Swanson farm, Eleanor wanted to stay forever. She pictured Hannah there, walking the paths through Mrs. Swanson's flower gardens, sitting on the bench under the cherry tree, naming birds by their songs, playing in the barn loft.

Hannah could help with the vegetable garden surely ample enough to feed all Burke Bay. Eleanor ate peas fresh from the pod—pods that opened with a satisfying pop.

Maeva pulled weeds as they went. She talked of thinning carrots, digging a hill or two of new potatoes and shelling peas for their traditional creamed dish for the Fourth.

From the gardens, they walked to a retreat in a stand of madronas, one with a bent trunk polished, Maeva said, from years of her sitting on it while she read, wrote poems, drew pictures of deer bedded down in the pasture grass or pheasants taking flight. Maeva picked up a large piece of curled bark, crumpled it, brushed her hands clean.

"We'll walk back to the tavern by way of the beach so you'll know that route, too. It's an easier walk than along the road if it's after dark. Even on the darkest, calmest nights you'll hear water movement over rocks or sand. You can hunker down behind a drift-log or tuck yourself into a stand of trees and listen to the sea. It's a comforting sound."

Before Eleanor left the farm, Mrs. Swanson served coffee and cookies, and fussed that it wasn't enough to keep them going on their beach walk. Eleanor marveled at the sense of safety she felt in the house. She'd followed Maeva upstairs to bedrooms, two now vacant though often used by an older brother, his wife and their new baby boy. All the rooms looked out at South Bay or over the gardens; all the beds were graced with handmade quilts.

"There's room; there's always enough room and plenty to eat here," Maeva said, and left it at that.

To her surprise Eleanor enjoyed the beach walk back to Burke Bay. They ducked under the plank road to climb up over the railings on the side where the road hugged the hill that rose above Carlson's Lagoon.

Maeva made the walk a geography lesson, checking to ensure Eleanor had a mental map of Puget Sound, the Kitsap Peninsula, the need to leave the Peninsula by ferry or by driving south through Belfair.

"Belfair," Eleanor said, "where Hood Canal comes to an end." She carried a map of Washington and Oregon in her head along with a good sense of ferry docks and train depots. She took pride in her ability to learn place names, to know leaving by ferry would be the only route that made sense in her circumstance.

The day before the Fourth three people whispered to Eleanor that Farley's car had been spotted in Bremerton, parked once, driving off the Seattle ferry another time. Irv Carlson, who'd seen it with his own eyes and recognized both car and license plate, said it could easily enough belong to someone else by now; Farley might have sold it. "That'd make some sense if he's decided to stay in these parts."

"No," Eleanor whispered back, "Farley would never sell that car."

That didn't mean he was using it to carry whiskey. Papa had suspected Farley was up to no good the first time he came out to the Keane ranch. She'd kept Papa's words buried for a long time, but they'd taken up residence in her conscious mind and she couldn't get them to leave again.

"Man's running liquor," Papa had said, but she'd been too naive and too enamored with Farley to listen.

She listened now. She'd worked out a plan of sorts with Astrid and Erling, who kept a written record that understated her wages a bit and showed they deducted the cost of rent and meals for her and Hannah. They had their own way of doing things. She no longer argued that they were too generous or too kind. They knew she might need to take Hannah and disappear, so they did what they could while they could.

She knew to the penny how much money she'd squirreled away and how much she could expect in wages.

The Fourth, a Tuesday, was busy as promised, with every cabin rented to folks from Seattle, all of them expecting fried chicken and potato salad picnics on the beach and a clambake to boot, so said Astrid.

The first firecrackers made Eleanor jump but by noon she was inured to them, sweating over the tavern's big black stove and counting the hours until she could fall into bed. Astrid, whose ankles grew swollen and red, worked alongside her. Erling waited tables inside the tavern and on the porch, and ran picnic lunches out to the beach.

"Ebbe will give us a hand soon as her bread's out of the oven," Astrid said. "I tried to hire them Federson twins, Iris and Rose, but they're too set on the Swanson-Jenson party. Most all the young folks around here go on over to South Bay Beach on the Fourth, leaving our bay here to those from out of town. Shame you can't join Maeva, like as not she and her mother could use your help in their kitchen."

Eleanor paused in the midst of peeling a cooked potato for the salad. "I wouldn't fit in with the others at their party."

"Nonsense. You'd fit just fine, you're Maeva's friend, she'd see to it you had a good time."

"True," Eleanor said, hoping to end that discussion. "Do you think I've boiled enough eggs?"

"It's hard to know what's enough to satisfy city folks. Might as well cook up all Ebbe brought down. Spuds, too, they all keep in the fridge."

Eleanor added wood to the stove, opened the kitchen windows and door to their widest, and stayed too busy to give Farley much thought or to keep a proper eye on Hannah, who darted in and out of the kitchen every few minutes. Her last time through, Hannah announced she was helping Erling serve and had collected a tip. Eleanor quit dicing eggs long enough to find a jar for Hannah's money and offer a silent prayer that Farley would never know.

By late afternoon, clouds moved in over the water. Erling added wood to the beach fire and moved his piano onto the tavern porch. He played lively songs, some of them over and over, through the afternoon and evening:

I'm Just Wild About Harry; Ma, he's Makin' Eyes at Me; Yes! We Have No Bananas; Ain't She Sweet.

The beach crowd sang along with him, most of them off-key and many making up words as they went. Night closed in; the tavern's lights bloomed. Erling played a few notes of *Night and Day*, announced the kitchen was closed and called Astrid and Eleanor to the porch to whistles and shouted thanks.

Eleanor watched a Roman candle shoot out over the bay. Firecrackers and Roman candles—some folks had money to burn.

Erling ran his fingers over the piano keys in a medley that settled into *Stardust*. He hummed for a time, then sang as he played.

And now the purple dust of twilight time
Steals across the meadows of my heart
High up in the sky the little stars climb
Always reminding me that we're apart

The smile Eleanor had dredged up at the crowd's appreciation dissolved. For a moment, unwanted tears stung her eyelids and made her face ache more than her feet and back. She edged her way past the piano and Erling to take up refuge in the brush above Whiskey Creek's lower pond. There, alone and chilled after a long day over a hot stove, she wept.

A minute later, or maybe an hour, she was jerked out of her self-pity by shouts and an abrupt end to the music. Unfinished notes of a song played in her head and fear sent her heart racing. An acrid smell wafted her way, the odor of burning wheat stubble. In the lull between shouts she heard a crackling sound and saw flames climbing the hillside toward the Romstads' home.

"Just dry grass," someone shouted.

"Keep it from the trees," another said.

She ran onto Dock Road, calling, "Hannah? Hannah!" Pain shot up her legs each time her feet hit the oil mat.

"Here, Mamma." Hannah ran to her with a dishpan sloshing water. Together they doused flames nearest them and ran back to the kitchen for more water, Hannah babbling about boys and firecrackers.

"Boys on the hill, you mean?" Eleanor felt giddy with relief that she'd found Hannah so quickly and even more so that boys with firecrackers, not Farley, started the blaze.

Twenty minutes later no flames could be seen, though men continued carrying seawater to hot spots and returning to the tavern porch to drink beer. Astrid complained to Erling that they were running low on the legal stuff. He told her not to fret, he'd handle that part, there was plenty enough to drink. Eleanor sat on the edge of the porch, leaned her back against a pillar and pulled Hannah onto her lap. It was the first time she'd heard Erling admit he kept illegal brew on the premises.

Fresh venison out of season. A few more clams or geoduck than the limit allowed. Illegal beer, or perhaps whiskey. The Romstads did what needed doing to keep their tavern in business. Farley Price did what needed doing to keep himself in drink.

Eleanor swallowed two aspirin tablets Astrid gave her to help with all the aches and pains, and settled into bed. Stretching out, preparing to sleep, made her more aware of every tired muscle. She stifled a groan, reached a hand across to pat Hannah, already asleep on the far side of the bed, and let herself drift.

Later, she would say she thought it was all a bad dream: Farley's hands clasping her wrists, jerking her upright; Farley's vile breath hitting her face.

"You belong to me, you're coming with me."

He said more, words as vile as his breath, slurred by all he'd had to drink. She managed to yell, "Hannah! The alarm!" before the blow to the side of her head left her dazed, uncertain where she was. Farley grasped Hannah's arm with his left hand while his right raised to deliver another blow.

Eleanor reached her right hand for the toggle switch that would set off the alarm. Farley grabbed her left arm and tugged. Her free hand caught the clock on the chair she used as a bedside table. Astrid's clock, silver-plate encased, some of the silver worn down to its nickel base. She swung her arm with strength mustered by rage, and planted it on Farley's left temple. Hannah stumbled free as Farley came at Eleanor with both fists.

"Bitch. You'll pay for that."

The last time she'd seen Farley she'd vowed she would fight if ever he came at her again. She clawed his face and wished her fingernails were longer, sharper, sharp as a bear's. Animal sounds, growls and moans, came up from her being and over them the sound of the alarm the Nordlunds installed. Farley swung one fist at Hannah, who had found the switch. A new wave of rage rolled through Eleanor's veins, followed by a wave of fear for her daughter.

"Run, Hannah." She didn't recognize her own voice, her strength. She had become an animal. She heard Hannah's bare feet slap the floor. Night air whooshed in through the open door.

Eleanor hit, bit, scratched, kicked and, through it all, growled and snarled. She tasted blood from her nose, smelled it—her own blood and some of Farley's. He twisted her right wrist, rendered it useless, though oddly she felt no pain. She sank her teeth into his hand and bit until she felt skin break and tasted his blood.

He'd reduced her to a rabid wolf worth the bullets it would take to kill. She kept fighting even when the first heavy footsteps landed on the cabin porch. She kept fighting until someone grabbed her from behind and wrested her from the carnage.

28

~ Alaska ~

*H*auk tucked the thick unopened letter he'd picked up at the cannery mail call into his shirt pocket and walked away from the unimaginative buildings that reeked of fish guts and human sweat to a spot where he could keep his eyes peeled for the *Katherine*, sister to the *NorthStar*, the boat he worked. He'd showered and shaved, but caught whiffs of boat galley when the wind lifted his hair. Fried bacon, fried potatoes, fried onions, fried mush, he couldn't distinguish them, the first providing grease for the others.

He'd signed on as cook but helped hand-haul seines, pick and toss fish into the hold, lift them out into the brailer when they tied up at the cannery dock. He scrubbed the galley to keep it clean and swabbed down decks to keep them safe. He knew his value aboard; his paycheck, when he collected it at the end of the season, would see him through fall and winter.

Lang did the same tasks aboard the *Katherine*. Each knew exactly what the other was doing almost to the minute. Their reputations had spread from Naknek to Egegik, not that there was much distance between the two rivers, and those reputations prodded captains of other boats to offer the brothers bribes to jump ship. Their own captains soon learned they needn't worry and spent their shore time trying to out-brag one another. Both brothers overheard the conversations more than once and gave a nod each time and a smile once or twice.

"Lang's the better of the two," the *Katherine's* captain said. "He's older, more experienced. Taught Hauk, true enough, but the youngster has some more learning to catch up."

"That's where you're wrong, the student's surpassed the teacher. Best damn cook on Bristol Bay." With that, the *NorthStar's* captain would light a fat, hand-rolled cigarette and draw in smoke and wink.

Hauk squinted as a boat broke the horizon. He cupped his eyes with his hands and watched for identifying characteristics as it motored toward the cannery dock. Every captain had a signature approach. The *Katherine* came in slow, swung wide and slipped into place as if towed by the wings of swooping gulls. The *NorthStar* made a gradual swing further out at sea and motored straight in.

Hauk waited until the fish were transferred from boat to dock before retracing his steps. Lang would want a shower and shave, though chances were good he'd want the letter first.

They came face-to-face on the leeward side of the shower shack, where they could talk without wind that whipped off the sea or across the tundra stealing their words. Hauk pulled the letter from his shirt pocket. "From Ilsa," he said, as if letters addressed to them ever came from anyone else. He'd hoped to hear from Maeva, but no luck.

Lang took the envelope with scale-dotted hands, hefted it as Hauk knew he would, and said, "It's addressed to you, too. Should have opened it, cut your worry in half by running your knife under the flap even if you didn't read a word."

"Your name's first." It wouldn't have mattered if Hauk's own name had been first or if Lang had retrieved the mail. Neither opened letters from their sister without the other present.

"All the same . . ." Lang slit the envelope, fanned the pages. "Eight. I think that's a record."

"Better begin with page one," Hauk said. He'd seen the name, *Eleanor*, written in Ilsa's loopy script, and tried to read over Lang's shoulder and brace him at the same time.

"There's been trouble down to the tavern, much as you boys speculated. Irv moved Eleanor and wee Hannah on out to Trigg's place where Millie can tend to them. No one in Burke Bay's seen the whites of

196

Farley Price's eyes since it all come to a head. Irv's sorry they didn't finish him on the spot, stuff him into his fancy car and push it off the end of the dock, though Erling says the bay's not deep enough there, nor the water fast enough, chances are he'd drift in on the bathing beach or right up to the pilings out behind my place.

Astrid's took to cussing like a logger. She loaded up Erling's shot gun and peppered the alarm you boys rigged, she was that undone by it all. She's the one would have shot Farley but for the fact he had a gun aimed at Eleanor. No civilized gun meant for hunting food for the family, but something that come up out of his pocket when Erling's hold on him slipped."

Lang jammed the first page of Ilsa's letter behind the last, handed the pages to Hauk, and ran a hand over his face. "How long before she gets to how bad Eleanor's hurt?"

"She's with Trigg and Millie, whatever happened she'll be safe." Hauk scanned their sister's writing, found the answer to Lang's question, read to himself before summarizing.

"Broken wrist. Irv got her to a doctor who set it. Looks like the doctor put a couple stitches above her upper lip. Here's something interesting."

"Irv said Eleanor fought Farley and left her mark. It seems she busted Astrid's bedside clock. Broke the face clean out of it. Astrid said more's the pity she didn't use the glass to poke him in the eye. The men and Astrid all think Farley left needing stitches himself. No one knows why he waved that gun around without firing it, but Erling's guessing it wasn't loaded, what with the cost of ammunition and the way Farley spends every cent on liquor. Walt Strom came into the store twice in one day looking for gossip, buying a little something to make his stop legitimate, and he let on that Orval Blevins has been asking after Farley. That tells me clear as the water in your well that Farley's not running Blevins's whiskey, and he's sure as shooting not milking Persson's cows, so he's like as not broke."

"Running for someone else," Lang said. "Good thing you and I weren't home, or Price would be dead. Who'd think you'd have to take time to give the other guy ammo for his gun to make a fight fair before you could fire off a round of your own?"

Hauk studied the cannery buildings, salt boxes with stingy windows perched on a stretch of salt marsh delta. "Could be the fight's all but over. Ilsa says once a woman stands up for herself like that there's not much left a man can do to keep his hold on her."

"Could be that leaves the man more desperate than before," Lang said.

Hauk had the same fear, though he wouldn't admit it aloud.

They read the letter through to its end, including a page about Maeva.

"It makes me heartsick to see Maeva so upset, worrying out loud about Eleanor and the child. She knows Irv got her out of here. 'Irv gave her money; I just know it,' Maeva said to me, 'and I want to send what I set aside, if he's in touch with her.' 'I'll pass that word along,' I said, near choking on my words. Then Maeva added she'd like to send books to Hannah, and she gave me a look with more than a little hint in it that she suspects Irv has Eleanor hid out somewhere—not off home to Kansas like we've been saying. We're spreading the word like manure, which is about what it is, but it's needed to convince any who might be carrying word to Farley.

We did all this talking in my kitchen, me and Maeva, over a cup of coffee and some cookies Mrs. Swanson sent over. I locked up the store so we'd have no eavesdroppers. Before she left, Maeva said one more thing you'd like to hear; she misses the both of you and sends her hello. 'Write them yourself,' I said, and she answered, 'I will. I owe Hauk a thank you letter for his thoughtfulness to me before they left.'

"Now, mind you, I didn't go prying into what thoughtfulness that might be, though it was on the tip of my tongue to ask when she spoke again. 'You said Eleanor didn't set off the alarm soon enough, but I don't think that's true. She set it off as soon as she could, and it brought help. She'll always remember the help.'"

Lang folded the letter, tucked it in its envelope, handed it to Hauk. "You hang on to this while I get cleaned up, then we'll go find us a drink one place or another in this goldarn Bone Dry state.

No beer, but honest to God drink, legal or not, legalities be damned. Goldarn Farley Price, I'd like to get my hands on him."

"A drink to forget Goldarn Farley Price, a tablet for writing Ilsa back and a meal neither of us has to cook." Hauk hoped writing a letter would bleed some of the fury out of his brother's veins.

"Meal won't be as good as our own," Lang said. "Might be we'll need more than one drink."

29

~ Truths and Secrets ~

Maeva straddled the bent branch of the madrona tree, settled her back against the trunk and picked at the hole in the knee of Jonas's overalls. They needed to be discarded, all but their buttons and buckles. Her mother would snip those off to store in the button can for future use, perhaps on a garment for Anders.

Sweet little Anders, born to a mother ill-prepared to care for him and a father too willing to leave both of them at the Swanson farm. Mother and son nestled-in the night before the Fourth of July beach party, and stayed. He'd been a month old.

Maeva and her mother took turns caring for Anders while Cynthia languished on the big front porch where she could catch a breeze off the water on warm afternoons, or in an upstairs bedroom wrapped in quilts to protect her from the dampness of the sea air on cool ones.

Cynthia, thin and pale, unable to nurse, given to tears, rallied each evening when Jonas returned to enjoy his mother's cooking. Rallied, drank Canadian whiskey Jonas managed to buy from a connection, and dozed off against his shoulder. Jonas carried her upstairs, tucked her in, drove off to return the next evening, and the next.

Though Maeva expected Jonas would take his wife and son home the weekend after the Fourth, he'd collected Cynthia for a drive. They left Anders behind. The following two weekends, the new parents set out after Friday's evening meal to give Cynthia a two-day rest from the baby. By late July, Maeva adjusted to the routine. She and her mother had a new baby to care for full time, a baby's mother to care for weekdays. They washed diapers, receiving blankets and baby gowns daily, and hung them on the line. They hoed, watered and harvested the vegetable garden. They cooked, cleaned and answered calls for food, bathing, clean sheets.

Maeva argued with Axel every night, once Anders had nodded off. Not argue so much as restate her right to choose her family's needs over his for one more year.

"I'm in mourning," she said. "It's my right to be sad and exhausted. Eleanor and Hannah are gone, Anders and Mom both need me, your family has one wedding to celebrate this summer."

"New Year's Eve," Axel said. "We'll marry in secret on New Year's Eve, celebrate as usual with my family. A wedding celebration only those closest to us will know about."

"Give me until Anders turns one. Surely by then Cynthia will be well enough to move home."

So it went until Axel left her in the madrona grove, angry that she'd lost interest in his caresses and kisses that aroused but didn't satisfy. He, not she, insisted on waiting until they married before consummating their love. She heard rocks tumbling in the ravine between the Swanson and Jenson properties—rocks he'd kicked loose to show his pique.

She toyed with the frayed edges of the overall's torn knee, contemplating what Axel really wanted, finding her answer as she might find a word in the dictionary. *Seduction.* The act of seducing the female who, in his view, had to be the weaker sex.

Though he claimed he wanted marriage and a family, she'd come to accept he wanted a wife who would be a social asset to Jenson's new land-transportation business, a speech writing asset in their political endeavors. He would stop short of intercourse to seduce her into marriage ahead of her time-table. For all she knew, his father already had an arrangement with a Justice of the Peace for New Year's Eve.

Night settled around the grove; the utility porch light blinked on, a beacon for her, a signal from her mother. Time to go inside. Her mother used electricity so sparingly that an outdoor light meant worry. She'd likely heard the tumbling rocks.

Maeva collected hoe and gloves, and made her way down the hill. Her mother met her at the door, said she'd heated water for a bath, took the worn coveralls and gave them a shake and an inspection.

"They're ready for the burn pile," Maeva said. "Or a bed for the barn cats." Worn denim was one of the few things her mother didn't use in the myriad ways she found for other worn garments: dust rags, rug strips, padding for pot holders, patches for a quilt. "I only need a little water, Mom."

She said the same thing before every bath. With electricity hooked up and the electric stove operating, the kitchen stayed cooler, but they traded away hot water. Pipes connected to coils behind the wood stove's fire box remained cold. "Cold and cold running water," Nels said, when their mother fussed about the cost of heating the kettle on the electric stove.

"We'll install a water-heater," Maeva said. "I'll use the money I set aside for Eleanor." She'd ask Hauk and Lang to install it when they returned from Alaska. Jonas warned her that heated water at the ready cost money, too. He didn't know how much stove-top heated water it took to wash the baby's things. Some days, Maeva wondered if he cared.

She bathed, dressed in summer pajamas. Anders lay asleep in his bassinet beside his grandmother's bed, a finger in his mouth. "Love," Maeva whispered. She fussed with his light blanket, though it needed no rearrangement, ran fingers over his head, dropped a kiss. When she looked down on the sleeping baby, the anger she sometimes felt toward Jonas and Cynthia flitted past her like a sated hummingbird darting from fuchsia to nest.

Both she and her mother would miss Anders when Cynthia came out of her lethargy and took him home. She tiptoed out of the bedroom, went looking for her mother, found her in the kitchen fussing over one last unwashed glass; she'd taken warm milk to Cynthia.

"It's almost eleven, Mom, you need some rest. I'll make up a bed on the front porch to listen for the baby tonight."

"My," her mother said. She let Maeva tuck her in with a hot-water bottle for her bad hip and adjust the window until the lace curtains stirred in the night air.

Maeva spread a sheet and blanket on the daybed on the front porch, plumped the pillows her mother sewed and stuffed with chicken-feather down, turned off the overhead light and settled with notebook and flashlight. She'd long since mastered reading and writing with a flashlight tucked high under her left arm. She considered flashlight batteries a staple as important to her as cinnamon to her mother.

The latest pages of her notebook teemed with snippets about marriage: Eleanor's to Farley; Jonas's to Cynthia; the long-married couples she'd known most of her life; the unmarried Ilsa Bakke and Irv Carlson, who lived together. She wrote about children, the reward of marriage, her mother said.

Nothing she wrote helped her find the answer she sought to her relationship with Axel. A secret marriage would let her continue teaching, thus continue supporting her mother and the farm. But it would be dishonest.

She started a letter to Hauk Nordlund, a serious man whose views she trusted. He called the front porch a verandah, one of the many little things she liked about him. The day before he left for Alaska he came to the Swanson farm with a gift for her; a fine drawing tablet, good pencils, boxed stationery and ink.

She looked at them daily, a gift given without expectations or rules for use attached. She kept them locked away, unused, in a small trunk in her room. One day soon she would find the words she sought, compose a letter to him, copy it onto stationery and drop it in the mail. One day—soon or it would be too late—she would say more than thank you. Saying so little at the time saved her the embarrassment of saying too much.

He'd offered to leave his car for her use in his absence and that, too, embarrassed her.

"I don't know how to drive."

"I'll teach you."

She wanted to say yes, but shook her head. "I'd worry about doing damage."

He'd accepted her answer, wished her a pleasant summer, turned down an invitation for dinner. She could open a letter by mentioning his offer of his car. When she put pen to paper the words that flowed were her worries about Eleanor. She wrote three paragraphs, read them, discovered they were about her sense of loss, her awareness that she could never protect Eleanor and Hannah from Farley Price. She scribbled over them so the page was a gray mass.

She could sketch over the scribble with a heavier hand, erase spots here and there, salvage the page. She turned off the flashlight and willed herself to sleep, but Eleanor remained at the front of her mind. Ebbe, Astrid and Ilsa knew more than they admitted about where Eleanor and Hannah had gone.

The next morning, Axel appeared between ferry runs, doffed his captain's cap to Maeva's mother who was off her feet long enough to give Anders a bottle, and kissed Maeva's cheek.

"Axel Jenson at your service, ladies. Maeva, would you care to prepare a sandwich to show you've forgiven me for last night's rock-thunder?" He dipped a finger in the butter she was moving from churn to butter molds. Rising loaves waited on the counter for their turn in the oven. An enamel dishpan filled with the last of the Royal Ann cherries waited in the sink for packing into jars. The washing machine labored in the utility room. It would continue to labor until someone threw the switch to pump out the wash water.

Maeva slapped away Axel's finger reaching for a second dip in the butter. "We're a little busy."

"Ah, so you are. And where, may I ask, is the fair Cynthia this morning?" He unwrapped the remains of yesterday's bread, slathered on butter and raspberry jam, waiting for an answer.

"She's truly not well, Axel," Maeva said. "She's not regaining her strength."

"Not surprising, the way you two let her sleep all day. Get her out of bed, I say, get her on her feet." He cut another slice of bread, coated it. "Well, I've got to run. See you this evening."

Maeva's mother said, "My." Maeva said, "I know, Mom." Neither mentioned the current hardship imposed by Jonas and Cynthia. Neither admitted the love they felt for Anders didn't erase the burden of caring for him. They didn't discuss the cost.

Late in the afternoon, Maeva rocked Anders and read to him to teach him the rhythm of written words. Her mother sewed, the treadle's hum providing harmony. The baby cuddled, content to listen, to feel loved.

Axel arrived for dinner, sparred with Jonas, teased Cynthia, played a game of checkers with Nels and left whistling when Maeva said she wanted an early night.

She climbed the stairs to her room, weary more from worry than work, to find Jonas's overalls, knee mended, draped across the end of her bed.

30

~ Tahuya ~

In the wee hours after her battle with Farley, Irv Carlson delivered Eleanor and Hannah to the home of a Bremerton doctor who set her wrist in a cast that covered most of her hand, sewed a cut above her lip, then left. His wife took over their care. She fed them, but otherwise ignored their presence.

Irv returned when darkness settled, loaded them in his car, and told them to scrunch down low, just in case. They drove several miles before he said, "Sit more comfortable, if you like. There's no one about out here."

"Where are we going?" Eleanor asked.

"Mouth of the Tahuya," Irv said. "Logging country. Nice river. Good folks, three children, one bound to be a playmate for Hannah." When Eleanor didn't reply, he added, "Astrid and Ebbe packed up your things."

Tahuya. Eleanor couldn't locate it on the map in her mind, the map created with fear that Farley would return to do Hannah and her harm no matter where she fled. She should have listened to Maeva, for Hannah's sake. Instead, she'd clung to the notion she'd be safe in Burke Bay, the place she'd grown to love, with people who'd become family. She brought danger to them, danger that would follow wherever she went.

The trip took almost two hours over rough roads, along moonlit water, across a short bridge that shook under their weight. Irv drove into a clearing with a building at its farthest reach. A dog, roused by their arrival, leaped at the car door, planted huge feet on the window near Irv's head and inched along as the car rolled to a stop deep in a stand of black trees.

"This here's Trigg Nordlund's place. Brother to Lang and Hauk, you'll see that soon enough when you get a good look at him. Brother to Ilsa, too, for that matter. Dog's name's Peavey on account of helping Trigg handle logs."

"Oh," Eleanor said, the same nothing word she'd overworked when she first met Ebbe Persson and Astrid Romstad. The dog's name made no sense. Nothing made sense. She wondered if Astrid and Ebbe had packed her money in with her things. She wondered how she'd earn her keep with a broken wrist. What good could she be in logging country even if her wrist were strong?

"Is Trigg Nordlund a nice man?" Hannah asked.

"Nice as they come," Irv said. He led them out of wooded darkness to the front of the building, where a door opened for them.

"Come in," a woman's voice said. "You're welcome here, and safe. I'm Millie Nordlund, Trigg's out on his boat."

It took Eleanor several hours to realize Irv Carlson had driven out to Tahuya earlier that day to prepare Millie and Trigg for her arrival. It took almost a week to understand that Trigg spent nights sleeping aboard the *Constance* to protect his log boom, not to make room for her in the one-bedroom cabin.

During that week, she watched and listened. The small building had been a bunkhouse up the river, used by men Trigg hired back when logging still paid a living wage. Lang and Hauk disassembled it, trucked it down to the river mouth where they put it back together in a design more comfortable for a family.

"There's another house up there," Millie said. "Roof, some wood walls, some canvas. Might be they'll bring that one on down, too, one of these days. We need the room." She spread a sheet on the davenport.

"Richard's six, he spends most nights on the boat with his dad, but the top bunk's his. Tommy has the lower bunk. He's four, he's our quiet one. Connie's about to outgrow the cradle we wedged into the bedroom corner, so we're needing that other building."

Eleanor fretted about being in the way. "You're kind to take us in, but we need to get to a city where I can find work." She rubbed the cast that immobilized her wrist.

"There's no rush. Irv figures you can help me with school for the boys. Trigg sees that as good news. He wants our three to make it through high school, but Richard can't start in first grade out here. Irv plans to come up with some books and lessons from Hannah's teacher."

"Maeva Swanson." Eleanor's skin itched down inside the cast, an annoyance she welcomed for its distraction from remembering Farley, the taste of blood, the sound of Hannah's bare feet running away from her. In the moment when she expected to kill or be killed, Eleanor offered up a prayer that Maeva would take Hannah as her own child.

While Eleanor spent that first week mustering up courage to go beyond the outhouse and clotheslines, both farther from the house than seemed prudent, Hannah followed Trigg and the boys wherever they went. She brought back tales of the beach, along with shells she'd found and clams she'd helped dig. She helped carry buckets of fresh water from up river.

"The river is called Tahuya and the big water is called Hood Canal, Mamma. Mr. Nordlund said it's part of Puget Sound. You should see his boat and all the logs and the little fish that swim under them. They swim in schools, did you know?"

Eleanor tacked that and other bits she collected onto her mind-map. Hood Canal, Belfair fifteen or so miles back. She hoped to head toward Portland, the city she'd decided would be big enough to hide them and safer than Seattle. She looked in Millie's mirror once a day, studied the bruises and swelling, the black threads above her lip, waiting to hear Hannah say, "Your face looks better today, Mamma."

Hannah assumed they were safe in this place with its river low and slow in summer dryness. Eleanor knew they weren't. She'd pieced the map together enough to know they were still on the Kitsap Peninsula, still trapped by the sea.

As Eleanor's face improved, so did her determination to help Millie with daily tasks. She held the scrub board in place with her left forearm, working clothes with her right hand. She shoved wood into the stove's firebox, took over several cooking tasks, though peeling potatoes almost brought her to tears. She lifted Connie, who'd just started toddling, onto a bed for a diaper change, managing the pins without poking the child.

She memorized sounds: Trigg's truck as it coughed to life; as it crossed the river bridge to make a milk and eggs run three miles along the Canal; his boat's engine when he idled it to pump out bilge water; Peavy's angry bark at swooping seagulls; his excitement when he and the children explored marsh grasses along the river mouth.

One night she asked Millie and Trigg what they'd do if Farley showed up. Give him a fighting chance to leave on his own, they said, but the likelihood of his finding his way to Tahuya was about equal to the Depression ending tomorrow.

On a warm morning, while she and Millie pinned sheets to the clothesline, Eleanor said, "Is Farley the reason why Trigg always carries that rifle?"

Millie shook her head. Sunlight caught red and gold strands in her chestnut curls. "Log poachers are why he packs that gun and why he sleeps on that boat. Now mind you, if a deer crosses his path, he won't hesitate to shoot it. We all grow tired of fish and clams along about this time of year."

Eleanor hung that Farley-worry on the line along with another sheet corner. She felt the cast lighten, her fingers grow more nimble.

"Fresh venison would be a nice change." She'd once fretted about Lang and Hauk when they killed a deer out of season for the Romstads to serve at the tavern. She laughed at the person she'd been.

That night Millie crumbled and fried a pound of pork sausage Trigg brought back from a trip across the Canal to Union, thickened it into what she called buckshot gravy, and made a double batch of biscuits. Hannah and the boys ate almost as much as Trigg. Eleanor surprised herself by accepting a third biscuit. Her appetite had returned.

"Would there be work in Union, do you think?" Eleanor asked Trigg. He'd poured a second cup of coffee and rolled a cigarette. "Once I get this cast off?"

Trigg's resemblance to Lang and Hauk went beyond blue eyes and sandy hair to mannerisms. He tilted his head, rubbed a hand over his chin and studied the air they breathed.

"I doubt there's anybody hiring anywhere right now. And I made a promise to Ilsa, by way of Irv, that I'd keep you and Hannah here, safe until Lang and Hauk come back from Alaska. Them two, Lang in particular, have some notion about seeing to your future."

Eleanor, who'd scooted forward on the kitchen bench, scooted back too far. Trigg caught her good arm, saving her from falling. He put his face in close to hers. "It don't seem to be no secret up in Burke Bay that Lang up and fell ass end over teakettle for you the first time he seen you. Can't say as I blame him. With them bruises all but faded away, you look enough like my Millie to be her sister."

Eleanor's hand shot up to her mouth.

"Sorry," Trigg said, "I shouldn't ought to use that language. Millie's all the time telling me 'back-side' works just as good as ass."

Eleanor replayed that conversation a dozen times before relating it to Millie. They were hilling potatoes in Millie's small garden while Connie slept in the shade.

"I guess you know the Nordlund brothers all love their potatoes," Millie said. "Word is Lang and Hauk planted an acre or two before they went up north. They wanted Trigg and us to stay at their place while they were gone. That got my vote, but Trigg wouldn't leave those rafted logs behind for moonlight loggers to steal."

"How would anyone steal them? And why?"

Millie straightened her bent back, shading her eyes with her hand. "I keep forgetting you're from Kansas, you fit right in with us so good. They steal logs by cutting cables and hooking them behind their own boat. As for why, well, there's more than one gypo mill around. Steal some logs, cut board lengths, throw up a house of sorts."

Eleanor pictured Keane cattle on an open range, some gone missing by round-up. "Log rustling," she said, pleased to

210

understand. "There's something I've wanted to talk about. Something Trigg said about Lang caring for me."

Millie listened, grinned, laughed. Connie stirred; both women quieted and watched the baby rearrange herself on the doubled quilt on the ground. Another sound drifted in. Millie's eyebrows knit. "Someone's coming. Get in the house. Take that hoe and get."

Fear paralyzed Eleanor for a moment before propelling her, hoe clamped in her good hand. Behind her, Millie called, "Trigg? Trigg!"

Hannah! Eleanor's shout was silent, a prayer. She closed the door, stood in the shadows by the window above the kitchen sink, hoe in her hand. A weapon, surely better than Astrid's clock.

Trigg came into the clearing, rifle pointed at the ground on his right side, Tommy marching on his left. Peavey passed them, barking. No Richard; no Hannah. Millie, with Connie on her hip, went to them, took Tommy's hand. They walked toward the river bridge. Fear gripped Eleanor by the throat. She couldn't swallow.

A vehicle inched its way around the bend; a black pickup, not a sand-colored coupe. An overloaded pickup, with a rope running from the front bumper across the roof. Trigg and Millie changed their gait. Both shouted "Hello."

The pickup stopped, the door opened. Irv Carlson stepped out, stretched his arms. Richard and Hannah came running from the woods. Eleanor slumped against the kitchen counter, her fingers locked around the hoe handle.

"There's no sense running off," Irv said. He perched with Eleanor on a log on the beach for a 'little talk' that grew long. "You've got another three weeks with this cast. After that, your wrist's going to need some time to strengthen up again, like as not. Wrists don't heal so easy."

Eleanor collected and discarded rocks near her feet. Gray, white, striated, smooth, rough. She liked them all well enough to keep, but she left them for another day. "I know you're right, it's just that I worry about bringing trouble to Trigg's family. And it's too far out to get work."

"You've got work, seems to me, back in Burke Bay. Astrid needs your help in the tavern, but it's more than that. She needs your company, yours and Hannah's. To her thinking, you two are daughter and granddaughter. She and Ebbe both are all broke up over your troubles. They took to you and Hannah; they're wanting you back. There's an emptiness with you gone."

Eleanor selected another rock, lobbed it into the water lapping a yard or so from their feet. Tears too determined to be blinked back ran down her cheeks. "There's still Farley. Anyone near me is in danger."

Irv nodded. "You're right about that, there's still Farley. Astrid thinks it's time you put out the divorce notice, get the law lined up on your side."

"The sea's smooth as glass," Eleanor said. "Still, it scares me so much my insides are all stirred up sitting here so close. I'm not sure I could cross to the other side even if that's where peace of mind waited. The law scares me the same way. I can daydream about being free of Farley, but I can't fill in the part that gets me free."

"You interested in a smoke? Might settle your insides." Irv dug in his shirt pocket for tobacco and papers.

Eleanor shook her head. "Irv, did you make that up about Astrid needing my help? And the daughter and granddaughter part?"

"Now why in the world would a man make up such a thing as that?" The left side of Irv's upper lip didn't close all the way to the lower, as though his cigarettes had made a permanent opening. He shook his head, ran his fingers through his thinning hair and struck a match on a rock.

"I thought maybe you just wanted to settle my insides."

"Now, you listen good. Your going left a hole in Burke Bay. Astrid needs you, so does Ebbe, both on account of the daughter thing. Maeva Swanson needs you as a sister of sorts, like Astrid and Ebbe and Ilsa are each to the other. Maeva's trying to sort out the sensibilities of marriage, so Ilsa tells me. I'm not up on what that means, but I'm certain about one thing. Like as not, there're other men worth loving back in Burke Bay, maybe you already care about one of them even though you're still married."

Eleanor stared across the Canal at the silhouette that was Union. In her mind's eye she saw Burke Bay, the tavern that night Irv's mill burned, herself dancing with Lang Nordlund. Tears she'd thought finished before Irv started his story streamed again.

"How can I belong to a place where I bring trouble?"

"You're not the one responsible for Farley's doings. That's on him. He's going to pay his dues one of these days. One way or another, he'll pay up."

31

~ Summer Woes ~

*T*hanks to Thelma, his smart little wife, Orval reconnected with a couple customers he'd feared lost to Farley Price and whatever distiller he'd took up with. The Silverdale outfit, Orval would bet money on that, but he wouldn't lose any more sleep gnawing that dry bone since he had his druggist back.

Thelma walked right up to the counter and asked for a remedy for colic. The two of them, concerned druggist and worried mother, got into a discussion that brought fire to Orval's ears and set his feet to itching, but he kept himself and the children in the wings, so to speak.

The druggist, who called himself Doc Sloan on account of his old man had used that title, kept his eyes on Thelma. She wore a summer dress she'd sewed up herself. It fit oh so nice over her milk factories and nipped right back in at her waist, and damned if she didn't turn her whole self every now and then to check on her babies.

Orval knew what she was about, she'd got him interested enough to sign his name to the marriage document with that turning and flouncing. With his ears burning, he nearly missed the part of the conversation about a mother taking a little something to settle her stomach.

"I take a little tonic every evening," Thelma said, her voice a notch above a whisper. "My husband, Orval Blevins, happens to make a fine tonic. I avail myself of a little to settle my stomach. We have an artesian well that sure enough makes a difference with tonic quality."

In truth, Thelma wouldn't touch his whiskey, she ate any darn thing she pleased, and the baby grew plumper and happier by the day. As for the artesian well business, the less known by others about his spot on Whiskey Creek, the better.

The druggist moved out from behind his counter to stand close to Thelma so as to whisper back. After a minute of them standing too close, whispering, Orval pinched the baby hard enough to set him crying. There's serious business and there's monkey business. He'd bet the serious part had been settled.

With that done, he drove himself and his family to a couple grocers he'd sold to in the past. The one on Arsenal Way gave Orval a signal to come around back. Turned out Thelma didn't need to do a thing. The other grocer, the one down in Charleston, jumped around like water drops in hot grease when they walked in the door, so Orval acted like he'd never before seen the place. He spent some time looking around, bought a bag of Bull Durham and rolling papers, and got himself and his family out of there.

All in all, things went along well enough in spite of rumors from down to the Bay about Farley Price raising a serious ruckus that sent his wife off in the dark of night. He got an update from Thelma, who'd taken to driving herself down to the mercantile, that Mrs. Price headed back to Kansas to a father who'd shoot Farley on sight.

Orval poked around a bit himself and came up with the same news which didn't much surprise him, being as it was Ilsa Bakke's story. Anybody in Burke Bay who told it any different would have to answer to her. The Anderson brothers at the garage said they got it from Irv Carlson, who'd know since he was the one drove her to the train. Still and all, it would have been Ilsa who sent Irv that direction.

Then, along about the first of August, things took a dark turn. *The Bremerton News-Searchlight* reported federal agents busted up a bootlegging operation at a Silverdale farm, arresting eight men and two women.

"Women," Thelma said loud enough for the Stroms down the creek to hear. "They locked women in the jail right along with the men."

"Now, Thelma, I'm almost certain they're not locked in the same cell. Fact is, I've been told the county's required to have separate cells."

That's as far as he got before Thelma whacked him with a wet rag, one that was none too clean.

"Don't be acting stupid with me, Orval Blevins, you know well enough what I mean." She tossed the rag into the sink and latched onto the handle of an iron skillet.

Orval, being far from stupid, backed himself out of reach, picking up Norma for insurance. Thelma would think twice before swinging a skillet at her daughter. With the girl child clutched to his chest, he tried reasoning.

"Them agents are out after the big operators. Look at what the paper wrote." He gathered the paper with his free hand and read the parts he wanted Thelma to think on. "Listen to this . . . 'A thousand-gallon whiskey still, the largest ever confiscated in the Pacific Northwest, producing three thousand gallons of moonshine a week.' Hell and damn, Thelma, the most I ever produced in my best week was forty-fifty gallons."

Thelma slammed the skillet back on the stove. Norma screamed. The baby, stuck in his sleeping basket, took to crying. Orval squeezed his eyes shut and saw his old grandpap shaking his head and pointing the finger of his right hand, reminding him about a woman's place.

I done told you, son, what the good Lord said about women. You keep 'em in the kitchen or you keep 'em in your bed.

Orval groaned. What good was Grandpap's word? There was Thelma, in the kitchen with no end of ammunition, including enough smarts to put words together faster and better than he could, him being more a thinking man. Trouble with thinking, it was hard to manage with wet rags and skillets being tossed around, one child screaming in your ear and another screaming off somewhere you didn't dare look for fear something else might come flying.

He took to patting Norma's back like he'd seen Thelma do no end of times, making shushing noises in the bargain.

While he patted, Thelma cooed, "There there, Teddy, Mommy's coming." Then she called for Norma to follow her, told Orval to start cleaning up the mess, and went off into the bedroom.

Orval backed himself up against a chair and plopped into it. "Hell and damn," he said, without the fire such words deserved. His legs shook.

He took up the newspaper again to give it another read and had to swat it once with the back of his hand to steady it long enough to look for names. There weren't none, just Silverdale farm. He knew which farm it would be, the very one where he'd stated his name and posted his address.

"Name's Blevins," he'd said, "I live up to Hidden Valley."

He'd gone on about cows eating up all the grass he had and the need to buy some hay, but chances were good the farmer saw through that. Paper said the federal agents were following up other leads in the area. That farmer could lead them agents right on up to the valley, right on up to his place.

He was still slumped in his chair chewing on his thoughts when Thelma came out of the bedroom. He checked her face for a smile that said she was sorry, but all he saw was tightness around her mouth.

"What are you doing, sitting here?" she said. "I told you to clean up the mess."

Orval poked pages of the paper together, that being the only mess he could see. Thelma kept a neat house. He hadn't got all the pages back in order before she made her intent known.

"Not in here; out there. Go on out there and get rid of all that apparatus and all those bottles. Pack them up and get them off this property."

"Now, just a minute, that all cost good money."

"It's going to cost a whole lot more if it's discovered. Get it loaded up and driven out of here. Your distilling and selling days are over. At least on this here piece of property."

"But Thelma, there's nowhere with water so good as here, you know that, you even bragged on it. 'Artesian well,' you said to Doc that day."

"A temporary lapse in judgment," she said, hands planted on her hips, "with my mind on feeding my babies. The second biggest mistake of my life,"

She left him to guess about the first mistake, though it didn't take too much work on his part to figure out she meant him. He struck out for the door at a pace slow enough to let her call him back. She didn't say a word.

While he inched his way through the blackberry tangle and under the fence he kept as a false property line, it came into his mind that a revenuer might be watching with field glasses. That gave him good cause for worry, though Thelma worried him more, so he went on in and went to work.

It was a nice little distillery, hunkered down in evergreens, well burbling close by. As he took the vapor tube loose from the collecting pot, he sent a silent apology to his grandpap. The collecting pot sloshed with the tail end of the last batch of whiskey. He poured it out into a jelly jar and sipped while he wrapped that pot and then the brewing pot in feed sacks. It took umpteen trips to get pots, kerosene stove, and one gunny sack of bottles out to his truck.

Once he had it all loaded, he went inside for his keys. "Thelma?" he called. When she didn't answer, he said "I'll be going now. On down to the Bay. Guess there's no choice but to dump the whole works off the end of the dock."

If he'd counted on her changing her mind, he'd counted wrong. He drove off giving some thought to hiding the whole shebang in Irv Carlson's mill, not the church part, the saw room. Trouble with that, Irv was in and out of the place the same as if he had real work, though everyone knew he lived with Ilsa Bakke and spent his days fishing or playing cards down to the tavern.

He gave a minute's thought to planting his equipment in the woods behind the school, but chances were that Wiley kid would find it and name him as the likely owner.

A hand other than his own took hold of his steering wheel and headed him north, not east to the bay. Old Grandpap stepping in, letting himself be known.

"Looks like you're needing me to keep an eye out, boy, you better come on up where I'm settled. Ain't nobody much poking around the back side of my place this time of night, and ain't likely to be lingering much any other time neither."

"Hell and damn," Orval said, when the message came clear. "The Hidden Valley cemetery, that's what Grandpap's telling me."

It took close to an hour to pack everything from the truck to the thick stand of trees behind the clearing filled with graves, one of them Grandma's and another old Grandpap's. Orval grunted and cussed a blue streak, quiet like so's not to raise the dead, as he lugged equipment into safe lodging at the base of a cedar tree likely old as Grandpap himself.

All the while he worked, Thelma flounced about in his head. Could be he shouldn't ought to have married her, half his age at the time, given her feistiness. Less than half now, himself nearing forty-one, her twenty-five, gaining on him every year. But married her he had and he got his Loyal, legally named Theodore. That assigned him an obligation to get his business up and running and in good order to pass along.

He was about to pull himself up by his bootstraps and head back on home when Farley Price strolled into his thoughts. Black overcoat, black hat pulled low, black unreadable eyes—all good signs the man could handle dark of night work like legging. That plus the fact he came out of Michigan where his old man got shot up by federal agents. Had Price told him that, or had Orval dreamed it up? A man who'd lost his daddy to revenuers wouldn't never give up names.

On the other hand, a man who needed drink day in and day out, one who'd hit his wife and child, couldn't be trusted. Every good man deserved to get drunk as a broom now and then, but them who leaned on alcohol like it was a crutch were a different matter.

Orval pushed himself to his feet, made his hands into fists and gritted his teeth. Farley Price, that's who gave up the Silverdale operation, he'd bet on it. The man needed to be dealt with. Fists, gun, an iron skillet, it wouldn't much matter.

"By God," Orval said, and chewed on that for a time. God might not get around to dealing with Farley Price soon enough. "By God, with my help."

On the drive down the valley road, Orval amended the last to, "My help and Thelma's." He knew he'd done a right smart thing when he married his feisty little wife.

32

~ Troubled Hearts ~

By the end of July, an unusually warm and dry month, the Swanson well was low and silty, the stream under the cool room little more than a trickle. The room no longer kept milk safely chilled for Anders.

Maeva removed Maidenhair fern from the wettest spots in the rocky bank above the beach, tucked in quart jars of milk and poked fern clumps around the jars as insulation. The cold spring water trickled on for a week or so and then gradually went dry.

Worry about Anders milk led her to spend the money she'd saved for a hot water heater on a small second hand refrigerator instead. Emil Jenson found it in Bremerton. He and Axel brought it by boat and carried it up the trail.

"Seems to me this should have been Jonas's responsibility," Axel said. "Both buying and moving this thing."

"True," Maeva said, lacking the energy to argue about Jonas. She sent them home with fresh churned butter and warm bread.

Through August, Nels collected gallon jugs of drinking and cooking water from Nordlund's well for the Swanson family's use. Along with water, he carried stories of wells going dry in Hidden Valley and Keyport, while Whiskey Creek stayed as broad and steady-flowing as ever. Folks with low wells gathered at the pond below the tavern to dip water or catch it as it tumbled over the falls from the upper pond. Most stopped for a beer with Erling or coffee with Astrid, asking for news of Eleanor. All got the same report; no one had heard from her.

"They're not talking, those wily women." Maeva spoke to breezes off the beach as much as to Nels, remembering in time to glance his way and smile. In her mind, she held a picture of Eleanor and Hannah safe somewhere, healing from their hurts. She needed that picture to get through the long days that began with freshening the cows' water trough and soaking the vegetables most taxed by heat.

Of late, her biggest worry was Cynthia's health. On a sweltering day in mid-August, she made a special trip to the Bremerton library where she sketched pictures of the human heart from a medical book, labeling the arteries, veins, and valves she'd drawn. She left with a certainty that the valves of Cynthia's heart had been damaged by rheumatic fever in her childhood.

Armed with her notes, she went to the Navy Yard gate to wait for the four o'clock whistle. Within seconds of its blast, men streamed out of shops, lunch buckets dangling at their sides or clasped under their arms so they could light cigarettes. Their stares and comments as they passed her didn't register. She was intent on spotting Jonas to show him her drawings, to share the depth of her concern that Cynthia might never be strong enough to care for their son.

She'd known Jonas all her life as the man of the family. She'd loved his laugh, but resented his bossiness and tight-fisted handling of money. She wasn't prepared for the fear that stole all handsomeness from his face when he saw her. Fear of bad news about Cynthia, she supposed, followed by concern for Anders or their mother. She waved and smiled. While she blinked, Jonas's face again became his own.

Someone in the crowd called, "Hey, Swanson." That was another thing Maeva didn't understand about men; their last name habit. Jonas waved the man off, grabbed her upper arm, and propelled her along the street. "What? What's happened? What brings you here?"

One *what* would have served. "Research," she said. "I've been at the library reading about heart disease." She half ran to keep stride with Jonas, well over six feet tall and long of leg. "Slow down so I can tell you what I think."

He scrubbed a hand over his face. "Cyn's having a hard time getting over the baby's birth. That's all."

They walked at a reasonable pace up Burwell Hill and halfway down the other side to Jonas's home. He seated her at the small table in the compact kitchen, took a beer from the refrigerator and sat across from her. When she looked at the beer, he frowned and stood again.

"Sorry. It's so darn hot. Didn't think you'd want one."

She shook her head. "I don't, but I'd like a glass of water."

"Sorry," he said again. He found a clean glass, let water run to cool it. "So, finish what you were saying while we walked. You think Cyn's heart was damaged by rheumatic fever."

Maeva took the glass, listened to the refrigerator hum, thought about water running down the drain. "Jonas, are you aware that Nels is hauling water from Whiskey Creek because our well's gone bad? Or that I squirreled food away in spring pockets on the beach to keep it cool? The cold room was failing. That's why I bought the refrigerator. We needed it to keep your son's milk safe. Do you ever notice that Mom or I tend Anders while we're cooking so you and Cynthia can cuddle and sip your whiskey?"

"Geez, Maeva, I'm tired when I get there, I work all day. I've been working all my life."

"We all work all day, all but Cynthia, who rouses herself when she hears your car. 'Ah, that's fine whiskey,' you say to her with your first sip. She agrees and leans against your chest. You and Cynthia sip whiskey, Mom and I tend Anders and scrub vegetables and cook whatever else we're fortunate enough to have or whatever you happen to bring. We tend Anders all day, Jonas. Cynthia rests all day."

Jonas closed his eyes. Maeva suspected he closed his ears too. He didn't want to hear about hardships at the farm, or about Cynthia's health. She'd answered him too fast, spoken with anger. It wouldn't help matters, but she was tired, too.

After what seemed an interminable wait, Jonas said, "What do you want me to do?"

Maeva opened her notebook to the heart drawing, pushed it in front of him and tapped the notes she'd written about valve damage. "Take her to a doctor in Seattle. One who knows more than Dr. Werner. They have heart specialists at Virginia Mason Hospital."

To his credit, Jonas studied her drawing and notes without making snide comments about wasting paper. She had the odd sense he read the words she hadn't copied from the medical text— *shortened life expectancy.* When he looked up, she saw his eyes were moist.

"Doc Werner has known her for years. He says her heart needs rest . . . time . . ." Jonas pulled a handkerchief from his pocket and wiped his eyes. "Beside that fever, bad hearts run in her family. Doc says you can't go inside a body and monkey around with a heart like you were digging for a sliver or something."

Maeva had never seen Jonas cry, but her immediate instinct to offer comfort got lost in impatience with his willingness to hand the problem, along with his soiled laundry, over to their mother and her. She'd washed and ironed that handkerchief and the clothes he wore. She tucked away both sympathy and anger for another day, and tried reason.

"Dr. Werner is an old man. You owe it to Cynthia and Anders to see a younger doctor. Virginia Mason's doctors work as a team."

"What if they have the same opinion? What then?"

She studied his face stained with dark whiskers, his eyes clouded with worry. "Then, I think you'll need to hire someone to care for Cynthia and Anders. They're too much for Mom. Can't you see that?"

Jonas leaned toward her so his face was too close and shouted, "You're a young woman, Maeva. Anders can't be too much for you."

She scooted her chair back to gain distance and heard herself shout in return. "School begins in a couple weeks, we're just getting into the heavy canning season, Anders will be crawling soon . . ."

Still shouting, he said, "Cynthia rocks him. She holds him most of the time he's awake, she tells me stories about him, how he smiles."

She wondered if he hoped interrupting her would make the truth go away. Her anger dissipated on a wave of sorrow. Tears bit her eyes. She shook her head. "No, Jonas, she doesn't. She may pause to glance at him on her way to the bathroom, but that's about all the energy she has for him."

Jonas's shoulders sagged. He leaned back, fixed his eyes on the small window, and spoke to the curtains. "I've worked all my life."

"So has Mom." Maeva wondered if he saw that both window and curtains needed washing. She put a hand on his arm. "For now, do two things for our mother's sake—get Cynthia an appointment in Seattle, and spend this weekend at the farm. Spend some time with your son and wife."

Jonas's eyes moved from window to her. He frowned. "To clean the well, you mean? You want me there to dig out the damn well."

"Nels and I have been digging out the well. I want you there to observe your wife and son. And one more thing, Jonas—I want you to stop bringing Cynthia whiskey."

"Doc Werner says it's good for her, it helps her blood circulate."

"Oh, Jonas." Maeva watched him finish his beer and heard, in the silence between them, what Jonas always said: he'd worked hard to support the family and the farm, provide money for their necessities, loan her the tuition for her college education. She answered in silence: the family managed with little so Jonas could buy nice clothes and a car; he'd enjoyed the privileges of the farm and their mother's labors, offered little help for several years; she'd paid him back the money he'd loaned her.

Silence followed them to the car, grew louder as they drove through Manette, and then Illahee. Maeva was about to speak when they turned onto the Swanson-Jenson Road. She closed her mouth when Jonas cleared his throat.

"If Cynthia doesn't get better . . . if she never regains her strength . . ."

Those words hung between them while he shifted gears and cleared his throat a second time.

". . . it seems to me you and Mom owe me the time it takes to see to Anders. I, of course, will provide for him. For his necessities."

"His necessities include love." She hadn't meant to shout. Jonas didn't answer until they reached the upper pasture.

"Frankly, Maeva, speaking of love, it's time for you to settle down. Quit dangling Axel. Get married, establish your own home. Take the boy as your own if Cynthia doesn't regain her strength."

Heat swept up her chest, neck, face. Chill followed, and the sense she might vomit. She spoke in a whisper. "You'd give up your son? Just like that? Like you gave me your old watch when you got a new one? Like you gave Mom your old washing machine and stove?"

Jonas slammed on the brakes. The car skidded on dry dirt and stopped in a cloud of dust that drifted into the apple orchard.

"Good Christ Almighty, what do you expect me to do, Maeva?" He made a fist, punched air, and slumped over the steering wheel.

She counted seconds in her head until she couldn't stand the silence. Both she and Jonas had said too much. She opened the door, eased it closed and headed for the house to help her mother with dinner. As she neared the barn, Nels stepped out with a milk pail in each hand.

"Edwina's going dry," he said. "Too old to bring fresh, good feed costs too much. Might be time to have Wes Wiley butcher her."

She shook her head. Nels nodded.

It was well past ten before Maeva had time to think about Edwina, though she and Nels had decided without speaking to buy more grain to get both old girls through the drought. She wasn't ready to have either of them butchered, though that day would come; they couldn't afford to keep dry cows around as pets.

When Jonas took his time following her, Maeva thought he might be looking over the garden, checking the water in the well, but his breath gave him away; he'd been sipping whiskey from his flask.

Cynthia, who'd grown impatient, walked as far as the bench under the Royal Ann tree to call his name. She waited there for him. Maeva had perched Anders, who fussed with heat rash and upset stomach, on her hip to free one hand for setting the table. Her mother drained water from steamed vegetables into a container for the next day's soup and arranged fried side pork on a platter.

Maeva took Anders, who kept fussing, to the front porch swing, away from kitchen heat. She sang Swedish lullabies, hummed past words she didn't know or substituted with English of her choice.

Anders relaxed, settled his forehead against her neck and made little sounds that were part pleasure, part pain. The milk, her mother had said. He's not doing so well with the milk; maybe the cows got into some weeds. Maybe they should buy the evaporated for his formula.

Axel showed up for dessert, raspberry jelly roll smothered with whipped cream. He found Maeva and Anders on the porch, made unkind comments about the baby's parents, asked if Maeva had shopped for new shoes for his sister's wedding now little more than a week away.

"Grain for the cows," she sang in Anders's ear, "and evaporated milk. No new shoes; no new shoes."

"What kind of song is that?" Axel asked.

"A made up one," she sang, though it was more truth than not. Raised voices, Jonas and Nels arguing about their mother's added burden, drifted their way from the kitchen. She held Anders with one ear cushioned from the sound and sang more inanities to the other. He squirmed, whimpered, and spit up his last feeding on the front of her blouse.

"Jonas is drunk, Cynthia's crying, Nels is mad, your mom's trying to calm everyone down and the baby's urping. I'm going down to the boat to listen to the wireless. You can join me there, once this mess is settled."

By the time the mess settled, Maeva had changed and sponge bathed Anders two more times, rocked him to sleep, rinsed his clothes and her blouse, read the Bremerton paper to her mother and convinced Jonas he shouldn't drive until he sobered up.

She made up a bed for him and Cynthia on the front porch before taking her notebook with the heart drawing and notes to her upstairs room. She meant only to jot down a few thoughts but found her worries and sorrows pouring out. When she read what she'd written, she realized it was more letter than journal entry—an honest appraisal of the challenges brought on by a dry summer, an ill sister-in-law, a nearly three month old baby.

After a moment's pondering, she took a sheet of stationery from the box Hauk had given her and, without practicing first what she would say, wrote, "Dear Hauk, I feel the need to talk with a friend about what the summer has wrought. At this moment, you seem to be the friend I need."

33

~ Dining Nook on Whiskey Creek ~

*T*heir first morning back from Alaska, Hauk and Lang needed to rest one hand on the counter top while lifting plates down from the cupboard with the other, grasp the table edge while pouring coffee, and hold their mugs with both hands.

"Sea legs have things on tilt," Hauk said. He studied the cozy room where they sat, French windows on three sides open to September breezes and the sound of the creek running to the bay. He liked to say he built the whimsical room onto the end of the kitchen to utilize windows salvaged from a house gutted by fire. In truth, he'd added it to take away from the box-look of his original house plan.

"Breakfast nook, Maeva wrote in that second letter you've about worn out," Lang said. "S'pose it's proper to eat lunch and dinner here?"

"Proper enough," Hauk said. "Call it lunch nook at noon and dining nook at night, if we like."

"How soon you plan to invite Maeva for a dinner meal in our dining nook?"

"I'll do the inviting today, when the school day ends. It's up to her how soon the meal will happen."

The two letters Hauk received from Maeva had suffered Alaska's fog-dampened weather and his fisherman hands. The pages were worn thin at the folds, the ink smeared in spots. He pulled them from his shirt pocket, opened and smoothed them on the table top, and found the page with Maeva's sketch of the house and nook.

"Read that part again, about the house," Lang said.

Hauk read, though he could have recited most any passage from memory. There hadn't been much reading material aboard the boats or at the cannery.

> *'Nels took me with him on an evening trip to do your watering. He wanted my opinion about your potatoes—dig them and put them down in your root cellar, or mound more dirt around them and hope bugs don't move in before you return. We agreed he should hill them for now. He worked and I sketched your house. I especially like your breakfast nook and hope my drawing does it justice."*

"You see," Lang said, "it's a love letter of sorts. She loves the breakfast nook."

"Likes," Hauk said. "She wrote like, not love."

"*Like* by itself means like. *Like* with a sketch means love. Closest thing either one of us ever got to a love letter."

Hauk shook his head. "That's a sad commentary."

"That's what I've been telling you for months. We could use girlfriends around here."

Hauk crossed the creek to the school yard and spent a few minutes in the playground shelter he and Lang built. Beams, bolts, hanging rings and swings all looked sturdy and safe. He sauntered toward the building when he heard the bell.

Children streamed out. Boys shouted terms of endearment to their friends: dimwit, dingbat, dunce. One climbed onto the porch rail and jumped. Miss Truax called a reprimand but the boy paid no attention.

Hauk heard Maeva's laugh, though she wasn't in sight. He smiled, easing the tension he felt along his jaw. He'd anticipated this visit to Maeva's classroom since her first letter reached him, and he'd worked up a set of nerves.

When the school grounds cleared, he climbed the steps, crossed porch and foyer, rapped his knuckles on her open classroom door and spoke her name. She looked up from her desk where she sorted papers torn from tablets.

"Hello, Hauk. Come in."

Spoken like they had an appointment and he was right on time.

"I've come to invite you for a cup of coffee in our breakfast nook. And a ride home, since you'll miss the *Aggie J* if you accept. Thought you could get in some driving practice."

Miss Truax appeared beside him. With that stealth, she could sneak up on a buck and grab it by the antlers. Helmer and Ebbe Persson, whom he'd heard coming from their first foot fall on the school steps, crossed the foyer and pushed their way past Miss Truax. From the looks of things, he should have brought coffee with him and called it a party.

"Miss Truax," he said. "Hauk Nordlund, if you've forgotten. Hello, Ebbe. Helmer."

Maeva smiled at him as if the others weren't there. "I'd like that, Hauk. The coffee and the driving practice. Nels and I have been spoiled with Lang's truck."

"If you've come to offer her a ride, you'll want to haul some water for Mrs. Swanson while you're at it," Helmer said.

"Excuse me," Miss Truax said, hand on her throat. "I'll return to my principal duties. Mr. Nordlund, you're always welcome, of course."

"You here on some sort of official business, Hauk?" Ebbe asked, eyes narrowed.

He shook his head. Ebbe was 'borrowing' books and materials from Maeva's classroom for Eleanor's use. He didn't want her to think the news about Eleanor's location was out.

"Hauk came to invite me for coffee," Maeva said.

Ebbe gave him a look that let him know she'd keep quiet about the borrowed books. "You'll be needing some fresh cream, then. I've got some downstairs in the fridge, I'll get it, and you two can get on out of here."

Five minutes later they descended the steps side-by-side, Hauk carrying a cream can, Maeva a bag filled with student papers and her good shoes. "They're on their fourth year," she'd said about the shoes as she stepped out of them into boots.

"I put a couple planks across the creek but boots are wise all the same." He'd brushed out a path to the edge of the school grounds, built a simple bridge and harbored hope Maeva would use it more than this one afternoon.

"I spent this season's new-shoe money on dressy pumps for Axel's sister's wedding. Against my better judgment but necessary to keep peace between Jensons and Swansons. Lovely impractical shoes, now tucked away in a box in my closet."

"Hmm," he said. He'd never mastered the art of small talk.

She laughed. "Shoes are a rather boring topic." She remarked on path, bridge, cedar and fir resin in the warm afternoon air. She took his offered hand to cross the creek and left hers in his the rest of the way to the house, where she removed the boots before going inside, though he insisted she needn't bother.

Lang poured boiling water through fresh ground coffee in a drip pot. "Heard you coming," he said.

Together they showed her through their house, kitchen first, with its wood burning range, large sink, long counters and space for a refrigerator when they decided to invest in one.

"Creek and root cellar work fine till then," Lang said.

They escorted her to the living room furnished with davenport and two arm chairs they'd purchased in Bremerton after they'd sold some timber, and two end tables they'd built themselves. They gave her time to remark on the hand-crafted furniture and oak floor before showing her the bedroom they shared.

That morning they'd discussed the possibility one or the other of them might want a private bedroom one day. Maybe even an entire separate house. By noon they'd decided how to add a couple bedrooms and a larger bath, and where a second house would be built.

"The washroom's not fancy," Hauk said. "Washroom and bathroom in one." A washing machine they called second hand, decent flush toilet and small sink consumed the space. A galvanized tub, hanging on a hook, came down for bathing.

The fragrance of brewing coffee drew them back to the kitchen. They settled in the nook. Lang poured coffee; Hauk found a pitcher for the cream.

"I love this little room." Maeva stirred cream in her coffee. "It's like a garden café."

Lang nodded. "That's what Hauk had in mind when he designed it." He gave Hauk's shin a tap with his foot, and mouthed 'love.'

Hauk remained stone still, though he too had heard the word and felt it touch his heart

Maeva looked from Hauk to Lang and back to Hauk. "Now," she said, "which one of you wants to tell me what you know about Eleanor?"

Lang shook his head, a breach of their unspoken arrangement that he answer questions put to them as a pair.

"You might as well tell me," Maeva said. "Ebbe's about as subtle as a swarm of bees setting up a hive atop my head. She buzzes in morning and afternoon, peeks over my shoulder at papers I'm sorting, snoops through them if she's given half a chance. Helmer is meant to distract me so she can have a look."

Lang chuckled. Hauk managed to maintain a straight face for several seconds before delight at Maeva's directness got the best of him.

"Eleanor's healing. She and Hannah are safe. Doing well enough. There's another child or two near the same age, so Hannah has playmates. School mates, so to speak, since we're talking about lessons."

Hauk noticed Maeva's eyes change from all green one second to gold specked the next, depending on the light. Depending on her mood too, he'd bet. He folded his arms across his chest. Lang shoved his chair back from the table, like as not trying to escape the scrutiny, or whatever was going through Maeva's mind and coming out through her eyes.

"I see," she said. "What about Farley? The last I heard, which came through Nels, neither he nor his car have been seen."

"That's what we've heard," Lang said.

Maeva's eyes narrowed. "He'll be back, but that's another matter. From now on, I'll prepare lessons for Hannah. I know her learning level and ability. As for the other child or two who are her school mates, it would help to know their ages and what formal schooling they've had."

"Close in age to Hannah, but no classroom experience," Hauk said.

"Okay, give me through the weekend to get some lessons and teaching suggestions together. I'll explain to Ebbe tomorrow, and I won't press for information."

They lingered over coffee, walked the grounds, filled jugs with water, and postponed her driving lessons for another time so she could get home to help her mother with Anders. "Rest your hand on the wheel to get a feel for steering and on the gearshift when I tell you," Hauk said. She leaned her shoulder against his to manage, and stayed there the entire drive, commenting on changes she felt in wheel and gears.

He walked her down to the house, where they smelled the wonders performed in the Swanson kitchen before they reached the porch. Mrs. Swanson said, "My. *Velcomen* home, we set another plate."

"Thank you," Hauk said, though he'd planned to decline such an offer. Maeva disappeared for a few minutes, reappeared in a different dress, with Anders perched on her hip. Jonas retrieved beer from the refrigerator and launched into a discussion of weather and problems with the well.

"I'll take a look at it, if you like," Hauk said. "Chances are you need to dig deeper for a more reliable spring if cleaning the well bottom isn't working."

"You look after dinner," Mrs. Swanson said. "We eat now."

Jonas lowered a rock-weighted rope, used for measuring depth, into the well and pulled it back out. "Barely wet," he said. "Silt's built up again."

Hauk tapped the timber walls. "Old well. Shallow. Looks like it's in line with the small stream that runs through your cool room."

"Right. It is."

"You say the bank above the beach is riddled with springs?"

Jonas nodded. "You heard Maeva say she used them to keep milk cold for my son until we had a heat wave that wouldn't let go."

"A man shouldn't have to dig too deep. Maybe clear the creek, increase its flow. My brother and I could give a day's labor, see where it gets us."

"I'd pay for the time it takes to evaluate the situation."

234

Hauk gave Jonas a nod. He understood the man's unspoken message—he wouldn't pay for any serious digging.

They returned to the house still busy with after-dinner clean-up, a hungry baby and an agitated Cynthia who couldn't calm little Anders. Mrs. Swanson took him, backed into a rocking chair and sang a Swedish lullaby. Maeva and Nels labored on in the kitchen. Jonas offered Hauk an after-dinner drink and smoke on the front porch.

Hauk shook his head. "I'll say my thanks and good night. You're still busy here."

Maeva grabbed a towel and dried her hands. "I'll walk you to your car."

The kitchen screen door slapped shut behind them. "Tell me what you suspect about the well," she said before they reached the wood shed.

"It's shallow, like I guessed. Smells earthy, which isn't dangerous but not what you want for drinking water. Should fill once the rain returns."

"Wes Wiley told me I should bring in a drilling rig."

"Wouldn't be a bad idea, if you can afford it."

"Not this year. I'm not even sure the school district can pay me. They've told all teachers to prepare for the worst."

He could offer her money from his Alaska wages, though he feared she'd be upset. "Lang and I will deepen the creek bed tomorrow, remove silt at the outflow. Beyond that, I can deliver water in a couple five gallon milk containers Ilsa has tucked back in her basement. Our well stays full no matter how much we draw."

She didn't refuse his offers as he'd expected. They'd passed the barn and started the climb toward the upper pasture before she spoke.

"Thank you, Hauk. You are indeed the friend I've needed." She took his hand. "You can see our troubles in a glance. They're even worse than when I wrote you the first time. Cynthia's so weak she can't hold her own baby for more than five minutes. Jonas finally took her to Seattle, to Virginia Mason. They confirmed she has a bad heart." She made an odd noise, part sigh, part moan. "Jonas drinks too much."

Hauk stopped walking. "I'll do anything I'm able to help you and your family, Maeva."

"I know. I trust you. It's a rare person who proves himself so trustworthy in so short a time."

She brushed his lips with hers, a butterfly kiss, and thanked him.

In spite of scant practice, he managed to drop her hands, circle her body with his arms and get their lips situated for a proper kiss, one in which she willingly participated.

"My," she said, when they separated, "thank you for that, too."

He studied her eyes, gave one nod. He knew enough to remain silent.

34

~ Artesian Well ~

Orval's pretty little wife came up with an idea that hadn't occurred to him, occupied as he was with setting up his brewery so far from the creek. She posted a *Drinking water for sale* sign on Hidden Valley Road. Customers stopped by with nickels and dimes to spend, carrots, spuds, apples or prunes to trade.

He took to worrying she'd fill the last of his good empty bottles, the ones he hadn't moved off the property, but it turned out she was too smart for that. She had folks bring their own containers and charged a quarter when they filled a copper canning kettle. Along with water, she handed out advice, no extra charge.

"Draw your well water for clothes washing and trough filling in early morning; then let the well rest and refill."

"Carry used wash water to vegetable and flower beds. A little suds kills off bugs that move in for a munch and gives plants a drink."

"Send the children down to Burke Bay for a bathe. Husbands, too, them being the ones crawling in between your own two sheets."

All the selling gave Orval cause for concern his own well might get low enough she'd send him off for a sea bathe, but water kept burbling up out of the ground begging to be used. He hadn't meant to get roped into her business, but hefting them canning kettles and hauling them gallon jugs was a mite much for Thelma, what with their girl child hanging on her skirts and his Loyal needing the breast every three four hours. In the end, hefting served his own interests. Orval needed the breast every now and again himself.

He went off most every day to have a sit-down visit with old Grandpap and found the quietude of the cemetery to his liking. It took him near on to two weeks to get the gist of what his grandpap had to say. In truth, that came more out of his own memory from back when they buried his grandmother.

> *"It's a Swede cemetery, for the most part, but they'll take me in when my time comes, what with me being legal-wed to your grandma. We all of us own the place. Them Swedes that staked it out made sure there's plenty enough room here, twice again what you see cleared for graves."*

That's what Grandpap had in mind. Set up operation on the uncleared cemetery land rightfully owned by the likes of them name of Blevins just as much as any others with folks buried there. Set it far enough back in the trees to go unnoticed, not so far as to break his back hauling water and makings in, hauling product back out.

He'd gotten his thinking straight before a letter showed up addressed to him and delivered to his mailbox without a stamp. No other name on the envelope, no names a'tall inside, but it came from Farley Price, sure as shooting.

> *If you're interested in talking business, meet me at the Maple Leaf. Thursday night, nine o'clock."*

Orval's feet took to itching so dang bad Thursday, he scratched till blood showed up on his socks. He didn't care to have much truck with a man who'd hit his wife and child. Worse'n hit, if rumors down to Burke Bay were true.

Still and all, he wouldn't be relying on a couple months worth of water sales to feed his family. Wasn't all that pleased about carrying product to Bremerton himself, neither. Grandpap had made mention of that clean on back to the night when Orval moved his brewing apparatus in under a cedar tree behind the cemetery's graves.

The Maple Leaf Tavern, with the lower part of its front windows painted over and next to no lights inside, made a good place to meet the likes of Farley Price. Orval conjectured the man must have taken up residence close enough to walk, since he didn't see no sand-colored car parked under the maple tree responsible for the tavern's name. He went inside, nonchalant as a man with sore feet could manage, and gave himself a good minute to adjust to the darkness before heading for the men's. When he came out, Price had moved from his perch on a stool at the end of the bar to a table off in a dark corner.

"Blevins." Price motioned with his head for Orval to sit, motioned with his hand for the bartender to bring a couple beers.

Orval sat, studied Price dressed out in black so it looked from a distance like a face and hands hovered without a body attached.

"You still cooking?" Price asked.

"Could be. You have a hand in that Silverdale raid?"

"You ought to know better."

"Leggers get caught, they give up shiners. Happens all the time."

"Seems to me I told you my daddy got shot full of holes by the law. Shot up so bad there wasn't much left to lay to rest. I might switch distillers to suit my own needs, but I don't barter with revenuers."

Orval eyed Price, who eyed him back. Neither spoke until filled glasses rested in front of them.

"What you have in mind?" Orval asked.

"Right now, I can move up to fifty gallons a week of your best. Twenty-five to thirty should keep us both on top of things, financially speaking, if you can't produce fifty."

"Why should I trust you to stick with me?"

Price shifted in his chair, the first indication he might be uncomfortable. "I been out of town, looking for my wife. Far enough out to know she didn't head back to her people. She'll show up, one of these days. I mean to stay close by. I've got contacts you need; you've got good product. Something to do with that water on your place."

"Cash money comes my way on delivery to you," Orval said. "None of this leaving product off somewhere. Keep your own imbibing limited to days you're not hauling. You show up in your cups, all bets are off."

Price narrowed his eyes and held off his answer long enough for Orval's feet to heat up like the floor'd caught fire.

"Deal," Price said. "You name time and place, I'll be there with cash for twenty-five gallons. Don't bother me with puny bottles. Make 'em all gallons."

Orval got down to serious work after that meeting. He built a blind for his fermenting tubs and collecting apparatus with scrap lumber he hauled in from here and there, some from Carlson's Mill, not truly scrap but not likely missed neither. Took hardly no time to have him a roof over his head for when the rains returned.

He rigged himself a new cooker that could burn oil or wood, smaller than the burner he and Grandpap had used since Orval's boyhood. Cooking in the wee hours, when hard working farm folks were abed, would be safe enough. Not many folks, hard working or not, meandered into a cemetery after dark.

His pretty little wife was smart enough to keep from asking questions about where he did his work, long as he kept it off their property. Only trouble with Thelma and her smarts, she started thinking down the road a whole lot farther than made sense, given the times.

"Here's a thought, Orval Blevins. You could lay pipe from our artesian well to folks both directions in the valley, put in a couple big pumps and sell water year-round. You're all the time moaning about new folks moving in without paying much attention to the troubles they have digging deep enough to hit water."

He let that settle in his brain long enough to get out tobacco and papers, and roll himself a smoke. "Now, why would folks buy water they can get free for the taking from their own wells?"

"I talk to the women who come here buying drinking water. Most complain about the cost of putting in a well that doesn't deliver adequate to their needs year round. None can afford to dig deeper, and there's no guarantee digging will get them more than another hole in the ground. Two or three tell me their pumps burned up trying to suck water out of dry earth. Farther they are from the creek, deeper they have to dig."

Orval had to smile at how cute she was when she got all het up. He had half a notion to nuzzle her a bit when she hit him with another thought, one he didn't like. No siree, he didn't like it a'tall.

"What's going to stop the government from coming out here and taking away the property with the well on it, and laying claim to the entire creek? I read about how they did that in Bremerton."

"Where'd you read a thing like that?"

"In the newspaper. Same paper you read."

Orval huffed his impatience. "The Navy Yard, you mean? They maybe done that when they added land to the yard. That's a whole lot different than clean out here in the country."

Thelma huffed right back. "You're so busy living in your grandfather's time you forget to think about the times Norma and Teddy will see. They won't be sneaking around selling moonshine; they'll be running a private water company, if you get your thinking straightened out sooner than later."

The fact that his stubborn little wife insisted on calling his Loyal by the wrong name near about brought on apoplexy.

"Now, Thelma," he said, working his way toward a sound argument in his own behalf.

"Never mind, Orval, talking to you just wastes my breath. I'll get a lawyer and get matters settled."

He stumbled backward two steps. "You mean to up and divorce me over your crazy notions?"

Thelma shook her head. "No, Orval, I mean to draw up business papers. Blevins Water Company. Lately it's getting to the point where that artesian well is the best reason I can find for having married you in the first place."

"Well, dang," Orval said, but Thelma had already scooted off to draw water into another neighbor's jug.

35

~ Ellie ~

When Eleanor could no longer tolerate the cast on her wrist, Trigg removed it with a hack saw and Millie's sewing shears. The plaster had grown dirty with cooking, handling firewood, using the scrub board and working in the garden. The tender skin revealed when Trigg broke the cast away looked like the underbelly of a garter snake Richard found in the garden and brought recoiling to the house to show her. She'd gasped, altogether satisfying Richard.

The pale skin exaggerated the tan on her exposed arm, reminding her of her mother's warnings. Summer sun turns skin leathery. Wear long sleeves, large hats to shade the face and neck. Ladies keep their skin soft.

Trigg turned and probed her unbound wrist with callused fingers. "Bend it down. Good. Bend back. Good. Move to the side. Now this way. Does this hurt? There's many wee bones in the wrist. First they knit themselves. Now they take on strength. No lifting for a time. Just flap a little, like a gull when it lifts from the beach."

Eleanor, who had little experience with doctors, found Trigg's ministrations kinder than those of the man who'd prepared the cast and stitched her upper lip. "Where did you learn about wrist bones?"

Trigg raised his head, squinting as though he needed to look beyond the walls for an answer. "On the dairy farm. We were a big family, we all learned. Hauk, who is our youngest, is our best at doctoring. He has the touch in his fingers. That comes to those who suffer pain young."

Eleanor listened to the story of Hauk's leg burns, the family's fear he might not walk again, how their sister Ilsa cared for him until he healed and walked and ran.

"Ilsa took over mothering them two boys, Hauk and Lang both, the day Hauk got burned. Three and five they were. She says without Lang she'd have never managed getting Hauk's legs working right. When you go on home to Burke Bay, you ask for a look at them legs. You'll see a story there good as any you read in the Bible."

Home to Burke Bay. The words hummed in Eleanor's brain for a week, a fortnight. Her wrist grew stronger by the day and with it thoughts of leaving to make her own life free of Farley Price. He'd stolen cattle from her father and stolen her ties to family and Kansas in the act. He'd transported her to a strange land where trees walled her in on one side, the sea held her hostage on the other. She'd grown to love the trees for their majesty, the fragrance they lent the air, the quiet security they provided. She still needed to make peace with the sea.

Before first light on a mid-September morning, Eleanor went alone to the rocky beach, around the headland, out of sight of Trigg's boat. Mist scarves trailed from trees on the bluff. The sea waited for daylight to determine its hue. She tested the water with her finger tips, rinsed her hands, splashed water on her face. She scrubbed her elbows with coarse sand, washed her feet and legs with sea water, searched for an oyster shell, filled it and sipped. The salty taste surprised her. A fish jumped, leaving concentric circles on the quiet surface. She drew in a deep breath and held it so she might define the scent of the sea.

Clean. Like sheets smell after drying in the breeze; like little Connie after her bath.

She'd been welcomed as a daughter in Burke Bay, respected for her talents and her personhood even when she'd expressed fear of her surroundings. She'd found friends. For all her talk of disappearing into a city, the weeks of hiding out at Tahuya, a place that consisted of a river mouth and nothing more, gave her time to reflect. If she ran now, she'd run forever. She needed to stand her ground against Farley.

She needed to go home.

Not yet, Trigg and Millie said. We wait for word from Irv and the others.

The river narrowed with waning summer, its once muddy edges crusted over like scabs on a wound. Trigg and the children hiked farther up river to chill the milk. Millie opened windows and the door to catch a breeze, and swatted flies with last year's newspapers. Eleanor settled Hannah and Richard at the table for school lessons, marveling at her daughter, who did much of the teaching. Tommy joined them, practiced printing his name and hid his smile when Hannah praised him.

"Print the first word with a capital, the rest small," Hannah said. "Help sound out the words, Mamma. That's how we learn." "Look, we can use dominoes for counting and adding." "We can draw around shells and leaves for art projects."

"I'm not fit to teach. I missed over half the school days each year," Eleanor confessed to Millie. "We couldn't get into town through the snow most of winter. Papa wanted me to board with a town family but Mamma let me stay home. She said she got too lonely without another female in the house."

"You're fit enough," Millie said. "And Hannah's a natural. Trigg and I are blessed to have you both with us for this time. Richard wants to catch up with Hannah. I doubt he would have progressed so fast in a classroom full of boys more interested in recess."

"We need more books, more tablets."

"I'll send Trigg across to Union to mail a letter off to Ilsa. She'll see to it."

A few days later, as afternoon heat pressed in on them, Irv Carlson's pickup rumbled over the bridge across the Tahuya River, coasted into the clearing, and coughed to a stop. Millie, first to hear the vehicle's approach, hushed Eleanor and the children and signaled for them to get up, get away from the table.

"It's Irv," Millie said, before the truck door slammed shut. "And Lang and Hauk with him."

Richard dashed outside, shouting, "Uncle Lang! Uncle Hauk!" Tommy, and then Hannah, followed. Eleanor, heart pounding and legs tingling from fear's rush, remained inside, watching Trigg cross the clearing in front of the house. He opened his gun, removed and pocketed the shell he kept at the ready, handed the weapon still broken open to Millie, then exchanged handshakes and back slaps with his brothers and Irv.

Eleanor's heart took up a new beat, excitement at seeing Lang. She admonished herself for her foolishness. Similar feelings led her into romance and hasty marriage, and delivered her seven years later to a hideout where her presence kept life a degree or two off kilter. No matter her self-talk, longing to be loved, to love in return, persisted. She wiped her damp palms on her skirt, the faded but serviceable denim riding skirt she'd carried from her old life, and made her way out to add her greeting.

In the midst of her shaky hello, Irv lifted her off the ground and swung her in a circle.

"Look at you. No cast, face as pretty as ever, and a light back on in your eyes."

Lang and Hauk unloaded boxes and bundles, naming off items—two chickens dressed out and wrapped in layered papers to keep them cold. Apples. Lard and flour and sugar. The table that served for meals and school lessons disappeared under boxes, none of which held books or tablets. Eleanor asked, but Millie didn't hear. She was handing out orders.

"Richard, you fire up the stove. Tommy, you help. Hannah, take Connie for me. Your mom and I have work to do. We'll get apple pies baking, applesauce cooking, chicken frying. It's going to get hot in here, but it's going to smell so good we could live a week extra just by breathing it in. The men can have a confab without us."

"What's a confab?" Hannah asked.

Millie gave her a hug. "A talk of serious matters, though you'd have to listen to what they don't say to understand its finer points. They're thinking ahead to winter."

"Winter," Eleanor said. The rains would return, the children would need to be inside most of the day. They were crowded without her and Hannah. Time to move on had come.

When the food was ready, the men moved table and benches outside, away from kitchen heat. Lang carried a gunnysack dripping seawater into the clearing, the same sack she'd seen him carry toward the beach earlier. Glass clanked. He pulled out brown quart bottles, some filled with home brewed beer, some with root beer for the children. They lifted their glasses in silent toasts, ate their chicken dinner with nods of pleasure.

Darkness eased in while they sipped coffee and ate pie. When the children were settled for the night, Trigg lit a kerosene lantern and set it at the far end of the table. He spoke as though calling a meeting to order.

"First, there's the matter of staying here through the winter. We're of two minds. One is shore up the cabin and stay put. Hope we don't get storms strong enough to break up the logs. They're protected pretty good here, if we don't get winds and high tides all in one."

"Bound to get them together," Hauk said. "One controls the other."

The men agreed. That was news to Eleanor, whose determination to feel comfortable with the sea dissolved like the salt she'd tasted when she brought the filled shell to her lips.

"The other notion," Trigg said, "is to move the logs to Irv's lagoon. No mills are buying. We're of a mind to consider that."

"And live where?" Millie watched Trigg through narrowed eyes.

"Here, till we find something in Burke Bay. Hauk figures he and Lang can have a decent place put up by Thanksgiving. They're wanting a second home on their property, one for each sometime down the road, plenty for all of us in the meantime."

"And Eleanor and Hannah?"

"That's the second matter that bears discussion," Trigg said. "One decision rests up against the other."

"I'm going back to Burke Bay to work for the Romstads, if they'll still have me."

"Romstads want you, soon as possible," Irv said, "but there's a bit of checking out to be done. Here's how the boys and me have worked it out. One of us will help Trigg start moving his logs. One of us stays out here while that's going on."

"Checking out what?" Millie said.

"Farley," Eleanor whispered.

Millie grabbed her hand and squeezed.

"No one's seen him," Irv said, "but Ilsa's got her sixth sense working overtime. She gets snippets from Walt Strom, who gets it from his wife, who gets it from Thelma Blevins, wife to Orval. Sometimes Ilsa gets it from Orval himself—the horse's mouth, so to speak. I'd trust how Ilsa puts two'n two together more'n anything I read in the news."

"Farley is my concern," Eleanor said.

"And ours," Irv said. "Farley made himself a concern to all of Burke Bay. None living there will tolerate such behavior in their midst. Falling-down drunk is one thing, there's more'n one been guilty of that over the years. Fights with fists to let off some steam are tolerated now and then. But when a man uses his strength against a woman and child, breaks bones and causes a need for stitches, bandies about a gun with threats, it's on all the rest to put the man back in order."

Trigg pushed aside the cooling coffee pot and poured another round of beer. "So, here's what we figured. Millie, Eleanor, and the children stay put out here. Hauk's here while I move logs. Once that's done, I come back. Hauk and Lang start building a small place on their property, down close to the pond and well house. We all move at once."

Millie released Eleanor's hand and slapped the table. "You're planning on letting Eleanor move back into one of the Romstad cabins? Where she nearly got killed?"

"No," Hauk said, "that's not how it's going to work. Eleanor and Hannah will move in with Lang and me. They'll have the bedroom to themselves. We'll bunk in the living room."

"No," Eleanor said. Firm, resounding. She stood as best she could between bench and table. "I can't let all of you keep making decisions for me." She stepped over the bench, kicked Millie's thigh in her haste to get away from them, stumbled toward the cabin. She'd pack her few things, waken Hannah and . . . and what? Borrow a flashlight to find her way down the road?

Lang caught up with her and grasped her upper arm. "Ellie," he whispered, "right or wrong, I have feelings for you. Hauk knows that. Hell, all sitting at the table know how I feel, and not one of us will leave you and Hannah at Farley's mercy."

"You can't . . . I can't . . ." Eleanor didn't know what she wanted to say; she was caught up in the endearment. *Ellie.*

"Listen for one minute before you say what can't be done. Ilsa, Ebbe and Astrid talked it over. They got Maeva involved. Astrid said it was like a quilting bee, patching in ideas and stitching them together."

Eleanor's heart pounded. Fear, hope, longing. "It's not right."

"No, none of it's right, not me falling in love with a married woman, not a husband bringing harm to his wife and child with his own hands, not these times that leave able-bodied men without work to support their families."

Millie appeared out of the dark. "The men are talking two months, Eleanor. Three at the most. We'll stay put out here for another two or three months. There's books and lessons for the children out there in Irv's truck just waiting for all of us to agree. Stay for the children. Stay for me. I couldn't bear it without another woman after this time we've had. I'm like your mother who needed you there during winter snow."

"Two months," Eleanor said, wondering if Lang was about to kiss her when Millie appeared. She knew how to handle a rifle. She needed to think about what taking a stand might involve and plan ahead for Hannah, in case she failed.

36

~ October Rains ~

October rains fall sweet on our farm, Maeva wrote, hoping words would help settle her troubled thoughts. She carried the kitchen rocker to the front porch where the sound and scent of rain might help Anders fall asleep. He snuggled against her, unmindful she was but a paternal aunt, so dubbed by Axel, who resented the infant for the time and attention he required.

Anders smiled and raised his arms to her when she returned from any absence: a day teaching, a half-day in Bremerton at the library, an hour in the garden. For her part, she found him easy to love, but she worried about her mother who cared for him and Cynthia in her absence.

She foisted aspirin tablets, touted by her doctor as a miracle drug, on her mother twice daily. She massaged her mother's back as demonstrated by a nurse; she rose in the night to refill the hot water bottle. The doctor said, "Your mother will live out her life with pain." She'd found books on anatomy, studied bones and joints, muscles and nerves and blood circulation to understand the damage wrought by old Dulcimer.

"What do you hope to accomplish with all this reading?" Axel asked, when she carted books home from the library.

"I need to understand."

His impatient groan registered deep in her being where it found company with other concerns she'd tucked away while lost in the pleasure of his kisses. She'd been kissed by Hauk, a kiss that brought longing, but longing for what? More kisses? And what did kissing have to do with love?

On a pleasant October afternoon, golden with the lowering sun and drifting maple leaves, Hauk and Ebbe chatted on the school porch while Maeva buttoned coats and reminded older children to watch younger ones on their walks up to the valley or down to the dock. Hauk's presence made her fumble-fingered. He, Lang and Irv Carlson had been away from Burke Bay for several days. She was certain he had news of Eleanor and Hannah.

When the children were gone, Hauk handed her a letter.

"They're both fine," he said. "I'll give Helmer a hand downstairs while you read. When you're finished, I'd like to drive you home."

She nodded, took the letter to her classroom.

Hannah and I are safe. We both miss you and all those we count friends in Burke Bay. Though I once planned to flee to Portland and then east, I am now determined to return to confront Farley. You've learned enough about my abrupt departure to know he broke my wrist, and that Irv Carlson drove Hannah and me to a safe place. I've recovered from the physical damage and do little things to earn our keep. There is no paying work where we're settled. I have too little money saved to pay rent or provide food. Hannah deserves a better life than I have given her thus far. I will not drag her off to suffer in a city.

Thank you for the lessons you sent. I'm discovering how much I need to learn just to help my child with her school work. Along with the lessons you prepared, Irv brought word that Astrid and Erling Romstad will welcome me back at the tavern when I'm able to return. They're so kind—kinder than I deserve.

You know by now, if you didn't before, that Lang and Hauk visited here with Irv. I want to tell you what I'm almost afraid to admit to myself. Lang has feelings for me, and I am attracted to him.

Hannah senses Lang's interest and tells me she likes him. My face heats at the shame I feel, and more at the fear. I have decided to seek a divorce, though I don't know how to proceed. Until I am free of my marriage bonds and healed in my heart, I will not succumb to my own foolish longings.

~

Maeva startled when Hauk tapped on her classroom door. She smiled when she saw him there, tucked the letter into its envelope and put it and a stack of students' papers into her canvas bag. "Hello, Hauk. I'll clean the blackboard and put the room in order a bit for Helmer."

"I'm not in a hurry, Maeva."

When they left the school, he led her to the driver's side door of his car. "You drive. Take a turn around the parking area to get the feel of the wheel."

She started his car, practiced breaking and shifting into reverse, and eased out onto School Road. He told her when to shift into second and third, how to ease her foot off the clutch; he didn't laugh when the car lurched, or when it stalled. He said, "Good," several times. By the time they crested Indian Hill, her heart rate had settled back to normal.

They talked only about the task at hand until she parked in Swanson's upper pasture. "Thank you," she said. "We've picked most of the apples for cider making this weekend coming. We'd like you and Lang to join us."

"Is this the annual Swanson-Jenson cider-pressing festival I've heard about from Irv and my sister? Complete with dancing in the woodshed?"

"It is."

"Will you give me a dance? Or will Axel claim them all?"

She looked at him, a man she considered a friend. She'd heard teasing in his question, saw seriousness in his eyes. "I'd like a dance with you, Hauk."

By early Saturday afternoon, apple pressing was in full swing. The round oak kitchen table was covered with a cloth Maeva's mother had starched and ironed to perfection. In her girlhood, she'd watched her mother do the cloth's fine embroidery and cut work during long winter nights. The cloth was smothered with food, dishes and cutlery neighbors brought for the festivities.

Jonas moved the old Victrola to the woodshed where he alternated tending it and competing for speed and output at the

251

crank on the oak cider press. Pocket watches came out. One man cranked, another counted turns, a third called, "Minute's up."

They placed bets, nickels and dimes, and bragged or moaned. They drank beer and last year's hard-cider. Women changed filter bags on the press and transferred juice from crocks and enamel dish pans to gallon jugs. At dusk they heaped plates with food and carried it to the men. "Enough drinking. Eat a bite."

Eating, drinking, pressing apples and sampling fresh cider gradually gave way to gathering empty plates, washing dishes, settling into a night of dancing and singing. The Nordlund brothers accompanied some of Jonas's records with their harmonicas and sang along to *Indian Love Call*.

Maeva danced at least once with every man present. She danced alone out of the woodshed, along the path to the house with stacked dirty dishes in her arms. A light mist caught the dim glow of electric lights Jonas had rigged, making the night magical. She returned with Anders on her left hip, hoping Jonas and Cynthia would hold him between them while they waltzed.

"Take the boy back inside to Mom," Jonas said. "He'll catch a chill out here."

Her steps felt heavier, the crunch of the shells louder, on her trip back to the house. A tear snuck out of one eye to mingle with rain on her face. Her mother, warmed bottle ready, took Anders from her and urged her to stay outside a bit longer.

Jonas cranked the Victrola and announced a special song for Cynthia. He crooned, "You're my everything," his eyes on hers. The crowd formed a circle around them to watch them dance on packed earth in misty light as though they'd gathered on the floor of a fine ballroom under a crystal chandelier. The music faded, the small crowd applauded. Cynthia clapped her hands and laughed with Jonas. He lifted her at her waist, twirled her once, twice.

Cynthia's laugh faded to a gurgle, a whimper. Her head fell, unhinged. Jonas whispered her name. "Cynthia?" Shouted, "Cynthia?" Keened "No! Noooo.

Wes Wiley yelled, "Get her to the house."

A woman's voice said, "A wet cloth."

Heart and valve sketches flashed through Maeva's conscious. She said, "Get her to the car, she needs a doctor," though she knew it was too late. Cynthia had risen from her lethargy for one last dance.

37

~ November Plans ~

It came as no surprise to Hauk that Maeva provided the voice of calm and reason in the moments after Cynthia's death. She'd ordered Jonas to get Cynthia into his car and asked Hauk to drive them to the hospital, though they all knew it was futile. She asked Lang and Nels to follow in Lang's truck, and ordered the remaining guests to go inside the house for fresh coffee.

He'd seen her only for driving lessons in the month since. He and Lang had the walls up and sub-roof on the house they were building by their pond. Irv Carlson scavenged for windows, trading off milled lumber here, cedar shakes and shingles there, picking up gossip along the way.

"I hear tell Jonas Swanson got himself a job offer at a shipyard in San Francisco," Irv said. He'd brought them four sash windows, all with pulley and cord problems, and one interior door abused with layers of cheap paint in colors never seen in the rainbow. "Maeva told you about that, Hauk?"

Hauk gave his head one shake and slid his hammer into the loop on his carpenter's apron. "Maeva talks about her mother and the boy, but she keeps Jonas out of the conversation." That wasn't the whole truth. She'd mentioned Jonas's increased drinking, her mother's concerns.

"Change of scene might be good for the man," Irv said. "Good for Mrs. Swanson, in the bargain, seeing as the man isn't much help with the wee babe."

"True enough," Hauk said.

"There's other news might be of more importance to you two," Irv said, once the windows had been unloaded and looked over. "Farley Price is pouring beer at a Bremerton joint. Breeze Inn, there at the end of Pacific. Sailor hang-out."

Lang's eyes narrowed to slits. "You seen him there yourself?"

"That I have, eyeball to eyeball. He could stare down a statue. 'What's your pleasure?' he said to me, without so much as a decent blink. 'A look-see with my own two eyes,' I said. 'Checking out hearsay.' 'Move along if you're not drinking,' he said. I gave him a nod. 'Glad to know your whereabouts, Price. Makes things a whole lot easier for me and my friends.' 'You and your friends be warned,' he said. 'Stay out of my way when I come for my wife.' 'That's her call,' I said, 'though you're in the wrong neck of the woods. She's long gone.'

"I meandered out on that note. Scoured the streets and parking lots ten blocks each direction, all but toward the water being as there's but one block that way, and never saw one automobile that wasn't black."

"He could have painted his, you consider that?" Lang said.

"Considered it good and hard. Looked over every coupe stem to stern, three in all, and none of them had the right license plate or the right smell."

Hauk studied the kitchen wall where he intended to hang open shelves until he could craft some decent doors, giving Lang time to loosen his fists and get the blood out of his eyes.

"Might not need to be in quite so much hurry to bring Eleanor and Hannah out here. Might want to deal with Price first."

"What do you have in mind?" Irv said.

Lang picked up a wood scrap and punted it out the door opening. "Take him out deer hunting."

"That'd work." Hauk let his reply hang out there while he kept his eyes on his brother. "Be a shame, though, to rot in jail over the likes of Farley Price."

"You got a better idea?"

"Not yet. Give me a couple minutes to think." It was the news he'd been hoping for. Price out in the open, his whereabouts more or less known. It gave them something to work with. Chances were good the man would stay put and wait for an opportunity to waylay his wife and child. He and Lang, along with Irv, the Romstads and a few others, needed to set up the opportunity.

After something less than two minutes, he said, "First off, one or another of us needs to hang around the Breeze every now and then. Get to know the man's hours, where he goes after work, where he's living. No need to be secretive. Let him know we're out and about."

Lang pursed his lips. "See if he spooks, is that what you're thinking? Get him to stand his ground or run?"

Hauk nodded and held back a grin. He'd taken his thought out of Lang's head and given it air.

"And if he stands his ground, what then? A little discussion, man-to-man?"

"That'd be your call, seeing as you're the older of us."

Lang took a turn studying the walls. "Okay, we'll give it a try. There's still plenty time to make another plan, need be. Might as well carry on here, consider finishing the roughed-in bathroom."

Hauk had drawn plans for two-bedrooms, bath between, and a decent size living room. They intended to hang a door on the bathroom and leave it closed until they could rustle up fixtures. He had the layout in mind for Eleanor and Hannah, but he didn't want them back in Burke Bay while the Farley Price matter remained unsettled.

Hauk and Lang discovered where Price lived that night when they sat in Lang's truck and watched the Breeze Inn. Price locked up about midnight, climbed stairs attached to the back side of the building, and unlocked another door.

"You notice how he stumbled on those steps?" Lang said.

"I noticed."

"You suppose that's due to sampling the wares? Or big feet?"

"Could be either," Hauk said. "Could be a flask he carries."

"A flask? Yeah, I'd put my money on the flask, if I were a betting man. Dang! I never much liked taking on a man who nips all day."

The next morning the brothers gave themselves the gift of a leisurely breakfast fit for working men: bacon, eggs, fried potatoes, plenty of toast and jam, a second pot of coffee. That second pot elevated the morning to a celebration of sorts and came in handy when Irv arrived, hungry for news of their night's adventure, gentleman enough to let them make him a couple pieces of toast, though chances were good Ilsa had fed him.

Hauk ran the pumice stone over the stove top, sprinkled fresh salt, cut two thick slabs of bread, and tended to toasting while Lang told the story. He delivered the toast on a china plate from a set Ilsa gave them and poured hot coffee all around. Irv slathered butter and blackberry jam on the toast before letting them know what more he had on his mind.

"I figure it's time to commiserate. Eleanor spoke to me about getting a divorce. Maybe she aired that thought when we were all together, it's getting hard for me to keep conversations sorted these days. Ilsa says it's time we get Maeva involved in researching the particulars of Eleanor's wishes, given none of us know much about the legalities. Astrid and Ebbe are of like minds."

"You figure Maeva can find all the particulars in the library?" Lang asked.

"I know Maeva well enough to trust she'll go to a lawyer, need be." Irv started on his second piece of toast.

"Talking to a lawyer could cost some money," Hauk said.

Irv nodded. "I've got some cash money I mean to press on her. And if that don't work, Maeva being the stubborn Swede she is, Ilsa's got a backup plan. Feed for the cows, sacks of flour, whatever else Swansons order, gets delivered to the farm without a bill attached."

Lang ran a hand over his face, a clear sign thoughts were falling into place inside his head. "I'll pay for the divorce itself, if Maeva can get things rolling."

"I'm in for half on that," Hauk said.

"Neither one of you is putting up a penny," Irv said. "Me and Ilsa have that covered."

Lang shot Hauk a look; Hauk raised his eyebrows and listened to his brother answer for both of them.

"We can agree to that only if there's something we can offer in fair trade."

"There will be. I'm thinking of starting up a saw or two in the mill, just to stay in practice. Keep them oiled up, so to speak."

Hauk saw Lang grin at that, and felt his own face muscles stretch a bit. Irv needed saws sharpened about as much as fish needed wings. "We're you're men for that job," he said. They shook hands all around. Norwegian business, they called it. Things had a way of evening out, maybe sooner than later, given Irv's next thought.

"Could be we'll want to cut some of Trigg's logs, buy ourselves more land here and there, put up houses and rent them out to folks who move here to take jobs in the Yard when they start hiring again."

"You see that day coming soon?"

"Not soon, maybe, but one of these days. Won't hurt to own the land and have the building underway when it comes. I've been pondering on Emil and Axel Jenson going in to land transportation. Figure we should be ready to provide homes for those they're expecting to ride their buses."

That afternoon Hauk waited in the schoolyard for Maeva. He noted a slump in her shoulders, slowness in her approach. She trudged across the muddy parking lot in a steady November rain, settled into his car on the passenger side with a sigh, said she wasn't up to a driving lesson that afternoon though she appreciated the ride.

"I'd be glad to drive you home every afternoon, Maeva."

She shook her head, her face turned away from him as though she were watching the view from the passenger's window. Fighting tears, he suspected. He drove in silence, uncertain how to broach the subject of divorce research. They'd crossed the plank road and climbed Indian Hill before she spoke.

"Jonas is on his way to San Francisco. You may have heard there's a chance he could take a job in the shipyard there."

"I heard."

"You haven't heard the rest. He wants me to adopt Anders. Not just help Mom rear him, but adopt him as my own with all the rights and responsibilities of parenthood."

"No, I hadn't heard that."

She made a sound much like a baby calf separated from its mother, a sound he'd heard often in his childhood. "He doesn't know where his future may lead, he doesn't want the financial burden just now. The way Jonas sees it, there's no real cost to bringing up a child on our farm. Jonas needs his money to maintain his house in Bremerton for the time being and pay rent while he's in California—if he takes the job."

Hauk's thoughts weren't fit to speak. He shifted into third gear at the top of the hill, placed his hand on Maeva's arm and glanced her way. "And what are your wishes?"

"My wishes? I wish my brother loved his son. Don't children deserve a father who loves them?" She wiped her fingers across her cheeks. "I'll see to Anders, of course, there's no question. Mom and I together." After the silence of another mile, she said, "Jonas gave me a notarized letter that declares me legal guardian of Anders until such time as an adoption can be finalized."

"Did you agree?" He knew without asking but wanted to keep her talking.

"Yes. To protect Anders, should medical or other needs arise. To save him from being given away to someone else. To save him from knowing the truth about his father."

They reached the Swanson-Jenson Road before Hauk sorted out the anguish underlying the matter. "You didn't know your father, did you?"

"No."

The word pierced the air. Hauk parked, watching Maeva without staring at her. He wanted to ask how Axel responded to the news. He wanted to offer his help in rearing Anders. He wanted to speak of his feelings for her, but he knew better. It wasn't time.

Maeva stared at the windshield. "What if Jonas changes his mind? What if he remarries and the new wife wants the child? Does he just march in with another notarized paper that takes Anders back? I looked into the law a bit. He'd have that right unless there's a legal adoption sanctioned by a court. I'd need to be married for that to happen, and I'm not giving up my teaching career, not even for Anders. Right now, I wonder why any woman in her right mind would want to be married."

Holding his tongue earlier had served him well. "I want to offer you comfort, Maeva, but I'm not much good in that department."

She squeezed his hand, smiled a bit. "You are a comfort. You listen without scoffing. I've never seen a demeaning look on your face, or on Lang's. I'm sorry to burden you. I didn't mean to, and I don't intend to broadcast my anger at Jonas to all of Burke Bay. Word will get out soon enough that I have legal guardianship of Anders. Those who know Jonas will form their own opinions."

Hauk sandwiched her hand between his two. "You've honored rather than burdened me. I had a favor to ask of you. Another legal matter."

"About Eleanor? About getting a divorce?" She smiled. "Don't look so stunned. Eleanor mentioned that in the letter you brought me. She said she didn't know how to proceed."

"That makes asking easier, though I'd decided I could do some research myself. You're coping with enough."

"I have a letter almost ready to send to her. She needs to file on the grounds of *Cruelty of Treatment*. She can give notice of no support requested, if she chooses. She has to declare an address of legal residence. I think she should use the Romstad's cabin address for that. The big problem is stating Farley's address, which she will also need."

"That's no longer a problem," Hauk said. "Farley Price has let himself be found."

38

~ Colored Up Whiskey ~

Now they were into November with rain enough to fill wells and barrels stuck out under eaves, Orval's spunky little wife didn't have to sell water. He'd figured that was a good thing until she took to gallivanting up and down the valley, visiting those she'd met. She named them off like a school child reciting her lessons, bandying about facts he didn't much care to know. It seemed any number of husbands had the gout, attacks of the gallbladder or dropsy. Worse news, Thelma made it her business to hand out advice to the wives on dietary adjustments to keep those husbands up on their feet tending to farm matters.

"Now what would you be knowing about any of that, Thelma? You never took up a nursing course."

"I know plenty, Orval Blevins, and you'd do well to listen to some of my knowledge. I got it from my granny, who tended to folks from Seabeck to Holly and inland to Crosby. She wrote it all down in her book."

With that she took down a hatbox she kept on the highest kitchen shelf and lifted out her favorite receipt book, its cover made of tablet-back cardboard, its pages strung together with gardening twine. He'd always figured it for a heap of stained pages, some loose and ratty at the edges, most not decipherable to untrained eyes, yet somehow the secret to Thelma's pie crusts and gingerbread, and such.

"Here," she said, opening the mess to a section marked by a cardboard divider, surrounded by a grayed, stretched-out garter.

"Granny wrote right here about foods that cause gout. Clams and clam chowder, oysters and oyster stew, anything overly full of cream and butter. Rich foods, she called them.

"And here's her remedies. 'Chew a piece of horseradish root or garlic. Make up tea of mustard, meadowsweet and comfrey. Eat buds of the quaking aspen. Past spring, when buds are gone, boil the leaves and bark. Nettle soup's powerful but needs care in gathering. Eat raw nettle leaves only in springtime.'"

"Hmm." Orval gave some thought to looking through the mess for liquor receipts. He'd heard tell Thelma's granny did some whiskey making for loggers out to Seabeck. Of late, he and Thelma had come to an understanding. She knew he'd set up his operation somewhere; he knew she expected him to keep it apart from the family. The fact that it paid the bills gave her no never mind.

"Your granny write any notes in there about coloring up whiskey?"

She heaved a sigh that hurt him like she'd punched him in the gut, shaking her head to show how upset she felt over the whole matter. He backed up a step. He shouldn't have asked the question. She gave him plenty time alone to go through that old hat box full of receipts.

"You've come up against the fact that whiskey sales will soon be legal. It's in the paper all the time, but you're still counting on selling moonshine."

"Now, Thelma, I haven't said a word about such a business. I was just making conversation, showing an interest in your granny."

The baby kicked up a fuss about then, best sound he'd heard all morning being as Thelma needed to turn her attention. She went off, talking over her shoulder, telling him to put his efforts into a water company. Way he figured, that's what he'd been doing all along. Good water made good product. Only problem, Farley Price had told him folks wanted whiskey that looked and tasted like the real thing.

He went on about his business more carefully than ever, driving off south from his place so's to make it look like he was headed for Bremerton, then circling around through Burke Bay proper to drive toward Keyport and circle back. Took more gas for the truck but eased Thelma's suspicions. He kept to that practice daytime and nighttime both, just in case.

He got color in one run by heating sugar to a nice golden color and adding it. To his mind, it gave his product a pleasant taste. He tried charring up some wood, dropping it still smoldering into an old wash tub and pouring his product over it. Scotch whiskey, he called it, and aged it a day or two in the bargain before corking up bottles. Seemed to him he lost a fair amount of liquor to that charred wood, thirsty as an old miner at day's end.

He burned himself more'n once in the production and took time to cuss out the government for messing up decent folks' lives with rearranged laws. Unfair practice, government taking away a man's business just like that. Prohibition made good sense, far as he was concerned. Gave the little man half a chance. Price said he had customers looking at cost comparisons, sales should continue with color and taste adjustments.

Yessiree, Orval had things humming along well enough. Good soil for growing grain and a good harvest this fall, couple cows on the place for milk, a gentleman's trade agreement with Walt Strom that sent ham and bacon to the Blevins family, and a clever little wife who kept the family fed and in decent clothes. He'd reel her in a bit on the visiting business in time. Better to tread lightly in that department.

He'd been treading lightly with Farley Price since their meeting at the Maple Leaf Tavern two or three months back. The man stuck to his end of their bargain, showed up with cash money, and sober enough to lend peace of mind to the exchange. Still and all, Orval stayed alert to signs, not just from Farley, and danged if he didn't come on a worrisome one on the full of the moon.

He sensed something not right when he drove on out of Hidden Valley Cemetery to head home for a little shut-eye. He hadn't traveled far enough to shift out of low gear when he came upon a pickup parked halfway in the ditch the other side of the road. A Chevy truck, could be a 1925 model, front bumper a length of wood. Two-by-four chunk, bolted on.

Orval drove on by slow enough to give the truck a good once-over, and felt the hair on the back of his neck stand up to take notice. The truck cab had a replacement roof, the bed a tarp cover. Could be a poacher out looking to bag a deer; could be a man out looking to raid a still. Or worse, a revenuer out to make an arrest.

Orval eased into second gear and drove on by. When he reached the valley road, he put his truck in third and drove like a bat out of hell. He'd heard his grandpap use that phrase more'n once and got himself a good firsthand reckoning what it meant.

He sped right on past his own place, on over to Silverdale, then to Bremerton, one eye on the rearview mirror the entire time. No truck came up behind him; no vehicle of any sort pulled out of side roads. He eased up to the curb alongside a waterfront dive, left the engine idling and pulled off his right boot to give his foot a good scratching.

If that Chevy pickup held revenuers, they'd let him run so they could put their energy into stealing his product and busting up his equipment. They'd know where to find him when they wanted their pound of flesh. Even if he boarded the first ferry to Seattle and headed north to Canada, they'd have the law on the lookout.

Somehow, the revenuer idea didn't quite jibe. They'd have a whole passel of men if they were out to bust up an operation—plenty enough men to do the busting and bringing down the operator. No, by golly, that parked pickup wasn't there on government business. More'n likely it was there to do some thieving. He shoved his foot back into its boot, pulled his deer rifle out from behind the seat, made a U-turn and headed for home. He had a wife and children to protect. He'd done that already, come to think of it, when he drove on by his place. Now he'd had time to mull over the situation, he'd go on home and take a stand.

"Thelma," he said, soon as he'd downed a cup of coffee, "there's something in the wind. To be on the safe side, you might want to gather up some clothes and things, and take yourself and the young ones on down to Strom's place for a few days." He'd bolted the doors, front and back, checked the window latches and had his rifle at the ready.

She turned from poking pabulum into the baby's mouth to give him a narrowed-eye look that darn near made him grab up his gun for protection.

"You come dragging in here at the crack of dawn, pack your rifle with you to the outhouse, you think I don't notice? I'm not going off to Strom's or anywhere else. Soon as Teddy's fed and bathed, I'll get granny's twenty-two out of the closet and sight it in. Nobody's getting near my babies. You take your fights elsewhere, you hear?"

She gave him a look meaner than a bobcat's before he so much as had time to rev up for his usual *Now, Thelma.*

"Fill your belly with the oatmeal I cooked and get yourself some sleep. From the looks of you, you're likely to shoot off a toe trying to get your gun raised."

Orval took his feisty little wife's advice, fell into bed determined to sleep with one eye and both ears open. He figured his old grandpap would put in his two cents worth. Soon as he called the old man to mind, he knew chances were good no one would come poking around his place, least not in the light of day. Once he'd slept a bit, he'd make a trip out past the cemetery, sniff the wind, take his time.

After a decent dinner, in spite of a go-round with Thelma regarding his occupation, Orval set out on his round-about route. Not much going on down to the bay. Couple lights on in the mercantile, three cars parked catawampus at the tavern like they'd been sipping before they showed up. He meandered north toward Keyport, zigged here and zagged there on forgotten logging roads, coming up to a dead end in a gulch below the woods where he'd moved his distillery.

He got his truck turned around so it faced out and set out on shank's mare, rifle at his side, finger on the trigger. He moved slow and quiet, never once cursing blackberry vines, resting a good ten minutes once he made it within spitting distance of his operation. If any humans had been there, they'd left no tracks he could see or smell. He eased on in, got a match out of a covered fruit jar, struck it and saw all in order just as he'd left it.

He was caught up in congratulating himself when he noticed a piece of brown paper sack poking out from under his collecting vat. That set his heart thumping, making it tough to find a decent breath. The match burned his finger tips. He dropped it, ground it out, lit another and took up the paper. He'd seen the writing once before.

You help me find my wife, I'll help you keep this place hidden. Start with Irv Carlson, his woman friend, and her brothers. Bring word with the next delivery.

Orval backed up against a wall and leaned into it so hard it dang near set the small building on tilt. It took a good long while to figure out he needed to send his gallivanting wife on down to the bay to cozy up with Mrs. Bakke. Smart woman like Thelma could learn answers to Mrs. Price's whereabouts without ever asking questions. Smart man such as himself knew when to let his wife take charge of matters.

39

~ Forever Lost ~

One or more of Maeva's mother's friends had come every day since Cynthia's death to offer food and comfort, rock Anders, peg diapers on the line or warm a bottle. They knew before it was announced that the baby would remain at the Swanson farm to be reared by his grandmother and aunt, though the particulars surprised them.

"San Francisco? Imagine that." From them Maeva learned a valuable lesson. To understand men, listen to women who'd lived half a century or more. They'd married men and reared sons.

They cuddled Anders, whispering, *"Föräldralös."* Parentless. Though Maeva knew the word's meaning, its sound spoken by their quick Swedish-tongues, tricked her brain. *Forever lost,* her unspoken fear that Anders would become a lost soul without a parent to love him.

Her mother shed quiet tears for Cynthia and kept a hankie ready for those moments when they came unbidden, but she wept aloud the Saturday morning Jonas came to the farm to say goodbye, the morning before he would drive away to San Francisco to work on a secret project in the shipyards.

Alma Swanson spoke to her first born in Swedish, harsh words Maeva couldn't follow except for her own name, though the anger and disappointment behind them needed no translation. In Alma's world, a parent did not abandon a child. She spoke, walked from her kitchen to her bedroom, closed her door and cried.

Maeva pressed Anders's head to her shoulder and hummed to soften the sound of his grandmother's pain. "*Föräldralös*," she said. "Sweet little boy." And to Jonas, in a whisper, "Go, then. Go have your life." She'd spent all the energy she could muster on him earlier in the woodshed, where she'd hoped for a reasonable discussion away from their mother.

"Cigarette?" he'd said, extending his pack of Lucky Strikes.

She attributed that to his inebriated state; he knew she didn't smoke. Sulfur from the ignited match drifted on the chilly air. The match fell, still burning. Smoke rose from wood chips purposely gathered and loosely piled, a mound she hadn't noticed when she'd entered the shed. Sulfur gave way to burning pitch and cedar. Jonas held her at arm's length.

"Burn the damn place. Funeral pyre for my wife," he said, words slurred.

She kicked at his shins, stomped on the sputtering flames. "Damn you, Jonas, damn you to hell!" Her tongue, unaccustomed to such words, spoke other words. "Deserter, duty shirker, drunkard."

She made a fist when he jerked her sleeve, swung upward toward his chin, struck his Adam's apple. It staggered him long enough to get his attention, get him out of the woodshed and onto the bench under the cherry tree. She clenched her fingers, rubbed her wrist, flexed her arm to ease the ache that traveled to her shoulder.

Now Jonas stood at the kitchen door, a bitter man with hard hazel eyes reddened by whiskey. "Marry Axel so you can adopt the boy." He slammed the door, stomped across the enclosed utility porch, opened and slammed another door.

His alcohol breath lingered. Maeva settled in the rocking chair, determined to soften the scene for Anders sake. Tears ran down her face, dampening the flannel blanket she'd wound too tightly. He squirmed, fussed, soon howled his displeasure at being bound.

"Never mind, little one." She unwound the blanket and dried her eyes with a corner warmed by the baby's body. "You'll own this farm one day. So says the father who just walked out of your life."

Jonas presumed he, as first born, would inherit the land their father acquired before he sent for their mother. The land, house, barn, woodshed and all that grew in the soil belonged to their father and, since his death, to Jonas. So he believed.

But he was wrong. The recorded deed, written in English, declared Alma Swanson owner by widowhood. Her will, written by a Bremerton attorney, declared, "Share and share alike," with the names of her four children recorded in her hand, dated and notarized.

Her mother emerged from her bedroom, eyes dry but puffy, and went straight to the old stove to build up the fire. "*Kaffe*," she said, grinding a handful of beans. She sliced bread for sandwiches, set out ingredients for gingerbread, sifted, added eggs, mixed.

"We bake in the old stove." She reclaimed the kitchen in less than an hour and sent messages by strength of her will and wind-carried scents to her friends along the beach. They came, wrapped against the November chill in layered sweaters, shawls over their heads. One, then another, held Anders and sang snippets of old country tunes.

"I'm going upstairs, Mom." Maeva left them to their Swedish conversation, their coffee and sugar cubes and gingerbread heaped with fresh whipped cream. She left so her mother could share her sadness with friends who understood, without censoring what she said for her daughter's sake.

In her room, Maeva took up the letter she'd been writing to Eleanor, the friend who fulfilled her needs just as those women downstairs fulfilled her mother's. The letter had grown to several pages over the weeks she'd been writing. She'd started it to explain divorce law, to name attorneys who would take such a case, to say she trusted Eleanor would follow her own good sense in the matter of Lang Nordlund.

She wrote now about Cynthia, the changes visited on her mother and herself, the fears she harbored about her inadequacies as a mother-substitute. She filled a page with the scene with Jonas, another with Axel's impatience with the situation, as though she had orchestrated it and could change it if she wished. In spite of no interest in Anders and irritation at Jonas, Axel showed up nightly for dinner or dessert and cuddling in front of the fire. Some nights she needed the cuddling, the respite from all she couldn't change.

After some pondering she added another sentence to the long letter.

"I wish you were here, settled again in Burke Bay where we could walk and talk."

A chill climbed her spine and slid down her arms as though her wish forebode danger. She set paper and pen aside, wrapped her favorite quilt tight, and tried to grasp a thread of the scene that flashed before her eyes. A layered scene: Farley Price, dressed in his long, black coat; the school building; Burke Bay viewed from the dip where Dock Road crossed Whiskey Creek.

That evening Nels came home with a message from Irv Carlson and Ilsa Bakke: They were ready to send the letter.

"I'm guessing you know what that means," Nels said, "and I'm further guessing I know what it means, myself. You have a letter to send to Eleanor and Irv is the mailman."

She made a concerted effort to nod without grinning, moved pots and pans on the stove while Nels ran the milk separator and their mother fed Anders mashed peas and carrots followed by applesauce. "Poor little Anders," she said, to cover her discomfort. "Peas and carrots without salt to make them tasty."

"We add good butter," her mother said.

Nels stepped out of the cool room. "And the rest of the message is Hauk will come over tomorrow afternoon to collect you for some sort of secret meeting at Mrs. Bakke's. They must be ready to bring Eleanor out of hiding."

~

They gathered in Ilsa Bakke's living quarters at the back of the mercantile: Ilsa and Irv, Astrid and Erling, Ebbe and Helmer, Hauk and Lang, Maeva. The room's windows looked over Burke Bay, east to the dock, south to the plank road and Indian Hill. The mercantile had been built against a slope with storage below.

Seaweed deposited by a high tide and odd bits of flotsam dotted the muddy earth that served as Ilsa's back yard. Irv's fishing boat floated alongside a raft of logs owned by Trigg Nordlund, though official word in Burke Bay was they belonged to Irv and would soon be unleashed and floated under the wood bridge into the mill lagoon.

Ilsa called them to the large table covered with a crocheted cloth. Maeva's heart beat a little fast; her underarms were moist. They were here to make a decision that could alter many lives.

Fine china cups and plates graced the table. Platters of cookies, bread, butter, jam, cream and sugar hid the cloth's center pattern. Ilsa poured coffee. "Pass the cream, Irv, it's fresh today. A little cream lightens the coffee, a little sip lightens the mood."

All at the table used cream. Ebbe and Astrid added sugar. Spoons settled on saucers. Irv dipped a cookie in his coffee and winked at Maeva. "Eleanor and Hannah are with Trigg Nordlund. No need to know just where that might be. I'll drive out tomorrow with your letter. Once Eleanor's read your legal advice, I'll do her bidding. She's in good health, body and mind both. She's ready to come home."

Astrid's eyes settled on Maeva. "Home's the cabin, same as before."

"Far as any are concerned, it is," Erling said. "They won't be spending their nights there, though none but us will know the truth of the arrangements. Most of their things will be in the cabin, should anyone choose to snoop."

Ilsa looked at her brothers, then around the table, her eyes stopping on each person as though she were counting them. "We're following the plan, more than less, that Irv and my brothers devised two months back. Hauk and Lang finish building the house beside their pond for Trigg and Millie and their wee babes. Lang helps Trigg move the rest of his logs and get them anchored here in the bay. When all's ready, Eleanor and Hannah move home to the Romstad's cabin, but they sleep at Lang and Hauk's, with one or the other of those boys, or sometimes Irv, keeping watch through the dark hours.

"Eleanor goes back to work in the tavern, but she's never to be alone. Hannah and Richard, Trigg and Millie's first-born, start school. Helmer and Ebbe pay close attention to the school just as always. I keep both ears open to gossip that wanders into the store."

Irv cleared his throat. "You can see, Maeva, we prepare for the worst. Farley Price will come looking for Eleanor and Hannah, we know that truth. We'll be ready. We've got the law on our side, though little help expected, given we're so far out in the country."

Maeva's coffee had gone cold. The layered scene she'd experienced in her bedroom the day before visited her again. She shivered, rubbed her arms, caught Hauk's eyes on her and had the odd sensation that his hands did the rubbing. His eyes softened, hinted at a smile. She lowered her head, felt heat in her cheeks that seconds ago seemed pricked by a thousand icy needles.

"There's one more thing I'll be passing along," Ilsa said. "Thelma Blevins came visiting the other afternoon, without her babies, mind you. 'Orval sent me,' she said, 'with orders to poke and probe as to what's going on with Eleanor Price and her child, but I'm the straight forward type. He's had a note from Farley Price, left off at Orval's place of business.'" Ilsa paused while Irv refilled her coffee cup. "She allowed that I'd be knowing what business she meant, and I agreed I was wise to the facts of that matter.

"'To my mind, it's a threat,' Thelma said. 'Farley wants information on the whereabouts of his wife and daughter in trade for keeping Orval's business private. What I've told Orval remains between him and me, though you can likely guess my thoughts on that whole mess. I'm just passing this much along to you for the sake of all concerned. Farley Price is lurking about, leaving off a note that mentioned Irv Carlson by name, and you and your brothers by relationship.'"

Around the table, eyes narrowed, mouths pursed. Maeva waited until she could wait no longer. "Filing for divorce is only the first step. Farley must be served with legal papers that advise him of the action before anything is really in motion. There's a long wait, a hearing so both parties can speak before a judge." She didn't say the rest, the troubling notion that divorce wouldn't stop Farley Price from mayhem and abuse.

Irv looked directly at Maeva. "Eleanor will see a lawyer soon as I can make such arrangements. Farley will be served soon after that as papers are readied. Some of us will take it upon ourselves to speak to him so we know he's informed that he's not welcome in Burke Bay. Once that's done, we're bringing Eleanor home to stand her ground. That's her wish, we've made our plans. It's the best we can come up with."

"Might want to give more thought to the school matter," Hauk said. "To Hannah and Richard starting school soon as they're settled. Price is a drunkard. His daughter makes an easy mark. So does Maeva. Might be we'll need to offer the school lessons in one or the other of our homes for a time."

"Hauk's right on that count," Helmer said. "Me and the missus need to take turns stationed at the school house. Ebbe's got her own gun and she'd not be afraid to use it."

Little laughs, along with nods, circled the table. Maeva smiled with the rest, a weak smile forced past the uncertainty of whether Helmer spoke in jest or seriousness. She'd like to think he had a sense of humor but the mental picture of Ebbe, or anyone armed with any sort of gun and on alert at the school, was too foreign.

Ilsa said, "My little brother is right. He's a wise one, is Hauk. The school bears close watching. Irv, you and the boys sort that out, but you keep guns out of sight."

Again, agreement all around, more coffee and cookies, Irv's comment that he might open the mill, cut a little lumber, have the brothers build another boat or two, another house or two. Maeva listened, hearing only bits and pieces. In her thinking, Hannah needed to return to school the very day she and her mother returned to Burke Bay. She needed normalcy back in her life.

She argued her point with Hauk on their drive back to the Swanson farm. Or more accurately, while she preached her view, he glanced her way with a set look about his mouth and no warmth whatsoever in his eyes.

"I can't imagine Hannah living so close and not returning to school," she said for the umpteenth time when Hauk stopped the car in the upper pasture. She turned to face him, took his arm in her hand, gave it a tug and put a little pepper in her tone. "I just can't imagine it, and I cannot permit guns on the school grounds."

Hauk looked at her so long without saying a word that she had half a notion she'd need to shake him to get him to hear. Finally, he took her hands, one and then the other, and rubbed his thumbs across her knuckles.

"It's a complicated matter, Maeva. Balancing danger and security for the children, and for you. The fact is, I've grown to love you. That aside, I won't let you be placed in unnecessary danger."

Her mouth opened but no words came. She'd been thinking about her chapped knuckles, and he'd declared his love.

40

~ Two Houses on Whiskey Creek ~

*H*auk had declared himself, watched a few tears spill and run down Maeva's cheeks, watched her swipe at them and smile in a way he'd describe as sweet, though that word seemed far too passive to associate with her.

"Love?" she said. "What is it? How do you know what you feel is love?"

He pondered her question and found himself making a speech. "I feel like smiling when I'm near you. I think about you while I'm working. It saddens me that I have too little to offer you, though I want to share what I have—time and help in rearing Anders, regardless of your decision about marriage."

She let a sound escape, almost a laugh. "Axel wants nothing to do with Anders."

"Well then." He left it at that, uncertain how to proceed. He'd declared himself, offered what he could, and gotten stuck.

Her brow knit in the way he'd come to recognize as thought-sorting; she fixed him with a worried look and spoke in a whisper.

"You've become such a trusted friend, Hauk. I don't want talk of love to get in the way of friendship."

He gave that a few beats. "Seems to me one is an important part of the other."

"Is it?" She looked at him with tilted head and surprise in her eyes, and placed the palm of her left hand on his face. "I'll give that some thought."

He walked her to the house, watched her with Anders, declined an invitation to stay for dinner and drove home wondering what she thought love involved. He'd gotten a look from Mrs. Swanson that told him she had him figured out. He wouldn't press for so much as courting privileges until he had ways and means to support her and Anders. The boy had become part of Maeva's life. Only a few days had passed since she'd said she couldn't understand why any woman in her right mind would want to be married. Still, he knew Axel remained in the picture.

He mentioned as much to Lang that evening when they were enjoying an after-dinner smoke and discussing the ins and outs of bringing Eleanor and Hannah back to Burke Bay. Each had a sharpened pencil in hand. Each had jotted notes on the tablet between them. Hauk figured how many feet of ogee molding he needed to cut to surround windows and doors, how much quarter-round to serve as baseboard. Lang noted shake requirements and chimney work.

"Goldarn Axel, he's got more than privilege on his side," Lang said. "Got the good looks women seem to like. Doesn't have the smarts though, not enough to suit Maeva in the long haul. I've watched her admire you a time or two when you spoke your thoughts about books you've read. More than a time or two when you put your carpentry skills to work on the Swanson house."

Hauk studied his pencil. It didn't need sharpening. Nothing to do but answer his brother. "She's known Axel all her life. Getting ahead of that is a steep hill to climb."

Lang nodded, took a final draw on his cigarette. "Come to think of it, you could be a few steps up that hill already. We've got a house here with a breakfast room she admires. You might tell her this house is yours alone. Offer it to her along with yourself living in it."

"House belongs to both of us," Hauk said.

"We've got another house that belongs to both of us, complete enough right now to keep out the rain. When time comes for choosing, one for you and one for me, which will you want?"

"Seems to me we're building the new one for Trigg and Millie."

"For a time. Trigg still wants us to put up a place for him on his Belfair property. Millie's keen on living there. Trigg's already moved wild rhodies and a dogwood tree onto that place for her."

"So, you've had the new place we're building in mind for yourself all along, now we know Eleanor's filing for divorce."

"Eleanor's still a married woman, but that would be my hope somewhere down the road."

Hauk shook his head. "Could be we're getting ahead of ourselves."

"Good idea to have that plan in place, same as the plan we're working on to protect Eleanor and Hannah when we move them back to Burke Bay," Lang said.

"How long you been cogitating this plan?"

Lang directed his gaze on Hauk. "Only recently. Been interested a year, though, give or take. Ever since that night I danced Eleanor around the tavern. How long you been looking fondly on Maeva?"

Hauk returned the look. "A day or two before that."

"A day or two, you say? How'd you get that much jump on me?"

"You can give Axel credit. You recall I went to the dock to meet the *Aggie J* when he needed a hand?" Lang nodded and Hauk went on. "Came eye to eye with Maeva that evening. That's all it took."

Lang pursed his lips. "Been taking some doing ever since."

"Could be time's on our side," Hauk said, hoping he was right.

41

~ Liquored-up Legger ~

Orval's old grandpap warned him about doing business with a liquored-up legger, and here he stood, boot toe to shoe tip with Farley Price, drunk as a boiled owl at four in the morning. Not that Price could stand. He leaned against the driver's side of the pickup with the two-by-four bumper, one and the same pickup Orval had saw that moonlit night not so long back. He pondered the whereabouts of the sand color coupe, though asking wouldn't be worth the breath it took.

"You're drunk," Orval said.

"Yeah, I had a few shots once my shift ended," Price said, words slurred, drool leaking from the corners of his mouth. "What's it to you?"

"I don't traffic with drunks."

Price dug in his overcoat pocket. "You don't traffic with me, you're out of business. I buy all you cook."

Orval shook his head and raised a hand to put a stop right then and there to any transaction, and found a pistol, not a wad of cash, waving in his face. Not even much of a pistol. "What the hell?"

"Make the transfer," Price said, words clear enough. "This delivery's on you. Last time we'll be doing business."

Orval knew a smart brewer never argued with a gun pointed his way, even when the gun was piss-ant size, and most particularly when the gun's holding hand flitted about like straw in the wind. He moved slow as a man could to the back of his truck, dug around in the load of farm rubbish, came out with a quart beer bottle, good size for swinging at a drunk man's head or hand, whichever made the better target. He heard the pistol's report, a pop more than a bang. His own good whiskey drenched his trousers.

"Told you sometime back, no puny bottles," Price said.

"Runnin' short of gallons," Orval said, voice none too steady, hand clasping the neck of the shattered quart, not much match for a gun. "Only had ten, rest are quarts."

"Unload the gallons two at a time," Price said. "Set 'em on the ground, then drive on out of here. Take the quarts back with you along with a message to Irv Carlson. Tell him I'm a good shot, drunk or sober, I'm saving a bullet for him."

Orval's feet itched so dang bad it took all his concentration to keep from wiggling out of his boots and taking up serious scratching then and there. He unloaded good product, ten gallons worth, not the end of the world, glass jugs a bigger loss than the whiskey itself.

He climbed into his truck, arms none too steady, legs cold and wet as a well digger's behind, and drove out of that secret meeting place. Seemed like old Grandpap sat there beside him, repeating his warning, while Orval wrenched his feet out of his boots.

Never argue with a pointed gun. Ain't no product worth dying over, boy.

Orval took care parking his truck once he made it to his place; backed clean into the stand of trees and tangle of berry vines so as to protect the fifty and some odd quarts of product still aboard, all colored up nice as you please. Now, where in tarnation was he going to unload fifty and some odd quarts?

He walked barefoot to the house, not minding the cold, damp ground. He peeled off his pants on the back porch where Thelma had a fancy wringer-washing machine hooked up—machine paid for by product sales—and dropped his socks atop his pants. After a few second's thought, he dropped his boots there, too. No money tucked in them and they'd need scraping to get rid of the mud.

He curled up on the overstuffed sofa Thelma had insisted on buying, his nerves still all frazzled, his head filled with good intents of figuring out what to do about his business. Next thing he knew there was an earthquake in the form of his fierce little wife tumbling him from his dreams onto the floor.

"Wake up, Orval Blevins, and explain the meaning of them stinking trousers of yours and the rest of that mess dumped on the back porch. And while you're at it, explain why your truck's backed into the berry vines and not parked out front where it belongs."

"Ow!" he said, working his way up to wakefulness.

"Never mind, it's not too hard to guess what's going on. You couldn't sell your product so you hauled it back here onto the very property where we're raising our babies. You get up and get it out of here or I'll turn you in to the sheriff myself."

Right on cue, the boy baby kicked up a fuss and the girl child took to whining.

"The man had a gun. Shot a bottle clean out of my hand. Coulda shot off my fingers or any number of other body parts." He gave thought to what body parts and pulled his knees up to his chest. Thelma started in again, but he spoke right over her, poured out the whole story, even the part about a bullet for Irv Carlson.

"That does it," Thelma said in a way that warned him his life was about to take a change, and quieted the children in the bargain. She stomped off to the kitchen. Maybe she meant to take up her gun and go after Farley Price herself. Half a minute later, dry pants and socks landed in his lap.

"Get yourself dressed and get that loaded truck off this property. Once that's done, you stop by Mrs. Bakke's store and tell your tale to Irv Carlson. While you're there, ask them where you might find work that's fit for a man with a wife and two babies."

Orval got himself dressed, his feet into mud caked boots, fired up the cranky truck and got out of there. He didn't much like hauling fifty quarts of whiskey back to his distillery in the light of day. He parked in the gulch below his building, hauled quarts of product uphill and got himself soaked clean through to the bone from all the wet trees and brush.

He knew he was a sorry sight when he walked into Mrs. Bakke's mercantile and asked the whereabouts of Irv Carlson. He smelled coffee brewing and bacon frying. His stomach grumbled.

"You been in a fight?" she said. "Or just drunk?"

"Now, Mrs. Bakke, I'm not a drinking man, no siree, though I sure could do with a cup of coffee."

She gave him a look that made him shift his feet once or twice, sort of like shifting gears to climb a hill. "Never mind that, just let Irv know I need to have a serious talk with him, man-to-man. Sooner the better."

"Let me guess," Mrs. Bakke said, eyes narrowed and hands on her hips. "You've had a run-in with Farley Price."

Now how in tarnation did she figure that out? "It's a matter for Irv, like I said. What might be a good time for me to drive back down here to meet up with him?"

Irv's voice carried out from somewhere at the back of the store. "Now's good a time as any. I'll bring you a mug of coffee, we'll go down to the feed storage room, leave Ilsa to her business."

Orval took close note of Irv loaded down with coffee mugs, cream pitcher, sugar bowl and spoons. He set the whole shebang on the counter where Mrs. Bakke tended to her customers. Orval took a mug, poured in cream, spooned in sugar, said his thanks and helped himself to a satisfying slurp, all the time studying Irv. The man was built thick through the chest and heavy in the belly, least aways that's how it looked with bib overalls up over a wool shirt.

They went out the main door, around the side of the building and down to the feed room. Irv unlocked a padlock, slid open the doors, found a switch and lit up the place. He waved a hand toward a stack of feed sacks. "Have a seat."

"No need, thanks just the same," Orval said. "I'll say my piece and get on back up to the valley. It's a message for you from the likes of Farley Price."

He made it brief, just the fact of Price saying he had a bullet meant for Irv, then somehow slid on in to telling where they met, the old truck with the two-by-four bumper, the bottle being shot out of his hand, how tough it was earning a decent living in these times. Might have kept more to the point if Irv hadn't kept nodding, encouraging like, through the whole sad story.

Irv rubbed his jaw up and down one side, then the other. "I been dropping in near every evening at the Bremerton tavern where Price works. Keeping an eye on him, so to speak. He's a bit upset over my helping his wife file for divorce. Full of threats, none of them pleasant to consider."

"Just so you know, he's got a gun up his sleeve," Orval said. "A puny pistol ain't much but it fires bullets all the same as something respectable."

"Oh, I've known that more or less for some time," Irv said. "You know, Blevins, you ought to take up a new line of work, times being what they are, whiskey sales soon to be legal, a man like Price on your behind. You might want to stop at Persson's farm and offer old Helmer help with his turkey harvest. He's having the devil's own time finding himself a decent hired hand. Might be good for you to do a neighborly deed. Comes in handy when you're wanting a deed done in return."

"I'll think on that," Orval said. "Right now I'd better get on home. Thelma will take to worrying."

"Be good for your wife if you got yourself out of the moonshine business before Farley Price or another like him pulls a gun again. Could be that some of us who have made it our business to deal with Price could use another man's help. Being close by at Persson's might be the very help we're looking for."

Orval nodded, unhappy with the conversation's direction.

"I expect you're handy with a gun yourself," Irv said. "Helmer and Ebbe Persson wouldn't be opposed to a hired hand with his own loaded gun at the ready in case Farley Price stops in to pay them a visit."

"Well, now, I can handle a gun. Not so sure about milking."

"You think on it, like you said. Give my regards to your wife. I expect we'll see her down here soon. She's taken a liking to Ilsa."

Orval nodded and headed for his truck. Dang his chatty little wife, she'd be the end of him doing business. If he had a business left, what with nobody to do the legging.

42

~ Moral Rectitude ~

$\mathcal{H}$auk had said he loved her. Maeva supposed he did, for he was a serious man who thought before he spoke. She'd meant to consider his words of love and friendship long into the night once she settled in her room. Instead, she fell asleep without worrying the fraying threads of the Swanson family's life, and slept better than any night since Cynthia's death.

Hauk waited after school the next day to give her another driving lesson. She'd expected to feel shy in his presence. To her surprise, she felt comfortable with him and behind the wheel of his car. She liked driving for the concentration it required.

She found herself hoping for a kiss, and got several separated by serious conversation. He walked her to the house, stayed for a cup of coffee, accepted a loaf of bread with proper thanks, and left shortly after Axel popped in.

That night she began a studied comparison of the two men—the manner of their appreciation for kindness extended by her mother when offering coffee, warm bread, a pleasant word. She compared all sorts of mannerisms before thinking about their kisses, both of which she'd sampled that afternoon and evening.

The reality of kissing two men the same day left her questioning her moral rectitude until thoughts gave way to feelings and her face muscles stretched into a grin. She enjoyed kissing, though promises that accompanied each man's kisses differed. She needed time to sort the differences. In the future, she would avoid kissing both on the same day.

The next several days she kissed neither, giving her brain time to work. Hauk stayed busy completing the small house he and Lang were building. Axel grumbled about Anders, working his way up to an ultimatum.

"I won't raise another man's child, Maeva. Make that clear to Jonas when he comes home for Thanksgiving. Either he moves back and sees to Anders himself, or he passes the baby along to Mrs. Hiram Smith, never mind her fox tails and bony chest."

Though she'd known how he felt, his words produced anger so profound she could have hit him with the fire poker. "Go home," she said. "Leave me to my life. Go find a woman who wants to be ordered around."

Axel waited on the *Aggie J* the next morning, grin in place, ready to be forgiven. She leaned away from his kiss, settled in the passenger hold, wrapped in worries. Jonas hadn't sent word of safe arrival or an address where he could be reached. Though her mother said little, her anxiety elevated each day.

Ebbe's news that morning drove other worries aside. "Orval Blevins showed up to our place and offered a hand with poking turkeys and dressing them out. Irv Carlson put him up to it, can you believe that one? The mister had some concerns, but Orval's a sober man for all that he's known for making whiskey. He's capable enough and don't complain half so much as Farley Price done about a little blood spattering his overalls. He's taking over for me on the milking, to boot."

"Orval Blevins?" Maeva's surprise pleased Ebbe.

"Not that Farley owned such a thing as overalls. He seemed above all that." Ebbe pushed straying gray hair away from her face. "But that's not the news that would be mattering most. Orval brought along his own shotgun and keeps it handy. I'm not knowing what all's been going on, but Irv's some riled up, so says Ilsa, and she's not one to pass idle gossip. Ilsa says we all need to keep the eyes in the back of our heads wide open."

"You mean when Hannah returns to school?"

"Then for certain, but now's none too soon. I'm betting Irv's gone and stirred up a hornets' nest, poking around in Bremerton like he's been doing."

That night Maeva passed along Ebbe's news to her mother, though she didn't mention guns.

"My," her mother said. Then, in mixed English and Swedish, she passed on truths Maeva had wondered about but never asked.

"Drink, it sometimes shows the truth hidden in the man. Jonas carried anger from the time he could walk and be sent out to feed the chickens. The same with your father all the years I knew him. Anger there, just waiting for an excuse. Drink too much, shout and throw things about, as if that makes life's problems disappear. Leave the mess and fall into bed."

"Our father drank too much?" She'd asked Jonas what he remembered, but his answers were vague. Eleanor had spoken of the anger Farley carried inside, and how it hid his truths.

"Not drink every day, like some we know," her mother said. "More like my own father in Sweden, and most all the uncles and neighbors. Save up sorrows and struggles for the weeks' end, drink too much and shout at those who have no choice but to listen. There were others who could drink, take up song and dance, at least while out in company."

"Axel's like that," Maeva said.

"Yes, like his father. Shouting or laughing, it doesn't much matter. Someone suffers."

"Wives," Maeva said. "Wives suffer."

"And children," her mother said. "Always, the children suffer the parents. Look at our wee Anders."

On Monday of Thanksgiving week, Maeva herded students through wind and rain that plagued late November days to the playground shelter for afternoon recess. Fresh air and exercise. This year's seventh and eighth grade students found recess boring. She missed Wesley Wiley.

Fifth and sixth grade boys, always a boisterous group, tried to outdo one another with gory tales of turkey slaughter, imitating noises they claimed to hear from Persson's farm. They whooped and hollered, hacked the air with sides of their hands and bragged about chopping off turkeys' heads. She tried to hush them and placate girls who complained that one boy or another hit the back of their necks and said, "Gobble gobble, you're dead, get ready for the oven."

"Children, let's remember the meaning of Thanksgiving. It's not about killing turkeys; it's about giving thanks for abundance and sharing."

"Thanks to God," Virginia Holmes said. "You left out the part about God, Miss Swanson.

"Of course, Virginia. Children, did you all hear?" They paid no attention. Virginia remained an annoyance, an unpopular child.

A tree branch snapped. Maeva turned from Virginia, scanned the woods beyond the playground, turned back to count heads. A year ago, Wesley, with Ralph Strom following, had gone off in the woods while she'd been distracted, and returned with the quart jar of home brewed beer.

No missing children this day; no wind strong enough to bring down branches. Still, she had an eerie feeling that she and the children were being watched, a sense of Farley Price, dressed all in black. She scanned the woods again, determined to drive his image from her mind. He stepped out from behind an old cedar tree, stood for a moment with hands in the pockets of his long black coat, and disappeared.

Disappeared, or dissolved? Real or nothing more than an apparition borne of worries?

"Children," she called, her voice sharp, her eyes focused on the tree she believed hid the man. She blew the playground whistle, three short tweets. What good was a weak whistle? "Children, we are returning to our classrooms immediately. Line up and go. Go now, no questions, no protests."

Some turned alarmed faces her way, likely hearing fear over the authority in her voice. They trusted her to be fair about recess. She rushed them toward the front of the building, wishing for real eyes in the back of her head, though she didn't need them. She felt the presence behind her, felt fear give way to fury. She would march the children into the building, lock the front doors and classrooms, and ring Miss Truax's bell until it drew attention at Persson's. Children, their curiosity aroused, turned to look behind them. She saw shock on their young faces, heard their gasps and odd sounds.

"Run!" she said. "Run and do not stop. Lock the doors. Tell Miss Truax to ring the bell."

They ran. She stopped and swung to face Farley Price, her stance meant to keep him from going any nearer the building. There they stood, her phantasm made real. The stench of alcohol surrounded him, a worse smell than lingered on Jonas the day he left for California. Stains honeycombed Farley's coat. He held a gun. She knew little about weapons. Though she'd never seen one quite so small, she assumed it worked.

"I want my wife. You tell me where she's hiding, I won't hurt you. You don't tell me, I shoot you and every child I can."

Though his voice rasped like a croaking bullfrog, his words were clear. Thoughts sharper than bullets pierced her brain and pounded behind her eyes. How many bullets could such a gun hold? If she fought and dodged and kicked, he might use them all on her. If she died, surely Jonas would come home to care for their mother and Anders. If not, Berta would step in. She opened her mouth, intent on calming Farley Price with words that showed she understood his sadness at the turn his life had taken.

But other words formed.

"Do you think shooting me will make your wife and child embrace you as a hero? Put that gun in your pocket if you wish to speak with me."

The school bell rang, clang clang clang, without pause, not the cl-clung when handled by Miss Truax. It rang loud and long.

"Now, listen here," Farley said, his saliva spewing her face, his breath so rancid it caused bile to rise to her mouth, "you and your friends are hiding my wife. She's my wife, I mean to . . ."

His next words went unheard, obliterated by a shot, surely the blast of a shotgun, not a pistol.

She waited for Farley Price to drop, for she'd felt nothing hit her.

Farley ran back the way he'd come, around the corner of the building toward the trail to the Nordlund's, coat hem flapping.

"Hauk! Lang!" She meant to shout, be heard through the trees, but the words slipped out as whispers, prayers for their safety.

Orval Blevins crashed through salal, Oregon grape and decaying maple leaves, yelling, "Price! Price!"

"Toward Nordlund's." She waved an arm.

Helmer Persson's truck, passenger door open, bounced through mud puddles and belched to a stop. Ebbe jumped out, rifle in hand. Helmer, with his own gun, followed Orval. The school bell clanged.

"The man is morally bereft," Maeva said to Ebbe, wondering if he'd always been so, or if being saturated in alcohol destroyed his rectitude.

43

~ Guns and Threats ~

When the gun shot sounded, Hauk was standing in a rowboat, jostling a hung-up log in the raft floating below their sister's store. Lang, in a separate rowboat, loosened cables that secured the raft. They worked with the incoming tide to herd logs from the center of the raft into the current that ran under the bridge to Carlson's mill pond.

"Shotgun!" Lang shouted.

They beached their rowboats, Hauk's on the south side of the bridge, Lang's on the north. Both ran for the truck. Hauk had more distance to cover and damaged legs that started every journey with stiffness, but he reached the truck only a heartbeat or two behind Lang.

"Could be somebody shot a turkey," Lang said, when the engine caught.

"Could be." Both knew better; both had expected an answering shot. Hauk shook his head, one shake, to dislodge the ugly picture his mind conjured.

The day before, while the brothers enjoyed a leisurely paced Sunday afternoon putting finishing touches on the new house, Irv Carlson drove in too fast, darn near right through the door, shouting before his truck quit chugging.

"Boys," Irv said, "better get ready for company. Ilsa's had a telephone call from Trigg. That down-on-its-luck pickup with the two-by-four bumper's been seen clean on out to Belfair. Word is its owner's been nosing around asking about a woman and girl. Asking for a Nordlund. Trigg got that news when he made a trip in for gasoline and gossip."

"Goldarn Farley Price." Lang punched his left palm with his right fist and kicked a couple rocks that needed to be raked away or lined up for a path.

Hauk gave the house a glance. "Better let the finishing go and get a move on cleaning."

They'd been at it nonstop ever since, sweeping up construction mess and washing windows so the small house would please the women, all while awaiting the afternoon incoming tide so Trigg's first log rafts could be moved to make way for one tied up at the bathing beach.

Hauk's first glimpse of the crowd standing in falling rain in front of the school got his blood flowing again. Helmer and Orval with guns; Maeva, surrounded by children, some crying, some jumping around playing guns with their arms. Maeva smiled his way. He gave a moment's thought to cutting through the children and gathering her up for a hug, but common sense, along with Lang's hand on his arm, stopped him from that foolishness. The community saw her as part of a couple with Axel Jenson. He had no right to put that picture on tilt in front of the entire school.

Helmer and Orval eased away from the children. Wind whistled through the trees between the school and Persson's farm. A few more leaves fell from the bigleaf maples. Maeva blew her playground whistle, arms waving children up the school steps.

"Figured you two would hear the shot," Helmer said. "Figured you'd come on foot from your place and get plowed into on the way by that fool Price."

Lang said, "We were down on the bay moving logs."

Helmer narrowed one eye. "Me and Ebbe come on the double in the truck and found Maeva staring off toward the trees. Blevins come through on foot."

"Fired in the air to warn him off," Orval said. "That piss-ant gun Price carries ain't much more'n a toy, but I can testify to the fact that it shoots real bullets." He lifted one booted foot and then the other. "Dang feet took to itching when that dang bell started up."

Helmer nodded. "Judgment call, shooting like you done. Maeva said it gave her the edge she needed since she took offense at the whole thing. Said she ordered Price to put the gun away if he wanted to speak with her, but he didn't pay her much mind till that blast went off. Ebbe's gone on inside the school to see to Miss Truax. Seems she upped and fainted."

Orval stirred up mud with his shifting feet. "Price took off so dang fast I couldn't get a bead on him. Persson said let him go, could be he'd run right into you two since he was heading back that direction. Said to wait for the rest of the men to help round him up somewhere off the school grounds."

"I figured on Irv Carlson and Erling Romstad at the least, and one or another of the boys from the garage," Helmer said. "Figured Nels Swanson woulda been here by now."

"Nels's out delivering feed somewhere for Ilsa," Lang said, "and John Anderson's either under a car or headfirst down inside one, and he's half deaf anyway. As for Irv and Erling, they drove on out to Tahuya this morning to give Trigg a hand."

Helmer fished a matchstick out of his shirt pocket and stuck it in his mouth. "You boys upping your time table some?"

Hauk gave a nod. "Thought we might get the new place finished and a stove hooked up in time to roast one of your turkeys for Thanksgiving dinner."

"Guess we ought to gather up our guns and comb the woods," Helmer said, "seeing as Price run off back behind the school. You boys locking up things these days?"

"It's locked," Hauk said. "But if you're asking, we've got a gun each in the truck."

Maeva wondered, as Helmer's truck rumbled down School Road, if Axel heard about the incident. She watched for him through the truck's slapping windshield wipers, saw him on the float alongside the *Aggie J*. He yelled at the children to hurry, though none needed to be told.

"I warned you, Maeva," he hissed, as he pulled her onto the bow deck. "You never listen and now look what's come of your friendship with that woman and her child. It's brought trouble to the school."

"That woman and her child are returning to Burke Bay tonight." She walked through the wheelhouse without explaining the rest of the story Helmer had related as he drove her and the South Bay children to the dock.

After dinner, Maeva settled her mother by the fire, Swedish newspaper and Bible in her lap. She'd managed to downplay the Farley Price incident until Nels came downstairs with a rifle that belonged to their father.

"*Gud i himmel,*" Maeva said, "put that back. We will not take up arms in our mother's home."

"All of Burke Bay is taking up arms, Maeva. I will take my turn guarding the school, the tavern, the dock, wherever."

"No guns. There's got to be a better way. Irv knows where Farley works. I'll go with him. We can talk to him together, offer him money."

Nels shook his head. "It's too late. Price is too far gone. You can't solve this one with words, Maeva."

"So you'll solve it with guns?"

Nels, a quiet young man, looked at her and nodded. "Farley Price held a gun aimed at you. You are my sister." He swiped at a tear.

Axel showed up about nine, looked at the closed door between the kitchen and living room, and asked if Anders was down for the night. He studied the long barrel rifle Nels had on the kitchen table, poked around in search of cookies or other dessert, and generally acted like an invited guest who'd parted with all present on good terms when, in fact, he'd left her at Wiley's Landing to see the children safely home while he continued to Jenson's Pier.

Axel and Nels talked about guns and posts. Maeva said, "I hope someone thinks about Hannah before they hunt down her father like he's a fox raiding the hen house."

Axel grabbed her wrist. "We're talking about a man who threatened you with a gun, for Christ's sake."

She pulled free. "Are you worried about my welfare, Axel? Or are you just mad at me?"

Axel's face darkened. He pounded a fist on the table. Gun parts jumped.

"What a stupid question. Of course it bothered me. If you'd listened to me in the first place, not taken pity on that woman and child . . ."

"Do not say another word about Eleanor. When I met her, I felt like I'd been given a rare gift, a woman who could become a life-long friend. I never had girl friends my age until I went to college, and then only two who came from similar circumstances. None of us had much time for friendship; we all had to work for room and board. In the time we had, I discovered what I'd missed. I've watched Mom's women friends since Cynthia's death. They got her through the bad days. They still do. I want a friendship like that."

Axel stood too close, breathing hard onto her face.

"Well, you'd better look elsewhere, Maeva, because we're not going to live in Burke Bay. Your position as my wife won't allow you to be bosom friends with a woman who cooks in a tavern."

Nels set the gun cleaning rod and cloth on the table, pushed back his chair and rose to stand between them. He put a hand on Axel's forearm.

"Take it easy. Maeva's been through enough for one day."

Axel pulled his arm free. "Your sister needs to get her head on straight if she's going to be my wife."

"Stop it," Maeva said. "Mom's in the other room."

Nels stepped back. "Maeva doesn't take well to threats. Maybe it's time you learned that, Axel. Maybe it's time you look elsewhere for a marionette."

Maeva's head jerked to look at Nels, over six feet tall. Thin. Wiry, some said. He was cleaning a gun to use for her protection while Axel tossed out threats and warnings.

"Go home, Axel," Maeva said. "I need to discuss matters with my family." Her mother and Anders could no longer be left alone.

44

~ Going Home ~

Over the months she'd been with them, Eleanor had learned to read Trigg and Millie's moods, even to sense their thoughts. She'd known before Trigg said, "Let the fire die out tonight soon as dinner dishes are washed," that they'd be leaving in the morning.

"We'd planned another week," Millie said.

"Lang and Hauk are ready, Millie." Trigg, with Richard at his side, disappeared into the darkness to take down clothes line, gather up the wash tub, decide whether to take or leave other items hanging on outside walls. Hannah and Tommy collected school supplies and items they'd used as toys, and arranged them in a cardboard box. Millie and Eleanor packed pots and pans in the oven; dishes, cups, glasses and eating utensils in two dishpans. They stacked clothes and towels in a blanket on Millie's bed and wrapped them like a present. They emptied cupboards, piling contents on the table.

"Do you think that's true? That Lang and Hauk are ready?" Eleanor asked. "Or do you think something's happened?"

Millie looked at Eleanor with narrowed eyes. "Something's happened. Trigg thinks he's helping matters by not saying. We'll have to wait for Irv to get the true story."

Nerves sent Eleanor to the outhouse every two hours through the night. She lay awake, Hannah's warm body against her back, waiting for dawn. She startled, and heard Millie's feet hit the bedroom floor, when Trigg came into the cabin before dawn with coffee brewed on the boat. The still steaming pot sitting on the cold stove and the mugs in their hands provided the only warmth they'd have that morning.

Trigg scrubbed a hand over his chin. "I'm keeping Richard with me, Millie, now no arguing. I need a hand aboard. We'll move out one more raft today. Jessie's coming out soon as he gets his gear together to keep watch here. He'll put up a tent out by the beach."

Millie's eyes closed for a moment too long for a blink. "I thought Jessie was helping move the rafts. I thought you went into Belfair to ask Jessie for help moving the rafts."

"We changed our plans a bit, what with the boys having the cabin ready and all."

Eleanor felt a chill start in her heart and travel to her hands holding a coffee mug. She looked at the dark brew and whispered, "Farley's around."

"Trigg?" Millie said.

Trigg looked at Millie, at Eleanor, at the window over the sink, back at Millie. "Aw, hell," he said, and gave his head a shake. "Jessie said someone's been poking around the garage and cafe asking questions. Said he drives a beat up old truck with a chunk of wood wired on the front. I called Ilsa. She put Irv on the phone. He and Erling Romstad will be here any time."

Loading the two trucks, Irv's and Trigg's, took forever, so it seemed to Eleanor who tried to keep Hannah, Tommy, and Connie occupied with stories of the Keane ranch and cowboys. Millie and Richard helped the men load everything that wasn't nailed down. Eleanor suffered waves of nausea. Her shaking hands dropped buttered and jellied bread on the needle-covered ground. She gulped in sea-scented air until the earth went on tilt. She stumbled without meaning to take a step.

She'd had a giggling spate when the men pried cupboards loose from the kitchen wall and set them on the floor. "Boxes," she said. "They're boxes now."

"Always been boxes," Trigg said. "Nail 'em together to haul food stuffs from camp to camp, unpack 'em and nail 'em up at the next site."

The two overloaded trucks covered with canvas reminded Eleanor of pictures of covered wagons. They'd gone less than ten miles when Irv turned left onto a narrow muddy road. Erling followed.

"Friends of Trigg and Millie," Erling said, as they approached a house with stone walls half-way up. "Ueland's. The missus expects us. She'll have coffee on."

The men parked the trucks in a stand of trees, ostensibly to keep them dry, though Eleanor suspected it might be to keep them hidden. Mrs. Ueland served vegetable soup, hard boiled eggs and gingerbread. They'd eaten, cleaned up the kitchen, and settled with a last cup of coffee before Eleanor understood they'd be staying until dark.

"Trigg stopped by here last night to let the Uelands know we'd come by today," Millie said. "They're our neighbors, Trigg's and mine. We own ten acres on the west side of their pasture."

Just after dark, they said goodbye to their hosts.

"You'll be back at work tomorrow," Erling said. "We're on our way home."

"Home," Eleanor said. She'd declared herself ready to stand her ground where Farley was concerned, but she'd tucked a letter into the things she'd packed; a letter written on children's tablet paper folded inside another sheet and sealed with wax dripped from a candle.

> *To all my friends: If I lose my battle with Farley, I'd like Hannah to stay with Maeva Swanson, if Maeva will have her. I'd like all of you to help Hannah grow up in Burke Bay. She seems to be a child who thrives with salt water and evergreen trees. Thank you for a thousand lessons I learned by being accepted in your community, your homes, and your hearts. Eleanor Keane Price.*

45

~ Neighborly Duty ~

Orval didn't much care for the idea of leaving his wife and babies untended while he joined up with a passel of men he didn't trust all that much, but his obstinate little wife grabbed up her own gun and told him to get going.

"I told you before, Orval Blevins, I can shoot the wings off a fly. Chances are good that Farley Price won't come around here anyway, since word is he's looking for his wife and child. He's not interested in the likes of me and mine. Now, you go on down to Burke Bay to do your neighborly duty."

So here he sat alongside Helmer Persson in the Burke Bay Tavern. Irv Carlson, who'd put himself in charge of things, introduced Eleanor Price and the child, then another woman and two young ones. After a bit, Mrs. Romstad took the women and children off somewhere so's the men could set up a plan.

Irv rapped a knife on the bar and said, "Chances are you've heard one version or another of the Farley Price story. He's some undone over the departure of Eleanor and Hannah from Burke Bay. They've been holed up out in Tahuya with Trigg and Millie Nordlund. You met Millie and two of their three children. You can like as not figure out that Trigg's a brother to Lang and Hauk, and all of them brothers to Ilsa Bakke. That makes them Burke Bay family.

"Some of us decided the time had come to bring Eleanor and Hannah back home. We invited Trigg and his family to come along out here where we could all join together to talk some sense into

Price. Trigg and the oldest boy are on their way by boat. He'll be anchoring across Dock Road soon as tides and a raft of logs allow.

"Times and things being what they are, we need to work together on all fronts. One of those fronts is the school. Nels Swanson has brought word that Maeva's opposed to all these guns. She'd like us to find a peaceful resolution. Some of us are pooling funds to help pay Price's transportation back to Detroit, which we have reason to believe is the place of his origin. I'm hoping to find him at the Breeze Inn Tavern in Bremerton later on today. Once we've had a meeting, we'll decide if his wife should have a talk with him. She's willing, but I'm not so certain that's going to work. We'll pass word along to all the folks who have taken an interest in this situation, let them know how our meeting goes. In the meantime, we need all of you to be on the lookout. Just don't go aiming those guns without good cause."

A spate of rain tapped the tavern windows. Someone said, "*Aggie J's* rounded Indian Hill Point."

Helmer Persson pushed back from the table. "I'll go on down to meet Maeva and the children. Drive them on up to school. I plan to stay put there, out on the porch in plain sight, until one of you spells me, or until Miss Truax rings the dismissal bell this afternoon. Ebbe's in charge at our place. Orval, we're expecting you back for evening milking."

"You'll get a breather, Helmer," Irv said. "We're going to do some moving around, give all our eyes a change of scenery. Now, we're open for discussion. Orval, let's start with you since you know a good bit more about Price's comings and goings than the rest of us."

Orval spun the barstool around. "I did have cause to meet up with Price a time or two over a private matter. Most of you like as not have some sense of our business. I'm not confirming, I'm not denying. Just admitting we came face to face now and again. Irv here knows most of the ins and outs of what transpired. Price fired off his piss-ant gun the last time we met up. I wish to hell I'd held off firing yesterday till I got close enough to wing him, but Miss Swanson stood between me and him. I blasted away to scare him off."

Dang, that was more words than he'd ever strung together in his entire life. His armpits took to itching dang near as bad as his feet. He sat back down, tugged off one boot and then the other, and worked his arms and shoulders around like he was loosening up his joints.

Irv said, "From all accounts, you did the right thing, Blevins. Like I said, we're hoping to keep it peaceful. Now that Axel Jenson's here, we'll get on to our plan."

Orval listened to the ins and outs of where Price's wife and child would be spending their days and nights. The teacher thought it best to get Hannah back in school and settled into a normal routine. The Nordlunds would be keeping close watch on her and their sister-in-law, who'd be settling into the new place the brothers built. Irv described the lay of the land, how the brothers had rigged an alarm system on the cabin just behind the tavern where Mrs. Price and the girl would be living, though not necessarily where they'd be sleeping. That gave him some cause for concern. Enough cause to clear his throat and speak up again.

"In my dealings with Price, I've found him able to sneak up in the dark. Moves quiet like. Wears them black clothes. Hard to see him coming."

"That brings up another point," Irv said. "The Nordlund boys plan to keep a light or two on through the night. Romstad's doing the same here at the tavern, Mrs. Bakke at the mercantile. We're hoping some of you volunteer to take a night watch. If my conversation with Price doesn't work out, I expect he'll come nosing around after dark."

With that, Irv pulled out a list, names, times and where to report, just like this here was the gosh dang army.

Orval grabbed up his boots. "I need to be moseying on home to my own wife and babies." He pulled on his right boot, hopped about trying to center his left foot over its boot, determined to get himself and his truck on out of there before Irv handed out assignments.

"I took that into account," Irv said, and tucked a piece of paper in under Orval's arm. "Got you scheduled daylight hours, some at the school, some down here on the tavern porch, some at the mercantile. Mrs. Bakke said to pass on her thanks in advance. She's fond of Thelma. Says it's about time you folks up in the valley got more involved with us folks down here on the bay. She'd be glad to have you bring Thelma and the children on down to her while you're helping out."

Orval got back out of his boots soon as he settled in his truck, and drove in his stocking feet. Irv set it up to give him time to check in at home and then hie on back down to take a shift at the school. Still and all, it showed him at home with Thelma and the babes from supper time on up to morning milking at Persson's place. He took his time leaving so's to get a clear picture of hiding spots around the tavern and cabins out back. He drove off slow, rumbled past the school house in first gear, gave Helmer a toot of his horn, and drove on apologizing out loud to his old grandpap's ghost.

Grandpap answered back, "*Hitch up them britches you got on, and do your duty in the name of Blevins. Man took a shot at you, only right you get a shot back at him. That there's the law of what's right and what ain't.*"

Dang, with Grandpap horning in, Orval might be the one required to do the shooting and thereby put himself in line for another bullet coming his way. Unless he counted the shot he already got off.

46

~ Sooner or Later ~

*H*auk and Lang waited at the Burke Bay Tavern for Irv, hoping he'd found Price, handed him a wad of cash, a divorce settlement, so to speak, and sent him on his way. They knew by the way Irv parked his truck, the time he took easing out of the cab, that the news wasn't good. They stepped off the tavern porch, met Irv at his tailgate, lined up so they could keep an eye on the tavern.

"Neither hide nor hair," Irv said. "Price hasn't been seen since his Saturday shift ended at midnight. Took his belongings and disappeared. Woman at the Breeze Inn said to follow my nose, he's heavy into drink."

"Saturday midnight," Hauk said. "Showed up at the school Monday afternoon reeking of alcohol. Maeva mentioned the stench." He fished his watch out of his pants pocket, checked the time though he knew it within five minutes based on darkness settling around them. "Any idea where Blevins does his cooking?"

Irv scowled, shook his head, checked his own watch and gave it a winding in the process. "The time he showed up at the store soaked to the skin and looking like the devil had danced on his grave, he only admitted to meeting up with Price and having a bottle of good liquor shot out of his hands. I'd a placed bets on him cooking on his own property up in the valley, off back in the trees beyond a tangle of berry vines, until I got a better sense of his wife. He might have cooked there for years, but not no more."

"Not on his property, but not too far from it, is that what you're guessing?" Lang asked.

Irv nodded. "Someplace where there's enough trees close together to keep smoke from a cooking fire near the ground. A place not easy to stumble across. One he'd figure Price couldn't find."

Hauk studied the tavern's profile in the darkening night, the small pool of light cast by a naked bulb at the back porch, shadow figures moving about in the kitchen. Onions cooking in the tavern and seaweed left by a high tide on the beach scented the night air.

"Blevins said this morning that Price can skulk about, wears black clothing. We're aware of that." Hauk had gotten him out of that long black coat not so many months back and settled him in cabin number four, up Church Road from where they stood. Drunk that time, too.

"If Price is hunkered down in the woods between the school and Keyport, you're the ones who'll have to find him. No better woodsmen around here than you two."

Lang rubbed his chin. "Find him and drag him out, or find him and shoot him? Hauk shoots, he's going to upset Maeva just when he's seeing some hope for friendship growing to courtship. I shoot, I'll make Eleanor a widow. What woman wants to start a new life with a man who killed her child's father?"

"Right, right, you're right. Nasty business."

Hauk gave that one nod. "The man has some woods' sense, drunk or not. Left no sign for us to follow yesterday." When they'd fanned out in the woods behind the school, they'd found no broken branches or trampled underbrush. Price could have walked down the creek to their pond and then out, but they saw no sign of disturbed terrain there either, and none on their driveway.

"Smoke him out or wait him out, those are our choices," Irv said. "Eleanor still insists she wants to talk with him. I'm still holding a wad of cash to send him on his way, should we be lucky enough to persuade him."

A wad of cash and the working end of a rifle barrel. They were playing a waiting game Hauk didn't like.

"Let life go on best it can the next few days," Lang said. "Eleanor agreed to send Hannah to school next Monday, after the Thanksgiving break. She and Maeva had a reunion of sorts this afternoon. I think they're counting on things coming to a head before Thanksgiving."

Irv narrowed his eyes. "Seems we're all of the same mind. Things will come to a head one way or another, likely sooner than later."

47

~ Sleepless Night ~

Eleanor still wanted to confront Farley, stand her ground, speak her mind and say goodbye to the sad life they'd made together. Most of all she wanted him to apologize to Hannah, leave their daughter with a sense that decency lingered somewhere in his damaged soul. A futile dream, she feared, but one that persisted even after she'd heard about the incident on the school grounds.

Farley threatened Maeva on Monday afternoon. Irv Carlson and Erling Romstad delivered Eleanor and Hannah to the Burke Bay Tavern on Monday night. Two dozen or more men gathered on Tuesday morning, guns loaded though not bragged about in front of women and children. That struck Eleanor as odd. In her ranch life, all men carried guns.

Astrid, Ebbe and Ilsa claimed they kept shotguns loaded with buckshot lest a thief, animal or human, darkened their doorstep. She'd seen Astrid sighting in Erling's long barrel Winchester, a gun much like the one that once belonged to great grandfather Keane.

Eleanor spent Tuesday night sleepless, settled with Hannah in Lang and Hauk's bedroom, aware of Lang's movements. She felt the change inside the house when he went out into the night, and waited for it to change back when he again came inside. She worried about electric lights left on, running up the bill; flushing the toilet in the wee hours when nerves, not a full bladder, lifted her from her bed; keeping a bathrobe handy lest she need to dash from the bedroom to confront a drunk and stupefied Farley.

Lang's nearness provided a sense of safety and unbridled longing for a lifetime with such a sense. She smelled him in his bed, in the blanket and quilt spread over fresh sheets and pillowcase crisp from the line, scented with air cleansed by cedar and fir. She settled in the slight trough his body left in the mattress, tried to clear her mind of worry and wishes long enough to offer a prayer.

"Guide the hands that carry guns. Let none other than me suffer for my sins. Help Hannah find her way."

At five o'clock Eleanor heard morning noises: wood added to the fire, stove lid settled back in place, water running. She rose when she smelled brewing coffee, wrapped and tied her robe and tiptoed into the kitchen.

Lang stood at the stove, hands open, palms down. "It's always darkest before the dawn," he said, without moving, without looking at her.

"You're cold," she said. "And wet."

"It's raining. Go back to bed."

"You've spent the night outside?"

"We built this place tight as we could. Hard to hear inside if something's moving about out there."

"Are you hungry? I'll fix you something to eat."

He looked at her then, a look she'd describe as stern, on the edge of exasperation. Her father's look. "Go back to bed, Ellie, and stay there till daylight. Take a cup of coffee with you if you like, but go on back to bed."

48

~ Log Raft on Burke Bay ~

Wednesday, the day before Thanksgiving break, a trying day made more so by a man with a gun on the school porch. Rain, a steady wind, children on edge, their eyes darting. Two fathers stationed at the back wall windows where they can watch the playground, the woods beyond.

So Maeva noted during the moments her students spent with their heads down on their desks, their eyes closed. No matter how clever her attempts at distraction, they wouldn't settle down to their lessons. They looked her way when she said, "Children," but in seconds their eyes went back to the two men. They spent their recesses and lunch in the basement where the noisy ones drove her to the brink of screaming and the silent ones tore at her heart.

The school foyer filled with parents and friends before the final bell. Hauk waited with Helmer Persson who called out names and counted noses. They packed South Bay children into Helmer's truck, sent Miss Truax and two children who lived next door to the place she rented in Irv's. Erling Romstad rode with Helmer, one rifle in hand, one leaning on the seat.

Hauk held his passenger door open for Maeva. His rain-soaked felt hat, low on his forehead, intensified his clear blue eyes, his unspoken message. He knew something more than he'd known yesterday. When they passed the tavern, Hauk nodded toward the bay where a wide bottom boat nudged up against rafted logs.

"Trigg's in with another raft."

She read that message: another hand, another pair of eyes.

"What else?" Maeva asked. "Other than your brother's arrival?"

"We found Blevins's distillery. Looks like Price found it too."

"And?"

"Nothing more. Nothing's changed."

Hauk walked her down the gangplank where Axel, Helmer and Erling were busy boarding children. Maeva clambered after them and stopped in the wheel house, her eyes squinted as if to take a picture of Trigg's boat and rafted logs. His boat's bow poked at one end of the raft, positioned to push rather than tow.

The picture, the way it changed the appearance of the bathing beach and bay, remained with Maeva. She made up a silly song about boats and logs while she rocked Anders.

Both picture and tune replayed through the evening. Several times she came close to mentioning Farley Price but bit her tongue to protect her mother from further worry. The kitchen smelled of cooked pumpkin for the next day's pies, toasted bread cubes for dressing, and vegetable soup they'd had for dinner.

At eight, Axel knocked on the kitchen door, opened it before she got there, and asked, "What's for dessert?" His question, his familiar grin, calmed her for the brief moment before he stepped inside with his loaded rifle.

Nels and Axel settled at the kitchen table with coffee and cookies, and insiders' conversation about the Burke Bay situation. They would guard the Swanson home through the night. Maeva collected information she would later sort and record in her notebook.

Hauk and Lang found a lean-to behind the Hidden Valley Cemetery, about two miles north of the school. Someone, quite likely Blevins, had made whiskey there. Another someone, Price they were certain, used it for shelter, smoked up the place trying to burn wet fir branches, and left behind empty sardine and tomato soup cans, assorted bottles, and cigarette butts.

They suspected Price saw them poking around and might have heard them coming. They made noise in hopes he'd fire his pistol, waste bullets and give up his location. They'd bet he found a new hideout, one closer to the tavern. They searched and would keep their eyes on Romstad's summer cabins, the storage rooms under the mercantile and garage, Carlson's mill, the old building at the end of the dock.

Maeva read over her notes, added an observation that Axel, and Nels to a lesser degree, seemed almost drunk on anticipation, eager for a showdown.

"There's no way Price can get to them, Maeva," Axel had said, his tone tinged with the superiority of one who had a gun at the ready.

A steady rain tapped on roof and windows through the night. Maeva wakened often, normal for her when worries piled up, listened for a time to the night sounds, burrowed deeper in her quilts and dozed to dream odd dreams. She rose early to help her mother make dressing, stuff the turkey, bake pumpkin and mincemeat pies, and fret over Jonas; they hadn't heard from him.

Berta and Garth, the only guests expected for dinner, arrived at noon and got so caught up in the Farley Price story they decided they would settle in at the farm until the situation was resolved. Somewhere, in the midst of preparing a feast worthy of far more than five adults and one baby, Berta told their mother and Maeva that she was expecting. She hoped to move home for a time when the baby arrived. The small place they rented was drafty and damp, unhealthy for a baby and mother and, by then, Garth might have gone elsewhere for work.

"Where?" Maeva asked.

"Maybe California. Where Jonas went. You're lucky you have a job that won't come to an end."

"We're only receiving half-pay for now, maybe less in January."

"Still," Berta said, "you know you'll be getting it someday. And you always know you have enough to eat."

"Mom always sees to it you get a share."

"Still," Berta said again, "if you start to run short here, we'll be the first to do without, by our own choosing."

Thanksgiving night, snow mixed with the steady rain. Sometime in the night one of the cows mooed a protest. Though Nels said they did that at times when the wind whistled through the barn walls, Garth feared it might be Farley Price come to wreak havoc on Swansons for Maeva befriending Eleanor.

He'd gone through several quarts of beer and half a bottle of cooking brandy he'd found in the back of a cupboard while he and Berta played cribbage.

"Nothing, nothing at all," Nels reported Friday evening and again Saturday, when he returned from his job at the Burke Bay Garage. "The tavern's closing early so everyone can get settled and men take up their posts. Romstads are opening on Sunday for breakfast and lunch. Lots of turkey soup to serve, and it gives folks a place to chew the fat and their fingernails."

Saturday night the rain stopped, the air turned colder, and the men, Axel included, speculated the cold would drive Farley Price from his hideout. The sun rose Sunday to a world frosted white, wilted flower beds, and water droplets frozen on evergreen trees.

Talk of an evening meal, turkey soup and warm bread, started over breakfast. By early afternoon, the rooms in the house had shrunk to the point Maeva felt suffocated. Garth and Nels played cribbage while Berta curled up with a book. Maeva put Anders down for a nap, filled a hot water bottle for her mother's hip, and talked her into a rest. She pulled Jonas's wool pants on under her skirt, took the navy surplus pea coat he'd left behind from the kitchen hook and headed out for a walk on the beach.

Frost nestled in nooks and crannies along the bank. Tiny icicles clustered in spots she'd hollowed out for milk and egg storage during August heat. Maidenhair fern drooped, its growing cycle ended for the season, its root clump ready for rest.

Jenson's Pier stood empty. Axel and the *Aggie J* hadn't returned from an afternoon run to Bremerton.

She meant to go only as far as Wiley's Landing and turn back, but her muscles had warmed with her brisk walk and her body and mind felt free. Low tide let her duck under the pier rather than cross its frosted surface. She walked on at a good pace, her body sweating, her face cool, and rounded Indian Hill Point, where she caught her first glimpse of the open bay, the dock and buildings. The air sang with perfect silence.

She needed to turn back, be there when Anders wakened, when the bread was ready for the oven, for a dozen things that needed doing on Sunday afternoon so she'd be ready for Monday morning.

A little farther on she saw the silvery plank road, all in shade, frost coated. She breathed in cold sea air and creosote, and decided to go on to the tavern, see Eleanor, spend some time with her, begin darning the hole ripped in their friendship.

She crossed the sand and rocks and ducked under the plank road to climb the slope on the land side. Half way up the slope she felt a presence, a chill like the one she'd experienced on the school playground. Instinct said turn, duck back under the road, run back to the Point.

Too late. A clamp had her left arm above the elbow, and a cold hard object poked the back of her head up under her knit cap. Farley Price. She recognized his smell, alcohol breath, alcohol emanating from every pore in his unwashed body, the rasping when he spoke.

"The teacher. My early Christmas present. You'll walk in front of me. Open doors, lower guns. No one in Burke Bay's going to risk you getting shot through the head. They'll give up my wife easy enough now."

He positioned her in front of him, her left arm clamped in his hand and twisted behind her back, her left ear near his chest. His breathing sounded like someone gargling. Breathing rales she'd learned somewhere.

He kept his right hand on the gun at her head. The adrenaline rush that came with his presence would trigger a headache. The gun at the base of her skull rested between the jutting bones she often massaged to alleviate headache pain.

"One of them will shoot you," she said.

"They'll have to shoot through you to get a bullet to me. Lucky for me you're a tall woman. Make a perfect shield. Now you ease yourself up over the rail onto the road. Up and over, no kicking or thrashing about or I'll have to put a bullet in your leg."

"I wouldn't stand quite as tall with a bullet in my leg. You should think about that."

Farley Price squeezed and tugged her forearm until it raised her already aching shoulder. The gun probed the back of her head. The occipital bone she rubbed when a headache formed.

"I heard all about you, how smart you are. Heard from my wife and kid, both the Perssons. If you're half so smart as they think, you'll keep your mouth shut and get up and over the rail and walk straight down the middle of the road."

She eased over the rail, her boots heavy, her legs still weak with fear, though that would gradually dissipate. They were an eighth-mile from the bridge over the inlet to Carlson's lagoon, another fifty yards or so to the front of the mercantile and Dock Road's intersection with the highway to Bremerton. She narrowed her eyes and focused on the tavern, the back of the mercantile and garage. No movement. Trigg's boat rested alongside his logs. If he was aboard, he wasn't looking her way.

No tire tracks showed on the frost-covered plank road. If she slipped, lost her balance for a moment, she might catch Farley off guard, have a chance to get one hand on the gun. Or he might shoot as she fell. She measured each step, an inch worm on a grass blade, and centered her thoughts on Eleanor.

"Do you expect Eleanor to be impressed with this behavior? Waving a gun, threatening to shoot me so others will do as you order? Do you think Hannah will admire you?"

The gun barrel jabbed harder. "Shut up. I'm warning you now, you say another word you're going to see your own blood running into the bay. I'm not interested in Hannah, she's just a kid, I never much liked kids. It's my wife I want. My wife! We're married, it's her job to be at my side, see to my needs." He twisted her arm harder as he spoke.

Maeva bit her lips, tasted blood. Truth of Farley's need found roots in her thoughts, and bloomed to understanding. He wanted a mother. A mother to cook his meals and comfort him, to mend torn clothing and tattered dreams.

They crossed the bridge, the narrow stream of water under it tranquil. As they rounded the slight bend to make their way in front of the mercantile, Farley pushed his body closer to hers. The rill in his chest intensified as he dragged in breath. She'd heard the same sound in Cynthia's breathing. Farley Price was sick, both in mind and body.

His hand that held her arm pushed against her shoulder blades. His other hand jammed harder against her head.

"You let out a word, even a sound, I'll have to hurt you."

Stupid, she thought. A stupid man, desperate, addled by drink, malnourished, walking her and himself into trouble.

A bell tinkled, signaling the mercantile door opening. Irv Carlson stepped onto the parking area, rifle at his side, finger on the trigger.

"Let her go, Price. There's six, eight, ten men with you in their sights. Just let her go and we'll set you up with a way out of here."

Maeva's heart thwacked her ribs. Men? Where?

Farley growled, "There's a bullet ready to take out her brain. You come on out here and walk on in front of us. Down to the tavern. Anyone moves funny, the gun goes off. You might take me down, but you lose your teacher. Your goddamn precious teacher."

"Listen to me . . ."

"Shut up, man, put that gun down and get in front of us. Now! I'm not telling you again."

Irv leaned the gun against the mercantile window, moved in front of Maeva, walked with his back straight, his head high, his arms out from his sides. She closed her eyes for a moment, clenched her teeth against crying out in pain. Her wrist. Her elbow. Her shoulder.

They passed the closed garage. If a man there had them in his sights, she couldn't see him. Cold wind blew off the bay onto Dock Road, cooling the sweat on her face. She released her lips from her teeth, gasped in a deep breath, saw movement out of the corner of her left eye. Lang Nordlund stepped off the tavern porch, onto the road, moved toward them.

"Tell him to back up, Carlson. Tell him he comes any closer, the teacher's dead."

"Back off, Lang," Irv said.

"Tell him to get my wife, bring her out here."

The tavern door opened before Lang had a chance to move. Eleanor, dressed in her blue denim skirt, blue chambray blouse, and bright red cardigan sweater, crossed the porch. Her hand flew to her mouth, then to cover her heart. "Noooo, Farley."

"We're going for a boat ride, Eleanor. Not another sound, now. You walk across the road, get down on the beach, get yourself over them logs and onto that boat. You and me are taking a boat ride, and the teacher here's coming along to see to our safe passage."

"Farley, listen, please . . ."

"You move your behind fast as you can onto that boat, Eleanor, or I'm shooting the teacher, and then I'm shooting this goddamn Lang Nordlund and Carlson, and any others I can get until one of them cuts me down. You want that, Eleanor? Or you want to do as you're told? You're my wife and it's goddamn time you started behaving like a wife."

Eleanor, hand on her mouth again, crossed Dock Road, jumped onto the sandy swimming beach, moved to the water's edge.

"Carlson, Nordlund, you two get down on the beach and walk yourselves out under the dock where others can't see you. The teacher and I will come down right behind you. That might be tricky, me getting her down there without the gun going off, so I suggest you move."

Irv and Lang moved. Where were the other men? How could they pick off Farley without shooting her?

Eleanor, one foot in the water, turned to face Maeva and Farley. Her face had lost all color, a ghost face framed with her dark hair streaked golden in the sun. Her mouth opened, her simple words whispered. "Please stop."

"Move your whoring ass, Eleanor, or I'll shoot this goddamn teacher and coat it with her blood."

Eleanor leaned onto the logs, crawled on hands and knees. Gut wrenching sobs shredded the silence as she inched her way to the *Constance*. Maeva watched the logs for shifting under Eleanor's weight and movement. None.

"Teacher, you sit your backside down on the bank edge and ease onto the sand." He gulped air and wheezed. "I'll do the same. I'm doing my best to keep this gun from firing."

Maeva moved as told, crossed the sand, stepped onto the first log attached at its ends to cross logs, thick through as the drift log on the beach, bark grooves deep enough to shelter small fish. She looked at Eleanor on board the *Constance*, slumped over like a heap of soiled laundry. Sit up, Eleanor, she silently implored. Dry those tears.

"Easy," Farley said, gun pushing against the back of her head so hard she felt needles stabbing her eyeballs. "Get your balance good before your next step. I know my way around log rafts."

Maeva moved her right foot onto the next log, loose inside the raft but too sturdy to rock. She counted ten seconds, moved her left foot. Farley stayed one log behind her, twisting, pushing, gasping. On the fourth log, she settled her right foot, brought her left past it, slipped to her knees, screamed and rammed her right elbow back hoping to hit Farley Price in his solar plexus, all in a second.

Pain ripped through her shoulder, rocketed into her head and down her spine. Seagulls squawked at her moan. The gun barrel moved to her right ear. She jerked her head left, heaved her strength into rocking and separating logs. They didn't move. She heard a popping sound like the weakest firecrackers Nels had for the Fourth of July. Felt heat on the side of her head. Heard an alarm blare. Heard Eleanor scream. Saw her stand. Saw fury replace fear in her eyes. Maeva fell forward, prone on the logs, right arm up and back, hand and fingers reaching for Farley's face, his eyes.

"Gun's still on her," Farley shouted, then growled to her, "Crawl, you goddamn bitch. Grab hold and crawl fast!"

Maeva stretched her right arm to its zenith, reaching for a hand hold, space between logs to manage she knew not what. The gun probed behind her ear. Jonas's soaked pants ripped at the knees.

An ear-splitting scream rocketed past her head, across the bay, echoed back. "Mama! Miss Swanson! Mamaaaa!"

Hannah. Sweet Hannah who loved books and reading, would live with this scene for the rest of her life. "That's your daughter, Farley Price. I'm going to push myself up now. I'll stand for my last dance. You can shoot me in the process, or you can stand up with me."

She made it to her feet, heard another popping sound followed by a blast, felt heat on her earlobe and a hundred bee stings on the backs of her legs. Bee stings, shoulder pain, blinding headache. Screams, blast and ping echoes. Inside logs moving. Nausea. She fell. Farley fell half beside her, half on top. She kicked at him, or tried to. Eleanor's screams met Hannah's, both reverberating.

Maeva tried to push herself free with her right arm, couldn't get more than her head lifted from the logs. Ragged edge pant legs above gnarled brown boots moved into her sight. The log beneath her rolled. Her right hand dipped into the icy waters of Burke Bay. Something, or someone, jerked it back. Farley moved, or was moved, freeing her legs. An arm found its way under her waist and lifted. A man who looked like Hauk Nordlund. Or perhaps like Lang.

Someday she would tell her children and grandchildren she'd once danced with five men on rafted logs on Burke Bay at the mouth of Whiskey Creek. She'd describe the men: Farley Price in a long black coat and once dandy black shoes, his coal black hair plastered to his head; Trigg Nordlund in logger pants, wool sweater, plaid shirt, red suspenders; Lang and Hauk Nordlund dressed almost the same as Trigg; Irv Carlson in bib overalls and his favorite shirt, one sewed for him by Eleanor Price.

"And me," she'd say. "Why I wore a skirt over Jonas's wool pants, and a navy pea coat and a cap my mother knit. Ladies always wore dresses to dances."

She'd write a story children could understand. An illustrated story that showed Astrid Romstad's shotgun still smoking, buckshot knocking Farley off his feet and peppering her in the process, a man saying "Sorry it took so long to reach you. I'm Trigg Nordlund, the one who rolled the logs. My brothers call me Dance Man."

She'd write the rest: Ilsa Bakke standing on the beach with Irv's gun he'd left propped against her store when he walked Dock Road in front of her and Farley. Erling Romstad running down the dock. Helmer and Ebbe Persson jumping out of the milk delivery truck before it stopped. Lang dragging Farley to the edge of the log raft, submerging his head in the bay. Irv and Hauk wrestling Lang away from Farley.

Trigg stepped aside. Hauk took his place, made a sling with his sweater, warm and scented by his body. He tended her bloodied earlobe and incessant shaking.

"Is Farley alive?" she asked.

"He is, more's the pity," Hauk said. "Coughing and spitting sea water. Lang helped him to a sip. You've lost a wee bit of your earlobe."

"It won't matter. I've never worn earrings."

49

~ Caravan ~

Orval Blevins came up out of a Sunday afternoon nap, much needed after a night out on watch and morning milking Persson's cows. There Thelma stood, his pretty little wife, holding her twenty-two and his shotgun by their barrels, both in one hand, and his son perched on her opposite hip.

"Have you gone deaf on me now, Orval Blevins? Didn't you hear that alarm? There's trouble down at the bay, and we're on our way. Here, you see to the guns so I can gather up Norma."

Orval scrambled to his feet, took the guns and a firm stand against Thelma and the children going anywhere. A firm stand cut off soon as he said, "Now, Thelma."

"You've got thirty seconds to get in the truck or I'll drive off and leave you here with our babies."

He made it to the truck in under fifteen seconds, boots in hand and no jacket against the cold air. He, his truck and family, and their guns, arrived at the tavern in time to catch on to the gist of the matter. They joined a caravan driving off to Harrison Hospital in Bremerton, Lang Nordund and Irv Carlson in Irv's truck, Farley Price wedged between them. Hauk Nordlund with the teacher alongside, his brother Trigg with Price's wife in the backseat. Romstads had Hannah with them in their car. Perssons brought up the rear.

John Andersson from the garage gathered up Ilsa Bakke and drove off toward Swanson's farm. Ilsa had said she'd see to Mrs. Swanson, make sure she sipped a little brandy with a cup of coffee.

Millie Nordlund and her three children stayed in the tavern to keep the coffee going and, like as not, bake a couple pies.

"It's about milking time," Orval said, preparing to head on home, but his feisty little wife had control of the guns.

"Helmer and Ebbe are up ahead in Helmer's truck. You can ride back with him if you're worried about his cows, but I don't plan to leave until I see Farley Price tied to a hospital bed or transported to jail."

"You don't know for sure what he done."

"Didn't you hear Astrid Romstad explaining? She said he shot at the teacher. He shot at you once, but there's no sense in trying to get you to tell the police. Now he's shot at someone farther on the right side of the law than you are on the wrong side. That calls for putting the man in jail, and I want to see him there."

"Why are you so het up about him going to jail?" Orval scratched his left foot with the toes of his right, giving his truck a bit too much gas.

"Slow down, Orval, and listen to what I've been telling you for months. We're going to start a water company and I need you around to do the labor. That fool Farley Price tried to kill you."

"What labor's that?" Orval asked, though he pondered the other part, the sound of her voice when she said Price tried to kill him.

"How do I know? I don't have it all figured out yet."

"That the only reason you want to keep me around? For the labor?"

"And for setting up a decent business to pass on to our son. Teddy needs a father he can brag on when he goes to school."

50

~ A Change in the Wind ~

Eleanor, as Farley's legal wife, provided the hospital staff with information they needed to admit him, followed by information for her own admission. A nurse swabbed her throat, gave her a lozenge for the irritation caused by screaming, administered a shot and left her with Ebbe watching over her.

"Where's Hannah?"

"With Astrid. Helmer and Erling, too, for that matter. Hannah's fine, now she's been told you'll be released soon."

"And Maeva?"

"Word is she's kicking up a fuss at being told she'll spend the night for observation. Nels borrowed his brother-in-law's car to bring Mrs. Swanson in for a visit. Maeva's sister Berta stayed behind with the baby."

"Oh," Eleanor said, thinking of all who were troubled by Farley's actions. "And Farley?"

"None too good. No visitors allowed, not even you, till they've got him stabilized."

Eleanor closed her eyes. Whatever the nurse had in the syringe made her feel sleepy

Hauk had his turn telling authorities the Farley Price story as he knew it. Near as he could gather, his story was identical to Lang's, and so close to Irv's and Erlings's and all the others, that the officer doing the questioning started writing *ditto* on his note pad.

Trigg had headed on back to Burke Bay to give Millie a hand with bachelors who'd come looking for gossip. Lang stayed put in the hospital waiting room, determined to see Eleanor. Hauk harbored similar hopes regarding Maeva.

Nels joined them, head shaking, eyes gleaming. "Maeva's on a tear, trying to get the nurses to release her, telling them our mother could better use the bed for a little rest. She got a nurse to take Mom's blood pressure, check her pulse and give her a calming pill. The nurse complained that it's taking at least two of them to keep Maeva contained. She's asked for you. Go on up, see if you can convince her she's got to spend the night. I'm taking Mom home."

Hauk glanced at Lang, saw him nod, and set off with his heart pounding harder, if possible, than when Farley held them all at bay with his pistol on Maeva.

She sat up in the narrow bed, smiled and held out her arms. He pressed against the bed's side, his arms around her shoulders, her head against his chest.

"Hauk," she said. "Dear Hauk," and kissed his neck.

He felt the dampness of her tears and fought back his own. "Love," he whispered, his arms tight around her, but not so tight to miss her head move down and up. A nod.

Maeva loosened her hold on Hauk and caught his hands in hers as he eased back from the bedside. He'd said *Love* at the very moment she accepted her feelings for him. She'd tell him soon. Not while in a hospital bed with a frowning nurse standing behind him.

"I have a request," she said. "Will you meet my class tomorrow if the hospital doesn't release me? The children will need a calming presence, and Miss Truax will need your help."

"Yes," he said, and touched his lips to her forehead.

The headache that began when Farley Price jabbed his gun at the back of her head grew worse. She threw up the aspirin the nurse gave her.

"Doctor ordered an injection, but the police want a statement first," the nurse said.

A city police detective and a sheriff's deputy questioned her for over an hour. When they left the nurse administered the injection and massaged her shoulders and neck with baby oil.

"There, you get some rest now. That awful man is handcuffed to his bed." She leaned closer and whispered, "He's got pneumonia. A serious case."

The hospital released Maeva just before noon the next day with orders to rest, sip broth and tea, and nibble on saltine crackers. Nels delivered her and those orders to their mother who shook her head.

"*Kaffe* first, for the headache. Buttered toast for the stomach. Chicken soup a little later."

Maeva held Anders while she sipped her coffee and fed him tiny bits of buttered toast. He grinned and drooled and bounced on her lap. She wept at the joy of being alive.

Axel blew into the kitchen without knocking. "I warned you, Maeva, but you wouldn't listen."

She drew in a deep breath. "I listened. I heard every word just as I've heard every warning and complaint you've uttered about my friend and her daughter since the day Hannah first stepped into my classroom. The day after Roosevelt's election when you were furious that a Democrat beat a Republican. I listen to you, Axel, but you don't hear my replies."

"That's ridiculous. Of course I hear. I'm trying to get you to see the big picture . . . the part you will have in business and politics as my wife."

He spat out *wife* like it was a curse word. His face had reddened, his hands had clenched. She'd never seen him so angry. She spoke softly, wanting to be kind, needing to be freed from the burden of their prolonged unofficial engagement.

"I can't marry you, Axel. You need a woman who sees the world the way you do."

"Oh, for Christ's sake!"

That's as far as he got before her mother appeared. "*Tyst.* No more words. You go now."

Axel went, possibly the first time he'd left the Swanson kitchen empty handed. He stayed away for two days, but returned to try his charm before accepting Maeva's decision and elicit her agreement to continue writing campaign speeches for his dad and himself. He remained a frequent visitor, kissed Maeva on her cheek when he bade her goodbye, and went whistling down the path.

It took until Christmas and the traditional Swanson-Jenson family gatherings for Maeva to see Axel as the friend he would remain once he gave up trying to change her into his concept of a Jenson wife.

Efteråt (from Maeva's journals)

~ The Whiskey Creek Water Company ~

Maeva returned to her classroom Tuesday morning where she and her students celebrated Hannah's return and welcomed Richard Nordlund, Trigg and Millie's oldest child, as a new student.

Orval Blevins continued milking for the Perssons while they advertised for a new hand.

Farley Price died of pneumonia five days after the incident on Burke Bay. Doctors who tended him let Eleanor see him for brief visits. He told her to go away. The official cause of death was listed as acute illness related to alcohol consumption, poor nutrition and exposure to the elements.

Thelma Blevins mentioned her water company idea to Ilsa Bakke who suggested a community meeting. By Christmas, Orval Blevins knew he'd be bottling and running drinking water for the rest of his days.

Pastor Holmes left the area in disgust, with promise of a new church in a community without Scandinavians or a creek.

Miss Truax went home to her people in Yakima—a sister, brother-in-law, nieces and nephews—for Christmas, and sent a letter of resignation to the school board. Maeva taught both classrooms, all 8 grades, from January to mid-June 1934, with volunteer help from Ebbe Persson, Millie Nordlund, one or another Nordlund brother, her brother Nels and most anyone else who stopped by the school to see if she needed a hand. She prepared all the lessons, had older students tutor younger ones, and did it all for half of one salary and a promissory note.

Eleanor and Hannah moved into the cabin vacated by the pastor and his family. It had two small bedrooms and a comfortable living area. Eleanor continued to cook at the tavern and tend the rental cabins for the Romstads, though she also helped Ilsa Bakke create a fabric and notions corner in the mercantile and accepted seamstress work.

Hauk and Lang built a footbridge from their place across the creek to the cabins so Trigg and Millie's children could visit Hannah without walking the long way around on roads used by cars. The three brothers took down a couple trees, built a slide and covered it with sheet metal Irv Carlson salvaged somewhere, hung swings from trees and laid out an obstacle course with worn through tires and peeled logs.

The Romstads turned Cabin Number One into an office for the water company, with a pleasant area for Thelma Blevins' children to play and nap while she oversaw the operation.

Trigg and Millie stayed on in Burke Bay for two years. Trigg, Lang and Hauk helped Irv Carlson mill Trigg's logs. Irv and Ilsa purchased small tracts of land, and the men built and sold homes.

Millie, possibly the best pie-maker ever born, baked pies for sale at Ilsa's store. She couldn't keep up, and wouldn't branch out far. Eleanor and Hannah, and a few trusted neighbors, first in Burke Bay and later in Belfair, baked for her under her supervision. Millie's Pies became the standard to meet in Kitsap County.

For two years The Whiskey Creek Water Company, funded by the myriad founders, sold only bottled water, much of it to Bremerton establishments for their water coolers, while assorted male laborers helped Orval Blevins lay pipe and position holding tanks for household delivery.

Maeva wrote advertising for the water company and served on the board of directors alongside Thelma Blevins, Astrid Romstad, Ilsa Bakke and Ebbe Persson. Thelma, as Chairman of the Board, put men in charge of labor and women in charge of management. No one argued with her decision.

Maeva Swanson married Hauk Nordlund, and Eleanor Keane Price married Lang Nordlund in a double ceremony in August 1936. Hauk and Maeva settled in the first Nordlund house, the one with the breakfast nook, and legally adopted Anders from her brother Jonas, who remarried and remained in California. Lang, Eleanor and Hannah moved into the house built for Trigg and Millie's use.

Nels Swanson gravitated from garage work to the grocery business. He brought a young bride to the Swanson farm where he built a small house for her and their two daughters.

Axel Jenson married Josephine (Josie) Winslow, sister of his brother-in-law, thus keeping the land transportation business in the family. He continued to skipper the *Aggie J* through December 6, 1941.

After the news of the Sunday morning bombing of Pearl Harbor on December 7, all able-bodied men either enlisted in the armed services or went to work in one of three naval facilities in the area. Axel and his dad soon added more buses to transport workers to the Navy Yard in Bremerton.

All three Nordlund brothers worked in the Navy Yard for a time, swing shift or graveyard, so they could continue milling lumber and building houses to meet the growing demand.

Maeva tutored children who needed extra assistance and taught drawing classes in the breakfast nook of the home she shared with Hauk. The school district called her back to the classroom in 1944. She and Hauk had two daughters by then, and another in 1947.

Eleanor managed both the tavern where she oversaw cooks and bartenders, and the seamstress and fabric business which grew into a school of its own. They added a daughter and son to their family.

Both women continued to serve on the board of The Whiskey Creek Water Company until their first born daughters stepped in to those positions under the joint directorship of Norma and Ted Blevins, Orval and Thelma's children.

The Whiskey Creek Water Company merged with a larger firm as the county grew.

About The Story

Burke Bay, the central setting for *The Whiskey Creek Water Company*, is the name of the small bay at Brownsville, Washington. Brownsville, in Kitsap County, is on the west side of Puget Sound, across from Seattle, with Bainbridge Island lying between.

Descriptions of the dock, tavern, mercantile and grade school (now a Grange hall) are accurate for the time, though none of them had Burke Bay in their name.

Hidden Valley of the story is based on Central Valley. There is a creek that meanders through the area, though I rerouted it and renamed it to suit the story. The cemetery mentioned is based on Island Lake Cemetery as I remember it from my childhood when it was a heavily wooded place.

The passenger launch, the *Aggie J*, is based on the *Chickeree*.

The plank road that plays a part in the story was replaced with a graded and blacktop road after World War II.

Kitsap County's historical writings mention several stills in the Silverdale and Central Valley area, and the difficulty revenuers had getting through wooded land and thick underbrush to locate them.

Though I didn't live through the Great Depression, my parents often mentioned that our family fared well thanks to the land and location. They grew their own vegetables and berries, maintained fruit trees, and relied on fish, clams and wild game to help provide nutritious meals.

And, as my dad always said, we had darn good water.

Acknowledgements

Thanks to Cheryl Ferguson Feeney and Ted Olinger for editorial comments during the final rewrite.

Thanks to my community of writers: Kathryn Arnold, Cheryl Ferguson Feeney, D. L. (Larry) Fowler, Richard Heller, Kathleen O'Brien, Ted Olinger, Colleen Slater and Frank Slater.

Thanks to my sisters Joyce Olsen Kelley and Susan Schnell, and to my daughter Marla Klipper.

CPSIA information can be obtained at www.ICGtesting.com
Printed in the USA
BVOW08s2226051213

338310BV00001B/4/P